The First Harvest

Anne Karppinen

An Inkd Pub book

Published by Inkd Publishing

254 SW Range Ave.

Madison, FL 32340

www.InkdPub.com

Cover art by MIBLart 2026

Contents

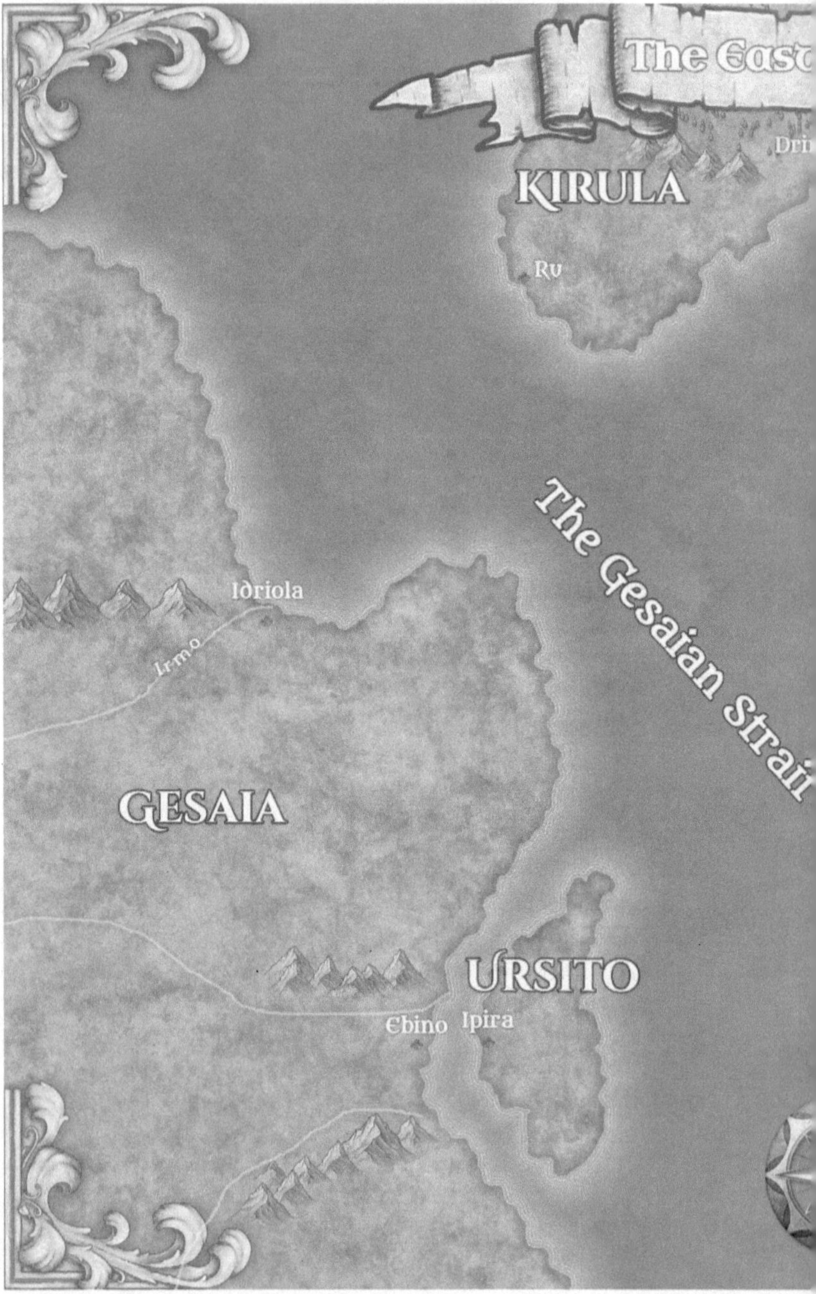

The East
Dri
KIRULA
Ru
The Gesaian Strai
Idriola
Irmo
GESAIA
URSITO
Ebino
Ipira

Islands
LUNEKEN
Tarel
Arrika
Auke
Hobra
Sabra
Jirda
Nebe
Sele
Sendal
Suro
Kaldona
Ruoke
Valja
Bitra
Kaknesa
EDERAI
Kols
Ibs
Krassmark
Davrbar
Belvim
ndina
Gidasoel
Haller
Zeiroa
Ervn
The Gvlf
of Ervn
Ollor
Oremel
Ardalbai

Prologue

Ardelei enters without knocking. Stepping out of the bright sunlight, she's immediately disoriented. It's hard to focus her eyes, or even understand the dimensions of the space she's entered. Her ears, too, are giving her unreliable information, which is even more alarming and unusual. A few frantic heartbeats and a good, long look later she's got her bearings again. Tidy rows of sparkling linen sheets hang between her and the other end of the room. No wonder both light and sound behave strangely in this attic space.

There's an airy, clean smell in the room that she can almost taste. Ardelei glances down at her grubby clothing, and her muddy boots that have already left a smudge mark on the rough wooden floorboards. She pauses for a while longer, waiting for a sign of some kind that tells her she's allowed to enter this space.

She listens to the house below her. On her way up the stairs, she passed small, shuttered windows. There are only two doors on this side of the building. One leading to the cellar, and the other opening to this large attic space. One by one, she starts picking up small notes sent by the unoccupied rooms: rats traversing the walls, a flock of sparrows settling down on the tin roof. From the tapestry of sounds it's now easy to pick out the clear melody made by the only other human in the house — and it's coming from the other end of the attic.

The song is complex and gritty, with an undertone of deep sorrow. An aural projection is bound to change over time, getting deeper and mellower with lived experience. Yet, songs rarely change beyond recognition — in that, they're similar to a person's face. Ardelei has rarely heard a dramatic shift in timbre like this one and is immediately on her guard again. Something truly traumatic has happened to the person projecting the song, not that long ago.

Ardelei is shaken, but not surprised.

She whistles a short greeting. At first, there's no response.

Then, "Just a minute. I'm literally up to my elbows in starch."

"I've come a long way," Ardelei says. "And I'm not in a particular hurry to go back. Take your time, Orandie."

There's another hesitant pause. "I know that voice." There's an abrupt sound of something heavy being dragged across the floor. Then, "Wait over there. It took me ages to get those sheets cleaned. Whatever it is those filthy nobs get up to in their bedchambers, they certainly aren't ashamed to advertise it. Or pay for my services, for that matter."

Ardelei grins. "Good for you."

Determined footsteps approach her across the room; Ardelei can follow the laundress's progress by the controlled swaying of the washing lines. Finally, the woman herself ducks out from under the last snow-white sheet.

"Ardelei Jolama!" she exclaims, clasping her headscarf for added effect. "It really is you, before my very eyes. How? Why?"

The two women embrace briefly. "Making the most of the situation," she says, chuckling. "But what's all this? I must say that my heart dropped to the soles of my feet when I walked into the Sunflower and found a complete stranger behind the bar."

Orandie glances down. "You know how it is. This hasn't been

an easy time for any of us. I'm one of the lucky ones. In a manner of speaking."

Ardelei takes a step back. She's been warned by her friend's altered music; yet, the change she sees in her appearance is even more drastic. Orandie has never been a tall woman, but she used to take up a lot more space before. It wasn't so much her physical girth, although that was considerable as well. It was more her incessant, bustling self-confidence that made her look larger than life. Now, she looks just like just another exhausted middle-aged woman working her fingers to the bone, living from one day to the next with no particular purpose.

Her friend clearly isn't eager to talk about her altered circumstances. She puts on a habitual smile that comes naturally to her after years of serving customers. "Is this a social call, or is there something you want?"

Ardelei gives her a genuine grin in return. "You know me too well."

"Well, in my experience people like you don't just drop by, particularly if they live on the other side of Ederai."

She breathes out carefully. "I could use a place to stay for the night. Several nights, if that can be managed. Somewhere quiet."

"Oh, there's plenty of space here. Most houses have a spare room or two." Orandie still doesn't meet her eyes, and her voice maintains the falsely jovial tone. "You can talk to the family next door. Their lodger decided he was better off back in Sendal. They're a decent lot — no small children, keep to themselves."

"Where are you staying yourself?"

Orandie gestures to the back of the room. "The air's very good here. And I have to say, most nights I'm so exhausted that it's a blessing I can just fall into bed with my boots on, right here, and pick up where I left off the next morning."

Ardelei suppresses a few immediate questions. "So, you do this for a living, then?" she finally asks. "And for the nobility, you say?"

"Not exactly a step up in the world, but we all need to eat, don't we? A much simpler business, compared to keeping an inn, that's for sure. All you need is a big tub and a bucket of lye to get started: at first, I used to hang my laundry on the riverside bushes to dry. So this," she glanced back," is a real improvement. As is the clientele."

"I can't imagine what you've been through."

A dark look. "No, you can't."

Orandie was right. The family next door is very happy to find a new lodger so quickly. Nobody asks any questions — particularly after Ardelei pays for her week's stay in advance in genuine silver. The eldest daughter shows her to the back of the house where she can choose from two identical bedrooms. Without a second thought, Ardelei chooses the one with larger windows. As the girl closes the door behind her, she tosses her bag onto the bed, and leans to look out the slightly grubby pane.

The city of Elandina has never held particular charms for her: the same goes for the entire country of Zeiroa. Yet, a port city has its uses. As always, Ardelei is drawn to the river. The broad stone bridges and the incessant traffic of boats give the otherwise placid city a sense of movement. As she watches, a lone barge makes its ponderous way up the Gidasoel. The nearest bridge still flies a ragged ribbon. For a few months, the northern side of the city was able to isolate itself from the infected south, and all roads and bridges were closed. Uselessly, as it turned out.

Ardelei turns her back on the city. This isn't perhaps the tranquil, comfortable place she's been hoping to find, but it'll have to do for the time being. Before blundering further, she needs to get her bearings, to understand this new version of the world she used to know so well. Or thought she used to know. The past year has overturned so many certainties. Including her sense of herself, and of her own place in the world.

Part One

The Sowing

Chapter 1

Haller - Rondei

The dogs were barking. Or not exactly: the sounds Lord Stainerau's hounds made encompassed every possible canine vocalization apart from the simple bark. They howled. They ululated. They growled and whined and yipped. Rondei stopped pretending to work and rested her head on her hands. She liked the animals. Like most people on Ederai, she'd grown up surrounded by dogs of many kinds — some working beasts and some beloved companions — and previously, she'd harbored very few negative feelings about them.

However, during her stay in Daurbar, the predictable, skull-reverberating racket had slowly begun to eat into her carefully constructed routines, and recently, even her ability to think. Every morning at sunrise, she was awakened by the almighty racket. At mealtimes, the hounds invariably goaded each other into an ever greater frenzy of sound. And at night, the last thing she heard was the chorus of serenading hounds.

Rondei stared out of her window, resting her eyes on the snow-capped peaks of the nearest mountains. She knew she was one of the lucky ones. She had a decent employer, comfortable lodgings, and regular days off for her own pursuits. She had known poverty, degradation, and grief enough to count her blessings every night as she drew a heavy quilt over her head in her private bedchamber. The time she had spent at the court of Daurbar had taught her much, and the fortifications had kept her and her son safe.

And yet, being shut in by the tall walls and the sheer, echoing mountainsides had begun to feel more like a life sentence than a luxury. Seeing the same faces day after day, hearing the courtiers' invariable opinions from one season to the next, and having no real equals to talk to, had started to stultify her own once so active mind. That, if anything, was making her rethink her future in the employ of Reutel Stainerau. She could stand boredom. She could even put up with closed-minded Hallerians if she had to. One thing she couldn't tolerate was a lack of freedom — both mental and physical.

She picked up her pencil and then put it down again. The storm of howling had driven out the perfectly balanced sentence she'd formulated during her morning walk. Now it was gone forever. And what was worse, she couldn't think of anything to replace it with. The paragraph lacked a conclusion. None was forthcoming.

At that precise moment Vejel decided to walk in. "Mother," he greeted her, and made to walk past her without further comment.

Rondei, however, wasn't in the mood to ignore him. She'd hoped the court would have a beneficial effect on her son, but the exposure to aristocratic life had unfortunately worked an opposite effect on him. Instead of becoming ambitious and vain, Vejel had somehow managed to turn into an even bigger slob. Today, it seemed that he hadn't bothered to comb his hair, and he'd swapped his court costume for a baggy number of indefinable color and cut. What was even more alarming was that some of the younger element at court seemed to be copying him.

"Come here," she indicated a chair next to her. "We need to talk."

He pulled a face.

"And stop grimacing like that. Gods know you are ugly enough already."

He dropped into the chair with the same lack of elegance he had entered the room. "Pot and kettle," he drawled.

She rolled her eyes. One talent Vejel had was for picking up the latest idioms of the young nobles and translating them into his native Nebian. "My lack of physical charms has never held me back, but that is only because I have other traits to liberally compensate for it. I am beginning to despair of you ever having any. What happened to the lessons with the head gardener?"

"He said he was too busy to teach me. But I'm getting really good at cards," the boy said after a moment's consideration. "And I'm the most accurate spitter of all Daurbar. Lord Stainerau himself said so."

"Well, that settles it. I am going to write to the rulers of Paishnal and offer your services as an ambassador. I am sure they will all bow down at the accuracy of your projectiles."

Vejel only gave her a lazy smile. He was used to her needling; she was used to his uselessness. Still, her son was of an age when lads usually go into apprenticeship, or apply to continue their studies. Vejel could read and write. His arithmetic was better than hers. However, he would never become a tutor like her, or pick up the manual skills to work at the printing press. For both, one needed an innate precision and a passion for words. As far as Rondei knew, her son had no passions whatsoever — unless one counted spitting.

"Did you get the paper?" she asked next, as Vejel showed signs of unfolding out of his chair.

A vacant look. "Um..."

"Vejel. You had one task today: to go to Lord Stainerau's steward and ask him if the consignment of Zeiroan paper had arrived. Do not tell me you forgot!"

"I didn't forget. Not exactly."

"No. You were far too busy spitting out of the window. Or teaching the younger boys to gamble." She raised her eyes to the ceiling once more. The baying of the hounds had stopped. "I have been thinking," she continued in a lower voice. "Once summer comes, and the gates are finally opened, as they say they will be, we are getting out of here. If Lord Stainerau agrees, of course," she added carefully.

Vejel blinked. "But... I was just getting to like it here." A pause, during which she could see the cogs laboriously turning in his mind. "I thought you liked it here, too."

"I do. But being too comfortable can sometimes lead to complacency. I also feel the court has only had a negative influence on your character."

"Lady Erden will be disappointed." This was his idea of a sneaky comeback.

"She might be," she shrugged. "And it gives me no pleasure to leave her. Yet, she is old enough to marry."

Vejel raised a skeptical eyebrow.

"She is. I have heard her uncle mention it twice now. There is no reason why she should not. After all, she is one of the most eligible ladies in the land." She heaved a sigh. "And when she does marry, I will be out of a job."

The dinner gong sounded. Rondei raised her head, and glancing at the clock, cursed under her breath. It was too late to change into her formal wear now. So immersed had she been in her writing that she'd forgotten that this late in spring the sun didn't sink past the mountaintops for a few hours yet. At the same time, she was pleased. The ennui of the past couple of weeks had lifted. In half a day she'd been able to produce as many pages as she usually churned out in a week. The mere thought of leaving Daurbar seemed to excite her brain, making ideas jostle into each other and form into completely new concepts.

With a practiced gesture, she locked her handwritten pages away and made her way to the wardrobe. She discarded her working robe onto the floor and pulled out a light coat of Gesaian linen, tying it with a silk sash. She liked simple, light-colored clothes that brought out the color of her eyes and skin and went together without a lot of thought. Despite her mind often being elsewhere, she still understood the worth of a good first impression. Also, as a member of the Hallerian court, her appearance reflected the status of her employer. She hunted around for the pair of tasseled slippers — her one nod to the latest fashions — and found them at the back of the wardrobe, curled out of shape.

Straightening up, she tried not to look directly at her hair. A turban? The gong sounded a second time. No time to look for one. She flattened the most unruly curls against her forehead - and watched them immediately spring back to their usual shape. The messy half-bun she'd been wearing since morning would have to do. Perhaps it would give the court something to talk about for the next few days. Gods knew they needed new topics of conversation. She tied a silk scarf around the back of her head, hoping it would keep most of her hair in place, and distract from the disaster that was going on at the front.

Rondei slid her way down the granite stairs, gratefully aware that she wasn't the last one to descend to the dining room. Nobles, by nature, weren't a punctual lot; yet, the Stainerau family followed a strict schedule that was mandated by the head of the clan. Anyone turning up late for a meal was shown right back out again. Anyone late out of bed wasn't allowed to join his lordship on his morning hunt. In this, as in many other things, Reutel Stainerau was a man after Rondei's own heart. At the same time, she was grateful that their relationship had never showed signs of developing past its present dimensions.

In the atrium Lady Erden stood patiently waiting, as was her habit, her hands clasped demurely in front of her. The girl's face lit up as soon as she spotted Rondei. The tutor took her pupil by the elbow and steered her into the dining room.

Before sitting down, Erden showed her the slate. *Do you like my robe?*

It is enchanting, she wrote in reply.

Much to her shame, Rondei had in fact paid no attention to the heavy, ivory-colored brocade. Lord Stainerau was clearly determined to put his niece on the marriage market — even before the gates were opened. In truth, the voluminous robe seemed to swallow up the slight girl. The fashionable silhouette worked best on a more mature woman, or at least one more used to carrying herself confidently upright. Rondei wiped her slate clean, but could think of nothing else to say to her pupil. Over time, the two of them had developed a rudimentary sign language; yet, in more crowded spaces it was more convenient — and more intimate — to write to each other.

Lord Stainerau entered. His was a presence that was impossible to miss. Tonight he, too, had discarded his usual uniform, and was wearing a tunic of embroidered Paishnali cotton and matching trousers. His thick, raven-black hair sat close to his head: another sign of his peaceful mood. He made no mention of his niece, but all through the meal he kept a keen eye on her, perhaps trying to see her as an outsider would.

It didn't surprise Rondei that he took her aside as soon as the meal ended. As the other courtiers settled to drink their colored liquors, Lord Stainerau, wineglass in hand, led her to the closest balcony. The evening was cool, but not unpleasantly so. After a long winter and an uncertain spring, summer was finally making its way across the mountains.

"So," he said, leaning his back on the banister, treating her to a view of his handsome profile. "Do you think she is ready?"

"For marriage? In my personal opinion, no one ever is."

Reutel Stainerau glanced at her sideways. He wasn't as immune to sarcasm as many of his countrymen, but he treated it with caution nevertheless. "She is old enough."

"Definitely, my lord. Old enough to bear living children, if that is what you mean."

"And anyway, I hear you are leaving us soon."

Her heart skipped a beat. "Who told you that, my lord?" The question was out of her mouth before she could stop it.

"It is common knowledge at court." He shrugged. "As your employer I would rather have heard it from your own lips, Mistress Galsi, but –"

"My lord," she said quickly. "I have been greatly honored by this post in your household, and it would please me to keep it for many years longer. I have realized, however, that my charge is now of age, and requires my services no longer. It is, for a woman of my position, second nature to think ahead, to prepare for all eventualities if you like." She swallowed. "This morning I told as much to my son. It was not in his place to report our conversation to anyone else, or indeed to add his own speculations to the matter. I hope your lordship forgives his rashness. As you know, he is young and thoughtless."

His lordship was now genuinely amused. He wasn't a cruel man, but he took pleasure in the discomfort of others — particularly those of lower rank. "Very well," he said, flashing his white teeth. "Apology accepted. And I have to say that I understand your situation. I wish I had a succession of nieces to offer you as pupils. You have worked wonders with Erden." He turned around and gestured over the mountains. "That not being the case, you have my permission to seek employment elsewhere."

"Thank you, my lord."

"Within the borders of Haller, naturally. We would not want someone of your talents straying too far."

A sleepless night followed. Rondei ran through the conversation in her head, trying to spot anything she might have missed – anything that might have given Lord Stainerau's final words a less binding effect. His expression had been neutral throughout. It was his habit to speak his mind with no premeditation. Yet, the underlying message had been clear: there were people at court watching her every move and listening to her every word. They read every page that emerged from her press. It was likely they knew what she was going to print even before she did.

Thus, her future had been decided without her consent. She wasn't allowed out of the country for the foreseeable future. In any other place on Ederai that would have been a rather empty threat. Where there was a wall, there was a haphazardly guarded door. Where there was a shuttered window, there was someone with a crowbar. And where there was a printing press, there was a receptive audience that kept a close eye on its favorite writer, ready to break her out of a prison cell if need be.

Haller, however, was a law unto itself. Surrounded by mountain ranges so unscalable that they could have been designed by the closed-minded Hallerians themselves, the country had been able to hold onto its ancient customs, and to force the rest of Ederai into accepting its rather unusual — and unusually powerful — position. In some other case, people would have let Haller stew in its own conservatism. It wasn't as if the well-being of the entire island depended on goat's milk and things made of straw.

Yet, the naturally fortified region had another strategic advantage — one born of the very mountains themselves. Deep under the unyielding rocks, some hundreds of years ago, the ancestors of the Stainerau family had discovered a treasure of unseen proportions, and had swiftly laid claim to it. Today, the entire economy of the country rested on the caves of glittering, white crystals that ran the length of the mountain ranges, providing well-being to the people of Ederai, and immeasurable wealth to the lords of Haller.

Salt. The lack of the precious commodity had made life on Ederai difficult at first: although easy to store and transport, it was also one of the most expensive materials in the Eastern Islands, as the fresh water of the Strait wouldn't yield any life-maintaining minerals. For hundreds of years, the islands had been dependent on their western neighbors who could mine salt out of their own, richer soil. Intrepid explorers had searched all mountain ranges, looking for saltwater lakes or promising cracks and crevices — in vain. It was only the sheer doggedness of the Steineraus that had finally yielded results, and granted their stubborn family a unique place in the ever-shifting alliances between the emerging nations.

It was also because of the salt trade that the well-fortified borders of Haller had become even more difficult to breach. All mountain passes were rigorously patrolled. The Pass of Krassmark was closest to the capital— and that naturally vulnerable location had been fortified to the point of absurdity. In a situation where a handful of salt was worth a month's pay for a laborer, guarding one's country was perhaps the only logical step to take. And Hallerians, she knew, were a supremely logical people.

Rondei stared at the ceiling where the shadows of trees traced themselves in the starlight. If the Pass of Krassmark did open at the start of summer as had been promised, more goods and people would start moving in from the outside. Yet, one needed a permit just to get out of Daurbar. Traditionally, anyone traveling out of the capital would have to do so without any belongings. They'd even have to change clothes to ensure they weren't trying to smuggle salt in their pockets or in the seams of their tunics.

Nowadays, the customs were somewhat more relaxed, but still one had to endure a thorough inspection at the Pass. Rondei was certain that her blockhead of a son would try to flaunt all possible rules and attempt to hide a bag of salt somewhere about his person, just because he'd think he could outsmart the guards. Not for the first time, she wondered if she could simply leave Vejel behind to lead his indolent, expectorating life in peace. That would make her a rotten mother, certainly, but it could also ensure his safety in the long run.

She rolled onto her side. How was it possible that the offspring of two very intelligent, worldly people could turn out to be such a raging mediocrity? Vejel wasn't completely unteachable. That, in a way, would have been a relief. At least then she could have gracefully admitted defeat and found him a steady, safe place to live out his life amid simple people and simple pleasures. Instead, she had a willful, aimless child on her hands – someone who in all likelihood would go blundering about all his existence, making one bad decision after another, and potentially endangering his loved ones in the process.

What had Ardelei said to her? *We all need to make our own mistakes.* Fair enough: Rondei had definitely had a share of hers. The crucial thing was, she'd learned from them. Every blunder and wrong turn she had made, she had sat herself down and analyzed the decision that had led to it. And sure enough, she had never made the same mistake again. Her only son was an example of that tendency. One mad infatuation had been enough, one desperate heartbreak. No man had ever caught her unawares again.

Had it been a mistake to come to Haller? She didn't think so. The serene safety the country had given her had been invaluable; she could only imagine the horrors the plague had wrought on its rampage across Ederai. Sheltered by the mountains and Lord Stainerau's inflexible laws, she'd been able to think in peace, and to arrive at conclusions she might not have otherwise reached. She had developed her skill as a tutor, too. Lady Erden was an excellent pupil, and to have been able to pull her out of her shell and to polish her into a court beauty was at least partly Rondei's doing.

Now, she would have to turn all her energies to achieving the next goal: getting out of Haller alive, with her most prized possessions untouched. Some of these possessions, however, she would have to leave behind.

In the days that followed, Rondei found her patience stretched almost to the breaking point. Although news of the outside world was becoming more frequent, and rumors of an approaching goods train had already caused a week's worth of excitement at court, mainly because of the Zeiroan fashion plates and bags of Paishnali tea it contained. No one else seemed to be particularly anxious to leave Haller, or to even hear tidings from beyond its borders.

Although loyalty to one's native place was a trait highly appreciated by any Ederaian, the inhabitants of the Mountain realm seemed to be taking this particular trait far beyond its natural limits. Self-contained as they were, they didn't see the benefit of traveling abroad, or learning from other nations — with the possible exception of Paishnal, which was comfortably far away to be ever seriously considered as a travel destination. Rondei had come to the conclusion that the only reason why Lord Stainerau had hired her as his niece's tutor was Erden's all-too evident handicap. The only person deemed fit enough to spend time with a pale deaf girl was a foreigner who'd for some inexplicable reason had cut ties with her own family in Nebe.

Rondei had been watching the southbound road for weeks: stubbornly, it failed to offer her a single glimpse of approaching merchants, or even Hallerian messengers. News continued to arrive through the *kullners*, as there was still fear that even paper could carry with itself seeds of the deadly disease. In one of the rare scientific journals she had been able to access during the isolation, an eminent Paishnali researcher reported her findings that the plague was ostensibly transmitted through invisibly tiny particles that could be carried over the air. Rondei hadn't shared the journal with anyone: she hadn't even dared to think what the consequences of such knowledge would be. Gods knew that the mountains were high enough.

At the beginning of the month of Azarole, she finally struck lucky. A Sendali diplomat had managed to wrangle his way into court — mainly with the help of his enormous patience (he had been quarantined for an entire month at the Pass, and didn't seem worse for wear after his ordeal) and his personal charm. At first, Rondei tried not to draw too much attention to herself: after all, she was one of the lesser members of the court. Yet, her international reputation inevitably drew Sir Babtei Abanta to her side.

They talked about places they both knew, and people whose names both were familiar with. Rondei was careful to draw Lady Erden into these conversations as well. A noblewoman should be able to converse with foreigners as fluently as with her own countryfolk. Her Sendali was slightly odd and littered with spelling errors, but Sir Babtei again turned on his famous tact, using his time to sketch the girl's portrait into the corner of his own slate.

From that evening on, Babtei Abanta was a firm favorite of Erden's, and was even admitted into her garden. Rondei didn't share her pupil's passion for horticulture but knew when to take advantage of a promising situation. As the girl showed the diplomat her prized yellow peonies, Rondei trailed behind, dropping in a Sendali word into the conversation now and then, careful not to seem too eager.

Sir Babtei, despite being patient, was also delightfully quick on the uptake. As he straightened from looking at yet another flowerbed, he said, "Weather permitting, I am returning to Valja at the end of the month. My personal luggage is limited, but there is always space for a few books, should you like to send something to your family."

Her heart skipped a beat. "I shall think about it," she said in the same disinterested tone. "Books are, after all, very precious."

"And you would know that, as a printer and an acclaimed author." He paused to write something admiring on his slate, and after Erden turned her attention to her treasured plants, he continued, "I would be honored if you would like to show me your press."

"The honor would be mine," Rondei smiled.

Three days later he strolled into the attic where her precious press was stationed. With him arrived a few Stainerau relatives, who before hadn't shown any interest in the workings of the machine. They didn't really do so now. As Rondei showed the stacks of paper, containers of ink, and boxes full of letters, the only one to pay close attention was the diplomat. Sir Babtei leaned over the metal frame with much the same posture as he had done while admiring Lady Erden's flowerbeds; this time, the expression on his face was that of admiring concentration.

Rondei humored her visitors, and printed sheets of paper with every individual's name and title in the curliest font available. As the nobles drifted out of the attic, comparing their sheets, she had the opportunity to give the diplomat a tightly stitched bundle.

"Is the Silver Hound still standing?" she asked.

Sir Babtei's eyes widened ever so slightly. "I believe so. It has been a while since I have been to that part of the city."

"Well, if it is still there, and the same people are running it, just leave the book behind the counter. Say it is for Ardelei Jolama. They will know what to do."

"Ardelei Jolama," he repeated. "And if they do not?"

"I would not like you to get into too much trouble over this one errand."

"No trouble at all, Mistress Galsi. I, too, know what it feels to be confined against one's will." He slipped the book into his breast pocket and strolled out of the attic room, whistling a carefree tune. Rondei recognized the melody and smiled.

Over the next couple of days, she managed to give him further instructions in case the Silver Hound wasn't a trusted drop-off location any longer. Still, the only person she could trust to pick up the book in Valja was her cousin Ardelei, and her wanderings were as unpredictable as the spring rains. Rondei wasn't certain if the island of Luneken had opened its bridges yet — or whether Ardelei had even spent the plague years confined to one place. The fact that her cousin might have succumbed to the disease didn't even cross her mind: Ardelei couldn't be brought down that easily. Like Rondei herself, the mage was a survivor.

Chapter 2

Sendal - Meropat

The sun was nearing its zenith, and Meropat Rugolata was getting increasingly desperate. They had been certain that an evening at the Smiling Vixen, followed by a lively romp with an adventure-seeking aristocrat would have yielded at least a rhyming couplet or two — but no. The epic poem they had promised Master Alikava two months ago wasn't materializing at the desired speed. In fact, it wasn't materializing at all.

Meropat was familiar with the concept of writer's block. Gods, they had watched colleagues grapple with dried-up inspiration too often to be completely ignorant of its existence. Yet, so far, they had thought themselves immune. While poets and playwrights had wept bitterly into their tankards, and hack novelists had considered slitting their wrists over unfinished manuscripts, Meropat had only ever needed to sit down, quill in hand, and in a few minutes the magic started happening. So to speak.

Now, leaning their throbbing head against a rather shaky palm, they had to admit that the dreaded disorder had caught up with them at last. And in a way, it was no wonder that it had. Lately, there had been very little call for lighthearted balladry, or even gravely philosophical, introspective sonnets. People had turned to art for consolation and commemoration, if they had done so at all. It was a rather absurd existence, aspiring to sell ditties from door to door when entire quarters were shut down for months, their inhabitants not even allowed to communicate with family members across the city.

During the direst times, Meropat had admitted defeat and looked for alternative ways of making ends meet. After a few false starts, an acquaintance had dropped a hint about a local printer needing an apprentice. As the plague burned through young people at a terrifying rate, finding semi-skilled workers who could stand upright was becoming a pressing problem. True to their nature, Meropat had jumped at the chance. After all, a poet is no stranger to the printing business, and messing about with ink and paper was much better than dealing with corpses or people who were in the process of burying them.

Right now, there wasn't exactly a lot of competition for apprenticeships. Still, printers had their pride, and becoming a member of their esteemed guild didn't happen without the right connections. Meropat, knowing this, had ensured the printer's approval by dropping the right name almost immediately after introducing themself.

"You know, as my dear friend Rondei Galsi always says, there's no sweeter smell than that of a freshly-printed page."

In fact, they and Rondei hadn't met for many years. Meropat found the woman's austere seriousness off-putting, and most likely Meropat's florid interest in the seedier aspects of life had never endeared them to Mistress Galsi. Still, the extraordinary few months they had once spent working for a common goal had brought them together in a way that meant being responsible for each other for the rest of their lives. Meropat was also certain that Rondei, too, had made use of their name often enough.

They soon found that earning a living through physical work had its advantages. Although their hands were busy, Meropat's mind was often occupied with the intricate task of fitting words and images tightly together in poetic form. More importantly, it kept body and soul together at a time when there was very little certainty of not waking up with a scorching fever and an unsightly lump or two about one's person.

And yet, there were downsides. The most obvious of these were the accommodations, which had seemed acceptable enough at first sight. Meropat's room was warm and for the most part comfortable. Meals were provided by the printer's wife. Although the quality of the food often left a lot to be desired, the quantity did compensate for this somewhat. Meropat had their own little desk, and a comfortable chair; the nearest public bath was a short stroll away. The only window did look into the dank back alley that joined the network of similar Brewers backstreets. Thus, a lamp had to be kept burning even during the day. All of these things they would have gradually learned to live with — particularly as paper and ink were never in short supply.

One thing their employer had forgotten to mention, however, was the occupation of the neighboring artisan. Meropat, being used to sub-par accommodations, had known better than to ask too many questions right away: improvements could be negotiated once the apprenticeship contract was older than a few months. They were learning the hard way, however, that in some cases it was worth a bit of hassle to ensure one's peace of mind. Next time, they would very emphatically enquire whether there were any instrument makers in the vicinity before signing any legally binding contracts.

Meropat loved music in all its forms and was an enthusiastic and experienced worshipper at the throne of the performing arts. They also understood the great variety of styles and instruments the world of music held; yet, being a Gesaian by birth, there were certain things their fine-tuned ear found difficult to accept. One of them was the inexplicable predilection of all Ederai people for the rudest of all possible noises. Most obnoxiously, they held one instrument dearer to their hearts than any other: the bagpipes.

In theory, the Ederai pipes were as delightful an invention as any. Having an instrument that could maintain its sound longer than the player could blow into it was a stroke of genius. Anyone who loved dancing understood that a reedy-voiced flute or a quiet guitar just wouldn't carry over the noises of a clamoring crowd. A timbre similar to the honking of a distressed goose was certainly one way of solving the problem.

Still, Meropat didn't understand why these cursed sacks of noise couldn't be made and sold somewhere outside the city walls; surely, the torment they caused was similar to the reek rising from a tannery, or the noisome emanations of a farm. It wasn't just the effects of the manufacture of the instruments, either: all potential buyers wanted to test all the available bagpipes — as loudly and as protractedly as possible. Meropat, a habitual haunter of taverns, often staggered back to their lodgings a fraction before sunrise, desperate for an hour or two of sleep before the day's printing work began. Unfortunately, the first customers came knocking at the neighbor's door at exactly that same early hour.

It was no wonder, then, that the muse had fled. There was no poetry found in the back room of a bagpipe shop — and definitely little romance. Master Galvonei Alikava had wished for a lofty epic on the exploits of his ancestors, and Meropat had promised him one in a moment of characteristic hubris. They had promised a finished work by the end of the month of Sycamore. Now, however, as the temperatures grew balmier, and the city slowly began to emerge from its enforced isolation, there were so many other things to do than to sit in the oppressive heat of one's chamber and listen to a prospective bagpiper blow raspberries through a narrow tube.

Just as Meropat was about to pick up the quill and try anyway, there was a knock at the door. Several possibilities ran through their mind, none of them particularly promising. They owed quite a lot of money to various people. Also, they had made some promises that they probably weren't going to be able to keep. Still, a free agent like them had to keep their mind — along with their door — open to all potential clients.

There was no second knock. A sign that the person outside was either not in a hurry, or was in possession of absolute certainty about Meropat's current whereabouts. Carefully, Meropat set down their dried-up quill and got to their still unsteady legs. Grumbling, they walked to the door and yanked it open.

The sunlight sliced at their eyeballs.

The face staring at them was unfamiliar, but not hostile looking. "Rugolata?" The young man made no move to introduce himself.

"I am." Very few people ever called Meropat by their last name — which was a blessing, come to think of it.

"Brother and Sister send their regards. Have you thought about their proposal?"

"I... have." A woman pushed a wheelbarrow past them. They both waited in silence; this also gave Meropat some precious time to think. "Listen, I'd rather not discuss this here. Could we meet somewhere a bit less... you know, later?"

The stranger's bland expression didn't waver. "There's a meeting at the Dormouse tonight. Most of the family will be there." He nodded and stalked away.

Meropat was left leaning on the doorframe, thoughts spinning uncomfortably around the remnants of their hangover. In a way, this was a relief. The visitor hadn't demanded money, or marriage, or anything else, really. Also, a night at the Dormouse was rarely a night wasted. The writing was going nowhere, anyway. Much better to think about something else entirely, and return to the manuscript tomorrow with a refreshed mind.

They closed the door quietly behind them. A chance meeting on New Year's Day had led to this; a few careless, drunken exclamations had been treated seriously, and remembered. The Siblings weren't jokers: that much had been clear from the encounter. What they wanted was something entirely new, and immense – and Meropat could tell that they had the drive to achieve anything they set their brilliant minds to.

Eolum and Ainaes Skovo were natural leaders, and drew into their orbit people similarly talented and passionate as themselves. Meropat had been deeply flattered by their attention, but hadn't really thought that a drunken market day meeting would have any serious repercussions. Politics wasn't a thing they tended to dabble in, and philosophy of the heavier kind tended to give them indigestion.

And yet somehow, here they were, dropped in the middle of some revolutionary intrigue. Desperately, they thought back to the foggy, cold spring day that had driven so many people indoors, trying to pin down what exactly had made them stand out from the holiday crowd. Usually, their imposing physique and dark skin were enough to gain interested glances, but this time Meropat had found themself in an unfamiliar tavern, crushed together with a group of young locals at the end of a long table. For a while they had just listened to the buzz of conversation around them, happy for the chance of warming themself in such attractive company, and finding new topics of conversation — a winning combination for a poet.

Although the meeting had started boisterously enough, the tenor of the conversation had soon shifted. During the forced isolation, people had mislaid some of their former politeness and now tended to go straight to the point – rather than dancing around it as would have been the old Sendali custom. With no prelude, someone had produced a soggy pamphlet and passed it around. Those who could read had taken in the text quickly and summarized it in an undertone for the benefit of their illiterate friends.

At first, Meropat had thought that this was just one of the usual semi-lewd attacks on the powers that be, or simply a juicy piece of local gossip. People could never resist either, and devoured such crudenesses with the sophistication of a dog eating its dinner. When the page had made its rounds, it had finally come to rest in Meropat's hand. They had glanced down at it, expecting a pornographic drawing and easy-to-read capital letters and exclamation marks. Instead, the piece of paper in front of them was elegantly put together, in three straight columns, and in very educated Sendali.

The title was "On the Power of the Common People and the Immediate and Radical Need for Change."

They had quickly scanned the page as they had seen others do. This was serious stuff. Meropat wasn't a particularly serious person, but they had a survivor's instinct that helped them blend into the surrounding crowd when necessary. They had kept their face solemn and passed the pamphlet to the next person with some appropriately grave comments, ready to forget the contents of the text as a new topic of conversation would arise.

They certainly would have, had it not been for the entrance of the Siblings. They didn't need to make themselves conspicuous. Their followers — and other like-minded people — recognized them immediately and made a space for them at the head of the table. Eolum and Ainaes Skovo looked so much alike they could have been twins. Meropat later learned that Eolum was a full year older than his sister. They had unremarkable Sendali features: olive skin, sleek black hair, and flat narrow faces. This, of course, was more of a blessing than a hindrance. Not only could the Siblings pass for each other, but they could also disguise themselves easily among the ordinary folk of Valja.

Meropat had kept their head down, still slightly disoriented by the turn of events. An artist, they had learned, was wise to remain neutral in matters of state. It wouldn't do to alienate potential patrons with inflammatory politics or even slightly contrary views. At the same time, and for the same reason, it was important to keep track of the different undercurrents of thought, so as not to fall out of fashion, or to make terrible gaffes around the more ideologically savvy.

They also recognized a fellow artist when they saw one. The Siblings might not seem anything out of the ordinary, but when they began to speak, they had a natural skill of drawing their listeners into their circle of enchanting words. Neither of them had been trained in rhetoric or public appearances, that was immediately clear. The language they used was ever so slightly uncouth, and their gestures lacked the precision of an educated speaker. What they had was raw, natural charisma — and, Meropat thought later — also a large dollop of untamed magic.

There were many different magics in the world — some of them codified, most of them not. You could study to be a mage, but that didn't mean that you could learn to increase your magical potential; it only meant you learned to harness and exploit your already existing powers. Many people preferred to use their magic as fuel for their life's work. It was one thing to be an outstanding singer, quite another to be an outstanding singer with a literally enchanting voice.

It seemed that the Skovos had learned to manipulate their magic in this way. Once the center of attention, they were captivating to look at, and even more so to listen to. Anything they said would have resonated with their young audience. More perilously, the Siblings had a clear purpose to their rhetoric, and they believed in their words with the conviction of the newly converted. When they spoke, their audience devoured every word, and lived their every sentiment. They had sighed, laughed, and eventually shed tears as one. It was a performance any actor would have envied.

Even though admiring, Meropat hadn't been so easily swayed. After all, a trained artist recognizes a colleague's tricks. They had drunk their beer, concentrating more on the spectacle itself than the actual content of the talk. But gradually, despite the armor of analytical thought that they wore, the passionate young people and their heightened emotion had had its effect, and the Siblings' words had wormed their way into Meropat's susceptible soul.

Eolum had leaned forward, pitching his voice even lower. "These are hard times, my friends. But they are also times of great hope: after all, sunrise always comes out of the darkest hour of night. There's an emptiness asking to be filled. There's momentum to be exploited. You've all felt it, haven't you?"

"Yes," the audience had whispered as one.

"It's time to leave the old world order behind. We saw that it has brought nothing but disease, hunger, and universal suffering. We Ederaians have always been considered stupid and backward. Why is that? Is it the fault of the people, or is it the fault of those who call themselves our leaders?"

Somewhat alarmingly, Meropat had heard their own voice saying, "It's the fault of both groups, to some extent."

Eolum's coal-black eyes had locked with theirs. "Well said. Our leaders are at fault, but we, the people also have our responsibility. We have the numbers behind us. We have the physical strength and the tools of our various trades on our side. And now, thanks to the horrible and unnecessary sacrifices of our countryfolk, we also have bargaining power over our betters. We can walk into any workshop in Valja and ask to be employed. We can negotiate our wages like never before. We can buy property and land with no questions asked." He had looked around, and had seemed to meet everyone's gaze at once. "What can't we do, friends? When all of us join forces, what is there that we can't achieve?"

"It's ours for the taking!" Ainaes had said. "And it will be ours!"

"Yes!" the audience had agreed.

Meropat, buzzing with inspiration and beer, had banged the table with their fist. "This is beautiful! This is right! This will be done!"

Some hours later, they had staggered out of the tavern in the company of their new-found friends, singing a version of what was to become the first anthem of the movement. Meropat's words, shouted out in a moment of foolish elation, were to haunt their author for years to come – painted on walls, used as code, and inevitably, sung in different versions in the streets of Valja and beyond. Many times, they wished they'd come up with something more elegant, but it was too late. Their most lasting legacy, their most recognized contribution to the culture of Ederai, was fated to be this triplet of rather mundane phrases.

The summer evening was warm. A languid breeze moved along the river, bringing with it the fresh scent of growing corn. The city, as always, exuded rather more unpleasant smells, but at least the streets were uncongested at this hour. Meropat stopped in one of the riverside bathhouses to refresh themselves and to enjoy a moment's peace before what they knew would be a very hectic night. Although the messenger hadn't said it explicitly, they knew that this wasn't going to be a mere social call. People like the Skovos didn't have friends. They had family members, and they had enemies. Nothing in between — choose a side, and stick with it. Meropat wasn't an admirer of such drastic divisions. They were still intrigued enough to keep the appointment.

The Dormouse was easy to miss. Like the animal that had given the tavern its name, it was small, drably colored, and nocturnal. It nestled between two much taller neighbors, and gave out no light. It was known as the haunt of apprentices and the poorer class of laborers, and thus was easily overlooked by everyone else. Lately, however, it had also become the headquarters of a widening group of revolutionaries.

Meropat soon learned that the Skovos didn't like to call themselves that. What they had in mind was something less violent, but even more earth-shattering. There had been some attempted coups and minor revolts in Sendal before, and even a short time when Valja had declared itself an independent city state. Still, the main lesson of those uprisings seemed to be a heightened consciousness of the perils of political unrest. People were reluctant to side with anyone they considered too radical, or potentially violent. Rather, they'd come to rely on the steady power of the Guilds, which over time had begun to take over all the administration of the city — without really consulting the citizens themselves.

For this reason, the Siblings had to tread carefully. They kept their message vague and easily digestible, and for the time being had avoided writing down anything incriminating. They criticized the status quo, but didn't point any fingers. They gathered sympathizers, but didn't assign them any specific roles. Unless, Meropat found, the Skovos considered you trustworthy and indispensable enough: then, you had a definite place within their inner circle.

Inside, the Dormouse was surprisingly cozy. Its clientele had learned not to pay any attention to new faces, and the burly man behind the bar only nodded knowingly when Meropat asked for the Siblings. They were led up a creaking flight of stairs into a private meeting room which had its windows open into the velvet night. They could see the river glinting in its deep bed; this was a reassuring sight somehow. Whatever the future that was being planned within these walls, outside, the natural world kept going as usual. The sun came up each morning and set at night; the long summer was about to start, bringing comfort to the survivors of the bitterest winter in living memory.

Meropat had been expecting a similar raucous meeting as they had witnessed earlier. They found their expectations dashed. This was going to be a much more intimate affair – a consultation between trusted comrades, rather than a stirring recruiting session. The poet was immediately on their guard. Surely, to become a member of the inner circle so quickly someone must have intervened, giving the Skovos some information on Meropat. After all, Valja wasn't their native city, and they hadn't been exactly politically active during their stay there. This raised even more disconcerting questions – but these would have to wait.

There were two other people in the room: an older man Meropat hadn't seen before, and Ainaes Skovo. The Sister — as she preferred to be called — beckoned to Meropat, pulling up a chair so that they could sit down next to her.

"I'm so glad you could make it," she said, smiling briefly and showing off a row of perfect white teeth.

"I was glad to be asked," said Meropat, somewhat warily.

"You must be wondering why we wanted to see you. I'm sorry for the abrupt invitation, but things have started moving fast, and we can't run around the streets as freely as we used to." She poured ale for both of them. The older man didn't join them. Meropat assumed that he was on bodyguard duty.

"I must confess that I am somewhat intrigued. What exactly is going on?"

Ainaes took a long draught out of her glass and said, "We'll explain everything in detail once Eolum and the others get here. But suffice it to say that your New Year's performance made quite an impression. I mean, there are still people asking us who you were, and how to get hold of you." She paused. "And I can tell you that it wasn't that easy to find that out for ourselves, even though we're very good at researching people's backgrounds."

Meropat took a gulp of ale to hide their consternation. It was true that they hadn't exactly made themselves conspicuous around Valja recently, but for an artist, visibility was everything. Furthermore, they doubted anyone could deliberately hide at the back of a bagpipe shop. "I've had to shut myself away for a few weeks — not for health reasons," they hastily added, "but for my work. I have an urgent commission, you see, and a well-known person such as myself sometimes has to dedicate themself entirely to their muse, otherwise inspiration — not to speak of funding — can run completely dry."

"I see," the Sister said drily. "Well, here we are nevertheless. Tell me, how *is* your muse at the moment? Do they feel ready for a new assignment?"

"Always," Meropat answered promptly. "What did you have in mind?"

"You work at a print shop, is that correct?"

"Yes, well, one has to earn one's daily bread somehow. During these past couple of years it hasn't been exactly easy to earn one's living through the performing arts."

Ainaes waved the explanations away impatiently. "The printer, what's his name? Do you know his affiliations?"

"Affiliations? Political, you mean?" Meropat scoffed. "He isn't interested in anything else but the number of printed pages that flows through his door. Master Keltuva is his name."

The sister and her retainer exchanged glances. The man gave another small shrug. "Never heard of him," Ainaes said. "Which, in this case, is a good thing. We don't want any troublemakers, and we definitely don't want anyone too closely allied with the Guilds."

At this point, Eolum arrived, followed by three people Meropat vaguely remembered from the earlier meeting. In passing, the Brother clapped Meropat on the shoulder. They watched the two leaders greet each other with a swift kiss.

Seeing their intent gaze, Ainaes said, "You've probably heard the rumors. Whether you believe them is your own business. I will only say this: Eolum is the only family I have. He is my second self, and closer to me than any other person will ever be."

"I can see that," Meropat said with a small calming gesture. "And I have nothing but admiration for the bond I see before me. People who leap to filthy conclusions have never experienced anything like it, and never will."

"Listen to the poet," Eolum said, including the others in his remark. "A silver tongue to go with that impressive figure. We could really use someone like you in the movement, Meropat. Are you willing to work for the Cause?"

Pleased and somewhat flustered by the direct question, Meropat took another sip of ale before answering. "I'm tremendously flattered, of course. I'd just like to know a bit more about the kind of work I'm supposed to be doing. Your sister mentioned Master Keltuva's printing press. Would I be required to make use of it for the Cause?"

Eolum gave an eloquent shrug. "In the future, perhaps. We are always looking for new ways to spread our message. At the moment, word of mouth is the safest, and most efficient."

"I thought literacy was relatively high in Valja," Meropat said.

"Most people can read, if it's nothing too complicated," said the Sister. "You saw the pamphlet we circulated earlier. But it's not just short texts like that — not anymore. There are some very interesting new thinkers in Nebe that we'd like to translate into Sendali. We've also heard of a woman who was writing some groundbreaking texts before the plague, which are now being read all over the Eastern Islands. What was her name? Rondel?"

"Rondei Galsi," said Meropat quietly.

All eyes were suddenly on their face. "You know Mistress Galsi?" asked Eolum almost breathlessly. His sister made a small squeak of excitement.

"Yes, Rondei and I go way back. Creative people seek each other out." As everyone was waiting for them to continue, they said, "Unfortunately I have no idea where she is right now. We have some friends in common. I could discreetly ask around."

"Could you?" Ainaes asked. "That would be a tremendous help."

The young people started talking shop amongst themselves, leaving Meropat to finish their beer in silence. It was twice now they had made use of Rondei's name to impress other people. Although Meropat wasn't particularly superstitious, the idea that this couldn't be a coincidence tugged on their already preoccupied mind. Mistress Galsi seemed to be the woman of the hour — and whether they liked it or not, Meropat needed to tie their name to hers. Not just for immediate profit, but to simply survive the increasingly unstable situation in Valja.

The seemingly interminable meeting finally over, Meropat made their excuses and tottered into the starlit street. Very little had been decided, as far as they could tell. That, of course, was the nature of most meetings. The Skovos had continued to beam on the poet, making vague remarks about commissioning a song from them, but mostly focusing on the shadowy and increasingly alluring figure of Mistress Galsi.

Meropat walked along the river, humming under their breath. They had enough on their plate. The damned epic was going nowhere, particularly as the printer was piling more duties on top of each other every day, and his neighbor was churning out more and more bagpipes by the hour. And now they had another task to see to — and not a paid one, either. In a bout of rashness that was quickly becoming habitual, they had mentioned they could try to find out the possible whereabouts of Rondei Galsi, and possibly even try to persuade her to work for the Skovos.

A slim ginger cat wandered past, greeting Meropat with an undertone miaow. Walking side by side with the animal, the poet shared their anxiousness aloud.

"This is a rotten mess and no mistake, kitty dearest. When was the last time I even saw this blasted woman? Three years ago? Four?"

The cat bumped against their leg.

"Could be. And can't say I made much of an impression on her. She certainly didn't make one on me. Dry, serious creature. But I suppose there's something about the texts she writes that makes people light up."

Purring.

Meropat stooped to pick up the cat and continued with their new friend towards the Brewers' Quarter. "I just wish I could keep my mouth shut sometimes. Would keep me out of a great deal of trouble."

"Oh, you bet," a low voice said behind them.

The cat climbed onto Meropat's shoulder, stiffening into a hissing arc. A man stepped out of the shadows — accompanied by a wolf-like dog.

"Heather!" they exclaimed with some relief, as the dog licked their hand. "And Bel," they nodded at the looming man. "What are you doing here, scaring innocent cats half to death?"

"Never mind that," said Beldor Amsta. "The question is, what in the name of all hells do you think you're doing, Meropat?"

Chapter 3

Sendal - Ardelei

The border guards were taking their time. The old couple who had preceded Ardelei into the small tin-roofed shed had come out some time ago, arguing in an undertone and trying hastily to put their disordered belongings to rights. The silver disc of the sun stared down at her from a cloudless sky. A queue was forming behind her, and Ardelei could hear people complaining about the dust and the heat in several languages. Many, like her, were traveling on foot — perhaps on their way to see friends and family members they hadn't been able to visit for months. All agreed that delays like this were highly unusual.

At last, a short, squat woman peered out of the shed and threw a lazy gesture at Ardelei, who had her introduction ready, and had loosened the strings of her bag in anticipation of an inspection. The inside of the tin-roofed hut was considerably hotter than the outside air, and smelled uncomfortably of half-digested garlic. It took a while for her to adjust her eyes, as well as her magic, in the enclosed space.

"Good day," she greeted the two other guards inside. While doing so, she took in the rather monotonous song they shared.

These were people who had worked together for a long time, and did not necessarily enjoy the experience.

"Your name and destination, please," the nearest guard said in a nasal voice, and in quite halting Sendali.

"Ardelei Jolama. I'm on my way to Valja." She handed her introduction to the man.

"Well," he said as if to himself, holding the small object aloft, and then turning it carefully in his fingers. "Won't you look at this."

Most introductions were made of fine but perishable materials: silk or linen in the case of aristocrats, leather for merchants and sailors. Before the plague, there had been a fashion for metal introductions — gold or silver — but even then, those were seen as tempting fate. A person's introduction, just like their life, is mutable, and eventually disposable.

In Arrika, there were more subtle ways of working introductions. Ardelei's current one was a solid spell. A song which described her origins, affiliations and various accomplishments, but only to those who had the ears to listen. The rest would have to rely on their other senses. To the untrained eye, it looked like a smooth stone which changed color ever so slightly from deep blue to radiant purple. It nestled comfortably on a palm, and on a summer's day it felt pleasantly cool to the touch. It gave off a subtle scent of pine which lingered in the air for a few moments. There were scented introductions as well, but in Ardelei's view it wasn't polite to stain other people's hands with cheap perfume.

The two other guards were now craning their necks as well. The Zeiroan reluctantly handed the introduction over. Even though she could have done it to ease the situation, Ardelei was careful not to add any more magic to the existing spell. Non-mages could rarely tell that they were being manipulated in this way, but the uncanny feeling of the material tended to get them uncomfortably interested in the origin of the object. Today, Ardelei would have preferred to get moving as quickly as possible.

The guards, however, had time to kill. They passed the introduction from hand to hand, commenting on its beauty and speculating on its source. As the sun moved higher, the poorly ventilated hut started to resemble a hammam.

At last, the stout Sendali woman looked up, handing back the introduction. "Valja, you said? What is your business there?"

"Merely personal," Ardelei smiled, pocketing the song-spell.

"Have family there?"

"You could say that." As the woman only continued staring at her, she said, "Yes."

"You don't mind if we take a look at your bag?" suggested the third guard, who had so far remained silent. He had a marked Zeiroan accent, but spoke Sendali much more fluently than his colleague. It was also clear to Ardelei that he not only had the keenest tongue, but also the sharpest ears of the lot. By his Hallerian-style uniform it was clear that he held the highest rank among them. Experience had taught her not to catch the attention of such people.

"Not at all. Go ahead."

Ardelei hoisted her bag onto the counter, and watched the taciturn guard expertly rifle through its contents. One by one, he selected out of the bag three items which he laid on the counter: a sachet of herbs, a stack of letters, and a tiny phial of clear liquid.

Without prompting, she identified the items. "Paishnali medicines: mostly painkillers," she said, pointing at the sachet and the small bottle. "Bought them in Elandina. I've kept the receipt, if you're interested."

"We're not," said the guard. "The letters?"

"Personal correspondence, as you would expect." She untied the bundle. "In several languages, as you can see. I have contacts all over Ederai, and beyond."

"What is your business in Valja?"

"Personal, as I said." She modulated her voice to a calmer register. There was a strange harmonic to the conversation, which, coupled with the unusually phlegmatic nature of the guards, made her nervous in turn. "What is going on in the city?"

The woman butted in. "Hopefully nothing. There's just some gossip going around, regarding the situation there. There usually is," she finished, at the sharp glance from her superior. "Gossip, I mean."

"The situation?" In Elandina, there had been very few tidings concerning Sendal in general. As far as Ardelei could tell, the country and its capital were as busy getting on their feet as the rest of the island was. "Has the plague returned?"

"Nothing like that," said the first man in his limping Sendali. "The Guilds are just having a spot of trouble."

He, in turn, was silenced by an angry wave from the officer. "Hold your tongue. That is nothing for us to worry about." His voice, however, told a different story. "Are you in any way connected to the Guilds of Valja?"

"No. As an Arrikan, I'm not allowed to hold any such affiliations. And anyway, it's over two years since I've been there."

"Very well." The officer stamped a piece of paper and gave it to her. "Give this to the city guards at the gate. Have a good day, madam."

Walking along the wide, dusty road northward Ardelei had time to reflect on the conversation. Since when was it necessary to hand in a document of entry at the city gate – and what purpose did the documents serve? The plague had changed many routines all over Ederai, but it seemed that something else was causing the increased vigilance in Valja. Before, no one had been particularly interested in people traveling on foot: it was only those arriving on carts or boats who caught the Guilds' attention, as the contents of those vehicles needed to be declared – and hopefully, taxed.

She had been meaning to enter the city quietly, find a place to stay, and only then look up her contacts. Now, it was becoming clear that she needed someone to give her a thorough briefing –

preferably before she even walked through the gates. As she stopped to fill her water bottle at a roadside fountain, she decided that sticking to her original plan wasn't wise, given the unclear circumstances. Instead of going straight into Valja, she would skirt the city from the east, getting her bearings on the way.

After a restless night under the stars, she made an early start, relying more on her ears than her eyes to find the right route. The song that made up this part of Sendal had always been a busy one, with the everyday noises of working people and their animals, the rattle of wheels and windmills, and the occasional birdsong weaving themselves into an easily recognizable tapestry of sound.

The natural noises were still there. An early-morning breeze whispered in the thistles of the abandoned fields on both sides of the road. Birds and insects went about their daily lives, and small animals rustled in the undergrowth. A hunting hawk circled ever upwards in the warming air, now and then giving voice to a high-pitched call. Ardelei passed the creaking ghost of a windmill, its arms listlessly swaying in the rising wind. Half an hour later, she saw a glimpse of a herd of wild cows disappearing into the nearby woods.

Although she had been prepared for such scenes, the sheer scope of the desolation chilled her to the very core. In the song of the land itself, she could hear a slow note of relief. The fields and forests had been left to their own ancient rhythms, finally released from the domination of the human hand. A part of her mourned the passing of the people who had put down roots here uncounted generations ago. Clearly, the survivors hadn't had the heart to remain, but had opted for a new life elsewhere.

She was forewarned of the abandoned village by the mourning stones that started appearing by the roadside at regular intervals. Some of them lay by themselves, covered in dust and light-green moss; these were somehow even more heartbreaking than the larger groups of stones of various sizes – many of which were frequently visited, their surfaces shiny clean, all surrounded by mounds of white pebbles.

As she walked, Ardelei began a slow mourning-song, partly to remind the land of its former inhabitants, but mainly to comfort herself. Her journey from Luneken to Zeiroa had been full of heartbreak and worry. On the ship, however, she'd been spared the reality of the abandoned land. In Elandina, she'd encountered many boarded-up shopfronts and seen gangs of orphaned children; yet, those sights had been tempered with the everyday bustle of a living city. Here, there was nothing else but herself and the altered harmony of the land around her.

She kept her eyes on the horizon. Although the empty villages she passed could give sustenance and shelter, she couldn't stop in any of them. Not for the fear of other travelers, or of any lingering disease. Her fear was that the songs of the small tragedies would start building up into a burden that would slow her down for the rest of her journey. For the time being, she'd decided to travel light – mainly because she didn't know how long that journey was going to be.

Darkness was gathering under the trees and around the roadside stones. Ardelei had walked the whole day under the scorching sky, barely stopping to eat. A new urgency was driving her — and it wasn't just the unease that hovered about the road. It felt as if the song of Ederai itself was changing – not in the usual slow way, but rapidly and with some discord. In the safety of Arrika, she'd been sheltered from such changes; now, she would have to try to modulate her own music to the new song she was sensing.

To fully understand these greater changes, she needed a safe space to stay for a while. She had long since dropped the mourning song, and concentrated on listening to the land around her, seeking to understand its underlying harmony and draw strength from it. Slowly, she started adding her own melody to the song of the road, gradually pitching her voice ever upwards, making use of the open sky above. In the past, she had rarely dared to use her magic so openly; right now, the few open ears wouldn't be concentrated on her feeble efforts.

Moving north, Ardelei pitched her voice ever higher, leaning on her magic where her natural register started to fail. Soon, the sound was inaudible even to her own ears. As the sun went down, and stars slid up one by one, there was a purple twilight moment. Gazing up, she could suddenly see dark shapes flitting above her, drawing nearer and then disappearing again. For a moment, she was at a loss – until she realized that her squeaking had fascinated a nearby colony of bats. She sang with the small creatures for a while to reassure them, and then left them to their nocturnal business.

Towards midnight, someone else finally responded to her call. Out of the woods, a sleek four-legged shape stalked towards her, stopping a dozen paces away. As Ardelei acknowledged it with a small change to her song, it turned and began leading her into the heart of the forest. She tried to keep up, but a day's trek and the two restless nights were beginning to weigh on her already tired legs. At first, she had to stop singing, just to be able to hear her guide's footfall on the dry forest floor. Finally, she gave up. The woods were a labyrinth of dark, tall shapes, with an uneven ground that kept trying to trip her up with roots and rocks.

"Heather!" she called. "Slow down."

A few moments passed. Then, she heard the approach of the dog, and soon felt its warm breath against her palm.

"It's good to see you, too," she said, as Heather licked her face with unabashed abandon. "I was beginning to fear you hadn't heard me."

Beldor Amsta was one of her oldest friends. Theirs was a relationship that didn't depend on constant communication. They met infrequently, often unexpectedly and without ceremony – and every time it felt as if they just picked up the conversation where they'd left off. Ardelei wasn't particularly concerned about how Bel occupied himself during these times apart, neither did she report her comings and goings to him. When they came together, they had better things to do.

Heather led her to a small lake that was surrounded by a grassy clearing. The water glittered in the starlight and smelled sweetly of summer. The dog drank noisily and wagged her tail as Ardelei stopped for a drink as well.

"A nice place you've got here," she said.

There was a house nearby, nestled among the ancient oaks and elms. It looked very comfortable, by Beldor's standards, which usually ranked invisibility above any other quality. Then again, there was a lot more choice at the moment, if one didn't believe in ghosts, or mind them. Yellow light poured out of the windows — a sign that he was expecting her. Otherwise, he was never keen to advertise his whereabouts.

Heather made her way to the porch and gave a small woof. The door opened wide, and light and the delicious smell of cooking meat poured out, making her immediately weak at the knees. Then there was Beldor: unchanged, as far as she could tell.

"Well," he said. "I was getting worried."

She knew he meant the dog; Heather never strayed far away from Bel, nor he from Heather. Yet, there was a note of unease that she'd never heard in his song before. "I'm glad to see you too. Anything in particular to be worried about?"

He stood aside to let her enter. She had just enough time to put down her bag before he drew her into a tight embrace, which turned into a long, knee-trembling kiss.

"You know," he finally said. "There's all kinds of strange folk abroad right now."

"I *don't* know," she said, mainly to Heather who was watching them raptly. "I thought I hadn't been away for that long, but now it seems that Ederai has changed beyond recognition."

"Perhaps it has." The strange, uncertain note sounded again. Then, he smiled. "But luckily, there are many things that have stayed the same."

Heather, always the more polite of the two, was anxious to give a tour of their new home, and Ardelei obliged. The inspection didn't take long. There were two rooms of equal size — one with a four-poster bed in it, the other with a stove, a table, and a neat stack of firewood. It looked as if the cottage had been looted at some point — or else the previous inhabitants had known they weren't coming back and had taken all their belongings with them. There were no curtains, no dishes on the shelves, and no candles in the holders. The yellow light Ardelei had seen came from two dusty oil lamps.

She turned to look at Beldor instead. Her friend looked the same as he'd always done: tall, spare, with straggly hair and beard. His skin had gotten darker with the summer sun, but he was still several shades lighter than her. The years they'd spent apart hadn't aged him at all. His green-brown eyes stared at her with the same boyish frankness she remembered from their first meeting, and the one streak of gray in his beard hadn't grown any wider. Then again, she'd always regarded him as somehow old for his years — in spirit, if not in appearance. He'd had to take care of himself from a young age, and didn't care what the world thought of him. He's chosen the luxury of freedom, but had paid a high price for it.

He was giving her a similar scrutiny, with a small smile playing at the corner of his mouth. Heather wagged her tail, just to show that she understood the nature of their game, too.

"Well?" she asked the two of them. "What do you see?"

"I see a woman who's on the run." He stepped closer to her again, touching her cheek with his dry fingertips. "I heard the rumors, but didn't believe them. There is so much nonsense around these days. And now —"

Ardelei blinked. "Your eyes are as keen as ever. Yet, rumors are rarely the whole truth. What have you heard?"

"Someone told me you'd left Luneken immediately after the bridges opened. That didn't surprise me. But then, someone else said that you'd run away, and had no intention of ever returning. How come?"

"The whole truth is always much more complicated than that." She closed her eyes for a moment. There was a buzzing sound in her head, and she felt faint for a moment. "I'll tell you tomorrow. Unless you're in a hurry to go somewhere?"

He laughed briefly. "You know me. Heather has more pressing engagements than I."

They sat down for a late-night meal, with Heather at the head of the table surreptitiously licking her lips in anticipation of her share. Although she was hungry, at first Ardelei found it hard to concentrate on the food: the sheer physical thrill of sharing a private space with Beldor resonated to her very core. His song had, from the first, harmonized closely with hers. They needed few words to say what they really meant, and rarely said anything more.

Through her song-sense she had quickly become aware of their differences, too. For all of her adult life, she had been tied to the Linduvan community, willingly serving those who needed her, and traveling around Ederai, and beyond, in the service of her order. She had friends in every major town, and readily learned the ways of others to increase her own knowledge. She had befriended many people for the skills they taught her, and for their eager acceptance of her own, hard-earned competence.

Bel, on the other hand, was a born loner. Even his beloved Heather had come to him by accident, and for a long time he'd tried to find her another master. Yet, the stubborn lavender-colored puppy had clung to him with such tenacity that finally he'd admitted defeat and opened his heart to her. Now, they were inseparable, and even their musics sounded alike.

Beldor traveled, too – indeed, Ardelei had never known him to have a permanent home. It wasn't entirely clear to her whether he was really Sendali by birth; perhaps he didn't quite know himself. He tolerated people around him, but would take no life-partner – and even friends found that he'd unceremoniously pack up and leave when he'd had enough of their company, even if that meant leaving his present lodgings behind.

Like her, Bel was a person of many skills. When times were hard, he made his living as a hunter – although he himself ate almost no meat and wore no fur. The animals he killed he either sold or gave to Heather. During the summer season, he gathered and sold medicinal herbs, and gave advice on how to use them. Ardelei herself had taught him some of that craft. And he, in turn, had introduced her to some of the rarer Sendali plants. Overall, he had always appeared content with his lot in life, and that is why Ardelei found her way to him year after year. In her profession, she'd learned to appreciate people like that above all else.

Of course, like most of her friends, Beldor wasn't quite what he seemed on the surface. Despite having disowned his sprawling merchant family, he still made use of the connections the Amstas had made over the centuries, trading all over the known world. He spoke several languages with the same reluctance he used his mother tongue, which gave him an unseen advantage as a diplomat. Mediating between hostile groups doesn't necessarily take many words, if one knows the right ones and the right time to use them.

Although he gave the appearance of complete independence, it was impossible for him, too, to live completely without human ties — and with said ties often came various obligations. His worldliness also meant that he rarely missed much. Even now, he was sending her concerned glances from under his black brows.

"It's true," she sighed, just to make him stop. "I've left Arrika, and I'm not going back. I can't."

He put his hand over hers. "I heard they selected a new leader."

"Darbei Kusvin." It was remarkably difficult to get the four syllables past her teeth. "A half-Hallerian traditionalist."

A pause. "I see. And you two don't agree."

"That's one way of putting it. I've never had anything against her, personally. But I couldn't just stand by when she started gathering supporters. In the end I decided that I should do the same. Unfortunately, turns out that she had more friends in the order than I did."

"Were you surprised?"

"Perhaps not." She put down her spoon; her appetite had abandoned her. "But I have to say that I was surprised at the vehemence of her supporters. And at the lengths they are ready to go to protect their own interests."

"That doesn't sound very traditional to me."

"You tell them. I tried to, and was shouted down, time and again. In the end I decided that Ederai means more to me than Arrika does."

Beldor didn't answer. He understood that the explanation she'd given was only the beginning of a much deeper story, and he had the patience to wait for the rest. Ardelei handed a piece of bread to Heather, who disappeared under the table. Beldor finished his ale.

"You know where the bedroom is. Make yourself comfortable. I'll take a swim, and will be right back."

She woke up before him, but stayed where she was, with his arm around her middle and his breath warm against her neck. In sleep, his music was barely there – but as always, Ardelei found it safe and soothing. She followed a patch of sunlight as it slowly moved across the floor, and listened to Heather's footsteps as the dog circled the cottage in search of mice, and defeated, settled on the porch to sleep. The seeming simplicity of Beldor's life had its attractions, but she knew that it was only a matter of time before the more complicated parts started to emerge.

He took a deep breath and moved closer. Barely emerged from sleep, he started kissing her neck with increasing intensity. His hard manhood was already pushing against her buttocks, and it wasn't long until he was moving inside her in a slow, leisurely way. She closed her eyes, letting his rhythm take over first her body, and then her entire consciousness. She'd needed this very badly – but even more so, she'd craved the brief moment of complete forgetfulness when nothing else existed but her own body and the body of the man beside her.

That, however, was always over far too quickly. As they lay entwined in the tangled sheets, Ardelei was aware of the expectation in every breath Beldor took. He was waiting for her to continue her dropped explanation. Most likely he, too, had something to tell her.

"Why are you here?" she began.

"This is a good place. Good fishing. Pretty good hunting, too. Heather enjoys the woods: there aren't many predators here. She's been working at a badger's nest for a couple of weeks now. I suspect the animals are long gone, but she seems to find a lot of amusement in just digging around, so I haven't stopped her."

Ardelei smiled. "Yes, but why are you here?"

A grunt. "You don't give up easily, do you?" He eased himself out of her, and rolled onto his back. "There are a couple of reasons."

"What's going on in Valja?" she asked, tired of fishing. "The border guards told me that the gates were as good as closed, and I got the impression that the Guilds are feeling threatened somehow – and not by the plague this time."

"Hm," he said. "The Guilds have discovered that those who control the gates, control everything else within the city as well. During the worst of the plague, the citizens were pretty happy to keep outsiders away, just as long as goods kept coming in. There was some talk of favoritism: that only certain merchants and certain farmers were allowed to sell food to Valja. Last summer, before harvest, there were some riots all over the city. Nothing came of it, at that time — mainly because there was another outbreak, and things quietened down."

Ardelei was quick to spot an opening. "So this time, something *is* happening?"

He didn't answer.

"How are you involved? Bel?"

"As little as possible. But I have some debts to pay, and my own interests to protect. Your interests, too."

She drew an annoyed breath and turned to look at him. His only response was a lazy grin. "Pray tell me, Beldor, how you've been protecting my interests while I've been away," she said in the most formal Sendali she could muster so early in the day.

"Mainly by not mentioning you to anyone. But I assume you're still friendly with that book printing cousin of yours?"

"Rondei? I am, as far as I know. We haven't been able to keep in touch since she took up the post in Daurbar. As I understand it, the Pass has been sealed shut these two years."

"Not entirely. She's been able to smuggle out some incendiary material and spread it all over Sendal, by the sound of it. Valja in particular."

"Why Valja of all places? They have the most printshops in northern Ederai. Why would they want her stuff so desperately?"

"Because it's just that. Her own stuff. Your cousin has started writing her own pamphlets, and I can tell you that it's not material fit for a schoolroom." He was looking unusually serious as he said, "Your cousin has turned into a revolutionary. And she's got a growing following among the young workers of Valja."

"So let me get this straight," Ardelei said. She was sitting on the dock, drying herself after a long, delicious swim. Beldor was still immersed in the water up to his neck. "Rondei has been working as a tutor for Lord Stainerau's niece, and all the while she's been writing political pamphlets behind his back?"

"Not only that, she's managed to smuggle out some of her writings — the latest one being a letter addressed to you."

She sat up straighter. "How did you come across the letter?"

"That is a long story." His head disappeared under the water. When it surfaced again, it was much closer to the shore. He strode out of the lake, shaking himself dry like a dog, before joining her on the dock. He kissed her shoulder, leaving a trail of water from his beard. "And it's better if you don't know the details. But I don't have the letter. The messenger would only give it to you in person."

"And where is the messenger?" Before he could answer, she'd already guessed. "Well, as it happens, I was on my way to Valja anyway."

The Sendali capital was in many ways as it had always been: crowded, smelly and unbearably loud. Ardelei's senses were soon overwhelmed, and she had to duck into an elegant little tavern just to be able to breathe. The young man behind the bar gave her a quick scrutiny, but at the sight of her purse he relaxed into a more customer-friendly attitude and mixed her a glass of switchel with a dollop of honey for good measure. Hearing her complaints about the noise, he commiserated, noting that the first week of a month was always busier than the rest — and in summertime, there were bound to be more people about anyway.

Having enjoyed her drink, Ardelei felt much more prepared for the throng. She was also minded to observe the city from a more neutral perspective: that, after all, had been part of her long training. A Linduvan mage was taught to see past surfaces, and to lay all preconceptions aside. A bustling marketplace, however, was very different from a meeting of serene minds. The short meeting with the Guild guards at the gate had already warned her of the particularly lively mood Valja had decided to put on after its long isolation.

Indeed, even at this relatively genteel part of town it was difficult to find a place to stand without being jostled from all sides by market-goers, cart-dogs and casual pickpockets. Very soon, Ardelei decided to drop her observation and move on. And anyway, she'd seen enough to understand the general mood of the city. The balmy heat of early summer had brought out the best and the worst of Valja; while the streets were unbearably busy, they were also lined with blossoming fruit trees and tubs of herbs which strewed their sweet odors into the lazily moving air. Children barged past her, wearing dirty summer linens, followed by yapping terriers and even smaller children desperate to keep up.

Following the flow of people and half-listening to their chatter, Ardelei suddenly realized that her usually unerring sense of direction had failed her. The quarter which she remembered hosting an abundance of small shops and a maze of interconnected marketplaces seemed to have vanished into thin air. The familiar cobbled streets still ran in a general north–south orientation, but most of the surrounding houses were gone. In the distance, she could hear the reassuring notes of the river Ruoke — but the rest of the song around her was in a completely different key. The wind blew unimpeded where tall walls used to stand, and she could still see some charred roofbeams sticking out of the nearest mound of rubble.

This wasn't a good place to linger. Whatever had happened here was already fading from living memory. Grass grew in the now-empty lots, and swallows darted out of glassless windows. Ardelei set her course towards the river, careful not to draw attention to herself. She'd already understood that while outsiders could enter Valja, they needed a good reason for their visit – otherwise, their documents would be stamped with a red circle indicating only a day's welcome. There were guards at street corners, ready to ask uncomfortable questions, and to escort any overstayed visitor out of the gates.

She didn't remember ever having visited the Silver Hound before, but she saw right away that it was the kind of place her cousin would feel right at home in. Although there was a certain grubbiness to the common room, it had large windows and bright oil lamps to illuminate all times of the day. Rondei would get anxious if she wasn't able to scribble things down when the mood took her, and it seemed that the current clientele shared her habits. The selection of comestibles was limited, as was that of drinks, but the prices seemed fair. Even in this lazy afternoon hour there were pale young persons lounging about, the necks of their shirts open, their long-fingered hands stained with ink.

Ardelei made it straight to the counter, which for the moment stood abandoned. She could hear noises coming from the cellar, and was eventually rewarded with the sight of a barrel of ale rolling into the room, followed by a peevish-looking woman.

"Can I do for you?" the innkeeper asked.

"I'd like to sample some of that ale, please," said Ardelei in her most jovial cadence. "If it's not too much trouble."

"Well," said the woman, wrestling the barrel into place behind the bar. "The weather's so hot that beer just seems to evaporate into thin air." She glared at the clientele, who had perked up at the entrance of the ale.

"Surely that's not a bad thing? I mean, business must have been rather slow over the past two winters."

"It was, and you didn't hear me complain." The innkeeper plonked a carelessly filled glass on the counter. "You're paying now or later?"

"Actually," Ardelei said, lowering her voice ever so slightly. "I came to collect something. A gift from a good friend of mine who had to leave in a hurry. A book, I believe."

The woman frowned. "Don't remember no book."

She worked the slightest hint of persuasion into her voice. "You could look."

Instead of following Ardelei's suggestion, the innkeeper turned and called in a shrill voice. In a moment, a gangly young man appeared — directly from the kitchen judging by his floury appearance.

"Lady wants a book," the woman said, nodding towards Ardelei.

The mage met the young man's bewildered eyes. "It was left by a friend of mine not many weeks ago. I'm Ardelei Jolama."

"A gentleman friend?" the youth asked hopefully.

"Yes," said Ardelei, without hesitation. In fact, the instructions Beldor had given her had been extremely minimalistic. Among other things, the gender of the hypothetical friend had been omitted. All she knew was that the sound of her own name should be enough to procure the parcel in question.

What Beldor had explained in some detail was that the Silver Hound operated as an underground post office of a kind. Those in the know could leave messages and even little parcels behind the counter, and the recipients could bail them out. After some rummaging, the young man handed her a linen-wrapped package with a small tag attached. Ardelei pressed a coin into the expectant hand, downed her ale, and made her way quietly out of the door.

With the parcel securely in her bag, she moved along the river, making sure to appear unhurried and in no way unsure of her destination. Following the smell of cooking, she eventually found the small street lined with nondescript boarding houses that had served her in similar situations many times before. This, at least, hadn't changed in the two years she had been out of Valja.

In her room — which had only the smallest excuse for a window, and a similar amount of insulation — Ardelei dumped the contents of her by now disordered bag onto the bed, and unceremoniously tore open the linen wrappings of the parcel. Rondei, she remembered, wasn't an enthusiastic needlewoman, but her stitches were as neat and unwavering as her handwriting. In the end, she had to sit down and unpick the work with the help of her small scissors.

The book was small, only the width of her palm. It was without a doubt her cousin's own work: unremarkable at first glance, but bound and printed with such immaculate care so as to be close to pure magic. Ardelei had always suspected that Mistress Galsi sublimated her frustrated sorcery into her work — and this was as good a proof as any. Rondei only sold her finest books to people who would appreciate them. Ardelei wondered what she'd have to pay for this unexpected gift from the Mountain realm.

The work itself was a Sendali translation of a classic tract on the nature of good and evil, written by the Hallerian philosopher Eberleis — a distant relative of Lord Stainerau, and thus in vogue in his court. Knowing her cousin's methods, Ardelei ran her fingertips carefully along the cover, then the binding, and finally the sturdy pages themselves, one by one. Nothing. No hidden pieces of paper woven into the back; no lumps or bumps anywhere. When held up to the light of the slowly setting sun, the pages only showed faint traces of Zeiroan watermarks — no code or other hidden symbols to be deciphered.

Nothing to it. She'd have to read the damn thing.

The light of the long summer's day was finally failing. Ardelei ordered a light supper into her room — delivered by a cowering child of indiscriminate gender — and ate without paying the meal any particular attention. Despite not being an admirer of golden-age Hallerian thought, she had to admit that old Eberleis had a clarity of expression many of her contemporaries could only have dreamed of. Then again, it could be that the scalpel-sharp style was the contribution of Rondei herself. The printer didn't have any scruples about tampering with her source material, as long as the result was elegant and comprehensible.

Ardelei lit a lamp, and after a while another one. The smell of oil was nauseating, but the brightness of the flame also made her see the book in front of her in a slightly different way. Turning the page, she became aware of a strange shadow some of the letters cast, as if they had been pressed onto the paper with more force, and with a different-colored ink. Ardelei wasn't a scholar by any means, but through Rondei she'd learned to appreciate the robust skill and subtle science that went into the production of books. Her cousin was particularly proud of the even quality of her printed pages: fonts were of the exact same size; lines were ruler-straight, and margins were equal and elegant everywhere.

Knowing this almost obsessive streak (perhaps having also made fun of it from time to time), Ardelei began turning the pages, looking for similar discrepancies. And sure enough, she found some. Not glaring ones — just ones that a mediocre printer wouldn't even have paid attention to. There was a slightly smaller letter at the end of a line. A bolded one in the middle of a word on the following page. A hanging line inelegantly jutting into the margin soon after.

With slightly trembling hands, Ardelei took out a pencil and a piece of paper, and started compiling words, and then sentences, out of the irregular elements of the book. Soon, it became clear how easy it was to miss them: Rondei, in her perfectionism, and perhaps also in fear of being found out, had made some of the irregularities extremely easy to miss. Finally, through a lot of squinting and swearing, and quite a lot of guesswork, Ardelei managed to decipher the message.

It was in Nebian, to begin with. Their mother tongue didn't have a standardized writing system, but Rondei had always preferred the Hallerian model to the more usual Sendali one. Ardelei had to keep this in mind as she divided words into sentences. The capitalization, she realized, also made a difference.

She paused for a moment. She had been so engrossed in her task that she had been able to filter out the nightly noises of the city around her. Now, as someone dropped a bottle onto the cobbles right outside her window, she was startled out of her cocoon of concentration. Simultaneously, she also became aware of the other occupants in the rooms around her. From above and below, as well as from left and right, emanated the insistent songs of half a dozen people – some sleeping, some worrying aloud, some silently pacing the narrow space. At least one couple in bed, trying to take joy in each other.

She glanced down on the sheet of paper in front of her. "Well," she said quietly to her dark reflection. "Good thing I wasn't planning on staying. This is becoming a theme, rather."

The paper spelled out the words, *Need a disguise and an introduction. Come to the Pass, ask to deliver a message to Lady Solsdar. If you need more information, find the messenger. Can be trusted, but not involved.*

Chapter 4

Haller - Rondei

There was a loud crash behind them, as if a large chunk of the mountainside had just sloughed off and rolled downhill. Their guide didn't even flinch; nor did he look back.

"Rocks. Usual at this time of year. Lucky we didn't stop for lunch there."

Rondei exchanged a glance with the older woman walking beside her. "Indeed."

The time and place of their midday meal had been fiercely debated all morning. Rondei wouldn't have been surprised if the clamor of their voices had precipitated this particular cascade of rocks in the first place. Hallerians were good at many things, but they excelled in debating the most insignificant things with indefatigable logic and great passion — and winning, whenever possible. This time, experience had won over volume.

The narrow path traveled upwards in winding loops. Rondei's linen shirt was already sticking to her skin – another sign that she'd been cooped up indoors for too long, occupying herself with exercises of the mind rather than those of the body. This order of things usually suited her fine. However, if her plan were to succeed, she'd need to be hardier than this, and much more flexible about the ankles.

Good thing that she'd set no definite date for her return to Daurbar. Lord Stainerau only knew that Mistress Galsi had expressed a wish to see more of her new home country, and profiting of the balmy weather, had gone hiking with some friends in the northwest. To this, even the usually querulous lord hadn't been able to find a counterargument: all Hallerians loved their mountains almost as much as they loved arguing about the best way to experience them.

She'd carefully chosen her companions, Lady Mittensel and Lady Solsdar — two women of stout opinions and similarly robust constitutions — and knew that she could trust them to stick to their plan with the obstinacy of old mastiffs. Had she been looking for sparkling conversation, or a boundless interest in the natural world, she would have chosen differently. This time, however, she'd settled for people with little imagination and a narrow field of interests. And, as it turned out, far stronger legs than hers.

The guide was another matter. Lord Stainerau had insisted on introducing her to one of his own trusted men who could navigate the deadly mountain passes in any condition. This was definitely a boon. Yet, Rondei had to keep in mind that the guide, who insisted on being called Ylm, was staunchly loyal to his lord, and would only follow a route carefully planned for foreign visitors. Rondei, however, wasn't dying to visit a salt mine. Neither was she passionate about rare, fragile mountain flowers which were reputed to have invigorating qualities if picked by starlight.

She had one simple goal: leaving Haller. And, with her methodical mind, she'd worked out a plan to accomplish that goal. People, she knew, were unpredictable and frail. Still, the biggest hurdle was turning out to be the land itself. There were blocked paths, impossibly steep climbs, and sudden ice storms that turned the entire landscape into a white, slippery desert.

And, just as that was getting predictable, it tried to kill one by throwing a massive boulder at one's head.

On their third evening, they stopped at a lakeside cabin which was perfectly suited for a party of four. After supper, as the two ladies sat on the porch, admiring the scenery, Rondei joined Ylm at the table. Their guide had a habit of going over their next day's route, even though he knew the paths like his roomy pockets. Rondei recognized a fellow lover of maps, and had made a point of studying the lie of the land with him — all the while trying not to appear too eager. This was quite easy to accomplish: they were still a long hike away from the border, and Ylm invariably dithered over the various routes in an infuriating way.

The map itself wasn't much to look at. It was a fourth-hand copy of an old, inaccurate chart of the mountains. Previous owners had scribbled comments and drawn in their own markings in different inks, indicating broken paths and places where landslides had destroyed a route for good.

Rondei also tried to make some small-talk. Unfortunately, Ylm insisted that his – and his family's – life was boring and ordinary, and never volunteered any information.

"How many children do you have?" she asked.

"Two." After a while he added, in a bout of uncharacteristic loquaciousness, "A girl and a boy."

"Who looks after them while you're working?" They'd already established that the children's mother had a farm to run, and took care of selling the produce as well, harnessing their dogs in front of a wagon once a week to take the milk and cheese to the local market.

"They look after themselves. They're not yet tall enough to lift the bolt on the door."

"I see."

Rondei remembered similar scenes from her childhood:

when her parents worked out of doors, she was left in charge of her younger siblings. At first, the smallest ones cried after their mother; after a while, everyone concentrated on trying to break out of the house. When that failed, they spent the day fighting amongst each other, finally falling asleep in an exhausted heap. More often than not, someone got hurt. Most of the time it was just scratches and bruises. Sometimes it was bleeding heads or broken bones. Rondei used to get a solid scolding from her parents anyway. She, as the eldest, should have been able to keep her siblings in check. Even when she was only two summers old, and the youngest was a baby in the cradle.

Growing up, she'd sworn that if one day she had children of her own, she'd look after them better. As Ylm started poring over the map again, she wondered whether she'd succeeded in that task. When Vejel was younger, she'd tried to keep him with her at all times and teach him her trade in the form of play; however, he'd always been a restless child who didn't get any pleasure from looking at woodcuts or playing with pieces of scrap paper. He was at his happiest running about with children of his own age, making an awful racket, and getting his clothes torn and muddy. Another thing he loved was eating. Rondei, whose tastes had always been frugal, was amazed at the joy a handful of sugar could produce in her son. Even now, Vejel seemed to live for the moments when he could gobble up leftover pieces of cake or steal a bit of marzipan from the kitchens.

Having left Daurbar behind, Rondei wasn't sure if she was ever going to see her son again. While making her preparations, she'd resolutely avoided thinking about their inevitable parting. She'd signed an apprenticeship contract in Vejel's name, thus making sure that Lord Stainerau would continue sheltering him under his roof even if she didn't return. She knew his lordship well enough to rely on his word, whatever happened to her.

With this decisive act, Rondei had made sure that Vejel would never leave Haller again. He didn't have the initiative or the cool boldness of his mother to go through with an escape;

most likely, he wouldn't be able to think of a valid reason to get himself a passport. His only concrete dream had been becoming a sailor. There was little chance of boarding a ship in a resolutely land-locked country; that, too, gave Rondei some satisfaction. The worst fate she could imagine for her son was ending up in some leaky, cramped merchant vessel with only hard tack to eat, bad rum to drink, and a watery grave to look forward to.

Still, there was no escaping the truth: she had abandoned her only child for her own personal happiness. True, he was old enough to begin an apprenticeship. In normal circumstances he would have been apprenticed years ago. Children often left home before their fifth birthday, either to go to school or to learn a trade. For some time, Rondei had deluded herself, thinking Vejel would calm down and one day wake up with a predilection for book printing.

Only during her time in Daurbar, seeing him romp around the grounds with friends he made with surprising ease, had she finally admitted the truth to herself. Her son would never take up her tools. He'd live out his life happily in service, not once thinking for himself. Therefore, when the time came, it had been easy to make the decision. If her only child was going to be a servant, why not choose the safest place on Ederai to do it in? Whether that made her a bad mother she didn't really care. Family ties, as strong as they were, could also serve as an anchor to tie a person down to a life of miserable drudgery. That was the last thing she wished for her lively boy.

In a few days their small group had moved from the sheer peaks of the northern mountains to a more hospitable, rolling landscape of western Haller. The Pass of Krassmark was still a week's journey away, but Rondei remained calm. It had never been her plan to march directly to the border and demand a way out. Instead, she played the long game, following the advice of a friend of hers, an ancient Stainerau cousin, who in their youth had spent all their summers in the Valley of Immits. From there, they'd told her, it was possible to make shorter trips all around the land that was dotted with crystalline lakes and the smallest pine trees anyone had ever seen.

From then on, she'd made pine trees her passion. She had scoured Lord Stainerau's library for books on dendrology, and exhausted her dinner partners with long explanations about the taxonomy of the pine family. She'd promised Lady Erden to find the tiniest tree in the mountains, and bring it back in a bottle.

Erden, too, would also have to survive without her from now on. That was an easier parting: her charge had been destined to marry all along, and their time together had been coming to its natural end. She liked to think that her tutoring had prepared Erden for a life outside her uncle's court, and that with her new-found confidence the girl could make her own mark on the staid society of Haller.

Ahead, Ylm was shouting and gesticulating vigorously. A rare occurrence on any day, as their guide was usually the one trying to shush his three companions in fear of landslides. He was pointing downwards, towards the emerald-green valley below that most certainly was Immits. The valley was sliced in half by a glinting river. The tiny green trees dotting the banks could only be the famous pygmy pines.

"Look at that!" sighed Lady Mittensel, shading her eyes with her hand. "Have you ever seen anything as enchanting as that?"

Sunset on the Northern Strait, perhaps. The first edition of Tokenari's The History of the Western Islands, Rondei thought. Aloud she said, "Indeed no. What a beautiful country this is."

Lady Solsdar sat down to rub her right ankle. The fashionable boots she'd chosen were magnificent to look at but gave very little actual support – thus making the progress of the entire group increasingly slow. Just two days ago, Ylm had threatened to find a dog big enough to carry her up a mountainside. "Charming," she said, her eyes still fixed on the offending limb. She was also looking decidedly pale. The days of vigorous walking were clearly taking their toll on her robust constitution.

Rondei smirked to herself, and then launched into a lecture on the astounding properties of the tiny pines.

In Immits, they immediately settled into a comfortable routine. With Ylm's help, they found another picturesque cabin, perched on the shore of a clear-watered lake, and made it their base camp. Rondei and Lady Mittensel — who was now insisting that she should be called her first name Bolrein — made daily hikes up the mountainsides and along the cool, glittering water. Rondei looked at a lot of very small pines, and her companion exclaimed over every sublime view with unvarying enthusiasm. They made sketches, and compared them over a glass of pear brandy in the evenings. They sang loud songs, but were careful not to interfere with the work of the *kullners* whose high voices echoed across the valley from morning to night.

Much to her chagrin, Lady Solsdar hadn't been able to join them yet. In addition to her swollen ankle, she had developed a gnawing pain in her stomach. Nothing too alarming, she assured her companions, but bothersome enough to stop her from getting out of bed most mornings. While the two others were gone, with or without Ylm, Lady Solsdar reclined on goose-down pillows, reading the novel she had brought along, and when she was feeling well enough, got up to putter in the kitchen with a show of cooking dinner for her returning friends.

What was even more annoying, instead of steadily improving as they'd all hoped it would, Lady Solsdar's condition grew ever so slightly worse by the day. Soon, she only got out of bed for meals, which others now had to cook in their entirety. She complained of pains in her eyes, and didn't feel like reading anymore. At night, she turned restlessly in her bed, now and then letting out a dainty moan. Rondei and Bolrein, healthily tired from their exertions, usually slept through these manifestations of pain. Thus, it was left to Ylm to check on her every hour or so, and to keep her company when she couldn't sleep.

On the morning of the fifth day, Rondei got up to find Lady Mittensel staring moodily into her cup of tea.

"What are we to do?" Bolrein's almond-shaped eyes were full of worry. "She needs a doctor. How are we to find one here, in the middle of nowhere?"

Rondei touched her hand reassuringly. "I'm already ahead of you. I asked Ylm yesterday where the nearest village was, and if they had a medic of some kind there." A small shrug. "Turns out the surest place to find a doctor is in Krass."

"That's too far away," Bolrein said, lowering her voice and glancing towards their sleeping companions. "We can't possibly carry her that far."

"No. But one or two of us can go to Krass to get the doctor."

"Of course." Lady Mittensel seemed relieved. "So, who's going?"

Rondei leaned her hands on her knees, drawing in one long breath after another. The air higher up in the mountains was more difficult to breathe somehow. Also, Ylm was setting a hard pace, and expecting her to follow without complaint. He'd promised to get them to Krass as swiftly as possible, and Rondei had seen genuine concern in his leathered face. Yet, she was beginning to suspect that Ylm set this punishing pace at least partly to test her. Thus, she had to be on her guard at all times. She'd stopped asking questions, and only spoke matters related to the route when they came up naturally. She kept reminding herself that she was doing this journey for her friend, and that she was anxious to get back to her as soon as possible.

It had taken a great deal of subtle wrangling to persuade the two ladies, as well as Ylm, that she was the best choice for the trip to Krass. While Lady Mittensel argued her more extensive experience in mountaineering and her better acquaintance of the habits of rural Hallerians, Rondei had countered by admitting that while she had spent most of her life in the flatlands, she was also the younger of the two, and on account of her profession, well conversant with the quirks of other people of her class.

All the while, she'd been careful to stress the long, loyal friendship between the Ladies Solsdar and Mittensel, stealthily increasing the guilt that Bolrein was bound to feel as she enjoyed her freedom in the open air. Neither she nor Rondei was a natural nurse, but Lady Solsdar was more comfortable being fussed over by someone of her own rank — and the way she gently held Bolrein's hand during these discussions was certainly working in Rondei's favor.

All the while, Rondei had been aware of Ylm hovering at the edges of their conversation. Careful not to take part, or to express a preference – but listening and remembering everything. In the end, she'd done the only thing she could to make the situation less awkward, and asked him a direct question.

"So, Ylm, you said the trip can be completed in five days. That seems like an optimistic estimate to me."

He had thought for a while. "As I said, if the weather holds, it's possible to get to Krass in two days, using the shortcuts I mentioned. If we manage to find a doctor quickly, we can't expect them to keep up such a hard pace, or to crawl on their hands and knees through the narrow passes, no matter how experienced a mountaineer they are. The easier route takes at least a day more." He knitted his bushy eyebrows. "And any one of us can always break a leg."

"Indeed," Rondei had smiled understandingly at him. She'd also avoided looking directly at Lady Mittensel's rather portly form.

"Whatever you decide, my ladies, I have to warn you that this won't be a pleasure trip by any means. Particularly if the weather turns foul."

"I think we both understand and accept that," Rondei had said meekly. By now, Ylm's predictions of bad weather were usually treated more as punctuation to his gloomy discourses, rather than actual forecasts.

Lady Mittensel had said nothing.

Fortunately, the weather had held so far. During the first day they'd walked from sunrise to sunset with very small breaks in between. This morning, Ylm had wakened her at the crack of dawn once more, scanning the sky above them and making contented noises. They'd been on the move since then, forcing their way along narrow paths, pushing through gaps between rocks, and sliding down sheer cliff-faces. All the while, neither of them had said a word.

Now, as they stopped for their midday meal, Rondei knew that one of them would have to break the silence. At this point, she felt it safest to start the conversation herself.

"I saw that you didn't need a map for this route," she began. "You know it well?"

"Was born near here," came the gruff reply.

She gave him a small smile, which he didn't return. "How did you come to work for Lord Stainerau?" she asked next.

"My uncle worked for him. He recommended me when he couldn't carry on the job anymore. This is no work for an old man."

"I can see that."

After some meditative chewing, he asked her the question she'd been expecting for some time. "Why are you anxious to get to Krass?" His pitch-black eyes met hers directly.

"Well, if we ignore the obvious answer," she said with practiced lightness, "and I hope I can be honest with you —" she waited until he gave her a reluctant nod, "I've discovered that I'm not that much of a hiker. It's not the exercise I resent, or these views. I just miss the bustle of people. I've always liked cities, and in Daurbar one is never alone. Suddenly, being here with only my two friends for company — and you, of course — I was getting nervous somehow. I think I just miss civilized life," she finished with a rueful grin. “I miss the feel of a freshly printed newspaper in my fingers.”

Ylm grunted and ate another piece of dried meat. “Fair enough. Krass isn’t much of a metropolis, so don’t get your hopes up.”

“As long as there’s a booksellers, I’ll feel right at home.”

There was a bookseller in Krass; Rondei made a note of its location as she and Ylm rushed down the main street. They’d made enquiries on the way, and had been told where Doctor Hilm’s practice — and hopefully the doctor herself — could be found. Rondei had a hard time concentrating on their mission. Not only was she anxious to get her hands on her post, she was also aware of the futility of their haste. Lady Solsdar’s health would have already taken a turn for the better, and thus lugging a medic all the way to Immits would be a waste of everyone’s time.

Krass was a small town, and they found the right door easily enough. Ylm knocked on it with his walking-staff and a solemn young man let them in, listened to their errand, and bade them to sit down for a moment.

“My mother will be with you as soon as she comes from her evening rounds,” he said, in a reassuring voice.

“Will she be long?” Rondei asked.

He gave her an eloquent shrug.

Ylm promptly settled to sleep in his chair; Rondei passed the time by looking out of the window, peering into the lives of the ordinary inhabitants of Krass. There wasn’t much she hadn’t seen hundreds of times before in dozens of other out-of-the-way towns. Workers coming home for their dinner – some walking with their heads held high, calling to their friends, most of them dragging their feet after a long day’s labor. A farmer with a dogcart loaded to the brim with newly-cut hay, swaying precariously in the middle of the road. A mother trying to persuade her toddler to leave a puddle alone.

It was easy to spot Doctor Hilm in the crowd. She walked with a brisk, authoritative step, and greeted almost everyone she passed. She had her bag slung across her shoulder, and a familiar-looking staff in one hand. She was wearing sturdy leather boots and a short walking-coat – as well as buff-colored trousers. Rondei understood that a lot of her work must take place outside of Krass, and that the more conservative element must have something to say about the figure she cut wherever she worked.

In this, as in many other things, Haller stood alone among the nations of Ederai. Elsewhere, all genders wore what was deemed practical – or fashionable – and very often this included a variation on the theme of a tunic and a pair of trousers. Court clothing was cut following the latest Paishnali styles and could be as cumbersome as it was colorful. In Haller, however, all nobles and most commoners clung to their own idea of what was seemly and modest. This included ankle-length skirts for women of a marriageable age.

Rondei, who didn't think about clothes if she could help it, didn't find it particularly taxing to put on a skirt for a formal occasion. Yet, she hadn't bowed to the customs of Daurbar completely, and for this trip had resolutely packed her sturdy Nebian clothes, rather than the more impractical Hallerian dress that her companions had tried to press on her. Just a few days of hiking had shown who had made the right choice.

There was a loud clattering noise. Doctor Hilm had entered her practice and thrown her staff into the nearest corner. Ylm started awake, nearly falling off his chair. This gave Rondei the chance to take lead of the conversation and its general tone. After a brief, polite greeting, she gave Doctor Hilm a thorough description of Lady Solsdar's unfortunate state, as well as the precise location of the patient.

"Do you think you would be able to help her?" she asked.

The medic, who all the while had been assessing her with her frank gaze, replied, "It is quite out of my usual range, and I know the route to Immits isn't the most comfortable. However, the situation sounds grave enough," she cocked her head, "and from your description of the symptoms I'm not able to immediately tell what might be ailing her. If nothing more pressing comes up, I'll join you in the morning. Do you have a place to stay?"

Rondei, who hadn't even thought of the matter, said, "Not really. Can you recommend something, Doctor?"

"I can recommend our downstairs bedroom to you, Mistress Galsi, and a comfortable bed in the kitchen to your guide. That way we will be able to breakfast at first light, and then be off." Before she strode into her office, she turned around and said, "Do join us for dinner. In an hour or so."

Rondei thanked the doctor, and left Ylm to familiarize himself with the house. She made a point of not hurrying out of the door, but stopped at a mirror to adjust her hat, and when she saw the doctor's son Jols in the hallway, she chatted to him a while about the Valley of Immits and her own research on the small pines. She asked the young man whether the bookseller's might still be open; he confirmed her suspicion that during the warm season, shops wouldn't close until sundown.

She retraced her steps back to the main street, again forcing herself to look at the other shop windows which boasted fine lace, bonnets, and jewels of various kinds. Along with the all-important salt crystals, miners often dredged up various other treasures from the depths of the mountains, including silver and gold, and deep-green emeralds. A jeweler tried to talk her into his shop, but Rondei rebuffed him curtly. She hadn't come to Krass to buy anything. She'd come to collect her freedom.

The booksellers' premises impressed her the moment she stepped in. From the outside, the place had looked dark and dingy, but that was perhaps because the display window had been draped in dark velvet, and the pane had been rather dusty. The shop itself was a large, high room with sparkling white walls and darkly gleaming shelves. The smell of ink always made her a bit weak at the knees, and she resisted the temptation to browse through the local varieties.

Instead, she made her way straight to the counter. Like most booksellers, this one also doubled as a post office.

A frail-looking man peered down at her. "How can I serve my lady?"

"I've come to see if there's any mail for myself or my companions." She gave all the three names of the hiking-party. Both of her companions were expecting well-wishing letters from Daurbar, and had also given her short missives to send back to the capital.

She duly received three bundles. She paid for twelve letters in all, and two parcels. The shopkeeper helped her wrap all of the mail in a large sheet of paper; the two largest pieces went into a basket she had borrowed from Doctor Hilm. Thanking the shopkeeper, she strode into the street – until she remembered to curb her enthusiasm, and dragged her feet back to the already familiar house.

Thankfully, Doctor Hilm was just as efficient with her dining as she was with all other aspects of her life. Rondei was first joined by Jols, who told her his mother had been called away urgently, and would dine when she was able. They had already established that the Doctor wasn't able to keep regular hours, and would invariably be dragged out of her bed, or would have to abandon a half-eaten breakfast when duty called.

Rondei was just rising from the table when Doctor Hilm returned. They chatted politely for a while, but as neither wanted to impose on the other, they agreed to meet again at breakfast. Ylm, too, seemed to want to stay out of the way. Rondei saw him pacing in the garden, and after confirming next day's travel arrangements with him, left him to it.

The room she'd been given was of picturesque proportions.

That is to say, it contained a narrow bed, a small desk and a chest of drawers. There was only one window, set high and deep in the wall. The floorboards squeaked with every step Rondei took. Very quickly, she decided to settle herself on the bed with her spoils.

To stretch out the suspense for a while longer, she first looked at her own mail. As she had expected, there was only one letter. A beautifully composed, long message from Lady Erden, who was full of news about her garden, her dogs, and her ever-growing list of suitors. Rondei smiled as her gaze skated over the elegant calligraphy. From an awkward, earnest creature her ward had grown up into a confident young lady who knew just how much emotion to put into a missive that could easily be read by a dozen people before it even reached the person it was addressed to. Rondei resolved to pen her an answer that same night. If everything went to plan, she wouldn't have the chance to correspond with Erden again — not while she remained with her uncle's household, at least.

All the while, Rondei's hand was resting on the tightly wrapped package with Lady Solsdar's name on it. She had recognized the handwriting instantly: otherwise she would have hesitated to unwrap the parcel. The package was a lot smaller than she had expected, leading her to fear that it had been tampered with. However, all of the seals were unbroken and the folds of the wrapping were crisp. It seemed that Ardelei had come up with a creative solution to her request – which wouldn't be the first time. Rondei's hand trembled slightly as she reached for her scissors. Her cousin had never been one to follow instructions to the letter, professing to know better than everyone else.

Two objects fell out of the package. One was an introduction: a no-nonsense, almost anonymous-looking oblong of dark blue linen. Rondei didn't recognize the insignia embroidered on its face, but was impressed with the tiny stitches and the vibrant colors of the threads. On the back, ears of golden corn marched diagonally across the blue field. The object had seen some use;

yet, it was as clean and presentable as it should be. She held the introduction close to her face, catching the tiniest hint of a lavender scent.

The other object could easily be mistaken for a pebble. It was dark gray in color, and shot through with lighter stripes. Rondei, having handled things like this in the past, hesitated for a while before picking it up. Ardelei had lectured her about solid spells often enough. Some of them would activate themselves at any careless touch, others would require some warming-up in the hands of the right person. Rondei had no doubt about the category her cousin's spell would fall into. Although Ardelei could be careless with instructions, she always made sure that her spells wouldn't fall into the wrong hands by mistake.

She wiped her palm on her trouser-leg and gingerly picked up the spell. As she'd been taught, she held it up to her lips, humming a note in what she hoped was a warm tone. Nothing happened. She tried again, lowering the pitch of the note ever so slightly. Sure enough, the spell began to grow warmer in her hands, and she had to set it down on the floor: the stone that had nestled comfortably in her hand was suddenly very hot — and expanding.

In a couple of minutes, she was looking at a life-sized representation of her cousin. Ardelei's image wavered, and it was hard to distinguish the colors she was wearing, yet there was no mistaking the almost painfully symmetrical face and the judgmental eyes, which didn't quite meet hers. Her musical voice echoed in Rondei's head — another jarring effect of the magic.

"This spell works only once, so be sure to remember everything I say," she began.

Rondei couldn't help rolling her eyes.

"There's another spell hidden in the introduction. Although it looks smaller, it's more powerful, and potentially risky. It's up to you whether you use it or not. The introduction itself should be enough to get you across the border. It belongs to a Nebian called Iekada Tamajei. Her husband is a salt merchant in Jirda;

they're very rich. You're good at stories, and know the situation in Haller better than I do. Make up a reason why Master Tamajei would have brought his wife along, and then abandoned her, leaving her to make her own way back to Nebe."

"Easy as pie," Rondei interjected dryly.

"That spell is for taking on the appearance of Iekada. It doesn't work on many people simultaneously, and only lasts for an hour or so. So choose your moment." Just as unceremoniously as she had appeared, Ardelei's wavering image winked out. The spell had crumbled into a handful of fine dust on the floor.

Rondei sat down on the bed with a thump, holding back tears. "Fantastic. Thank you, cousin Ardelei. That is helpful indeed."

Night fell. Rondei lay in her narrow bed, listening to the nightly noises of Krass. Now and then someone would pass the house. She heard several dogs as well as people making their way home. A nightingale serenaded the neighborhood from a nearby tree. The mountains looming over the town produced their own slow music. Water cascaded endlessly downhill. The wind pushed past smooth rock-faces, and birds and animals punctuated the flow of sound with their sudden cries.

All the while, Rondei's mind was whirring in ever-widening circles. Ardelei's decision to send her a spell instead of a change of clothes irked her at first. Soon, however, she began to understand her cousin's reasoning. The mage had correctly judged the mood in Haller. If a suspiciously large parcel arrived from the outside, it was much more likely to be opened and reported to higher authorities, compared to a mundane-looking parcel that seemed only to contain some Nebian pebbles.

Although her cousin hadn't said as much, Rondei also understood that the initial plan still stood. In some ways, having the appearance of a completely different person would also enhance the scheme. The fewer people that saw and recognized her, the more time would pass before someone would sound the alarm. Rondei had never been much of a play-actor. She suspected that Ardelei remembered this, and had worked out a way for her cousin to not embarrass herself – and everyone else – in trying to bluff her way across the border.

Rondei was always at her best when she could act independently. Other people were a liability. They were either more stupid, more slow — or in the case of Ardelei, more creative than her, and thus liable to create unforeseen problems. Rondei had already devised several versions of her plan, and was able to adapt this new turn to its confines. However, she couldn't help wondering how many people in Sendal were already aware of her movements. The too-clever-for-his-own-good diplomat Babtei for one. Ardelei's unkempt lover Beldor Amsta — and his dog — for another. Rondei sighed, and turned over in her lumpy bed. Notoriety was the last thing she wanted. For the moment, at least.

Morning found her calm and clear-headed, if not well-rested. It was often the case that despite all her anxious fretting beforehand, when the moment to take action came, she found herself almost resigned to her fate, with no other option but to see the plan through. She had done all she could: once the events started rolling, she would be swept up in them, for better or for worse. As the sky started to lighten, Rondei got dressed, scraped her hair into a tight bun, and before going down to breakfast, drank down the vial of light-blue liquid that had been nestling among her cosmetics.

It didn't surprise her to find Ylm already hovering about the dining room, not sure of his welcome. Just as he and Rondei sat down, Doctor Hilm burst in from the kitchen, carrying a smoldering frying-pan in front of her.

"Morning," she greeted them with her customary gruff cheer.

"Hope you like your eggs singed. Ten years I've lived in this house, and the stove and I still aren't the best of friends."

Ylm made a polite noise and claimed his portion of the eggs with the practicality of a habitual traveler. Rondei was about to do the same – but instead of reaching for her plate, she suddenly doubled over and was violently sick on the floor.

The good thing about staying at the house of a medical practitioner was that no one seemed at all scandalized. Doctor Hilm got up calmly and fetched a basin, telling Rondei to use it the next time she felt a wave of nausea coming over her. Ylm removed himself and his breakfast into the smoky kitchen, while the doctor woke up her son to do the cleaning for her. In the meanwhile, she marched Rondei, basin and all, back into her bedroom.

"So you say this came on with no warning whatsoever, and that this has nothing to do with your monthly cycle — or the lack thereof. Are you in any pain at all?" the doctor asked her, peering into her face, but careful to keep her distance.

"Not really," Rondei managed. "My insides just feel really disordered."

"I can tell. Did Lady Solsdar exhibit similar symptoms?"

She pretended to cast her mind back. "She did complain of nausea. Nothing quite this violent happened, however. That I know of."

"Diseases take different routes with different people. Some only have a sore throat, others are in bed for weeks with a fever. Could be the same here." She looked down on Rondei. "Whatever it is, it is clear that you are not able to join us today, Mistress Galsi. My home is your home as long as you need it."

"You are too kind," she said wretchedly. "And you and Ylm go ahead. I do not mind waiting here, but I do worry for Lady Solsdar."

"I will speak to Ylm. I am sure he will agree."

Ylm agreed. He didn't come to see her — after her spectacular performance at breakfast, she didn't think he would — but he sent a kind word, saying he would be back when Doctor

Hilm's business was done in Immits. The Doctor herself made Rondei down a glass of some murky substance, which nearly made her retch again.

"I have left instructions with my son. He is almost as good a medic as I am, having observed me all his life. You will be in safe hands, Mistress Galsi."

"I cannot thank you enough, Doctor. I am sorry to be such an inconvenience to you."

"Do not mention it: after all, no one forced this life on me. It is my passion, and always has been."

"I am glad to hear it," Rondei said to herself, listening to Doctor Hilm's heavy footsteps on the stairs.

Chapter 5

Haller - Ardelei

"**The next** time I see Lord Stainerau, I'll have a word with him," Ardelei said, leaning against a tall rock. "Several words, in fact. I can understand that he wants his people and his precious salt to be safe, but this is ridiculous."

Heather looked up at her, lolling her long lilac tongue.

"Or I might ask you to do it. He's fond of dogs."

"His dogs," Bel reminded her. He, like Heather, seemed to enjoy the trip along the steep, stony paths that went up and up, towards the perpetually cloudy sky. "Lord Stainerau's precious hounds are cooped up like the ladies of his house: no outsider is allowed to set eyes on them without his permission."

He was exaggerating, of course, but Ardelei understood his point and didn't argue it. Indeed, she had no breath left to argue anything; they'd been steadily climbing for three days, with no end in sight. What in the distance had looked like a single row of smooth, triangular mountains had turned out to be a wilderness of jagged rock stretching in all directions — but mainly upwards. Beldor had warned her about the route, saying that only the most desperate of travelers tried to cross the mountains directly from the north. She wasn't certain of her desperation, but she knew the geography of Ederai well enough to estimate that all alternative routes would take at least twice as long, and would bring them in close contact with other people.

She was also wondering, not for the first time, why she'd taken on this foolish mission. She liked her cousin, but owed her no favors. Both of them had made it certain over the years that no such debts remained unpaid. Rondei was perfectly capable of extricating herself from any situation if she so wished: sending for Ardelei only made the process quicker. This of course had piqued Ardelei's interest. Rondei was in a hurry to get out of Haller. It was understandable that after two years of isolation, she'd want to travel and to see her family and friends. But to go against the iron will of her employer, and to risk his wrath was uncharacteristic of Ardelei's cool, calculating cousin.

Ardelei had seen enough of Valja, and sensed the new tenseness of the atmosphere, to understand that something was changing in the city, and perhaps in the entire country itself. The Guilds that had steered Sendal for centuries and exercised their power during the plague were being challenged. This wasn't the first time. There was always a revolt or two bubbling in Valja – but right now, the main challenge didn't come from rival merchants or foreign powers, but from the underclass of the city itself. Tired of the continuing restrictions and aware of their new power, the landless workers, young apprentices, and domestic servants were plotting to make their influence felt once and for all.

What still mystified Ardelei was the passion that the mere mention of Mistress Galsi's name seemed to excite among the revolutionary youth of Valja. So far in her life, Rondei had only dabbled in Nebian politics, and had printed and sold other people's radically-worded pamphlets. As far as Ardelei was aware, before the plague, she hadn't produced a single tract herself, or hadn't been particularly interested in the condition of the workers in the rest of Ederai. And now, seemingly overnight, several of her texts were circulating in the Sendali capital, only to be snatched up and read by any working person discontented with their lot.

She'd have time enough to quiz her cousin on her change of heart, and to draw her own conclusions about her motives. Still, the diplomat in her wanted to understand the bigger picture.

"You said you'd met the Skovos," she said to Beldor that evening as they made camp under a narrow stone ledge. "What are they like?"

Bel, as was his habit, took his time. "Young," he said at last. "Troublemakers — the kind of people who don't easily find their place in the world, and go about making things difficult for others as well."

"So you don't agree with them?"

"I agree that the Guilds have far too much power, and have been abusing their privileges far too long. They said they'd ease the passage of people and goods once the summer begins, but we're three months into the warm season, and nothing has changed."

She studied his impassive face. "What about the rest of it? Bringing down the old world order and beginning anew?"

He scoffed. "As I said, they're young and hot headed. They'll learn the hard way that the world can't be changed overnight. If at all. Money runs the world. That never changes."

Ardelei smiled to herself. As much as he claimed to disown his merchant roots, he could never truly escape the ideas he'd grown up with. "But they're not against money. They'd just like to spread it out a bit more evenly."

"You can spread it out as thinly as you like. In a few years it's again gathering in the pockets of some greedy bastard who's not keen on sharing."

They fell asleep rolled in Bel's cloak. The night was pleasantly cool, and for a while Ardelei listened to the wind moving against the rocks, and tracked Heather as the dog made her way back to the cave, and finally settled next to the sleeping friends with a theatrical sigh. Ardelei took comfort in the physical presence of

Bel and Heather, and in this simple life they could lead together, if only for a few weeks.

It felt good to have a clear goal, too — and that was perhaps why she'd thrown herself so eagerly into this foolish project. She'd have to face the consequences of her actions soon enough – but right now, she could pretend to be just as free as Bel and Heather were.

"That's the path that leads to the Pass," Beldor said, coming back from his scouting trip. "Do we want to approach right now? It looks quite crowded down there."

"Then perhaps we'll stay here a while longer. There's no hurry. The first spell has been spent, but I haven't felt the second one activating yet. We don't want to draw attention to ourselves at this point. Let's wait and rest."

Heather agreed. The dog had found the legbone of some long-deceased sheep and was worrying it in a leisurely way.

Ardelei sat down. "This place always takes my breath away. I do understand why the Staineraus want to keep it to themselves."

Bel raised a sardonic eyebrow. "I thought that went against all of your Linduvan teachings."

"I'm not Linduvan anymore," she said as lightly as she could. "Might as well try out new ways of thinking."

"You can't be both a Sendali revolutionary and a Hallerian isolationist."

"Why not? Even revolutionaries need a place to live. Why not find an isolated spot to start a new community altogether?"

"I suppose there are uninhabited islands farther east," he said.

She let out a long breath. "I think I've had enough of small islands for the time being."

They moved closer to the Pass, choosing a secluded place where they could peer down on the lower paths without being spotted themselves. Ardelei let the music of the mountains drift over her: it was one of the slowest songs there was, made up of water and stone resonating in the caves and fissures all around them. It also served as a background for the much more obvious, human sounds that passed from valley to valley. Hallerians had developed and codified *kullning* — a messaging system that relied on the high head tones which easily carried over the otherwise restrictive peaks. There were melodies for different everyday messages, and an even more sophisticated system of notes and pauses which could be understood as words.

Ardelei, however, was more tuned to the voices that produced the piercing songs. While there was a certain urgency to the messages, the kullners didn't sound particularly agitated. These were ordinary events crossing Haller from north to south, and from east to west. Births and deaths. Lost and found animals and possessions. Tidings about the planting of crops and requests for nails and ploughshares.

Deep down, she admired the self-contained nature of Haller. The plague had made no dent on the Mountain kingdom; they'd gotten used to their independence from the rest of Ederai, and the travel restrictions they put in place were entirely for the benefit of their own people. The salt trade continued, somewhat more cautiously than before, but goods arriving from the outside were subjected to such a long quarantine that all perishable foodstuffs stopped moving across the border altogether. People, too, found themselves turned back at the border, unless they had a Hallerian passport – and those who did were quarantined just as surely as their goods were. The draconian measures had worked: the plague hadn't been able to find its way into the Mountain realm.

Luneken, the island where Ardelei had spent most of her adult life, could never aspire to such complete isolation. Easily reachable by boat and bridge, it had made openness its watchword — partly to avoid the sinister reputation religious and magical communities often gathered around them. Linduvan mages weren't a secret society: they were an open-minded group of people who were ever willing to take on new members and learn new skills. Every Linduvan was a teacher and a pupil at the same time. Everyone took part in the growing and the preparation of food, and in the making and mending of clothes. Everyone made sure that the rest of the islanders considered them a helpful addition to their number: a boon, not a threat.

She took a deep breath. That, at least, had been the initial idea. Over the years, the non-hierarchical system had begun to erode, and the head of the Linduvan community had grown in power and influence. Ederai, the larger island to the south, was a confederation of small states which, after enduring decades of devastating wars, had decided to enforce peace between all of its political entities. For this, the people of Ederai needed diplomats who could help mediate any conflicts before they reached the critical stage. Linduvans, being neutral in their eyes, had seemed the perfect people for the task.

Thus, the Linduvan community embraced a double task: they taught and studied magic, and sought to understand the world through its manifold powers. But they also learned the ways of diplomacy, studying the history and languages of the Ederaian nations, never favoring any of them over the others. Naturally, some Linduvans were more adept mages than they were diplomats. Some were skilled in neither, and preferred to serve the community in some other way.

There were some rare persons, however, who excelled in both the more practical study of magic and the more academic skill of diplomacy. People like that were highly prized. Magic can be used for many things, but most of all it enhances already existing talents. A diplomat trained in magic knows how to manipulate the atmosphere of a meeting; in rare cases, they also know how to manipulate the participants. Needless to say, people like that don't advertise their skills outside of their community. They're also bound by the strict codes of the Linduvan order, and suffer dire consequences should they break them.

Ardelei, having taken her vows to heart, had always striven to work for the good of the greatest number of people, even if this conflicted with the well-being of her own community. As the plague first started making its way across Ederai, there were many Linduvans who felt it their responsibility to head south to help. However, those hopefuls — Ardelei among them — soon realized that the new strain of the disease held no respect for their traditional cures, and moved at a frightening speed from the port cities ever inwards. Many mages lost their lives in their struggle to ease the suffering of the afflicted. Very soon, most of those still alive returned to Arrika, and in the end accepted the petition of Luneken's non-mages to close all bridges and block all ports. They stewed in their enforced isolation for nearly two years. Some took it in their stride. The healers worked on cures for the plague and its after-effects; the more artistically-minded turned their experiences into harrowing songs and images. Some, like Ardelei, plunged themselves into physical labor so that during the day they'd have no time to think – and only at night could they dream of a better world where people wouldn't turn their backs on the suffering of others, if they dreamed at all.

There were those, however, who thought that the Linduvan community had been too slow to act, and that it had been foolish to even think that the plague could be stopped by any human means. They looked into the world of dreams and visions. They fasted and deprived themselves of sleep; they tried to find a way to appease the realm beyond, and to stop anything similar from ever happening again.

Many of the latter group also saw the plague as a particular punishment for the people of Ederai. They didn't listen to those who tried to explain that boats had always carried diseases effortlessly from one island to another. They saw the best and safest option to be complete isolationism, the turning away from all things mundane, and striving towards a better, purer life in the safety of Arrika. They looked down on the non-mages, claiming even against existing evidence that the Linduvans had been on the island first.

From the start, Ardelei had fought passionately against such views. She'd argued and explained, used violent words and gentle ones; she had persuaded and cajoled with her most honeyed tones until she grew hoarse. She'd wanted to break the isolation earlier, to allow those who wished to seek their surviving family members and friends to return to Ederai. She'd reminded her fellow Linduvans that most of them were from Ederai, and in no way better or more deserving than their siblings in the south. She'd reminded them that the sole reason their community was tolerated on Luneken was because they'd taken on the burden of reconciling the fractious peoples of Ederai, thus also assuring the safety of the northern island.

She'd gained sympathizers and friends through her impassioned speeches. For a while, she'd believed that through the power of her voice alone she could sway the entire community, and that together they could have created a magic more powerful and more long-lasting than anything that had ever been achieved in Arrika. During that heady time, she'd let herself be persuaded to pitch herself against Darbei Kusvin — the spokesperson for the isolationist group. By that time, it was clear that their long-time leader, Obelie Kalangi, wasn't going to see the next warm season, and that a new leader would have to be elected soon. Passions ran high, and Ardelei allowed herself to be swept up in the swell of heightened words and emotions.

Certainly, she said some things that she later came to regret. She counted on people who turned out to be untrustworthy; she trusted her secrets to people who turned out to be disloyal. Yet, there was no other way she could have run her campaign. She wasn't a calculating schemer like her cousin Rondei, neither was she a slippery turncoat who made empty promises just to win popularity.

She'd taken a risk and lost. There was no shame in that. Still, she hadn't realized at the time just how high the stakes were. She'd thought that once the passions cooled, they could all settle down to live together, just as they'd done so far — just like they'd taught generations of people to do. But she'd miscalculated the ruthlessness of Darbei Kusvin.

The sun was going down. Heather had moved on to another foraged bone, and was licking it clean with tender concentration. Beldor was about to say something when Ardelei silenced him with a swift gesture.

"There. The second spell."

She knew Rondei was going to be sour about disregarding her request for a change of clothes. Yet, in the short time she'd had to arrange her cousin's escape, both she and Bel had agreed that trying to get a large, suspicious parcel through the Hallerian customs would very likely get Rondei and her friends in trouble. Instead, Ardelei had settled on a shape-shifting spell sewn into a counterfeit introduction — a neat piece of magic she'd rarely had the chance to use herself.

She'd avoided any detailed instructions, knowing the suspicious mindset of the Hallerian border guards. Rondei knew enough about magic to be able to activate both spells in the correct way – the first by her voice, and the second by swallowing it. It was the second spell that slightly worried Ardelei, partly because it was so invasive. Still, she relied on the steeliness of Rondei's bowels almost as much as she did on her cousin's cool judgment.

Crossing the border at dusk would have its advantages: even if the illusion didn't hold up, other travelers might not be able to recognize Rondei for the fugitive she was. Ardelei had already made sure that the real Iekada Tamajei wouldn't be accompanying her husband on this trip. Through his contacts, Beldor had found out that Mistress Tamajei had just been brought to bed with her fifth child, and even if her confinement hadn't been so near, the four existing children would have kept her firmly in Jirda.

Ardelei left Bel and Heather in their hiding place, and made her way down the mountainside towards the Pass of Krassmark. Very little seemed to have changed since her last visit. Apart from merchants with long-established routes and watertight permits, very few outsiders were ever admitted across the border, plague or no plague. Even now, the only traveler making his way towards the first checkpoint was a man with a cartload of grain. The Pass closed at sundown. Ardelei hoped that her cousin would already be handing her introduction to the last set of guards on the Hallerian side of the border.

She had no intention of crossing. Indeed, she hoped to interfere with the guards and other travelers as little as possible. Instead, she began to hum intensely under her breath. The dogs pulling the grain cart glanced in her direction, but as she stopped in her tracks, they forgot about her. She strewed careful notes around her, building a nebulous shield of sound. Soon, anyone passing an armspan away wouldn't be able to see her. The shield was effective but not very flexible; it worked best when she stood still. Thus, she strengthened the spell with a few more harmonics and started making her way ever so slowly towards the Pass, hoping the guards would be focused on the grain merchant for the moment.

The Hallerian border was unlike any other on Ederai — or indeed anywhere Ardelei had been. It wasn't one specific spot where one could cross from one country to another. Neither was it a clear succession of huts and offices where various pieces of paper needed to be signed and stamped, and goods declared. Rather, the Pass of Krassmark was a labyrinth of roads, buildings and booths. Individual travelers chose one route, groups another. Merchants who had their passports and permits in order could navigate a relatively straightforward course between tollhouses and checkpoints – but only those who came into Haller from the outside.

From within the country, the procedure was as byzantine as it was unforgiving. So jealously did the rulers of Haller protect their precious salt that even now, all travelers had to strip off all their clothes and turn them inside out in front of two guards — one standing in front, the other at the back. All possessions were similarly ransacked at a separate checkpoint, and later on a third set of guards would subject the traveler to dozens of detailed questions about their destination, duration of stay, and the possessions they were taking with them. The failure to answer any of these questions satisfactorily usually resulted in the denial of a permit. The attempt to smuggle salt — even in the tiniest quantities — usually resulted in the loss of a nose.

It was no wonder, then, that most Hallerians decided to stay put, and encouraged all foreigners to do the same. As far as Ardelei was aware, there had never been a large-scale effort to smuggle people and goods across the mountains. Partly this was due to the harsh conditions of the land itself; partly it depended on the obedient nature of Hallerians. It had long been the custom of the Lords of Haller to organize hunts in the farthest regions of the land. While ostensibly they were hunting for blue deer, everyone knew that the real quarry was smugglers.

Ardelei stopped to listen. The shield restricted her hearing somewhat, and its undertone buzzing interfered with her senses. Still, her listening skills were extraordinarily acute, and even in her encumbered state she could easily pick up the song of the surrounding land. It was calm. The merchant had already entered the Pass with his dogs, and the only sound nearby was the rattling of wheels on gravel.

She increased her pace. Without documents, she couldn't risk entering the Pass itself, but she could work her magic on the guards from a safe distance in case Rondei's disguise started to fail. As she watched the merchant exchanging greetings with the straight-backed guards of the checkpoint, she tried to remember why she'd agreed to help her cousin in the first place.

If they got caught, what remained of her long-wrought diplomacy with Reutel Stainerau and his family would vanish into thin air in a heartbeat. For years, she'd sacrificed her time and resources negotiating with the stubborn Lord of Haller, spending endless hours dining with his tedious court, strewing careless charm in all directions, while at the same time trying to convince the Hallerian nobles of the virtues of the Linduvan Order and the benefits of opening borders to traveling diplomats.

Slowly, her efforts had begun to bear fruit. Young mages had made tentative trips to Haller, learning its language and history in the impressive libraries of the capital. There had been some flirtations during hunting trips, and friendships wrought over card games. For a while it had seemed that the hard nut in the middle of Ederai had been ready for cracking. Then the plague had arrived, swiping the board clean overnight.

And now the borders were just as tightly shut as they'd been at the beginning of her acquaintance with Lord Stainerau. She'd come to realize that for his lordship salt, or even money, didn't matter as much as the idea of containment. In his private life, Reutel Stainerau enjoyed Gesaian wines and Paishnali fabrics as much as the next nobleman. He read widely, and in her discussions with him, Ardelei had discovered a keen mind ever open to new ideas. To him, however, it was enough to let his own thoughts travel freely. Granting such freedoms to the rest of Hallerians was as unthinkable as the complete opening of his borders.

At the end of a particularly heated debate, she had decided to push him.

"In other words, you are a despot, allowing yourself liberties but not even imagining your people would enjoy the same privileges," she had said.

He'd met her gaze levelly, his voice a pleasant purr. "Why would they enjoy them? Most of them are illiterate peasants. They work the land and know only the simple pleasures of the bed and the table. Why should I promise them any more, knowing full well the world does not provide wealth and education to all?"

"So you are saying that people born to a humble state should not seek to better themselves? To lift themselves out of that state?"

A merry grin. "I would definitely not say it in the present company." He had gestured towards the nearest window. "Out there, there are schools enough. Those fortunate and motivated enough can raise themselves out of the common muck. Then again, such people are dangerous. They know that circumstances can be changed."

"And you don't like change?"

"Who does? We all like the safety of a good routine. Would you rather wear an old pair of boots for a day's hike, or change into a new pair each day?" At her rhetorical gesture, he continued, "Tradition is a great stabilizer. Depending on the tradition, of course. The Sendali tradition is to riot every few decades and get a few thousand good workers killed in the process. The Hallerian way is definitely more boring, but in my view it is also the more humane way in the long run. Everyone knows their place. No one goes hungry. No one needs to emigrate in search of a better life. Does that sound like a people living under a tyrannical rule?"

"It does not. And I don't think you a tyrant for the things you do. We both know, however, that one can do harm not only through direct action, but through failing to act. By not giving your people options you are smothering them with a false sense of security." She had met his eyes again over the rim of her wineglass. "Change does not necessarily barge in overnight. One day, you may look over the mountains and see that the rest of Ederai has moved on, and that there is no way you can catch up with them."

"I do not quite understand you."

In truth, she hadn't quite understood the deeper meaning of her words back then. She'd wanted to appear wise and prophetic, and had perhaps succeeded. After that meeting, Reutel Stainerau had begun inviting more foreign diplomats to his court. He'd continued long-dropped trade negotiations with Kirula, seeking a new market for Hallerian gemstones — and eventually succeeding. And, sometime later, he'd started looking for a tutor for his niece Erden.

Darkness was falling. The tops of the mountains changed color from orange to lilac. The valleys surrounding the Pass were already wreathed in long shadows. Ardelei tried not to fidget. She'd experienced the crossing of the Hallerian border often enough, and even with her diplomatic immunity had had to endure all of its humiliating stages — although she'd been allowed to wear a shift while the salt guards had gone through the rest of her clothes. A Nebian merchant's wife, with or without her husband, would have to answer many more questions and negotiate the succession of booths without any concessions.

The mountainsides began to fade into the falling darkness. If Rondei didn't make it to the last checkpoint before dusk, her chance of crossing the border in disguise would be gone for good. Getting caught between booths meant going back to where she'd started from. Ardelei took a few more steps towards the guards who now had their backs to her, sensing the disturbance before she heard it. There was some commotion on the Hallerian side: a group of travelers was making its way out of the Pass, shouting as they came.

The song around her grew confused and discordant. The travelers had been confident they would get out of Haller before sunset, but something had delayed them: now the border was closing in front of their eyes. Ardelei kept her focus on the nearest guards — the two people standing between the travelers and their freedom. Standing unmoving in the shadows, she knew she wasn't likely to be spotted, and so she risked letting go of her invisibility and began directing the full force of her song towards the already distracted guards.

Magic is an imprecise power. It can be used to move things —

sometimes even people — and the most skillful mages can turn spells into physical objects. Some have been known to shift their own shape, even though Ardelei had never seen it done. Her magic was best at moving the minds and hearts of people. Her song could make a person act against their will, or feel emotions far removed from their present ones. With her voice, she could bring forgetfulness or fear. She could soothe or incite, while her victims were none the wiser, and had little recollection of the events afterwards. The only drawback of this power was that it couldn't be contained in a bottle or trapped in a spell-stone. She had to stand at close proximity to her targets to reach their ears.

She began by bending the song of the valley itself into a more tranquil, monotonous shape. From its notes, she started building a blanket of sound she could throw over the two hesitant guards, making their minds more malleable and less suspicious. She could hear their ongoing negotiation with the travelers. Ardelei could pick up the accents of Zeiroa and Nebe above others. All of the speakers were agitated, which made the guards even more adamant in turn. No one was listening to anyone else: no one was willing to take orders or suggestions. Still, the border closed at sunset: that was the unbending law of Haller.

"But that's not our fault!" a Zeiroan merchant was wailing. "It was your colleagues. They insisted on searching everyone's bags twice!"

"That is normal," said the younger of the guards. "All of us are only following orders."

"You have to come back tomorrow," said the older.

"You must be joking!" This seemed to be the general consensus among the travelers. Yet, everyone knew that humor wasn't a regular weapon in the Hallerian arsenal.

The spell wasn't complete yet; still, Ardelei had to act before the rest of the guards came to the aid of their harassed colleagues. She picked up a stone and lobbed it towards the checkpoint. It was much easier to latch the spell onto people when you had their attention.

As she raised her voice, starting to weave the two outside minds into one, compliant whole, out of the corner of her eye she saw a woman launching into a run. Someone else shouted, and decided to follow her. Luckily, the texture of the spell didn't waver, even though Ardelei's concentration was now split between tracking the movements of the fleeing travelers, and placating the confused minds of the guards. She took a couple of more steps forward so that Rondei could recognize her. For both of them, any pretension of a disguise would be futile from now on.

As more people started to make their way across the border, followed by angry orders and more confused shouts, she knew it was time to abandon the spell as well. There was no way she could catch and hold the attention of the half a dozen guards who were now making their way to the scene, launching themselves over the carts and loading their crossbows. Ardelei had to concentrate on finding and protecting her cousin.

The first of these was easily done. The woman she'd seen vaulting the barrier was indeed Rondei. Although her clothes were Hallerian, she carried herself in a very familiar way. As she got closer, Ardelei could tell that even the remnants of the disguising spell had by now worn away. She whistled a two-note greeting.

In the dim evening light, Rondei appeared both tired and elated. "What kept you? We nearly got shot."

"I had a spell trained on you," Ardelei said, taking her cousin by the shoulders and steering Rondei up the path in front of her. "Come on: Bel and Heather are waiting. And keep dodging those crossbow bolts. I can't use my magic right now."

"It is good to see you too," Rondei panted, but did as she was told.

They'd only managed to run a few steps before a tall shape appeared on the path. The border guards had their own shortcuts through the Pass, and at least one of them had been thinking with his feet. Ardelei didn't see the beginning of the tussle, but Rondei was somehow able to wrest the guard's crossbow from his grasp and throw it into a nearby ravine. The man had the upper hand – quite literally – as he was taller than Rondei and standing above her on the steep path. She, however, was used to fighting from a disadvantaged position, and managed to kick his legs from under him.

Ardelei picked up a stone and unceremoniously knocked the guard unconscious. "Well done," she smiled. "But you got lucky. The next ones will be better prepared."

"I should have kept the crossbow," Rondei said. "Hallerian weapons are rare. Could have started my pension fund on that."

"Wouldn't start thinking about pensions before we're safely over the mountains. And, if we get out of here, you'll be thanking yourself you don't have any extra weight to lug around. It'll take days to get to level ground."

"I know. And I am used to this landscape by now. Been hiking up and down the Valley of Immits for the past weeks, with all my possessions on my back. I have become quite the –"

Rondei never finished the sentence. In the darkness, she'd made a small sidestep which sent her sprawling on all fours on the path. Almost at the same time, two guards tumbled out of the shadows – somewhat taken aback by the sudden appearance of the two women, but quickly catching up with the situation. Neither of them was armed, which gave them the first advantage. They had their hands free to grab Rondei right off the path.

Ardelei tried to find an opportunity to use her stone again, but both guards were wearing snug felt hats, and kept turning their heads to avoid her blows. Rondei clawed at their faces, while trying to trip them up by hanging onto their arms and legs with all her weight. In the dim light, this made a strange tableau, particularly as the struggle mostly went on in complete silence. At last Rondei managed to bite a guard's hand, making him cry out in pain and let go of her arm. Still, it seemed the wrestling might go on for a good while, giving more guards the opportunity to come to their colleague's aid.

"Do something!" Rondei shouted in Nebian. "Throw a spell. Lob a stone. Or just stand and stare – that can frighten people in the right circumstances."

"I've already used too much magic tonight. If I form another spell, you'll have to carry me up this path. I wonder –"

One of the guards gave a strangled yell. Something heavy and hairy had plummeted down the mountainside, aiming for the nearest exposed throat. Ardelei wrestled Rondei free from the remaining — now terrified — guard, and once again began pushing her cousin uphill. The man tried to follow on his hands and knees, but gave a hissing grunt and rolled gently downwards.

From her labored breathing, Ardelei could hear that her cousin was hurt. "What happened?" she asked.

"I twisted my ankle. Nothing major. I can walk. Is that who I think it is?"

"Yes. Heather took down the first guard, and Bel shot the second. I told them to keep themselves hidden nearby."

"Do you know what?" Rondei replied. "That spell of yours. Started fading within half an hour." She stopped to catch her breath and then continued at a slower pace. "Good thing no one got a good look at me before the border. Would have given them quite a shock."

"Well, good thing that didn't happen, then. In my experience, people don't pay a lot of attention to each other's faces anyway. You were still wearing the same clothes and behaving in the same way as before. Most likely no one even noticed."

"Yes, well," another long pause. "You had not counted on the fact that I might run into someone I knew."

"And did you?"

"I did indeed. There was a Sendali merchant I had worked with before. He used to bring me inks. Imagine his surprise, running into Mistress Galsi in the Pass of Krassmark. Had to keep my face hidden in my scarf every time he looked in my direction."

"So he didn't recognize you?"

"Hard to say. Luckily, the Pass was closing, and everyone was getting really riled up. It was easy to stoke that emotion, and to keep out of the way."

"That seems to be your way," Ardelei couldn't help remarking.

"Pardon?"

"I know what you've been doing, Rondei. The books and pamphlets you've been writing. Valja is getting pretty riled up as well."

Rondei turned to look at her. Her eyes were barely visible, but the flash of the whites told Ardelei that her cousin was excited, quite despite herself. "They have been reading my works?"

"Yes, and burned down houses and shops. Homeless families. Parentless children. You know," she breathed out. "The usual."

"They have already started rioting?"

Ardelei tried to get on top of her own, sudden irritation. "I rather believe they've never stopped. Which is, I suppose, why you chose Valja in the first place."

"How am I getting a feeling that you do not entirely approve of my exploits, cousin dear?" Rondei asked in her customary drawl. "I do not need your approval — or that of your order. As you say, I have always preferred to work alone, and from the sidelines. That tends to give the best view."

"Aye. And the surest escape." They had reached a fork in the path. Ardelei thought it best to stop and wait for Bel and Heather, and decide which route to take together. "Speaking of, is that where you're headed right now? Valja?"

"I suppose so." Rondei was leaning heavily on the nearest rock, resting her weight on one foot. "Although, if what you say is true and the revolt is already spent, I might have to reconsider my options."

"It's not spent, as far as I know. It will only take the sound of your name to galvanize the most discontented into action. I wonder what they'll do at the sight of your face."

Someone whispered a greeting: Beldor had joined them. Heather followed at his heels, licking her chops.

"Beldor," the printer nodded at him. "That was an impressive shot."

"It was touch and go in the murk," he admitted. "Luckily, the fellow was making quite a lot of noise at that point."

"Well done, Heather," Ardelei smiled at the dog. "I trust you both got out of the scrap without injuries." At Bel's noncommittal grunt, she turned to her cousin once more. "How's your ankle, Rondei? We need to keep going as long as there's the smallest glint of light. It's a clear night, so we should have enough starlight for a couple of hours at least. Do you think you can walk that far?"

"I can," Rondei said. "I did not come all this way to sit down at the first hurdle, only to be dragged back to that prison again."

Chapter 6

Sendal - Meropat

Footsteps thudded across the floor. Meropat raised their head, and after some deliberation, opened their eyes. By the sound of the determined walk, they deduced a loud shout would soon follow – and raised voices were something they were trying to avoid right now. The workshop was oppressive as it was. The midday sun was beating on the tin roof, and the open windows let in air that had been breathed out by too many people. The smell of ink and hot metal was enough to turn their stomach. Dealing with shouty men was more than Meropat could handle at the moment.

Neither were they looking to infuriate their employer. Ever since their first meeting with the Skovos, they had been trying to find out about Master Keltuva's affiliations, and whether these would be negotiable. Like all law-abiding printers, Master Keltuva paid his tithes to the Guilds; still, he'd never struck Meropat as a particularly enthusiastic navigator of the city's political currents. The printing press was his pride and joy. Every night, Meropat saw him pull a dust-sheet over it with all the tenderness of a devoted father.

Master Keltuva did have children of his own, but having gotten them relatively late in life, had no one to train up as his follower yet. Thus, he had to rely on a miscellany of apprentices and other temporary help. Mistress Keltuva, a flighty, giggly specimen, wasn't of much help in the daily running of the business, as she professed no interest in bookkeeping or proofreading. Meropat was beginning to suspect the woman didn't even know how to read.

This had made it easy to make themselves indispensable to Master Keltuva. Meropat had their considerable charm to fall back on, but their solid experience in the production of texts and the selling of their wares alone would have endeared them to the master printer. Also, it seemed that after years of uncertainty, business was finally picking up. There was work for all skilled people, and where there was work, there were wages. Soon, those wages would be flowing in the direction of Master Keltuva as well. People wanted to read books and newspapers, and they wanted their own texts published.

Meropat was wondering when the flow of cash would reach their own pockets. As the cursed epic was still refusing to materialize, they had been reduced to living hand-to-mouth. A romantic existence, no doubt, but not a desirable one for someone of Meropat's caliber. This was one of the reasons they had come up with a tentative plan to bring Master Keltuva and the Skovos together. If the printer proved open to the Siblings' ideas, Meropat could claim a commission, or at least could touch their friends for a loan from time to time on the understanding that they'd given the revolutionaries a steady source of income.

They were feeling rather optimistic: after all, they'd used Rondei Galsi's name as an introduction to their apprenticeship. Not even the most unpolitical printer in the city of Valja could pretend ignorance about her affiliations. Everyone in the trade recognized the excellence of her books and pamphlets – and many used the excuse of learning about her printing techniques for perusing the content of her own texts as well.

Master Keltuva swaggered across the workshop, idly running his finger along the shelf of newly arrived pots of ink. He was a small, rotund man with a tuft of gray hair on either side of his otherwise egg-bald head. As usual, he was wearing an expression of vacant goodwill. Meropat had grown to distrust that expression. Their employer might seem good-natured — and for the most part, he was — yet he could fly into a red-hot rage at the drop of a hat if his orders weren't followed to the letter.

"Meropat," he said by way of greeting. "Any news?"

"None," they answered in a rather feeble voice. "It's been unusually quiet today. A Nebian lady dropped in to ask about maps, but I told her that's not our specialty."

"Indeed it is not. Anyone can draw squiggly lines across a page. Making your texts regular and easy to read: that's where the real skill lies. Never forget that, young Meropat."

"I won't."

Master Keltuva called almost everyone by the epithet "young," just as long as they were lower down the social rank than he was. Meropat had never actually told him how old they were – mainly because people of their age tended to be firmly established in a trade, and most had settled down long since. Establishing and settling had never appealed to Meropat. They were much more interested in becoming and diversifying.

"Can I ask you a question, Master?" they began, knowing that their employer was usually only too happy to share what he considered to be his extensive knowledge.

"Anytime." He took up a newspaper and sat down in a sunny spot.

"This is a rather delicate matter, and I hope you don't mind me broaching it." At an encouraging gesture, they went on. "I have been speaking to some young people who would like to get their texts printed. It seems, however, that some of their ideas go against the Guild guidelines. Now, as a foreigner, I don't always quite understand the finesses of Sendali thought, so I thought it best to consult you first before giving them an answer."

Master Keltuva smiled indulgently. "You did well, young Meropat. I have noted your ignorance of our politics, and I have to say that it is one of the reasons why I took you on as an apprentice. I've had enough hotheads. A printing press is a dangerous implement, you know," he gestured towards the machine. "Whatever you feed into it becomes immortal. One sheet of paper is easily destroyed. But what about ten? A hundred? A thousand copies of the same sheet? The printed word is impossible to kill, and that's why people fear it. That's also why the Guilds regulate what can be printed."

"But they don't read every page, do they?"

"No, that would be impossible. There are dozens of printers on Scribe Street alone. Just imagine how many pages they produce in a day. No — instead, the Guilds rely on random checks. Sometimes, they come and pay us a visit. That's pretty rare nowadays. They just usually collect the stuff that goes around in the streets and check the watermarks. That way, if there are some dodgy things printed, they know who produced them."

"Makes sense," Meropat said, pretending to ponder the new information. "But suppose you use someone else's watermark? Or none? After all, it's only here in Sendal that printers are obliged to use them."

"That's been done. But the punishment for being caught with blank paper is much higher than that of printing an incendiary leaflet using your own watermark. I don't know anyone who'd be willing to risk it."

"What if you accidentally print on blank paper? Or use someone else's mark?"

"They don't care. If you're caught, it's your fault for not checking your paper properly. Or for letting someone else use your press."

"Sounds a bit unfair to me, to be honest," Meropat said mildly. "People make mistakes."

Master Keltuva shrugged. "Law is law. But I have to say that compared to the rest of Ederai, our laws are on the strict side.

And I've heard that in places like Idriola you can pretty much print what you like."

"Well, not exactly, but if you print controversial texts in Gesaia, it's only the writer who gets into trouble, not the printer. After all, they're just doing their job."

The master printer looked confused for a moment. Then, "Ah, of course, I had almost forgotten that I have a living, breathing Gesaian in my service now. That perhaps explains some of your more... well, different views."

Meropat paused for a moment to wonder what these views might be. They'd been careful not to involve their master in their private life, and had avoided all discussions of politics or religion. Yet, while it was possible to remain quiet, one tended to put one's disagreement into facial expressions and gestures that were less easy to police. It was also true that Meropat had begun to cultivate a rather unconventional circle of friends in Valja, and that these friends had some very catching views.

Seeing their confusion, Master Keltuva went on in a kinder voice, "I didn't mean any harm by that — please don't think I did. It's just that I've lived all my life in this city. I can usually tell what my neighbor will say just by looking at his face, and most likely he can do the same with me. Things change slowly here."

As he didn't go on, Meropat thought it safe to ask, "Do you think that's a good thing?"

"On the whole, I do. In my time, I've seen that it's no good blundering into things you don't understand. But then again, I've seen that often things change without a warning anyway. Take the plague, for instance. There are some that say that it could have been prevented, or that a cure could have been come up with, if only the authorities had acted more quickly, or with the well-being of their people in mind. And I say that I at least partially agree."

The bell rang, and a father with two children entered the shop, wanting to see the latest Zeiroan prints. As Master Keltuva helped the children select some for their mother's birthday, Meropat removed themself to the storeroom for a quiet reflection. The dim coolness of the room eased their hangover somewhat; at the same time, they were grateful for the interruption. If the clients hadn't barged in just then, it would have been all too easy to lead the conversation deeper into Master Keltuva's personal politics.

This, Meropat now understood, would have been a mistake. It wasn't wise to make someone confide too many things at once. The two of them had made a good start, and Meropat would give the master printer some time to decide whether to take them further into his confidence. After all, as an outsider, they served as a mirror to the staid practices of Valjan society. Next time, they could perhaps start steering the conversation deeper into Keltuva's own convictions. After all, he seemed much more flexible in his views that many other people of his background Meropat had talked to.

This also meant that the Skovos would have to wait for an answer. Not that Meropat wasn't already helping them in other ways. The fierce hangover, for instance, was a direct consequence of last night's foray into the city's riverside society at its most authentic. Not the clean, well-behaved inns they were usually invited to, but the grubby, dimly lit, and infinitely more exciting public houses most Valjan workers frequented. Places that were full of noise, license – and a palpable sense of growing discontent egged on by the Siblings.

The Skovos were recognized everywhere, and to Meropat's glee, no one in their retinue had to pay for their refreshments. Even though the surroundings seemed insalubrious, the beer was invariably strong, and the food simple but tasty. And so it was that despite years of practice, Meropat had found themself reeling drunk after only three hours of socializing – and, as often happens in these cases, hadn't been able to stop themself in time.

They'd learned early on that the Siblings were creatures of the night. Although they inevitably did business in sunlight, too, they truly came to life in the dark, cracking jokes and calling out to their friends. Even their appearance seemed somehow more attractive after sundown.

"It runs in their blood," someone had remarked when Meropat had once, rather carelessly, mentioned this. "Better not think too much about it."

"What does that mean?"

"It only means that before we lot came here and took over, there were creatures of a very different kind living on Ederai. Some say that our blood mingled with theirs." At Meropat's skeptical look, the woman had gone on, "That's the story, anyway. Lots of similar ones about. As I said, don't think about it if you want to sleep at night."

Meropat didn't believe in the existence of primaeval dark creatures, but the story was too resonant to let go. So, with the reluctant agreement of the Skovos, they began spreading the rumor that there was something more to the Siblings than met the eye. A hint of rare magic never went amiss, and the added link to the mysterious ancestors of Ederai was a touch of genius. The Skovos were born of the ancient bloodline of the island. Perhaps they had access to knowledge and powers other people could only dream of. Thus, only a fool would cross them deliberately. Only a fool would ignore them.

Meropat leaned their forehead against the nearest shelf. It was well and good spinning songs and cheap stories for the Siblings; that was something that came naturally to them. However, this wasn't the way Meropat wanted to see their reputation spread all over Ederai. They'd come to take the island by storm, combining their native Gesaian elegance with the raw talent that had no homeland. So far, their audience had proven somewhat hard of hearing. The pestilence hadn't helped matters, either. They needed to come up with something big before the momentum of their arrival was entirely spent.

In the following days, Meropat continued their subtle campaign with Master Keltuva. They weren't really acting out of the goodness of their heart. During another midnight meeting, Ainaes had turned to them, her dark eyes fierce with the revolutionary flame that only seemed to grow brighter with every passing day.

"What's going on at the printshop? Is the owner ripe for the picking, or are we wasting our time with him?"

"He's ripening. I just need a couple of more days: I feel he's about to trust me."

"Oh Meropat," the Sister had sighed. "Ever the romantic. I admire your talents, and your artistic passion – we all do – but those aren't going to be enough in the long run. You can't dawdle. The iron is hot. Strike it."

On their way home, they'd begun a ballad that used the imagery of the forge to talk about the hard times that had brought about the revolt. They tried to keep the words simple. The Skovos were quick to criticize anything that might go over the heads of ordinary laborers. Meropat didn't necessarily agree with this point of view; sometimes, a striking pair of lyrical words conveyed the message better than ten plain ones. Still, they were an artisan and strove to please the people who paid them.

Or at least paid for their food and drink. The revolution wasn't exactly a lucrative occupation. It was a maw that sucked in all available resources, and spat out exhausted people. Meropat had seen workers come in after ten hours of labor, down a glass of beer and eat a hunk of bread, and put in another two or three hours of work for the Skovos. Meropat, a part-time apprentice, flushed with shame thinking about all the idle hours they had to themself in the noisy but otherwise comfortable room.

They were also somewhat wary of the feverish tone in Ainaes's voice. For some weeks now, the Siblings had been talking about an event that would spark their revolt: something big and unmistakably violent — something the Guilds would have to acknowledge and respond to with equal force. Valja had seen violence before; this wasn't even the first riot since the beginning of the plague. Thus, the Skovos needed to make their mark with decisive action. Many of the workers Meropat had seen toiling in the back rooms of pubs weren't writing passionate texts or embroidering banners. They were making weapons: sharpening stakes and kitchen knives, putting together bows and fletching arrows. On their days off, they sneaked out of Valja to practice shooting in the nearby woods and meadows.

Realizing the true nature of the movement, Meropat had sat themself down for a serious talk. Being involved in the revolt had been entertaining and educational so far: full of meetings, high passions and rousing words. Often the heightened atmosphere had led to passionate encounters in alleyways and in the back rooms of taverns. Above all, Meropat had enjoyed the magnetic company of the two leaders. Like all creative artists, they'd reveled in the aura of the Siblings, and bathed in its reflected glory. Now, however, the time had come to stop talking and pick up a weapon. The time had come to destroy other peoples' property – and to maim and kill the owners of said property.

Meropat had already made it clear to the Siblings that this wasn't what they'd joined the movement for. In a group as extensive as theirs, there had to be different roles for different kinds of people. As a Gesaian they knew that an army needed someone to cook and launder for the soldiers, to draw their maps and plan their routes. Meropat hadn't volunteered for the front lines. They saw their role as an entertainer and inspirer, someone to soothe troubled minds and lift weary hearts.

Eolum had given them a crooked smile. "I hear you: I, too, have studied Gesaian history. And I know you well enough to know that you're not the fighting type. Yet, when you join a revolution, you do it with the intention of overthrowing those in power. We both know that doesn't happen just because someone wrote a rousing song or pretty poem. We don't get results just by organizing demonstrations and giving passionate speeches. In order to depose something as powerful as the Guilds of Valja, we need to shed blood. Lots of it."

"It sounds as if you think you'll enjoy it."

"You know me. I'm not a violent man, but I feel more for my people than I do for those bastards who sit in their stone houses, content to let the rest of us be taken by hunger, fire and plague. They've killed too many of us over the centuries — most through indirect means. Which is worse, Meropat: taking someone's life knowingly, looking them in the eye, or never knowing how many people have perished because of a policy you made?"

They'd leaned back. "I'd love to debate philosophy with you, but I don't think that's what's going on here. You've already made up your mind, and I commend you for it. You're an honest man, Eolum, and a man who stands behind his beliefs. You might find it difficult to understand people whose positions aren't so clear-cut. I, for example, am a foreigner here. My people haven't suffered in the hands of the Guilds. I've joined you because I see your struggle, and I find it worthwhile. Yet, I can't commit to the revolution like you can. Look at these hands," they'd said rather dramatically, showing their ink-stained fingers to the young man. "Touch them. They might be black with the work I do, but they're smooth and delicate. These aren't killing hands."

Eolum had held their hand for a while. The touch had been pleasant enough, but there was no tenderness or any promise of further caresses in it. Indeed, for all his political passion, Eolum seemed devoid of any physical attraction. As far as Meropat knew, he'd had no sweethearts, and he always accompanied his sister back home after meetings. They didn't believe the nastiest rumors that circulated about the Skovos: they'd seen many types of affection in their time, and both Siblings seemed as chaste as two stones by the roadside. Their one overwhelming passion was the well-being of the workers: nothing else – no one else – mattered.

This would be the last moment to step off the boat before it launched. After this, they would be fully committed to the revolution, and anything that happened would happen in their name. Victory or defeat, Meropat Rugolata would be someone associated with the revolt against the Guilds, and nothing they did would erase those pages from existence. Like Master Keltuva had said, the written word endured, particularly when immortalized in print.

They'd been looking for a smooth pathway into renown. Now, one stretched right in front of them, promising undying fame and quite probable — if short-lived — glory. It promised friendship and excitement, and a multitude of mouths to sing their songs and chant their slogans. It also promised death — or at least injury and disgrace in the hands of the guards. It promised the end of their short-lived apprenticeship, and any association with the well-to-do of Valja. Indeed, once their allegiances became clear to the general public, no self-respecting merchant or aristocrat would associate with them ever again.

Meropat had always been impulsive. They'd left Gesaia on a whim, after a patron had insulted their meticulously put-together collection of quatrains. They'd stormed off, swearing not to return until the high aristocracy of Idriola begged them on their knees to come back to court. They'd settled in Valja in a bout of similar indignation, having failed to impress the upper crust of Zeiroan society in Erun, and having rather embarrassingly run out of money in the process. Sendal had seemed like a good choice at the time, and its main city full of fair prospects.

Then the plague had started sweeping over the island, and a city with sturdy walls and a government that looked after the interests of its people seemed like a prudent choice. Even if Valja wasn't necessarily full of potential patrons anymore, it had seemed self-sufficient enough compared to many other towns on Ederai. The city's rebellious history had also appealed to Meropat. Surely, the smoldering flame would help the citizens burn through the disease faster than in more peaceful places.

That hadn't turned out to be exactly true, but the strict measures of the Guilds had meant that for a few months, the city had remained plague-free, and its people had been able to enjoy relative freedom within the gates. The disease, however, outsmarted the Members of the Assembly in the end, and soon there were special guards going round, splashing white paint on the doors of homes and workshops of the afflicted. Anyone suspected of having caught the disease was supposed to wear a strip of white linen around their neck; very few did, which led to the next phase where the infected were sealed into their homes until everyone indoors got better, or died. There came a time when the only people who dared to move freely were the medics — others were either prisoners in their homes, or afraid of becoming so.

Meropat had been lucky in their choice of lodgings that time round. In their early days in Valja, they'd befriended a hairdresser's apprentice who'd recommended renting a room next to hers. The boarding house was full of workers, and as the stricter measures began to confine people in their homes and workplaces, many had been trapped on their masters' premises. Week by week, the rooms began to empty; very few of those who caught the plague ever came back.

It soon became clear that young people were most vulnerable to the disease. Through some cruel twist of fate, the plague often took down the most active, leaving countless families without their young folk, and many masters without a trained workforce. For Meropat, it had meant the loss of a friendly community – but it also left them in a room with a lot of uninfected air to breathe.

Now that the disease was retreating, the lack of apprentices gave people like the Skovos a new weapon. Valja was a shadow of its former self. Sure enough, there were children playing in the streets, and middle-aged people trying to return to their old routines. Many older people had succumbed not to the plague, but to other diseases that took over their weakened bodies afterwards. Many died of hunger or cold when there was no one left to look after them.

As trade picked up, the city started to feel the lack of its young workers. The survivors found out that they could ask for better wages and conditions in exchange for their labor. Some masters granted these things straight away, particularly as newspapers reported that elsewhere in Ederai the circumstances had also changed to favor apprentices. In Valja, the ever-present Guilds were reluctant to improve the situation, claiming that they were looking out for the interests of all citizens, not just aiming to raise the wages of those who seemed unwilling to work otherwise.

So far, Meropat had only seen that the Guilds' protectionism extended to those with a vote; people with no legal way of steering public opinion were left to fend for themselves. Only those with their own businesses could apply for a Guild membership, and usually only those with a high enough income would be invited to join. It was no wonder that Valja had seen so many revolts in the past — and no wonder, Meropat thought, that all of those revolts had failed. The Guilds could afford their own guards, and equipped them with the most effective weapons available. Since the arrival of the plague, the number of guards had doubled – and showed no signs of going down, even when people were no longer falling ill.

After the siesta, they decided to stroll down to the riverside — first to visit a bathhouse, and afterwards to take a turn along the Parade. Meropat wasn't one for exercise for its own sake, but staying holed up in the bagpipy room wasn't going to give them much pleasure, and definitely wouldn't help in getting their overheated thoughts in order.

It turned out that the outdoors wasn't much of an improvement. Although the long warm season was only beginning, the streets of the Brewers' Quarter were hazy with dust, and reeked of refuse. They passed an old woman watering her plants, and stopped for a while to commiserate the lack of rain.

Meropat turned north. Nearer to the river the air would be cooler, and the streets packed with people desperate for shade. Many innkeepers had set up tables outdoors, next to the sweating stone walls of their buildings, or else hung fluttering cloths to protect their customers from the glare of the sun. Many Valjans preferred to cross the river and picnic under the plane trees on the green. The best places were jealously guarded, and Meropat had heard of fistfights erupting if a long-established boundary was carelessly crossed. If Valja had had any theatres worth writing for, Meropat would have produced a witty comedy on the topic. As it was, the Sendali capital was almost totally oblivious to the pleasures of the noblest of the performing arts, and thus Meropat only made up pieces of dialogue for their own amusement.

The sun's white disc dragged itself across the searing sky. As a Gesaian, Meropat had gotten used to piercingly hot midsummer days and sweltering nights. The afternoon heat of Valja was nothing compared to the windless days in Idriola when the very cobblestones seemed about to melt and run into the Strait. In Gesaia, however, people could enjoy cool drinks and flavored ices in the Paishnali fashion. In Sendal, it didn't even seem to cross anyone's mind to offer such refreshments for love or money. The only concession to the hot season was switchel — a nauseating concoction made up of water, vinegar and honey, which Meropat had learned to steer clear of.

Just as Meropat was thinking of setting up trade negotiations with Haller for the import rights of the ice that permanently graced the tops of their highest mountains, someone hailed them. A well-dressed, pale-skinned man with a very prominent nose and a shock of reddish-brown hair.

"Meropat Rugolata, I presume?" he called in a sing-song voice.

"I am," they answered warily.

"Could I just talk to you for a minute? I believe we have friends in common."

Doubting this, but having picked up a Hallerian accent, they decided to oblige. Who knew if this was someone with connections to very high mountains? "I have friends all over the Eastern Isles. Who do you mean, exactly? And what do I call you?"

"You don't have to call me anything," the man said with a wink. Meropat suspected he was drunk — or else, acting drunk. They were quickly coming to the conclusion that Hallerians weren't particularly accomplished thespians, either. "And the business I have to discuss is not one for the open street. Here's an inn: what do you think?"

Meropat looked up. The Silver Scissors. The name didn't ring a bell. "Well, there's a first time for everything. The drinks are on you?"

The Hallerian pointed them to a secluded corner of the rather pleasant-looking establishment, and soon joined Meropat carrying two beaded glasses of something greenish.

"Mint tea," he said. "Straight from the cellar."

Meropat, wary of all Ederaian drinks, first sniffed, and then plucked up the courage to sip the cool liquid. Despite its innocuous name, there was something stronger in the glass than just summer herbs. They said as much.

"Oh yes. There's vodka as well. Seeing that we are in Sendal."

"Are you trying to get me drunk?" Meropat had used this line many times in the past, usually with a teasing cadence; right now, they were deadly serious.

"Perhaps. You look somewhat tense, my friend." He reached out to touch Meropat's arm. "I'm just trying to talk to you."

Leaning back from the touch, they said, "I'm not your friend."

Perhaps it was the oppressive heat; perhaps it was the load of worry they'd been carrying for weeks. Still, Meropat wasn't feeling at all chummy — which was rare enough. In their line of work a free drink and a casual chat in an intimate setting rarely went amiss. Now, however, their instincts were screaming to get out of the conversation as quickly as possible. Their instincts were rarely wrong.

The curly-haired Hallerian bared his teeth in a rather predatory smile. "Well, in that case, we can go straight to business. I think you know why I am here."

Meropat met his gaze. "I have no idea why you are here."

"As I said, we have friends in common. Or acquaintances, rather. I have never called Mistress Galsi a friend, and I'm sure she would return the compliment. As you have." He raised his glass at Meropat.

"Rondei Galsi?" They shrugged. "Haven't seen her in ages."

"That does not surprise me. She has been working in Daurbar. Still, for a woman like her it's no problem communicating with her co-conspirators across the mountains."

"Her what?" Meropat was keeping their voice deliberately low.

"You know what I mean. She came to our court, using Lord Stainerau's goodwill as a shield under which she could weave her disgusting plots. She said she needed a printing press, and she was given one, so that she could teach us her trade." A dramatic pause. "She never did. Instead, she used her free time — not to mention Lord Stainerau's paper and ink – to print revolutionary texts, which are now circulating all over Sendal."

"I don't know why you're telling me all this. I've met Mistress Galsi only once in my life, and as I said, that was long ago. I didn't particularly sympathize with her views then, and I doubt I would do so now."

"Yes, but you artistic types are always drawn to each other, and to ideas of freedom and equality. I'm sure that someone you know has been in touch with Rondei Galsi even if you haven't. All I'm asking is for you to cast your net wide."

Meropat took a small sip of the drink. "Are you asking me to spy for Lord Stainerau? Here in Valja?"

"That is an unattractive word, my friend. *Gathering information* is much better, hm? Lord Stainerau has been badly let down by this woman. We just want to learn how deep the deception runs." The Hallerian leaned back, and his face assumed an expression of studied guile. "You can also remind her friends that her son is still in Daurbar. Whatever she expected him to do has failed. He has very readily renounced any ties to her, and has pledged life-long loyalty to the Stainerau family. It's not possible, however, to fully trust in the word of someone brought up by a traitor. Therefore, Vejèl Galsi will remain under house arrest until his mother returns to stand a fair trial in Daurbar." He gave them another grimace. "Just something for you to think about."

Meropat blinked at him, struggling to keep a straight face. The idiot probably thought that as soon as this absurd meeting was over, Meropat would run to the hiding place of Rondei's friends to breathlessly relate the message word for word.

"That's a strange tune you're singing," they said, as some response was expected. "I don't know how you found me, but I assure you, you're wasting your time." Pushing back their chair, they continued, "It has been fascinating talking to you, but I'm already late for an appointment. Thank you for the tea. It was... surprising." They took their leave with the smallest of parting gestures, careful not to hurry their steps as they got out into the street.

The Hallerian chose not to follow. Most likely, this was also part of the plan: behind the corner of the Scissors, the less conspicuous members of the group would be lurking, waiting to slip after Meropat. Not wanting to encourage them, they made an exaggeratedly slow and showy beeline for the river. As the sun started to roll towards the horizon, the temperatures were dropping to a perfect strolling temperature. Bathing would have to wait. They didn't want to get caught unawares in a hammam with only a damp towel for protection.

As Meropat had expected, the riverside and the Parade were pullulating with people. Built only a few years before the plague, the Parade — an elevated walkway that connected the four bridges on the southern side of the river — was a place designed for the city's well-to-do to show off their summer fashions. However, it had more recently become a prowling-ground of young apprentices who, more often than not, sat in small groups on the wooden benches after work, staring moodily into the water while singing long, slow songs about unreliable lovers and ungenerous masters.

On days off the scene was livelier, and it was difficult to even make one's way from one bridge to another; finding an unoccupied bench was impossible. Even on this regular workday evening, Meropat found that they didn't need to slow down their pace on purpose. They'd slipped into a stream of people strolling westwards. On the other side of the walkway a similar current was moving in the opposite direction. They followed the crowd, happy to blend into its carefree mood and the press of young bodies.

They were also beginning to enjoy the look of the young couple walking directly in front of them. Although forced by the throng to walk one behind the other, they still managed to hold hands and even steal a kiss from time to time. The girl, catching Meropat's eye, blew them a kiss as well— which they obviously had to catch and return with great courtesy. With a wink and a wave she passed on the kiss to her beau.

This made the young man turn around as well. Soon the three of them were having a lively conversation about nothing in particular. None of them was minded to talk about their work; no one even mentioned the oppressive weather. This hour was theirs alone, and it was full of joy. Meropat sang snatches of jolly songs while the young man made a show of dancing. The girl, tired of the laws of gravity, leaped onto the handrail and walked a few paces, careful not to tread on the hands of other strollers. Not wanting to get separated from her companions, she also made her way back the same way.

In no time at all, Meropat had secured a place at their picnic. Under an ancient plane tree they made the acquaintance of several similarly carefree young people, and bought their evening meal and drink with witty anecdotes and romantic ditties. There was a round of rapid introductions, but Meropat, true to their habit, let names fly in one ear and out of the other. For them, this group was one entity – a happy, youthful embodiment of everything that was beautiful and free in the city of Valja.

As the evening deepened around them, Meropat was reminded that not all of the city's working people were desperately unhappy with their lot. Most likely, these youngsters would grow up to be hard-working heads of families, and still remember how to toast with abandon or take a turn on the dance floor. Not one person mentioned the Skovos, or even skirted the ideas the Siblings so religiously discussed, night after night. Politics and riots interested the picnickers as much as the inner life of the tree they were leaning on — which is to say, not at all.

Their head buzzing with cheap Zeiroan wine and carefree talk, Meropat found that they could breathe freely for the first time in weeks. They could admit to themself that they were growing tired of the serious Siblings. While they admired the passion that drove the Cause, they found themself despairing of the matter-of-factness of the two leaders, and the message they were so desperate to stamp onto everyone else. Nothing mattered but the coming revolution; there was no greater goal in life than the complete overthrowing of the Guilds and everything they stood for.

This, unfortunately, included a lot of things Meropat quite liked as well. Generally speaking, they enjoyed the clean, well-ordered streets, and the regulated trade which brought in goods from all corners of the known world. They enjoyed dining in an efficiently run household, even if that meant that many people had to sweat in the kitchens to get the food on the table. The fine fabrics, rare foods and expensive liqueurs that made up a dinner party were for Meropat a sign of a life well spent. It would be difficult to imagine the Skovos sitting to dine like that.

As darkness fell, their resolution became stronger. Once they got home, they'd send a message through one of their contacts, informing the Siblings of their decision to leave the Cause. Although its core was true and its followers admirable, Meropat just couldn't find it in themself to fight to the death — theirs or somebody else's — for all its ruthless goals. It would also be safer for Master Keltuva not to get dragged into the murky business of the revolution. Let him keep his dreary routines. After all, they were of his own choosing.

They were taking the long way back. Their new friends lived all over the Brewers, and the thinning group had been making its way from door to door, shedding members on the way—unwilling to admit that the evening was coming to an end, and also clinging together for more practical reasons. Even though there were numerous night guards in Valja, these rarely bothered to ensure the safety of the poorer population. Indeed, more often than not, revelers like themselves found the guard actively pursuing them in search of a quick brawl.

Meropat, in the unpleasant state of fading inebriation, was deliberating on whether it would be wiser to continue straight to their lodgings, or to make the night stretch on a tiny bit longer by stepping into a nearby tavern for one last drink. Their companions — two haberdasher's apprentices and a dainty Nebian lady's maid who'd recently come to town with her mistress — were loudly arguing in favor of the latter plan. Knowing the price they'd pay for it on the morrow, Meropat acquiesced anyway. Who were they to say no to the folly of youth?

The Valjan apprentices spotted a shortcut to their regular inn. The alleyways between houses were so narrow that the four of them had to walk in single file, much like they'd done earlier on the Parade. They sang outrageous songs, and banged their elbows against the windowless brick walls. Meropat was grateful for the extra support. The youngsters, despite their drunkenness, were very swift on their feet.

As they were walking in the middle of the group — the apprentices leading the way, and the Nebian servant bringing up the rear — it took them a while to notice that they weren't alone.

The alleyway was almost pitch-dark. The sun had set hours ago, and starlight reached only sporadically into the depths of the alley. Suddenly, the girl behind them gave a strangled yelp, her legs buckling from under her.

It appeared that someone had grabbed the girl from behind and was dragging her into the shadows. Meropat turned around to let the apprentices know what was going on – and realized that they had been attacked from the opposite direction. Judging that the two of them could take care of themself better than the lone girl, Meropat turned to follow the abductor. Easy enough at first, as the alleyway continued back with no branchings.

They kept their left hand on the brick wall, while reaching under their clothes with their right. Never one for casual brawling, Meropat had nevertheless learned to take care of themselves from quite an early age. Tall and well-built, they had an immediate advantage over many an opponent. They had also discovered that few people expected a jovial bard to whip out a blade and know how to wield it. It had been worth it, however, to pay for private lessons with the best knife-fighters in Idriola.

Unwilling to blunder any further in the dark by themself, they stopped to listen and to catch their breath. Judging by the noises, the apprentices, too, had had some practice in hand-to-hand fighting. From ahead, Meropat could hear nothing. Either the assailants had found an open door and stepped into a house, or they were lying in wait somewhere close by. What they'd done to silence the serving-girl didn't bear thinking about.

"Show yourselves!" Meropat called, just to steady their own nerves.

"Keep walking," someone answered in a low voice. "We won't hurt you."

"What have you done to the girl?" they asked, doing as they'd been told. Staying put really wasn't an option anyway.

"Don't worry about her. We just want to talk to you."

Where have I heard that before? Although Meropat had sobered up remarkably quickly, the events of the day were a merry jumble. Too many meetings: too many new faces and topics of conversation to be kept straight.

A boot nail scraped against a cobblestone behind them. Without thinking, Meropat flattened themself against the wall and swung their right arm towards the unseen person. Unfortunately, his night-vision was much better than theirs, and he stepped back deftly.

"Come on," the voice continued as if nothing had happened. "Just follow us and you'll be fine."

"Where are we going?" Meropat asked, trying to still their hammering heart.

"You'll see."

The smugness of the voice was grating. "Where's the girl? Promise she won't come to any harm, and I'll go with you. I've only just met these people: they know nothing, I swear."

One of the apprentices had managed to fight free of his assailants, and was making his way towards Meropat. He bowled into the booted man, causing both of them to tumble to the ground. In the general confusion Meropat lunged forwards as well, desperate to find a way out of the maze. After a dozen or so steps, they saw that the alleyway branched in two directions; the alley on the left was slightly wider, and so Meropat decided to follow it in hopes of it leading to a nearby street.

Instead, they found themself in a rectangular well formed by the backs of three houses. In a way, their instinct had been correct, as this was also the way the second group of assailants had taken. Meropat could hear the servant girl's muffled protests as someone was trying to tie her hands. Again, following their instincts, Meropat launched themself into the middle of the group. They'd counted three strangers in the dim light.

Meropat shouldered the smallest of these men to the ground, at the same time setting free the serving-girl he'd been holding. The Nebian was light on her feet and quick with her thinking, too. In a heartbeat, she was haring back into the alleyway as silently as a cloud. This unfortunately left Meropat alone with the three assailants.

"Well, you've got me now," they told the nearest person. "If you have any questions, ask them now. Otherwise, I'll give you a taste of my blade."

"Fancy your chances, do you, Gesaian?"

"Not particularly, but it's not my style to come quietly." Meropat raised their knife once more, poised to strike at the slightest movement in their direction.

"Oh, don't we know that," said the person they'd knocked over before as he kicked Meropat in the stomach.

Without even drawing a breath, Meropat rolled away from the group and put their back against the nearest wall. The first person to reach them got a knife to the throat and fell back, gurgling horribly. The next, spurred on by sheer momentum, got his head bashed against the bricks; he didn't even make a sound as he went down. What would have happened to the third man even Meropat couldn't tell. When their instruction-honed instincts took over, there was no time to make elaborate plans.

There were suddenly many more people in the small space. There were shouts and grunts, and orders in at least three languages. The city guard had arrived, bringing with them someone with enough magical ability to cast a daylight spell over the scene for a few seconds. In that time, in the fluorescent flash of element magic, the main points of interest became obvious. There was a person lying on the ground in a pool of blood. Another was shaking his head in an experimental way. The third member of the matching group had collided with a guard, and had deemed it wisest to drop to his knees.

Which left Meropat in a rather compromising position. They still held the knife that had slashed at least one throat, standing next to a wall that had evidently ruined another man's face. The thing to do, they knew instinctively as well as intellectually, was to talk fast. The guards rarely asked questions — that was for the city's judiciary to do — but their opinion on your innocence had a lot of bearing on where, and with whom, they chose to house for the night.

"Good evening, gentlemen," they began, their voice a low purr. "I'm so glad you arrived so quickly. You saw that I was just about to be completely overwhelmed by these ruffians." They shook their sleeves, sheathing the knife in the process. "There are two other young friends of mine who could also use your help. They were pursued from the other end of the alleyway."

The head of the guards stepped clear of the still kneeling man and walked unhurriedly towards Meropat. They could see the cold glint of amusement in the man's eyes – a second before his fist came flying out of nowhere, connecting with Meropat's cheekbone. Another, more vicious blow, knocked them unconscious.

Chapter 7

Sendal - Rondei

There was a smell of something burning. Rondei sighed and got up from her desk, rolling her shoulders. Some days, she'd give her left hand for some of the peace and solitude she'd experienced in Daurbar. Although Sendal had a much freer atmosphere than its mountain neighbor, it was also full of people — and people meant distractions. She made her way to the kitchen where the stench was emanating from.

"Sorry," Ainali looked up from the smoking stove. "The milk overheated."

"And whose job is it to watch the pot so that it does not overheat?" Rondei asked, rhetorically.

The girl answered anyway. "Mine. I'm sorry. I was —"

Rondei reached for a piece of bread. Lunch would be late again. "Never mind. Just remember what I hired you for."

"Yes, Mistress Galsi," Ainali said, hanging her head.

Rondei headed back up the stairs. She'd also forgotten how problematic servants were. The bad ones needed disciplining, and eventually ran away. The good ones knew their worth and were uppity and always asking for more wages. The majority — the indifferent ones — were slow learners who toiled unthinkingly at whatever task their employer set for them. Which of course led her to the underlying question: was it right to keep a servant in her house, while at the same time churning out pamphlets calling for all workers to rebel against their masters?

In her head, she justified her decision by arguing that she had always treated her maids fairly, and paid them good wages. She made a point of remembering their full names, their family backgrounds and all other details they saw necessary to divulge to their employer. The reality was that a desperately busy woman like herself just couldn't manage without a maid. Rondei's days were filled with studying, writing, editing, and wrangling with booksellers, which in itself would have been a full-time occupation for a less experienced person.

With no children and no husband in her household, who would do her cooking, cleaning, shopping and laundering for her? No one but herself. Every hour spent away from her desk was an unproductive hour in her line of work. Also, any maid worth their salt knew exactly where to buy the freshest and most inexpensive produce in town. Rondei, who kept moving about, had no time to start learning these things anew every time she landed in a new place.

Before she'd reached the top stair, a loud knock reverberated through the narrow house. Rondei wasn't expecting company. Ardelei and Bel were the only people of her acquaintance who knew that she'd taken up residence in Kaldona, and neither of them would stand on the doorstep long enough to knock.

"I'll get it!" she shouted in the direction of the kitchen. Gods knew Ainali didn't need any more distractions.

"Am I speaking to Mistress Galsi?" A bright-eyed messenger-girl enquired as soon as the door opened.

"You are." Rondei crossed her arms, scanning the street behind the messenger. "How did you find me?"

"In Kaldona everyone knows everyone else. Your landlady is a friend of Professor Dubele. He's requesting your presence at Oremel College this evening. A dinner, if that would be acceptable, Mistress Galsi."

The reek of burned milk still lingering in her nostrils, Rondei took the piece of paper she was offered and said without hesitation, "That would be more than acceptable. Thank Professor Dubele for his invitation. I will see him at dinner."

Rondei found an almost illicit elation in walking the twilight streets of Kaldona, savoring the smell of ripening fruit and baked earth. Inns and taverns had opened their doors for the night, tables and chairs spilling out, settling in shadowy corners and under the branches of tall trees. People moved in a leisurely way, carrying trays of food and large pitchers of chilled wine, calling out to their friends across the street and in windows. Rondei smiled and nodded at a few friendly-looking faces.

Many heads turned in her direction as she passed: a lone woman in a sparklingly white robe and fluttering headscarf was enough to attract attention in any town. Rondei met all eyes fearlessly. It was likely she'd run into someone she knew sooner or later, and wasn't going to shrink from such meetings. She'd chosen Kaldona for several reasons. Most had something to do with the Academy that had proven friendly to her ideas in the past and was, even now, courting her very person. She also knew that Lord Stainerau had very little influence in this city famous for its fierce independence.

Although it had been some years since she'd passed the gates of Sendal's second city, it was easy to find her way around the winding streets. The plague had made a dent in the population of Kaldona, but the situation had remained calm even during the worst times — perhaps due to the reassuring presence of the academicians, and the general feeling of security that permeated the city. It had strong walls, but unlike the capital which had slammed its gates shut at the first sign of illness, Kaldona had taken in all those in need of shelter or healing.

In Kaldona, there had been no riots or looting. The Colleges had made sure that there was enough bread for everyone, and that what medicines there were would also be distributed fairly among the populace. Those who had caught the plague had been welcome at the public hospital; those who had preferred to see the disease through at home had been left to do so in peace. Most infected houses chose to communicate with the outside world with the use of colorful cloths; no one's front door was boarded shut by the authorities.

Thus, all the old houses were still standing, and there was no trace of barricades or broken windows. The skyline of the city was dominated by the slim tower of Sandom College, glinting indigo in the gathering dusk. Instead of making her way directly towards it, Rondei kept to the main street. She could afford a few moments of browsing local wares: another luxury she had denied herself so far. All the shops were open. And like the tavern-keepers, most proprietors had moved their business outside for the summer months. Rondei had to keep her hands in her pockets so as not to touch the pyramids of books and maps, swathes of cloth and barrelfuls of Paishnali spices she passed. Behind one counter a young girl was embroidering introductions, reminding Rondei that she was in need of a new one, having shed her former identity along with her Hallerian credentials.

One of the printshop owners she passed was an old Nebian acquaintance of hers, and she promised the woman to come back on the morrow. It wasn't just that she was looking for a regular collaborator to print her texts: Rondei had money to spend. Lord Stainerau had been an unexpectedly generous employer, and during her years in Haller Rondei hadn't had many opportunities to squander her savings. Always mindful of the day when she'd leave Daurbar, she'd resisted suggestions of placing all of her money in the care of a local bank. Instead, she'd spent many an evening sewing small pouches and money-belts, and gradually filling them with her earnings.

Thus, crossing the border to Sendal she'd not only carried her revolutionary ideas with her: she'd also brought a great sum of money — some in Hallerian notes, some in silver coins. She'd done so without a twinge of remorse. After all, she'd had to leave behind her two most precious possessions, her son Vejel, and her printing press.

Gods forgive her, she'd only missed one of them so far.

The gates of Oremel College were already closed for the night; luckily, the gatekeeper was willing to let her in at the smallest glimpse of her invitation. Once inside, Rondei did what she always had to do when entering the Academy: she stood still, hands on hips, taking in the calm splendor of the buildings. Oremel was a relatively new construction, and had been designed by a Paishnali architect to reflect the current fashions. The Western influence was evident everywhere — from the gravity-defying, intricately decorated walls and porticoes to the dazzling color scheme.

Every building shimmered like a jewel, poised in a bed of vibrant green grass, ready to outshine its neighbor. Yet, the general impression was harmonious and inviting. In between, there were small piazzas complete with tinkling fountains, and quiet gardens filled with fruit trees and flowering shrubs. Birds sang from secluded places, and cicadas were slowly winding down their whirring calls. Someone played a flute from an open window, imitating the birdsong; soon, the melodies intertwined in a cascade of harmonious notes.

Rondei wiped away a tear that had unexpectedly rolled down her cheek. In her darkest moments, she had thought she'd never see the splendor of Oremel again. Despite her fondness for it, she'd never be able to call any of the Colleges her home. Only formally educated academicians could do so, and Rondei had gathered her learning from various places and tutors over the years, never having enough money to pay for more than one semester at a time. Although she was welcomed as a visiting scholar, she'd never stand in one of the echoing lecture halls of the Academy of Kaldona, surrounded by people who'd hang onto her every word, ready to challenge or admire her.

Before, she'd been grateful for even such small academic honors — after all, the College Library alone was a wonder to behold. Now, she was becoming increasingly uncomfortable with the idea of locking up books and isolating them from the general public. If revolutions were possible in cities, surely they were possible within institutions such as the Academy, too. If the plague had taught her one thing, it was that change was an inevitable part of life.

One rather unexpected change was that the old world of oral traditions seemed to be quickly vanishing. Previously, most children had gotten their learning from songs and tales that told them how the world worked, where their families came from, how to follow weather signs on land and water, how to cure illnesses, how to bring babies into the world and how to take the dead out of it. Now, many of the singers of those songs, grandparents and other elders, were suddenly gone, and their long wisdom disappearing.

All around Ederai, scholars and non-academicians alike agreed that it was high time to start writing ancient words and traditions down before they died out completely. More importantly, many thought that it was time to teach all children to read and write so that they themselves could decide what information was worth recording for future generations.

Rondei had heard encouraging reports of people setting up village schools in far-flung places that had so far resisted organized education, or had been deemed too insignificant to warrant a tutor. At the same time, there was a seemingly never-ending demand for books and writing implements. Some of her friends had been setting up libraries in provincial towns: spaces that had books for learning and for leisure, all for a small subscription. It wouldn't take long before the most curious of these newly literate young people would start arriving at the Academies, clamoring to be admitted.

Rondei found herself in front of the Library — another Paishnali confection with a multicolored dome that hovered above the building like an indolent soap bubble. Starlight silhouetted the building's unblemished whiteness against the velvet sky. She drew a deep breath. How did something as perfect as this have a right to exist?

"Mistress Galsi," someone said behind her in Nebian. "And just on time. You have not lost your admirable punctuality."

"Professor Dubele," she said, turning and making a slight bow. "I was just admiring the Library. It is even more enchanting than I remember it." She refrained from saying what she really thought: that the small man in front of her had grown smaller and grayer. The past years hadn't treated her particularly kindly, either. She, however, had never been vain about her appearance.

"We had the exterior cleaned and whitewashed just last summer. That perhaps explains it." He shrugged mournfully. "Do not ask about the expense."

"In that case, I will ask the other obvious question: why am I here?"

"Because I wanted to see you? No?" Dubele raised an eyebrow at her skeptical expression. "I will explain over dinner. As you can probably guess, it is not a matter I can discuss freely out here."

"I guessed as much, yes."

Professor Dubele's private quarters were on the top floor of an emerald-green building. From his windows there was a view of a charming quadrangle that, at this hour, was illuminated with dozens of multicolored lanterns. The food, when it arrived, was as sumptuous as the surroundings — and likewise heavily influenced by Paishnali tastes. The sauces were hot, the rice was sweet and tinted with saffron, and the small savory pastries melted in the mouth. Several dishes were served one after the other, all laid on a low rosewood table.

Rondei, a natural ascetic as she was, had learned to appreciate spices during her Hallerian stay. The mountain people believed in plain, hearty food, and served Western-influenced dishes on high days only — and even then, with some modifications. There was no risk of sweating over a curry at Lord Stainerau's table. The Hallerians also ate a lot more meat than the other East Islanders, and valued hunting as a noble skill. Here, following the Paishnali example, all dishes were vegetarian. This, too, Rondei appreciated; where she'd grown up, meat was usually reserved for the working dogs.

Professor Dubele, sitting cross-legged on an embroidered cushion, accepted her compliments calmly. "Many would prefer the traditional fare, but I feel that there are certain fashions worth following. Anyway, the Paishnali trade is picking up again, and we have been flooded with spices and other condiments. The cooks need to put them somewhere."

Rondei smiled at this hyperbole: surely, no one forced Oremel College to buy exported spices. "I seem to remember that there was a lot of bread and brown sauce where I grew up. If we wanted some fruit, we had to climb a tree to get it. My mother was never one for making preserves, or growing herbs."

"Yes, we did not seem to be able to appreciate our own produce until the Westerners came along and started buying the stuff off our hands. Funny how that always seems to be the case." He took a sip of his iced tea and leaned back. "But it was not really the Paishnali I wanted to talk to you about."

"I thought as much."

"I heard you had given Lord Stainerau the slip." He stroked his moustache meditatively. "A very brave thing to do."

"And a very stupid thing, according to most people. But believe me, it was the only way. His lordship was planning to keep me in Daurbar indefinitely. Two years of isolation was enough. I found that the body craves freedom almost as badly as the mind does."

"Well said." He cleared his throat and looked down at his hands. Then, "About these pamphlets of yours."

A wave of involuntary excitement washed over her. "You have read them?"

"Not all. Only the ones that have lately been circulating in the city. I suppose you have distributors elsewhere as well?"

"Naturally. All eggs in one basket is a bad publishing policy. Before I left for Haller, I entrusted several manuscripts with different friends all over Ederai. As far as I know, most have been published since— along with some smaller works I managed to get across the border before even the smugglers gave up."

The Professor met her eyes. "This is incendiary stuff, Rondei. You know what is going on in Valja?"

"I am aware of the situation." She had to smile at his mildly scandalized expression. "And I can only take one small part of the credit. I did not start the fire: I may have only fanned the flames here and there."

"Do you think you are safe here?"

She drew a careful breath. "I do not know. Am I?"

Another elegant shrug. "You know that the Valjan Guilds have no power here. But they have people who can make your life difficult, one way or another. Lord Stainerau has a long memory, too – and a long arm."

"But would he really reach across his own borders? Risk conflict with Sendal to grab at an insignificant scribbler like me?"

"Insignificant?" Dubele frowned. "He does not seem to think so. Also, we are short of diplomats at the moment. Have you spoken to your cousin Ardelei lately?"

Rondei bit back an angry reply. Instead, she said, "I know she has left Arrika for good."

In truth, she had been deeply shaken when Ardelei had told her how she had been forced out of the Linduvan community. It seemed that the enforced isolation of the past two years would be a permanent way of life for the Linduvans – which might be good for their own spiritual well-being, but bad news for the rest of the Eastern Islands. For centuries, Arrikan mages had sat at negotiations, serving as neutral diplomats, easing quarrels between the different nations before they could escalate into warfare.

"This is a bad time for navel-gazing," opined Dubele. "If the Linduvans refuse to continue their peace-brokering, other people will step in to take their place. And not always with similarly selfless intentions."

Rondei took a large gulp of tea. "Who?"

The academician made a belittling gesture. "I have heard nothing official. But it seems that representatives of the Brotherhood of Light have been making enthusiastic noises about replacing the Linduvans."

"Ye gods. Who would want the Brotherhood to mediate for them in matters of conflict? And here on Ederai, of all places?"

"For exactly that reason, it seems. As a Gesaian community, they can set themselves up as a neutral negotiating partner, much like the Linduvans have." He touched his moustache. "Which, in matters of state, they theoretically are."

"But in matters of religion, they definitely are not," she continued. "I also have a distinct impression that the Brothers do not approve of educated women. Or printing presses. Or reading in general."

"That is one of the reasons I thought I would get in touch with you. You understand what is at stake. You also have connections to people like Ardelei Jolama."

She paused to think for a few seconds. "So you are saying that instead of writing about revolutions, I should avoid conflicts altogether?"

"Not necessarily. I was young once. I understand the drive for change, and I see that this is a very good time for new ideas and new practices, particularly in places like Valja. However, I just wish to remind you that there are also opposing forces at play: where there is change, there is resistance to change." He met her eyes. "I am not asking you to stop writing. I am just suggesting that every once in a while you look up from your work. It is not just the Guilds that are opposed to your ideas; it is the Brotherhood of Light as well. In time, there may be others."

Kaldona had a very different face once darkness had fallen; between pools of welcoming lamplight there were long stretches of impenetrable murk. Perhaps Rondei's own agitation also conjured up shadows where there were none. She was not usually one for public drinking, but now she felt that a glass of wine in a well-lit beer garden would be justified, just to take her mind off the bigger picture Professor Dubele had painted for her. She was beginning to realize that she had been somewhat naïve in her single-minded pursuits – and that her time in Haller had cut her off from important sources of information.

She found a table close to a boisterous group of students and sat down with her wineglass, content just to be in the presence of such carefree young people. It was difficult to turn off her thoughts, however, and the laughter and loud talk around her made Rondei conscious of her own solitude. The wine did very little to ease her mind: it just made her more jittery and uncomfortable.

It had perhaps been a mistake to choose Kaldona as her safe haven. There were too many clever people here — people who wished to use her for their own purposes. She surmised that Professor Dubele's invitation wouldn't be an isolated incident: everyone would want a piece of the famous Nebian lady printer and her similarly incendiary friends. This, she admitted to herself, had been her initial dream, too: to find a place where she would get maximum publicity for minimum effort.

The quality of the publicity she was now offered, however, wasn't at all what she had expected. It was one thing to be consulted by respected academicians, quite another to be implicated in their schemes. Whatever Dubele had in mind would involve political intrigue, and having slipped from under the thumb of one willful lord, Rondei wasn't looking for anything similar in Sendal. Let cousin Ardelei flit from court to court, trailing a string of admirers and detractors. Mistress Galsi had only one goal in mind: to ease the plight of the working poor, through the most direct means possible.

This, of course, led her to the underlying question: if revolution was what she wanted, why had she chosen to be happily cloistered within the respectful walls of Kaldona? While she was sitting here in her cool summer linens, sipping expensive Gesaian wine, the Siblings might be putting their lives on the line to depose the Guilds. Was Rondei Galsi a hypocrite?

She contemplated the darkness of the wine in the crystal glass. Early on, she had decided that her life would be a cerebral one. Having grown up on a farm, she knew the demands of physical labor. She had pulled herself up by her bootstraps, working night and day for printers and booksellers, and at the same time scraping out the best education a girl like her could hope to get.

It had always been her mind that set her apart from other people. In any given situation, she was most likely the cleverest person in the room. That didn't make her any better than the rest, but it meant that she didn't need to break her back to earn her daily bread. She could think for other people – and she did. She formulated ideas, found the right words to express them, and manipulated bits of metal and wood to print them onto blemishless paper. In a similar way, she didn't need to pick up a weapon to fight for what she believed in: she motivated other people to do that for her.

Would she be of better use in Valja? Would people need to see her in order to follow her ideas? She didn't think so. The Cause already had its convincing, youthful faces and fearless leaders in the Skovos. They wouldn't need any competition from a middle-aged woman who didn't even know how to shoot. What they needed more was support from all over Ederai – and that was what Rondei was mustering through her pamphlets.

Just as she was finding her peace of mind once more, someone plonked down their tankard on the table.

"Mistress Galsi?" the person asked, and sat down opposite her.

"What do you want?" Rondei asked, somewhat startled.

"I have a message for you." The messenger was a small, leather-faced woman, who met Rondei's eyes fearlessly.

She did need a lot of coaxing, however. "Go on," she said.

The woman reached into her pocket and took out two small squares of paper. She swiftly transferred them into Rondei's hand, and stepping back into the shadows, was gone.

Chapter 8

Kirula - Ardelei

A **keen** west wind swept across the harbor, whipping up waves and bobbing boats like so many corks. The sun had barely risen, and because of the inclement weather, most sailors and fisherfolk had decided to sleep in. Ardelei walked to the end of the longest pier, gazing south across the restless Strait. The way to Idriola was short. She'd been planning to use that route, as she'd done many times before. Now, it seemed that the way south was a coward's way.

Since leaving Rondei in Dugda, and saying farewell to Bel and Heather near Kaknesa, she'd sworn to concentrate on her own concerns. Mainly, avoiding Hallerians, and resisting the urge to meddle with the running of the Linduvan community. Traveling had always been her way of re-focusing herself and her worn-out magic. A change of scenery usually jolted her out of any rut she might have fallen into, and the new faces and musics around her forced her to turn outwards.

In Kaknesa, she'd scoured the harbor and taverns for any news of ships on their way to Gesaia. She'd made many promises to visit her friend Ondala din Rettimiso once the travel restrictions were lifted, and had expected to find a suitable vessel fairly soon. It turned out, however, that most captains were still reluctant to take casual travelers onboard. Ardelei, travelling without her Arrikan immunity for the first time in a decade, found that without an official invitation from the court of Idriola, no one was willing to wave her through customs.

Thus, settling for the next best option, she'd boarded a merchant boat en route to Kirula. The northern island was one of the least exciting places Ardelei knew, yet it boasted one clear advantage. The harbor of the capital city of Ru had always had lively connections to Gesaia. From there it would be easier to find passage to Idriola, invitation or no invitation.

Once on Kirula, Ardelei had found that the unchanging dullness of Ru actually soothed her nerves. Relying on her instincts, she decided not to hurry her departure. At first, she didn't even seek out her local friends, preferring to stay in her anonymous boarding house, taking her meals in the small dining room, speaking to no one. Most mornings, she woke up with the sun and took a walk in the harbor. At that early hour, the only creatures awake were the gulls and the ever-present cats. Slowly, as the winds picked up, the merchants started their day, and the fisherfolk prepared their nets and boats.

This morning, even the long-haired harbor cats preferred to stay out of the wind. Ardelei, having filled her lungs with the slightly fishy air of the Strait, also turned back towards the town. She found an open teahouse and took full advantage of its selection of sugary cakes and piping-hot biscuits. Having lived frugally for the past weeks, the sweetness rushed directly into her veins. The songs of the people around her suddenly sounded a lot more welcoming, too. She concluded that it was time to end her self-imposed solitude.

The high street of Ru ran up the hill, leading directly away from the harbor. It was the only paved road in the entire town. Everyone wishing to be anyone built their houses along this, by now unnecessarily long, thoroughfare. It took Ardelei quite a while to arrive at the house she was looking for. On the way, she noted that most of the townhouses were inhabited, and most shops boasted clean, unbroken windows. Kirula had weathered the plague much better than the other Eastern Islands, maybe because even the disease hadn't been bothered to travel such a long way to such an unexciting destination.

Before knocking on the familiar door, Ardelei decided to amend her attitude. Living on Luneken, she'd learned to consider Kirula her home island's rural cousin – smaller, poorer and less interesting in every way. Now, as a person with no fixed abode, she couldn't afford such arrogance. After all, Ru had already given her what other, more exciting places hadn't been able to provide. Over her stay on Kirula, she'd started to accept her present situation and had begun to look for alternate ways of making use of her education and experience.

A young boy answered the door. Ardelei handed him her shimmering introduction and was immediately shown into the front room. Here, little had changed since her last visit. The narrow space was overhung with drooping bookcases, leaving barely enough room for two Paishnali-style divans and a spindly table. She was prepared to wait for some time and started idly looking through the latest additions to her friend's collection: easily spotted because the topmost layer was also the most recent.

The boy came back carrying a pot of tea and a bowl full of dried fruit. "Mistress Meldo will be with you in a moment," he said, carefully enunciating the Sendali words. "She asked to make yourself comfortable in the meanwhile."

Ardelei thanked him with a smile. Eskim had always chosen bright young people as her servants, giving them a first-class education along with an occupation. Several had gone on to study at the Gesaian and Ederaian academies. One had even made his way to Arrika.

Just as the boy exited, his mistress wheeled her way into the front room, followed by a pair of immaculately white lapdogs. "What do my eyes see!" she stopped in front of Ardelei who stooped ever so slightly to kiss her cheek. "You're looking well, considering."

"So are you, considering," she countered. The dogs whirred excitedly around her legs, making small yipping noises.

This had been their greeting for almost as long as they'd known each other. For all those years, Ardelei had been busy traveling around the Eastern Isles, making use of her considerable energy and various talents. Eskim, on the other hand, had slowly lost the use of her legs. The illness that gnawed at her limbs had never touched her brain, however. She'd been the brightest scholar Ardelei had ever met, and had continued her studies even after leaving the Linduvan community, mainly through correspondence with academicians all over Ederai and beyond.

Eskim maneuvered her wheelchair next to the small table and went about the ceremony of pouring tea. The teapot was of pink Paishnali porcelain, as were the cups. A silver spoon nestled daintily on the saucer.

"Pretty, aren't they?" asked Eskim. "My brother insists on sending me all this stuff."

"And how is your brother?" Ardelei knew that, despite her reluctance to admit it, her friend had always enjoyed having beautiful things— and beautiful people — around her. "Prosperous, I take it? Married?"

"Yes, and yes. He chose to stay in Gatra when the plague first started making its rounds. Cutting his losses, he called it. Later on, we found out that there was another, more pressing reason. He'd got some local merchant's daughter pregnant, and at the same time was busy joining her family business there. Now they've got another baby on the way, and it seems that he will stay in Paishnal for the rest of his life."

Ardelei, remembering the nature of the relationship between Eskim and her brother, said, "Which leaves you free to do whatever you like."

Eskim burst into laughter. "Exactly! And good riddance to him," she continued, hiccupping slightly. The two dogs, wanting to share her merriment, hopped onto her lap one after the other. "Let him continue sending me teapots, meanwhile I can get on with my work. I haven't had a sulphur bath in years, nor drunk any disgusting waters, either." She looked at her legs. "I always knew that once I sat down in this chair I'd never get up again. And I've made my peace with that."

"You have?"

She rolled her eyes. "Most days it feels that way. It was different when I was younger. I longed to ride a horse, or to swim in the Strait, or to dance with all the pretty young men I could reach. Now, I live inside my head. That has always been my strongest body part anyway, bar one." She cackled at Ardelei's expression.

They drank some tea and nibbled on the dried fruit. Ardelei was patient: Eskim was not. "So, they kicked you out," she said casually. "I suppose you've already got your revenge planned out?"

Ardelei shrugged. "I suppose I do." She took another sip of tea. "I intend to live happily on my own, relying on the things I learned in Arrika and the friends I made when I worked for the Linduvans. I'll build my life anew and never look back."

Eskim whistled. "You do come up with the most astonishing nonsense, Mistress Jolama." On cue, the dogs tilted their heads at the visitor.

She put her teacup down carefully. "What else am I supposed to do? Raise an army and lay siege on Arrika? Spread nasty rumors about the new leader and her supporters? Pine for the old days for the rest of my life?" She looked her friend in the eye. "You never did any of these things."

A raised eyebrow. "I might have done some of them."

"How big was the army?" Ardelei grinned.

"Not big enough." Eskim tipped her cotton headscarf away from her face. "But the rumors did circulate for years. And none of you ever found out where they came from."

"We had an idea. But this is different. You had to leave a place you loved. I doubt I'd even recognize Arrika if I went back now. It was already changing beyond recognition when I was there." She paused. "Physically as well. People started building stone houses with fences around them. They had their own private gardens. Children weren't allowed to run in and out of other people's homes anymore. Now they have to knock, and wipe their feet, and ask nicely."

"So no bitterness there whatsoever."

"Of course I'm bitter. I wanted to change the place I loved for the better. But even knowing what I know now, I wouldn't do things differently. If the Linduvan community doesn't respect the rules it was built on, it's not for me alone to push it back to its roots. It's the people who make Arrika."

"That new bitch is definitely shaking things up."

Alerted by the acidic tone in Eskim's voice, Ardelei quickly asked, "What do you mean? What has she done?"

"I'm not sure if I'm the right person to tell you..."

"You're dying to tell me, Eskim. Say it!"

Her friend shooed the dogs off her lap, and took up her writing desk. Inside, there was a tumble of letters. It took her some time to find the one she was looking for.

"This is from an acquaintance of mine. For reasons you can imagine, I'll let them remain anonymous. Suffice it to say that the Linduvan community has set up some new rules and restrictions. There's a list of names at both bridges of the people who have been permanently banned from entering the island." She looked up. "Yours is among them."

"This doesn't surprise me." Yet it did, deep down. She hadn't expected such vindictiveness from Darbei Kusvin. She'd already given up everything she had. Now, the woman who led the Linduvans had barred her way to the entire island. This meant that Darbei had not only the Arrikan community, but the non-mages of Luneken behind her.

Eskim had arrived at the same conclusion. "She's determined to take over the whole island, if you ask me."

"What is she going to do with it?"

"Who knows? But I know an ambitious bitch when I see one. Ederai had better watch out."

Walking back down the hill, Ardelei realized that her hands were shaking. She'd known that a visit to Eskim was going to raise some difficult topics: she'd thought she'd be ready to confront them. Yet, knowing that the place she'd called home for nearly ten years was now closed to her for good made her suddenly feel unanchored. Before, she'd started getting used to the idea that she'd have to spend some months, years even, with no permanent home. Traveling with Bel and Heather she'd thought she could learn to enjoy such an unfettered life.

But even Bel had his family in Valja to call on if things got truly difficult. He'd chosen his homelessness himself. Ardelei had been forced out of Arrika by people she'd thought she could trust. A lot of her life had been spent on the road, staying with friends and acquaintances way past her welcome. This had been possible because everyone, including herself, had known that she had a home, and a well-established community to return to. Arrikan mages may not be particularly high in status, but they had their recognized and respected place in the world, and a clear purpose.

Unlike her friend Eskim, she had no meddling family to fall back on, either. Once she'd left her parents' farm in Nebe, she had never looked back, and had never tried to get in touch with her remaining kin. Her parents had done their best to keep their children alive, and had even allowed them to be rudimentarily educated by an itinerant tutor. When they died, one of her numerous uncles had used his connections to find her a place in Arrika. This was a relief all round, as her magical talent had been prominent from early on, and hadn't exactly endeared her to the other villagers.

Thus, joining the Linduvans hadn't been her own choice.

Then again, she knew she was one of the few lucky ones. The children of carpenters learned to work with wood, while the children of cobblers studied shoemaking. The children of farmers inevitably learned to work the land they were tied to. Being able to escape a life of physical toil was a luxury in itself. Learning to work her magic together with other like-minded people, and later learning the intricate art of diplomacy, had been unthinkable for a girl like her. And, somehow, she had made that life hers.

Now, she'd have to build her life anew. She had many skills to fall back on. Sooner or later, she'd have to attach herself to some household or government. Itinerant mages weren't generally tolerated, not even on Gesaia. Ardelei had no intention of selling her talents to the highest bidder, but she knew she'd have to start looking for some employment soon. The money she'd saved and put away into several banks wouldn't last forever, and a life of aimless wandering didn't suit her. She'd gotten used to having a clear direction, and a place to call home.

Returning to her lodgings, she found a letter waiting for her. Ardelei recognized the sender immediately. She didn't know many people who could afford such thick, creamy paper and soot-black ink, or could boast such an elegant hand. It took all her willpower to wait until the door of her room had closed after her to tear open the seal.

My Dearest, Most Highly Learned Friend, it started. The Duchess had always had a penchant for hyperbole.

Having received your Letter dated 25th of the 4th, I was very glad to learn that your Endeavour reached its desired Conclusion. Had I known your full Plan beforehand, I would have been even more apprehensive. My Dealings with the Realm of Haller have been cursory to say the Least – yet, I am well acquainted with the forceful Nature of Reutel Stainerau.

We have received rather worrying Communications from the

Sendali Capital of late. I trust you do not mean to reside there in the near Future? Or encourage any of your Nearest and Dearest to do so? I do feel for the people of Valja, but I cannot say I approve of their chosen Methods.

Time is short, as always, so I shall leave you with this: if you are going to extend your Sojourn in Ru, I do recommend looking up a Gesaian Gentleman by the name of Ebarilla Olvite. You may find that you have some Friends in Common.

Yours, in Eternal Friendship,

Ondala din Rettimiso

Ardelei folded the letter in two, pursing her lips. The Duchess of Idriola, who almost single-handedly ruled the entire island of Gesaia, could turn out elegant phrases which, to a casual observer, conveyed only vacuous good intentions. However, the relationship between Ardelei and Ondala din Rettimiso had never been a casual one, and over the years the two women had come up with a style of correspondence that didn't involve complex codes or secret messengers. Usually, the less was said, the weightier the message.

This time, the main gist Ardelei got was the importance of looking up Sir Olvite. From him, she'd get a fuller picture of the goings-on at the court of Idriola , and possibly those in Valja as well. Since her short visit, she hadn't deemed it necessary to return to the Sendali capital, nor did she think her cousin was foolhardy enough to have settled there. Rondei appreciated comfortable lodgings and a peaceful working environment – and both were in short supply in a city poised for a rebellion.

Ebarilla Olvite looked every bit the Gesaian gentleman. His clothes were expensive but not flashy, and he carried himself with admirable ease. Outdoors, he wore a lined cloak, and covered his head with a small silk hat. When he took off the outer layer to step indoors, he could have passed for a member of the Brotherhood of Light. Yet, despite the lack of ostentation, there was nothing monastic about his bearing or manners. He had an Ederaian-style introduction, which was a study in expensive understatement. The white oblong of silk he handed to Ardelei had his family insignia embroidered in fine thread, with only a hint of gold and silver worked in to catch the light.

Ardelei was glad she was wearing gloves and was eager to hand back the introduction as soon as was politely possible. Her own introduction engrossed Sir Olvite for much longer. He clearly had no magic, but could appreciate the object for the work of art it was.

"The Duchess sends her regards," he said finally in a deep voice that resonated pleasantly against Ardelei's song-sense. "Do not ask me how she knew you would be on Kirula, Mistress Jolama."

"Lady Ondala and I go way back. Some time ago, I tutored her in magic, and discovered that she had some talent in foresight. As you probably know, these things are never precise. But let us say that she has a keener instinct than most."

"I agree."

He led her along a carpeted corridor which led to a small library. The Gesaians, keen travelers as they were, had set up boarding houses for their countrypeople all over the Eastern Islands. In these establishments one could imagine oneself back at home, with none of the strangenesses that otherwise accompanied international travel. This one, called the Pearl of Alizanda, was a tall building which immediately stood out from its neighbors due to its austere elegance and sparkling sheet-glass windows.

To Ardelei, crossing the threshold had felt eerily like stepping into a townhouse in Idriola. There had been Gesaian servants ready to welcome her, and to hand her a glass of wine while she waited for Sir Olvite to return from his daily constitutional. She'd been fairly certain she'd find him at the Alizanda. All Gesaians she knew preferred the luxuries of their own island to the more prosaic realities of the places they landed in. Naturally, the less wealthy had to make do with lodgings closer to the harbor. Sir Ebarilla Olvite, it was immediately clear, could have bought the entire building had he been so inclined.

His air of effortless courtesy put Ardelei immediately at her ease. Generally, Gesaians liked to display their superiority in every way. Sir Olvite had no need for such snobbery. He invited her to take a look at the collection of manuscripts in the library. This would give them a perfect excuse for meeting, and also tickled Ardelei's scholarly curiosity. She'd been to the Alizanda a few times, but so far hadn't been able to penetrate farther than the glittering vestibule.

"These are all Paishnali texts from the second century, translated by our finest scholars." He indicated a shelf full of scrolls. "Mathematics, astronomy, poetry. You name it."

"Music?" she asked hopefully.

"Ah," he smiled. "Of course. These are treatises on the ancient music systems of the Western Isles. Fascinating. The instruments alone: there is so much to learn."

"Do you play?" she asked, carefully unrolling a crackling piece of papyrus. The courtly Gesaian script was difficult to read, but the illustrations spoke for themselves.

"I am an enthusiastic amateur. My brother builds instruments, and my children have learned to play most of them. I have less spare time than my brother."

She didn't ask. She didn't need to. She recognized a spy— or, to put it more diplomatically, a member of the Duchess's inner circle — when she met one. Ondala din Rettimiso had a veritable network of such people spread all over the Eastern Isles. And if things were going as planned, in the most important Paishnali cities as well. The country that depended on trade with all its neighbors also needed to keep up to date with the goings-on in all the important ports and ruling houses. The Rettimiso family was a newcomer to the high aristocracy of Idriola: for that reason, they needed to be particularly careful about the alliances they made.

As the library stayed resolutely unoccupied, she dared to lead the discussion to more personal matters. "The Duchess intimated that we might have some friends in common."

Sir Olvite grinned. "Oh, I am sure we do. As I understand it, you have stayed extended periods in Idriola. However," he touched his nose, "I think I understand who the Duchess means." He glanced out of the window as if there might be someone sitting on the ledge outside. "Because I have friends in Sendal as well. Some *artistic* friends, let us call them."

It didn't take long for Ardelei to understand who he meant. "I am not sure I can call them a friend by any means. A friend of a friend, perhaps."

"That is often good enough. They and I," he made a complicated gesture, "are related. You know how our family trees entwine: we are all cousins to some degree on Gesaia." He sobered. "The person I am talking about is not just important because of the blood we share. They have accrued a political importance quite beyond their control, to put it mildly."

Ardelei nodded. She'd heard about Meropat Rugolata from both Rondei and Beldor. Bel knew them better, and had seen them in Valja some weeks ago. She'd understood that the poet had got themself entangled in the Cause, and had quickly risen through the ranks and become a member of the Siblings' inner circle. She hadn't been aware of their connections to Gesaian aristocracy, at least to the extent that the Duchess's spymaster would be personally interested in their whereabouts.

Having worked with his ilk before, Ardelei was careful not to divulge anything. It was basic tactics to introduce a common "friend," and get the other person to tell everything they knew – often not realizing that the first person wasn't contributing anything new to the conversation.

"What do you want me to do, exactly?"

Another warm smile. "I would not presume, Mistress Jolama.

But, if you find yourself going that way in the near future, both the Duchess and I would appreciate it if you found out on which charges exactly they are held by the Guilds."

"They have been arrested? When?"

"A couple of days ago. There was an unfortunate run-in with some foreign elements, which gave the city guard an opportunity to seize them. Clearly, their association with the Siblings had not gone unnoticed."

Ardelei looked out of the window. The day had turned gray again. "You do realize, Sir Olvite, that I'm no longer in a position to make official inquiries."

"I am perfectly aware of that. And that is one of the reasons why you are just the right person for the task. Having no official affiliations, you will only appear to be interested in Meropat's well-being as a friend."

Her song-sense picked up only the slightest change in the general harmony of the room; yet, it felt as if a window had suddenly been slammed shut, robbing her of air. "Are you — is the Duchess suggesting that I work for her from now on?" She couldn't meet the man's steady gaze.

"That you will need to establish with the Duchess herself. This is only a ... small favor we ask. All expenses paid, naturally."

A velvet purse landed on the nearby table with a respectable clink. Despite having great faith in banks and the paper money they produced and circulated, most Gesaians still preferred to pay with solid gold, or with blocks of salt, in the case of heftier transactions. Ardelei stared at the handful of coins that was literally within her reach. Was this what her life was to be like from now on? Small commissions, furtive journeys from one island to another, loyalties rapidly earned and as rapidly forgotten.

Ebarilla Olvite was a patient man. Even his music didn't betray any sense of urgency. He had all the time in the world to persuade her. Or perhaps he already knew what she only gradually realized — that Ondala din Rettimiso wasn't just offering her a one-off job. The Duchess of Idriola was reminding her of the ties of loyalty and friendship that stretched years into the past, and could extend similarly into the future. That Ondala had realized Ardelei's difficult situation, and was looking for a way to support her without wounding her pride.

Ardelei read some of this in Sir Olvite's open gaze. "Very well," she said, still not looking at the velvet purse. "I might as well make Valja my next destination. After all, I have other friends whose interests are tied to that city as well."

"The Duchess told me you were a person with a keen intellect," he said. "I will give you all the information you need."

"Speaking of," she said, having seen the opening, "can you tell me what is going on in Idriola? The Duchess isn't usually reticent. In her last letter, she didn't say a word about the situation at her court. I'm worried."

"You should be. You, of all people, realize how tenuous her position is. All this time she has had to play the different factions against each other to remain where she is. Most of her status has come from her husband who, we have to admit, is not getting any younger."

"There is no heir, still," she finished his thought. "How is that a problem, all of a sudden?"

"Perhaps during the plague people became more keenly aware of their limited lifespans. Perhaps, also, some of those nobles who were carried off by the disease were replaced by younger, shrewder representatives of their houses. Not everyone has reconciled themselves to an upstart Duchess, someone who is an unbeliever to boot."

Ardelei felt cold all of a sudden. She'd been hearing about the renewed zeal of the Brotherhood of Light from all over Ederai. In its native Gesaia the Brotherhood would naturally have an even stronger foothold, and a considerable say in the daily lives of its nobility as well. "Are the Brothers directly meddling with her government?"

"No. Brother l'Oremel may not have many traits to recommend him, but his traditional views have proved a blessing in this sense. He has forbidden any of the members of the Brotherhood from even taking an interest in politics. The High Priest of Ipira is a devout man and leads through example. Unfortunately, not all of the Brothers are willing to follow."

"I see. Well, as I understand it, the Duchess has always been able to negotiate with Brother l'Oremel on equal terms. Are you suggesting that he might risk losing his position within the Brotherhood if he continues to accommodate her?"

"I hope not: he is a liked man both within his order and without. It is indeed the more radical fringes that the Duchess is worried about. The younger Brothers are frustrated that right now, people are returning to their old lives, and also giving up on the belief in their God. These radicals are looking for like-minded people among the aristocracy in order to solidify the standing of the Brotherhood on all levels of power in Gesaia."

Over the years, Ardelei had had her share of dealings with the Brotherhood of Light. Most of these had been respectful, or at least efficiently neutral: on Ederai in particular, every state had its own traditional version of religion, some more than one, and these had learned to co-exist, just as the respective states had. The Linduvan mages and Brothers of Ipira had often sat down at negotiating tables together, mediating for different groups. Perhaps because they lived so far apart, they had been able to discuss their differing world views rather like academics would discuss their theories: passionately but with mutual respect.

When the plague first hit Ederai, many people had turned to the religious communities for help and comfort. Some had been quickly disillusioned. No matter how hard they prayed, sacrificed, or sang, their loved ones kept falling ill and dying. Some of the more radical members of the Brotherhood of Light had begun parading through the streets of bigger cities, calling for everyone to repent their wrongdoings and turn to the One True God. The pantheistic Nebians had laughed at them. The practical citizens of Sendal had asked why most of the Brothers had retreated behind their monastery walls, leaving everyone else to die. The Hallerians, as was their habit, simply ignored them.

"Well," Ardelei said, "I've known the Duchess for many years. Not once have I seen her back down from a conflict. Very rarely have I seen her lose. It seems that the harder she is pushed, the harder she pushes back. I admire her for it. I wish I could help her in this particular fight, but in the present circumstances it seems that I'm better off in Sendal."

"That is my opinion as well, Mistress Jolama," said the old spy.

Chapter 9

Sendal - Meropat

Someone was whistling outside. The slightly off-key noise didn't sound like a signal or a greeting –it was just a way of passing the time while idling around the Square. It didn't take Meropat long to recognize the tune. "The Last Harvest" had a very distinctive, flowing melody. A week ago, the Siblings had asked them to write new lyrics to that tune. Something bittersweet yet simple to fit the tone of the original song. Everyone in Sendal knew versions of the melody, and thus it would be easy to turn it into one of the Cause's anthems.

Meropat hadn't had time to even finish the first draft. Partly, it had been the fault of their own waning enthusiasm, and partly just the fact that they'd had quite a lot on their plate. Now, as they had nothing else to do, they hummed along to the rousing refrain and tried to find a good rhyme for "workers." That had proved their stumbling block many times before, and wasn't proving fruitful now. "Laborers" wasn't any better.

A glossy, fat fly barged in through the grilled window. It spent a while banging indignantly into walls — and into Meropat's person — before it found an escape through the door. A guard had stepped in, carrying a mug of ale and a slice of bread the size of Meropat's palm.

"Any chance of pen and paper?" they asked casually. The guards were a sullen lot who didn't take kindly to requests for more ale, more varied food, or visiting rights. "I feel a ballad coming on."

The young woman glanced at them uncertainly. "You have a right to one letter, prisoner. No more." She turned to go.

"But it's not a letter I'm writing. It's a work of art."

"You'll need to ask the judge at the hearing tomorrow. This is none of my business." The door clanged shut behind her.

Meropat didn't know what to think of the hearing. On the one hand, anything that would alleviate the boredom of the cell would be an improvement. All the so-called political prisoners were kept apart from the other inhabitants of the Guardhouse. Their cells had thick walls and small, sparsely spaced windows so that they wouldn't be able to communicate with each other. A naturally sociable person, Meropat was beginning to feel the strain of solitude after two days and nights of isolation.

On the other hand, the actual purpose of the hearing was a complete mystery to them. They hadn't been told the nature of the charges against them – or even if there were any specific charges at this point. The identity of the people who'd attacked them in the alleyway might have been revealed to the authorities in the meanwhile, leading to some awkwardness with their Hallerian counterparts. Meropat could only hope that the young people who'd accompanied them had got away. If not, their testimony would probably incriminate Meropat even further.

What had become abundantly clear was that the Skovos had decided to throw Meropat over. Since their arrest, there hadn't been the tiniest of hints that the Siblings knew of their plight and were working to set them free. If a bluebottle could make its way into their cell through the opened shutter, surely a message could be dropped through the bars, or a guard could be corrupted to carry a small piece of paper. Someone could tap a short code against the metal shutter in the night, or sing a song in passing.

The bread was gone in three bites. The ale lasted slightly

longer because it was musty and flat. Still, it was thirst that demoralized a person much faster than the lack of food, and Meropat wasn't built for fasting. As they drained the last drops of the beer, they heard the persistent notes of "The Last Harvest" echoing against the walls of the surrounding houses. They put down the mug carefully, pursing their lips. Surely, it wasn't a coincidence that the person had parked themself just within hearing range to whistle that particular song, over and over again.

Hope dawned — that most treacherous of emotions.

The next morning, Meropat had barely time to gulp down their breakfast ale when they heard the sound of purposefully marching feet. A group of guards made its way through the maze of corridors, and came to a halt at their cell door. With no word of greeting or explanation, Meropat was hauled by the elbows up to the ground floor, out the door, across the Main Square — the unimaginative name always gave Meropat a twinge of despair — and in through one of the numerous doors that dotted the complex of buildings that was the Guildhall.

The heads of the numerous guilds rarely met at the Hall nowadays. Some time ago, the interconnected buildings had been given over to the everyday administration of the city, and housed an army of clerks, as well as judges, tax collectors and other people of varying importance. Only the upper floor of the oldest part of the Hall was reserved for the ceremonial use of the Guilds. Meropat found themself being dragged up just one flight of stairs and into a disappointingly small space.

They'd been expecting a spectacle. In fact, for most of the previous night, they'd been preparing a heartrending speech for the people of Valja to hear and remember. They'd pictured the galleries filled to the brim with curious onlookers, as well as the inevitable representatives of the press, pens and sketching-blocks at the ready. They'd even imagined the faces of the Skovos, somewhere in the crowd, looking directly at Meropat, scintillating with hope.

They should have known better. The authorities of Valja had got used to dealing with political prisoners of various sorts: they knew that nothing stirred the hearts of the populace more than the sight of a martyr. It was much better to get on with the questioning and sentencing in private: corporal punishments and executions, should any be required, could then be carried out in public for the edification of the common folk.

The timbred room contained five people in serious silk robes sitting behind a low table, and now and then glancing at Meropat and the guards. The space was already stuffy: it had no windows, and the only ventilation came through narrow slits close to the floor. Meropat counted three sweating pewter jugs on the table, but only five cups. One of the lawyers saw them looking, and grinned.

"Shall we begin?" the man asked, ostentatiously pouring himself a cup of switchel and draining it in long gulps.

The person sitting in the middle, a nondescript-looking woman of no particular age, looked up. So far, she'd been in deep conversation with a younger woman to her left. "We might as well. Thank you, Belvei. I will take it from here."

The man shot an irritated glance in her direction, but settled quietly to pour himself another drink and enjoy it. The guards behind Meropat stood to attention as the members of the court identified themselves: a secretary, three lawyers, and a judge.

"Judge Laikova," said the woman, enunciating each syllable carefully, as if she wasn't already known to everyone in the room, including Meropat.

The secretary scribbled away in shorthand.

Despite being a relative newcomer to Valja, Meropat knew enough of Judge Laikova's reputation to become immediately nervous. She'd been the youngest ever lawyer to graduate from the University of Erun and had gone on to finish her studies in Mandiora, again climbing through the academic ranks in record time. Despite hailing from an obscure village in eastern Sendal, she had started her career on Gesaia, and could easily have continued her stellar ascent there, working to further the causes of wealthy bankers and aristocrats.

To the people of Ederai, however, family is everything. Not just the immediate parents and cousins, but the entire bloodline connecting hundreds of people to their common ancestors and the land that had given them life. It didn't do to shake oneself free of one's roots like dog shakes off fleas. Without a home village, a last name, and a long list of relatives, one might as well be dead. Pemonai Laikova, too, had eventually decided to return to her native land, and had devoted herself to promoting the well-being of her people.

Or at least some of her people. The Skovos had told Meropat that Judge Laikova was, despite her humble origins, a stout ally of the Members of the Assembly, and a stern believer in the status quo. She'd been the one to sign the order to close the gates of Valja when the plague first came knocking. She'd been among the last to admit that the outbreak was over, and to let people roam the streets once more. She knew the law of her native land by heart, and used it to uphold the rights of those in power.

The Skovos had told Meropat other grim stories of Judge Laikova's work, and thus it wasn't a surprise that she'd been chosen to handle their case. They knew to expect no sympathy from her, or the other people in the room.

"You are Meropat Orteta Gobadelo din Rugolata of Mandiora?" the secretary asked.

"Yes," they said, flinching slightly, as they always did at the sound of their full name. The Ederaian custom of burdening a person with only two names had always seemed a much more merciful practice to them.

As the preliminaries were over, the Judge raised her head. "Do you know why you are here, Mistrum Rugolata?"

"Not exactly," Meropat answered. Beforehand, they'd decided to try to be as curt and courteous as possible, but as always in situations where other people's undivided attention was upon them, it was difficult to keep to this decision. "I mean, I assume it has something to do with the altercation three nights ago."

The switchel-drinking lawyer squinted at them. "An 'altercation' you call it?"

"It very much felt like one."

The young woman on Judge Laikova's left side frowned slightly. "Just answer the questions, Mistrum Rugolata."

"What were you doing in that part of town, so late at night?" Laikova continued as if nothing had happened. "Earlier you have stated that you live in the back room of a print shop on Scribe Street."

"I was going home, my lady. I had been spending the evening with some friends on the riverside. We ate, drank, and made merry until we all realized it was time to go home. So we did. We kept each other company to be safer."

"And these friends of yours. What are they called?"

Meropat made a wide gesture. "In truth, I'd only met them that night. There was such a large group of these delightful young people that I didn't have the opportunity to exchange introductions with everyone."

The judge went on, "What did you talk about, with these *friends* of yours, Mistrum Rugolata?"

"Oh, the usual. Nothing in particular, that is. It was a beautiful summer's evening. They are beautiful young people, as I said. You don't talk about serious matters with people like that, particularly after a long day's toil."

Some glances were exchanged by the lawyers. The oldest of the group, a tall, spare man with a curly beard, spoke for the first time. "And is it your habit to otherwise talk about serious matters with people you meet on the town?"

Sensing the leading nature of the questions, Meropat raised their chin. "I'm one of the least serious people around, sir. When

I'm not working, I try to surround myself with like-minded people and talk nonsense with them."

"Like the Skovos?" said the switchel-drinker.

"I've met them, too," they admitted. "A bit too serious for my liking, though."

"But that hasn't stopped you from working for the Cause, has it?" the lawyer pursued. "Writing them songs and tracts and whatnot."

"I'm a poet. Generally, I write for whoever pays me."

"So you admit to working for the Skovos."

"I don't," Meropat said stoutly. "I admit to taking part in some of their meetings, and exchanging ideas with them, but I deny having written tracts or pamphlets, or indeed, whatnot for the Skovos. I'm not in their employ."

Judge Laikova, who had been leaning back and observing Meropat through her glistening spectacles, spoke again. "Are you acquainted with Rondei Galsi?"

As always, the name sent a small shiver down their spine. "I've met her once. That was years ago. We haven't kept in touch."

"I see." A pause — just long enough to make Meropat admire her performance. "How is it possible, then, that her works have been circulating all over Ederai these past years, even though she has been in the employ of Lord Reutel Stainerau in Daurbar?"

"I couldn't say. If I had to guess, I'd say that she's been making use of her own printing press before she left for Haller, and perhaps even during her stay there."

"You work for a printer, don't you?" asked the bearded lawyer.

"I do." Meropat remained looking at him, as if they couldn't work out the connection between the circulating pamphlets and Master Keltuva's shop.

"Have you received manuscripts from Mistress Galsi?" he continued. "Or any other materials which you then have circulated in Valja?"

"No, sir. I'm a printer's apprentice: I'm not allowed to use the press unsupervised. And anyway, as I said, I haven't kept in touch with Mistress Galsi. Nor do I have common acquaintances with her, as far as I'm aware."

"You are friendly with Beldor Amsta?" asked the young woman.

"I wouldn't use that word. I know him, but I don't keep in touch with him, either. And he doesn't live in Valja as far as I know."

"You are correct," interjected the younger man who'd finished his drink. "Master Amsta doesn't seem to live anywhere in particular. He's also renounced his ties to one of the oldest families in Valja. People like that are dangerous, Mistrum Rugolata. You, as a newcomer to our city, should be aware of this." The pale lawyer received a reprimanding glance from the judge, and picked up his cup again – at least partly to cover his confusion.

Judge Laikova regarded Meropat in turn. It wasn't so much her job to ask questions — that was what the other lawyers were for. She was there to observe, to follow the letter of the law, and to give her final judgment on the character of the accused. Meropat had rarely felt so exposed. The feeling of acute discomfort was partly related to their appearance. They were still wearing the clothes they'd been arrested in, and had had no chance of cleaning themself up at any point. For the most part, however, it was because they felt Judge Laikova's gaze boring into their very spirit, weighing the truthfulness of every word they uttered, listening for any false cadences in their speech.

"You are a Gesaian, Mistrum Rugolata. What does your family think of your decision to move to Ederai?" she asked in a voice that was almost kind.

Meropat drew a careful breath. "I couldn't say, my lady."

"You do not keep in touch with them? Or they do not keep in touch with you?"

They had to smile at her astuteness. Or, perhaps, the quality of her research. Judge Laikova had, after all, a sizable network of learned colleagues all over Gesaia. "The feeling *is* mutual, I think it's safe to say. My family has never approved of my choice of career. I have never approved of their closed-mindedness." They'd never been ashamed of their decision to follow their muse; however, in the present company, admitting to severing their family ties for such a frivolous reason cost them some dignity.

"And do you find that the decision was worth it?"

They blinked. "My lady, I don't see how this is relevant."

"This is my court," Judge Laikova replied, in the same resonant voice. "I decide what is relevant." She made a show of sifting through the documents in front of her. "It has come to my attention that your family is not in any way insignificant, and that losing their protection might not have been a very intelligent thing to do in the long run. The Duchess has been quite selective in picking out her favorites, and it seems that the Rugolatas are among that privileged few."

"I wouldn't know anything about that. I've never met the Duchess, and thus have not formed an opinion on her."

"Surely, you have an opinion on the ruler of your home island?"

"I try not to get mixed up in political matters, my lady."

"Indeed."

"Do you recognize this?" she held out a tattered broadsheet.

Meropat leaned forward to read the title. "Never seen it in my life. My master would give me a hiding if he saw me printing something as shoddy as that."

"It is not the print work I am talking about, and you know it." She dipped her head to read a few lines from the sheet. "'Rise up together / sister and brother / Help one another / to break all the chains.' Sound familiar?"

They shrugged. "I might have heard people singing it around town. Not a particularly successful rhyme, if you ask me. Definitely not original. The scansion is also questionable to say the least."

"You wrote this, Mistrum Rugolata. This, and many other

similar, disgusting little ditties." She tilted her head. "Do you think this is a worthwhile pursuit for someone of your background and talents? Do you think your family would be proud of you if they found out that this is how you spend your time nowadays?"

Meropat looked down at their shaking hands. They didn't trust themself to speak for some time, taking deep, calming breaths. Who was this hypocrite of a woman to question their life choices? They'd left Gesaia to get away from exactly these kinds of shaming tactics.

"What is it exactly I am accused of?" they asked, pulling their shoulders back and meeting the judge's eyes once more. "Songwriting? Pamphleteering? Whatever it is, I don't think you have the right to keep me locked up on made-up charges."

Judge Laikova gave them a wry smile. "We do not need to make up charges. Believe me, you are not that important. This, however, is only a preliminary hearing. The trial itself will take place in a week. Should you require an advocate, Mistrum Rugolata, you have time to procure one." As Meropat continued staring at her, she elaborated. "As you can imagine, at this point in time it is not wise to put people like you on public trial. We are here to find out the extent of your treasonous acts, and your collusion with well-known rebels. Should you want to make a confession now, it would speed things up considerably."

"I have nothing to confess. Indeed, I would like to press charges against the ruffians who attacked me in the alleyway. Have *they* been arrested?"

The bearded lawyer pretended to go through his documents. "That is a matter for a different hearing, Mistrum Rugolata. The man you stabbed is still fighting for his life. Should he die, his relatives may want to take the matter further."

Meropat blinked. "But there were three of them. Your guards saw them as they arrived. They attacked me and my companions out of the blue. And, if you ask me, their relatives may not be able to press charges, on account of being Hallerian."

An icy silence descended. Meropat knew they'd made a mistake. They were in trouble enough without drawing the Mountain spies into the matter. Yet, they'd sworn to keep to the truth, and the truth was that the assailants hadn't been Sendali. No matter how it might complicate things, they had to fight for their rights now that they had the slightest chance of doing so. After all, their face still bore the bruises of the so-called altercation. Some caused by the city guards, and some by the Hallerians.

Judge Laikova drew an audible breath. "As my colleague said, this hearing is not about the unfortunate incident in the alleyway. You are here to answer our questions about your association with the Skovos."

"In that case, I have nothing else to say to you," Meropat said. "And I would like to get in touch with my advocate."

"I warmly suggest you do."

Back in the glisteningly hot cell, Meropat tried to gather their thoughts. This was a mess and no mistake: what they'd thought of as the main point of interest — the attack on them and their friends — was just an afterthought for Judge Laikova and her team of lawyers. The main charge obviously had to do with collusion with the Skovos. If the Siblings chose to launch the planned revolt any time soon, the consequences would be fatal to Meropat.

Later a guard dropped by carrying the usual bread-and-ale midday meal, as well as a piece of paper and a nub of a pencil.

"Write to your advocate, if you have one," he said. "Keep it short."

"Thanks. I will."

"And don't try to hide that pencil. I *will* find it, and won't make it comfortable for you," the man added over his shoulder.

Meropat twirled the pencil in their fingers. For a long time, they remained staring at the blank page, fighting back tears.

What was the use of having the wretched pencil, if they had no one to write to? There were advocates aplenty in the city and in the smaller towns all around Sendal, but Meropat had very resolutely avoided any association with legal practitioners after leaving their home island. Not that they'd set out to break the law deliberately; that was a crass and unnecessary thing to do. Rather, Meropat considered the letter of the law a piece of writing like any other. Something to be considered, debated, and ultimately forgotten.

Their father, of course, would have disagreed heartily. The Rugolatas were a well-respected family, and their rapid rise through the ranks was at least partly due to this pristine image. Ondala din Rettimiso had looked for allies unsullied by the centuries of political intrigue in Gesaia. And while doing so, she'd made liberal use of their money during her spectacular ascent from relative obscurity to the highest position in the country. Meropat's father, by then in charge of the family bank, had been more than happy to back the Duchess in her fight against the other noble families of Mandiora – and had been one of the first to benefit from her rise. He'd even had the audacity to add the aristocratic syllable "din" to the family name, just to emphasize the point.

Meropat had no doubt that their father had associates in Valja as well. After all, there were branches of Gesaian banks all over Ederai. It would be the work of a few minutes to pen a letter to the manager of one of these banks, and to ask for help. Or why not write directly to Mandiora? Din Rugolata Senior wouldn't be thrilled to hear that his only child had landed in a Sendali prison on political charges. He'd also do his utmost to get them out and safely back to their home island where he could stop them from getting into any more trouble.

They leaned their head against the rough, sweating bricks of the wall behind them. They wrote for a living. Over the years they'd written things they weren't particularly proud of, for people they hadn't felt comfortable associating with. But that was how patronage worked. In order to let the muse flourish, it was sometimes necessary to lower one's standards. Producing mediocre work for indifferent strangers was something Meropat could live with, just as long as it kept body and soul together.

There were things, however, they'd never abase themself with writing. On the night they'd decided to leave Gesaia for good, they'd gone to see their father. Not for advice or a blessing, and definitely not in the hope of any kind of apology. They'd climbed up the spiraling staircase, all the way to the top, just because they didn't want their parent to think that they were afraid of him. Meropat already knew that they'd let their father down in the most concrete way possible. They'd refused to even consider a life in the Gesaian capital, working together with their father to further the family fortunes.

Their father had only had a few minutes between meetings. That had been enough for them both. Meropat, already dressed for a journey, their bags waiting in a hired cab outside, had bowed stiffly and announced their intentions. Their father had barely raised his eyes from the figures he was studying.

When Meropat was done, he'd glanced in their direction and said, "I knew I should have married a second time when I had the chance. That, I fear, will be the biggest regret of my life."

When the guard came back, Meropat was in deep concentration. It took them a while to understand that the man was talking to them.

"No, it's not ready yet," they said impatiently.

Had the guard been able to read, he'd noticed immediately that the text the prisoner was writing was not a letter. The words were grouped together in the center of the page, and there were some crossings-out and rewriting along the margins. The guard, however, was neither literate nor interested in the scribblings of prisoners. He was already thinking of the end of his shift, his dinner, and the day off he'd have tomorrow.

As the man shuffled away, Meropat looked at the words they'd produced with fresh eyes. It was far from perfect yet, but the ballad was finally coming together. Out of the fear and indignation of the past days, they'd been able to refine sentiments that were both acute and universal. They wished they'd had another, pristine sheet of paper to transfer the stanzas onto, but in the lack of one, they tried to make their script as legible as possible.

Just before sunset, they moved close to the small slit of a window. The shutters would be closed for the night. They'd also noticed that for the past two evenings, the curfew bugle had been sounded once again — something people had gotten used to during the plague. Now, the city was deemed unsafe again after sundown.

Meropat guessed the reason. Thus, before all doors were barred for the night, and all fires died down, they reached up towards the metal grill of the window and whistled the first four notes of "The Last Harvest." Without waiting for a reply, they pushed the rolled-up piece of paper through the bars.

Part Two

The Reaping

Chapter 10

Sendal - Rondei

From the moment Ardelei entered Valja, she understood why the merchants she'd met on the way had been reluctant to even mention the name of the Sendali capital, let alone set foot in it. The city was a tinderbox waiting for the flare of a match. The Guilds knew it, too. She'd had to spend some uncomfortable hours at the city gate, first patiently waiting with a quickly dwindling crowd to get to the first checkpoint, then in stages of mounting exasperation as she was shunted from one officer of the guard to the next.

To make matters worse, no one knew for certain whether people like her were allowed into the city in the first place. Had anyone really stopped to think about the matter, they would have quickly come up with a negative. Ardelei herself definitely would have. She had no Sendali passport, and her reasons for entering the capital were decidedly vague. She'd decided not to use her Gesaian letter of recommendation until it was strictly necessary. She didn't want it to become common knowledge that the services of Linduvan mages were for sale these days, and likely to be used in negotiations for the lives of known revolutionaries.

Thus, it was only when the captain of the guard had taken too keen an interest in her belongings that she had produced the letter, together with her introduction. Even then, the pinched-faced woman had taken a long time to make up her mind. Finally, she'd looked up from her desk and handed back Ardelei's documents with a pointed sigh.

"Two days, that's as long as I can give you. If you need to stay beyond that time, report back to me and we'll reassess the situation."

This morning, Ardelei guessed that the reassessment of her situation was the least of the captain's worries. The first day of the month of Portia had dawned early, and it had dawned hot. Over the past weeks, the sun had already baked the city dry. The streets were cracked, the walls of buildings glowed with heat, and from the earliest hour there were long, snaking queues to all of the city's public wells and fountains. The Ruoke ran so low in its bed that only the smallest barges could get past all the city's locks, and the water of the river was beginning to take on a decidedly yellowish hue. Bathing, that favorite pastime of all citizens, was becoming a chore.

It wasn't just the weather that made Valja feel like the inside of a shaken beehive. As Ardelei struck up a conversation with a young couple at a trickling fountain, she discovered the extent of the city's new emergency laws. In addition to a curfew, there were many other restrictions on movement and public behavior.

"Gatherings of more than four people are now banned," the young man was saying. "And the guard can search your belongings at any time."

"I just passed a printshop with a bar across its door," Ardelei said. "Is that happening all over the city?"

The girl hesitated. "I think they're all closed now. At least until they find out who's been distributing all those pamphlets."

Ardelei knew better than to press them on the matter. "But how is the oath-taking going to happen if people aren't allowed to gather in groups?"

"It isn't," the man said simply.

"Not at all?"

"Oath Day has been postponed. Until further notice."

This was shocking news even to an outsider. The city of Valja followed the ages-old principle whereby the Guilds looked after the interests of the citizens, and the citizens let the Guilds rule over them. To uphold this custom, the two groups swore loyalty to each other once a year on the first day of the month of Portia. Even during the worst of the plague, guards had gone from house to house, reading out the oath, and listening to people's replies through closed doors, or receiving their affirmations by notes pushed through mail slots.

Today, then, was going to be the first time in the history of the city when the Guilds had deemed their own safety more important than the continuation of one of the fundamental traditions Valja stood on. Ardelei couldn't help but think of it in those terms. As far as she could see, Valjans were as eager as ever to renew the Oath and to get on with their lives once more. There was, of course, a smaller group of those who had been waiting for this opportunity to make their stance known to the entire city, and to encourage others in their opinion that the Guilds weren't actually looking after common interests anymore.

Through her contacts, Ardelei had learned that the Siblings had managed to recruit and radicalize an impressive number of the city's young population. Yet, it was one thing to shout about revolution in a safe place, surrounded by your closest, like-minded friends. It was quite another thing to march out into the open and repeat those same slogans when your parents and employers were watching. From experience, Ardelei also knew that most people shrank from direct violence if they hadn't been specifically trained for it.

As the day wore on, the song of the city was growing more and more frenzied. Usually, hot summer days didn't encourage people to loiter at street corners or spend time in open piazzas. For this reason, most meetings went on in the shade of deep stone walls and in the coolness of cellars. As she made her way towards the river, Ardelei became aware of an underground hum. It was if the streets themselves were responding to the discomfort of the citizens, and the houses trembled with barely suppressed rage.

She knew then that she was going in the wrong direction entirely. Instead of getting her bearings and deliberating on the best strategy — her usual way of doing things — she'd have to make up her mind and act before it was too late. Oath Day was one of the most important events in the Valjan calendar. She was sure that this year, too, the citizens were going to mark it in some way, whether the Guilds approved or not.

Judge Laikova's chambers were a study in understated elegance. Although situated in the centuries-old Guild Hall, they felt both timeless and modern at the same time. The paneled walls were painted in cool pastel shades, and the only ornaments in the waiting room were two large Zeiroan prints depicting minimal flower arrangements. The furniture was equally sparse and unwelcoming. The straight-backed Gesaian chairs and the tiny, shiny sideboard were only there to be looked at. It didn't even cross Ardelei's mind to sit down as she waited for her summons.

Eventually, a harassed-looking secretary waved her through Judge Laikova's door – only to tell her that she'd have to wait some more.

"Lady Laikova has been detained on her way back to the Old Town," the woman said, with a frown that seemed habitual. "I'm really sorry. Today's been a bit of a mess."

"I see," Ardelei said with a small smile. "But I just came that way myself, and there doesn't seem to be that much traffic today. Not within the city walls at least."

"Oh, it's not the traffic. As you probably know, the city gates are closed."

"I didn't know. How long for?"

A small shrug. "Until tomorrow morning, at least." She put on a bright, official expression. "But we're used to it. That's how it was during the plague. At first, they issued the closing anew for each day. Soon, we realized that it was going to be more or less permanent. So we settled down to endure it. And in the end, it wasn't so bad."

"But the plague's gone now, more or less?" Ardelei persisted. "I thought the temporary laws had been overturned."

"Oh no, there hasn't really been time for that. The Guilds have been so busy with other matters that they've postponed many such decisions until further notice."

"So the Guilds are still allowed to run the city based on the plague laws?" Through years of training, Ardelei had learned to control the timbre of her voice. Yet, it was difficult not to let a note of disapproval leak into the question – particularly when faced with the impermeably bright mask of her interlocutor.

The secretary went blithely on. "Yes, thank the gods. Today we're very grateful for that little oversight."

Ardelei didn't need to ask why. She was growing increasingly uncomfortable, both physically and mentally. Partly, it was due to the sun, which was moving over the roof, and reaching its scorching fingers towards Judge Laikova's windows. Although the building was stoutly shuttered, Ardelei could almost hear sunlight battering on the slatted wood, looking for a way in. As the secretary bustled out to get her a cool drink, the owner of the chambers finally made her way through another door — and didn't seem at all surprised to find the room already occupied.

Ardelei stood up instinctively. She'd been in the presence of powerful people often enough not to get overwhelmed by their often forcefully self-important music. Judge Laikova was different, however. Even though her physical stature was slight, and she walked with a nervous gait, there was something about the resonance that told Ardelei instantly that this was a person who was used to getting her way. When Lady Laikova met her eyes, she had to steel herself to hold the gaze for an uncomfortable moment. Both of them stepped forward at the same time.

"Ardelei Jolama, is that right?" Judge Laikova said. Her voice was deep, and she enunciated each word with practiced care. "Please take a seat. I am sure Rusnava has already offered you some refreshments."

"Yes. Thank you." She had been about to present her introduction, but as the other woman didn't see the need to do so, placed both her hands on the armrests of her very comfortable chair. She was beginning to understand the rules of the game they were about to play.

"I have to say that I usually prefer people to make appointments well in advance, but this I hear is a particular case."

"It's not my habit to drop in unannounced, either," Ardelei said with another cool smile. "But yes, as you say, Lady Laikova, I have come upon a rather pressing matter. I'm also aware that you're extremely busy, so let me tell you straight away why I am here. Is Mistrum Meropat Rugolata still held prisoner by the Guilds?"

Judge Laikova blinked. "What is Mistrum Rugolata to you?"

"That is beyond the point. You are aware that they have some very influential friends in Gesaia?"

She leaned back in her chair. Then a broad smile spread over her face. "Well, well. So, the bankers of Mandiora have finally decided to bring the errant child back to the fold? I am not altogether surprised."

"If that were the case, I'm sure they'd prefer to deal with the matter themselves. This is something else."

The secretary clattered in once again, bearing a tray with two tall glasses on it. Ardelei guessed that her way of constantly making noise was essential when serving Lady Laikova: otherwise, she would have been permanently ignored. She made a point of thanking Rusnava before taking a sip of the switchel and meeting the judge's eyes once more.

"What are the charges against Mistrum Rugolata?"

Judge Laikova glanced towards the window. "Nothing official yet. The hearing is in a few days, and the case is still being prepared."

"That's what I've understood. Yet, in order for there to be a hearing, there needs to be an official charge — or at least a crime that's been committed against someone. Thus, I have to ask you again, Lady Laikova: is there any such charge, or indeed a crime? Who is the plaintiff, if there is one?"

"If you have been sent by whom I think you have, Mistress Jolama, you do not need to pretend to be ignorant, or indeed stupid. Surely, we do not need to waste each other's time on these frivolous details."

Ardelei narrowed her eyes. "On the contrary. Holding a Gesaian subject prisoner on vague charges is far from frivolous. I understand that there was a fight, and several people — not all of them Sendali — were injured. Can you confirm this?"

She'd known beforehand that the interview with Judge Laikova was going to strain even her practiced diplomatic nerves. Sir Olvite had been able to give her only the bare bones of Meropat's case, along with some unconfirmed rumors about their alleged involvement in the Cause, and a rather muddled tale involving three Hallerian spies and an alleyway. She also knew enough of Lady Laikova's reputation to guess that the judge wasn't going to yield any details of the case easily, if at all. In delicate situations like this, she couldn't rely on her magic, and could only use her own song to shield herself from Judge Laikova's overwhelming music.

"I can confirm no such thing. As I said, the investigation is still ongoing, and I am not at liberty to divulge any details to outsiders. If Mistrum Rugolata had named an advocate, I might be able to negotiate, but as I understand, they have refused to do so."

Ardelei gave her a civil smile. "An advocate has been named. He couldn't join us today, but I'll inform him of all the things we discuss presently." She took another sip of her drink. There was enough vinegar in it to make her gums ache.

Judge Laikova raised an eyebrow ever so slightly. She'd been pointedly ignoring the switchel from the moment it had been placed in front of her. "I had not been informed. Who is the advocate?"

"Upine Rankomai," she answered, not entirely without smugness. Being connected to Gesaian aristocracy had its advantages, including having one of the most experienced Sendali lawyers at one's disposal. "I'll have a meeting with him later today, provided that he has been able to make it through the gates."

"Well," the judge leaned back in her chair. "I thought from the start that this was going to be an unusual case." She paused for effect. "Seeing that the former Head of Ebino College himself has involved himself in this mess, you will not mind me asking you a second time. Who cares so much for this wretched scribbler that they are willing to go through all this trouble and expense?"

"Mistrum Rugolata has friends all over the Eastern Isles," Ardelei said. "Not all of them want their names bandied about in the criminal courts of Sendal. But, seeing that he already has committed himself, I don't mind reminding you that Master Rankomai, and his College, have always had close ties to Gesaia."

"Those connections have not escaped me." Judge Laikova's tone was icy. She and Master Rankomai undoubtedly went back, too.

"Lady Laikova, let me be absolutely clear. I understand why you're unable, or unwilling, to discuss the details of Mistrum Rugolata's case with me. Yet, I've been given to understand that they languish in the most uncomfortable of conditions during the hottest months of the year. Surely, if they are to be an important witness, or if they are being accused of a crime themself, you will see to their well-being in the meanwhile? Surely, you will be able to keep them from dying of thirst, at least?"

"What are you implying, Mistress Jolama?"

"I meant what I said." She modulated her voice to a slightly friendlier tone. "I think it is in your best interests, too, to make sure they are comfortable. Mistrum Rugolata's friends in Sendal, and abroad, would no doubt be upset if they were being unfairly treated."

The judge flashed her an annoyed grin. "So you keep insinuating, Mistress Jolama. What you may not have understood is that the number of *your* influential friends has been decreasing of late, as has your general usefulness."

Ardelei let the taunt slide. "During my career I have learned to keep friends close, and enemies closer, Lady Laikova. And, even more importantly, to tell one from the other." Pushing her chair back, she got to her feet as gracefully as she could. "You'll be hearing from Master Rankomai presently. Good Oath Day to you."

Ardelei sat down for a late luncheon, trying to overwhelm the unpleasant taste of the interview with some cold spicy soup. She couldn't say that she felt particularly proud of herself. While during her career as a diplomat she'd learned to use all available weapons in her arsenal, vague threats and insinuations had never been her favorite negotiating tactic, mainly because that made it far too easy for the opposing side to call her bluff. Luckily, this time she'd had something to show for her big words. She just hoped that the help she'd been counting on would materialize before Meropat's trial.

Contacting Upine Rankomai had been Sir Olvite's idea. The two men had struck up a friendship in Idriola, and Ardelei had got the sense that the lawyer owed some debt to the Gesaian spymaster. She doubted that a long loyalty alone could persuade a retired academician to abandon his comfortable life in Kaldona and rush to the aid of some obscure young poet in a city on the brink of a rebellion.

She wondered if Master Rankomai had even been able to get through the gates of Valja. She feared that knowing the situation inside the city, he wouldn't have tried very hard before turning back. She'd worded her message in rather vague terms. These days, one couldn't be too careful, even when sending coded missives through trusted messengers. Then again, the messenger she'd chosen was one of the best. Even though often abrupt and impatient, her cousin Rondei also had a wide vocabulary to draw on, and a passion that could sway the most reluctant of hearts.

While eating, she'd had her mind on the morning's matters, and hadn't paid a lot of attention to the people around her. As she left the restaurant, however, she was taken aback by the abrupt behavior of the waiters. On these desperately hot days everyone's nerves got frayed easily. She'd paid for her food in Sendali coin, spoken the local language, and had happily eaten up her soup. Yet, when she whistled politely on her way out, the nearest waiter only stared blankly at her. Walking away, she could have sworn he muttered "Good riddance!" under his breath.

This was warning enough. In the present circumstances, a moment's carelessness could be costly, particularly to an outsider such as herself. She found a shop window and checked her appearance on its filmy surface. At first glance, everything was as it should be. Her clothes were neat and neutral enough, and she carried nothing that could be construed as a weapon. She'd been careful to leave even her small bag at her lodgings, mainly to avoid the repeated and now customary rummagings by the city guards. She ran her hand over her head – and finally understood what had so offended the restaurant staff earlier. Most Sendali women wore their hair long, and covered it with a scarf or a hat during the summer months. Bareheaded, she'd advertised herself as an obvious outsider.

Ardelei had got used to her appearance announcing her affiliations. The simple, homespun Arrikan clothes she was wearing were definitely still practical, but also swiftly going out of fashion. Most people who could afford Paishnali fabrics wanted to show them off at all times, and it was becoming more fashionable to ornament one's person with bangles and other pieces of silver jewels in the Western style. Young people experimented with kohl, and braided their hair in elaborate ways.

She must look odd indeed — and perhaps even arrogant —

with her closely-cropped hair, gray tunic and hose, and worn leather sandals. She wasn't immune to beautiful things, and enjoyed wearing different court costumes when custom so demanded. Yet, she preferred to keep her hair short for practical reasons, and to buy clothes that suited any weather Ederai decided to throw at her. For years, her Linduvan uniform had been a subtle way of showing off her credentials. Now, it seemed that anything deemed too novel or foreign was perceived as a threat in Valja.

She'd been planning to retire to her anonymous lodgings for a siesta. Now, listening to the harmonics of the city around her, she concluded that resting might not be an option in the near future. Outwardly, little had changed. Most houses were resolutely shuttered, and most shops were closing for the afternoon. Still, on her way towards the river, every eye turned in her direction. Even though she sought to make her own music as soothing as possible, very few people answered the greeting note she hummed. Even fewer would look her in the eye. All around her, doors banged close and screens descended over shopfronts.

Valja was preparing for another siege. This time, however, the enemy was already within the city walls. A loud sound could be the signal that kicked off a storm of violence. The song of the city rang like bugles and drums. In their walled gardens, people were lining up sandbags and buckets of water. Some were preparing their weapons. All were praying to their gods. Some prayed for victory; others asked for peace. Most just wanted this terrible day to be over.

Even though she was preoccupied with thoughts of violence, Ardelei heard the guard coming from streets away. His music was frantic with conflicting emotions, and his makeshift armor had been thrown on in a hurry. Having no reason to get away from him, she only slowed down her steps until the young man caught up.

"Stop right there!" he shouted from behind her, quite needlessly.

She gave him her papers, and showed him her introduction. "I was on my way to see a friend," she said, before he could ask. "She lives in Fletchers' Street."

"What's your business in Valja?" he asked. He, too, had trouble meeting her gaze.

"I'm in the employ of Ebarilla Olvite." Her papers said as much.

He squinted at her documents. "Why are you in Valja?" he persisted. "Gesaians have no business here."

She blinked at the bold statement. "I go where my master sends me." Which was more or less true. "I'm not Gesaian."

He looked at her; her face, her hair, her modest gray tunic. "Yeah, I thought as much. I think my captain would like to have a word with you."

She adjusted her music ever so slightly, soothing his jittery nerves and suggesting a calmer solution to the potential conflict that was swirling around him. "I don't think I have anything to say to your captain," she purred. "But you could do something for me."

This time, his pale eyes met hers. "I'm not supposed to leave my patrol."

"I'm not asking you to."

The door opened a sliver. Ardelei could see one green eye peering nervously at her. "Seisikei, it's me," she said to the eye. "You've been very helpful: thank you. Go safely." This to the guard, who walked off in a rather unsteady manner.

"Ardelei Jolama, you do have the strangest sense of timing!" The door shut and then opened again, and on the doorstep stood Seisikei Gimse, as exquisite as ever. She was wearing a peacock-colored robe that shimmered in the sunlight. "How long has it been?"

"Two years, at least," Ardelei said, pushing her way past the mage into the cool interior of the echoing house. "Where are your servants?"

"I've sent most of them away to the country. Only the cook and the gardener remain. They're the only ones I can trust."

"Lucky for you, then: you won't have to go hungry."

"How like you to go straight into the practicalities, Ardelei."

The two women had started their training at almost the same time. While Ardelei had been a wide-eyed Nebian bumpkin eager to grasp at every piece of knowledge thrown at her, Seisikei had clashed with her teachers from their first lesson onwards, refusing to do any physical work, and flirting with anything that moved on two legs. Neither had been particularly popular at first, or even considered to have a lot of promise, magical or diplomatic. Yet, over time, both had distinguished themselves. Through hard work in Ardelei's case, and through carefully chosen allies and sheer personal charisma in Seisikei's.

They had never been friends — not exactly. That would have been too much to ask, perhaps, given their wildly differing temperaments and lifestyles. Yet, they respected each other and had forged a working relationship over the years. While Ardelei was at ease moving about the Eastern Isles, listening to complaints and mediating between different interests, Seisikei preferred to stay in her native Valja, using her vast network of acquaintances to stay on top of the rumors and political gossip that traveled along the Strait.

"How is it possible that this house seems bigger every time I visit?" Ardelei couldn't help craning her neck upwards. The vestibule had doorways on either side, and a wide granite staircase leading to two upper levels. Dark wood and velvet had been used to magnificent effect. Their opulence was lightened by delicate silver ornaments and stained-glass lanterns that hung from the ceiling, glinting as they slowly turned on their chains.

"It looks bigger because it is," Seisikei replied in her low voice, without quite being able to suppress a smile. "Our neighbors died, and their children were anxious to get rid of the house. So we bought it and knocked down a few walls."

"How I am not surprised." Other people's misfortune always seemed to tilt the scales in Seisikei's favor. "And your wife?"

"Serkinel's got a new ship. I suppose I won't be seeing too much of her this summer."

Seisikei had done what very few mages could or wanted to do. She'd married young, and had chosen her partner mainly for practical reasons. She and Serkinel were third cousins, which meant that Serkinel's family wealth was also already partly Seisikei's. They'd bought a dark, dilapidated townhouse with a complex of similarly rundown warehouses nearby. Over the years, while Seisikei was busy fixing the house to her liking and consolidating her diplomatic network all over the Eastern Isles, Serkinel had occupied herself with renovating and then filling each of the warehouses with merchandise. As far as Ardelei knew, the Gimses were among the richest families in northern Ederai.

"I'm not going to ask you why you're here," Seisikei continued, gesturing outside. "As this is hardly a courtesy visit."

"It isn't. I need your help." Ardelei met her own eyes in a gilt-edged mirror. "Or, at least some sartorial advice. People don't seem too friendly towards Linduvans anymore."

Mistress Gimse ran a practiced eye over her colleague's appearance. "Well, you do look a bit frayed, if you don't mind me saying so. And a headscarf wouldn't go amiss. Since the plague people have become much more traditional."

"Meaning that I look like a revolutionary if I go around bareheaded?"

"More or less. Eccentricity of any sort isn't really encouraged right now."

"So how come you're still alive?"

As Seisikei had gone through life making and following her own rules, the austere Linduvan styles had made no impression on her fashion sense, either. A rather small, stout person, she liked to add to her height with Western-style turbans, and wear ample caftans so as to take up more space in any room she entered. The jewelery she wore was also carefully chosen, and often conspicuous. After all, what was the point of being wealthy if you couldn't show off your possessions?

"I'm a citizen of Valja with Guild connections, whether they like it or not," Seisikei grew somewhat more serious. "And whether I like it or not. I can tell you, when the gates finally opened, I was among the first clamoring to get out to the city. I appreciated the safety as much as the next person, but having to spend two years with no one but Valjans for company I nearly went mad."

"Couldn't Serkinel smuggle you out every now and then? I assume she was allowed to continue her trade." The Gimses were one of the few non-Hallerian merchant houses Lord Stainerau trusted with his business, and Seisikei's family had made most of their now considerable wealth in trading salt and other luxury items.

"You cannot imagine how many times I dreamed of doing just that. But you know how strict the rules are. All of our company's carts and ships are inspected for contraband coming *and* going, almost as if they were leaving Haller itself. And you of all people should know all about Hallerian security measures."

The change in the harmony around her had already warned Ardelei that there was a third person somewhere nearby. Thus, she only turned her head as the slight figure of her cousin entered the vestibule. "Hello, Rondei. I was rather hoping I'd meet you here."

Chapter 11

Sendal - Rondei

"**A**nd how was Master Rankomai?" Ardelei wanted to know. For once, her cousin looked somewhat blurred around the edges.

Rondei watched her eat another apricot before answering. "As he always is. Busy." She thought back to their rather hurried first meeting in Kaldona. "But glad to be of service. It seemed to me that he was not too surprised to be approached."

"I bet that man's been itching to find an excuse to return to Valja," Seisikei opined. "After all, as far as I know, he's published almost exclusively on civil unrest and things of that sort since his retirement."

"One does not need to observe a revolt in order to theorize about it," Rondei said.

"No, and you're the living proof of it, Mistress Galsi," her hostess continued without missing a beat. Even though Rondei couldn't say she wholeheartedly agreed with Seisikei Gimse's lifestyle, she had to admire her brazen intellect. "But I'm just saying that Upine Rankomai has more than one reason for being here."

"One of them undoubtedly being Judge Laikova," Ardelei said. "I heard her say as much this morning."

Seisikei grimaced. "Yes, such bad luck for your friend to be riddled with that old mastiff. She'll make their life as difficult as she's able, just out of spite."

There was a moment of rather tense silence. Ardelei, with her impeccable timing, was the first to open her mouth. "Meropat is Rondei's friend, not mine."

"They are not exactly a friend," Rondei hedged. She was getting flustered in spite of herself, and checked the emotion before continuing, "But seeing that they got into trouble partly through my work, I feel obligated to help them."

Seisikei tilted her head in the way most people probably found endearing. Rondei, who had seen enough court coquetry to last a lifetime, tried to avoid looking directly at her. "How curious," her hostess was saying. "Neither of you claim friendship with Mistrum Rugolata: yet you come to their aid at the drop of a hat. Please explain."

Her cousin looked somewhat pained. "Suffice it to say that there are third parties interested in Meropat's fate. And the fate of other people like Meropat in Valja right now."

"Third parties? Gesaian parties, you mean?" Seisikei shot back. "What's this, Ardelei? Have you turned mercenary in your middle age?"

"Let's say that I owed some favors. And I have time on my hands, being middle-aged and otherwise idle."

Seisikei grinned. "If I were you I'd spend that time as far away from Sendal as possible. But I've met the Duchess, too. She's a very difficult woman to refuse."

Ardelei's expression showed just how close to the mark Seisikei had hit. "It's more complicated than that." She wiped her fruit-stained fingers on a damp napkin. "And I've only been told the bare bones of the case anyway."

Rondei leaned back on her divan. "So this is how you're planning to live from now on? In the pocket of the Duchess?"

"Not at all. But times are unpredictable, and we all have to make a living somehow." Her cousin's voice was infuriatingly calm. "I was wondering what *you* are getting out of this,

Rondei? I thought you'd made yourself comfortable in Kaldona."

"I thought so too. It was you who summoned me to Valja, remember?"

"I most definitely did not. I asked you to get in touch with Master Rankomai, and to get *him* to Valja by all means possible. Not at all the same thing."

Rondei drew a calming breath. She didn't really want to get into an argument with Ardelei right now. Arguing with diplomats was a spectacular waste of time, but the revelation of Gesaian meddling in Meropat's case rankled her with unexpected keenness. She'd come to Valja expecting the city to be sealed to all outside influences, and buzzing only with its own violent concerns. She should have known better. After all, a great deal of the unease in the city stemmed from the ideas she had circulated earlier, all the way from the safety of Daurbar.

A bell tinkled in the distance. As most of the servants were gone, Seisikei had to get up to answer the door herself. This gave Rondei an opportunity to apologize to her cousin. "We are all on edge," she said as an explanation. "And you are right, at least partly. I did debate the question with myself for the longest time, but in the end I decided that if one is willing to write about a revolution, one should also be obliged to experience it firsthand."

Ardelei accepted the apology with a small gesture. Then, "Are you in touch with the Siblings at all? If I'm allowed to ask."

"Questions are a path to wisdom," Rondei smiled at the cliché. "Not directly. When I first moved to Kaldona, I established a kind of correspondence with them, but nothing really came of it. I am not surprised." As her cousin seemed to expect more information, she said, "The Guilds have clamped down on the postal system, as well as the newspapers. All printshops have been forced to shut down, too."

"I'm supposing that those experiments with sympathetic ink have come to nothing?" Ardelei asked idly.

Rondei scoffed. "That was just an idea some Zeiroan printers had."

"There were some foreign mages involved, too, as I understand it — and a great deal of foreign funds. I mean, that would be a radical invention: being able to communicate instantly over any distance, using only pen and paper."

"Yes. Well, they could never get the ink to work. And they tried writing on other things, too: mirrors, silk, sheets of ice. They could not even transmit across a room, let alone the entire island." She pursed her lips. "If you ask me, they should have focused on those things that already work, and tried perfecting them. Invisible inks, for one. Most of those are already too well known to be of any practical use."

"Invisible pigeons?" Ardelei suggested, while shooting a warning glance towards the vestibule. "It would be a pain to clean after them."

Knowing the acuteness of her cousin's senses, Rondei went along with the change of tone. "So, I hear you visited Ru. Tedious as usual?"

Their hostess soon reappeared, looking uncharacteristically flushed. She sat down on her low chair and poured a liberal helping of wine with a shaking hand.

"What's happening?" Ardelei asked. "Has it begun?"

"It's beginning. Groups of people are gathering in the Old Town, breaking windows and carrying torches." She grimaced. "As if it isn't hot enough already."

An icy thrill ran down Rondei's spine. As she understood it, this was going to be a rehearsal of a kind. A message sent to the Guilds to see how harshly they would respond, and to see if anyone would step forward from the usually anonymous body of administrators. "What are we going to do about Meropat? Is it safer to leave them in prison?"

"Do you have a plan on how to break them out quickly and safely while there's a riot going on?" asked Ardelei. "No? In that case, I think they might be safer where they are. I've tried my best to get them legal help, and I don't think that in the present circumstances I can do more. At least not when there's a mob trying to burn down the Guildhall."

"A *mob* you call them?" she couldn't resist. "Whose side are you on, Ardelei?"

"I'm used to being on no one's side, remember," the mage said with some asperity. "Your writings started this, Rondei. Are *you* prepared to take to the streets for the Cause? Are you prepared to see innocent people get burned for the sake of something your mind created, and your own hand wrote down?"

Knowing that Ardelei was only trying to provoke her in her turn, Rondei said, "I stand behind every word I wrote. I believe that the common people should have a say in the way this city and this country are run. I also know that the Guilds are not going to yield their power willingly – particularly as they were allowed to run the city almost unrestrained for the duration of the plague. I knew that in the end it could come to this. I was prepared for some loss of life and property." As Ardelei didn't respond, she went on. "I am not a fighter. Other people, inspired by my words, picked up the banner and took to the streets. If they are now going to pick up their weapons, too, I cannot blame them. And if they are going to kill someone, I understand why that has to happen. Yet, I am not going to take part in that killing myself. I never was."

"So," said a voice from the vestibule. "Your zeal has some limits, after all, Mistress Galsi. I am heartened to hear it."

The three women got to their feet as one. Ardelei had probably been aware of the presence of the fourth person, but hadn't thought it necessary to warn her companions. Seisikei didn't seem too surprised, either. She and the newcomer had clearly met before, thus Rondei was the only one whose heart jumped into her throat at the sight of this unexpected stranger.

The man standing in the doorway would have been easy to overlook in any other circumstances. Everything about him spoke of mediocrity. He was of medium height, built rather slightly. His skin was medium brown, as was his hair. He was wearing clothes that most Valjans resorted to during the summer months — an off-white linen tunic and loose trousers. He was clean-shaven and wore no ornaments. Yet, there was something about him that told Rondei that this unremarkableness wasn't accidental, but rather the result of years of careful cultivation.

He was also clearly enjoying the discomfort his sudden appearance had caused. "You aren't going to introduce me, Mistress Gimse?"

Seisikei physically shook herself, as if waking up from a dream, or shrugging off a spell. "Yes, goodness me, where are my manners? Master Taraskil, this is my colleague Ardelei Jolama. I understand that you have met Mistress Galsi?"

"I only know her by reputation," he smiled, barely nodding at Ardelei, and concentrating his attention fully on Rondei again.

"In that case, Rondei: this is Beljone Taraskil, a Guild Secretary."

There was an awkward silence. Ardelei once again took the lead, giving the Secretary a cool, diplomatic nod. "Pleasure to meet you, Master Taraskil. Is this an official visit?"

Master Taraskil gave her another lopsided smile. "Not exactly. This isn't really the right moment for those, wouldn't you agree?" As she didn't answer, he went on, "Indeed no. I only came to let Mistress Gimse know that things were heating up in the Old Town. You must forgive me for not letting myself out as soon as I had finished the glass of wine you so kindly offered me," he said to Seisikei. "I also freely admit to eavesdropping on your conversation."

"Why?" Rondei couldn't help asking.

"Let us say that it goes with the job," he said. "Gathering information, that is. In this case, I thought I'd make my presence known to you, as our interests seem to run in a common direction."

"Guild Secretary isn't an official position," Seisikei explained.

"Or at least, it doesn't involve traditional secretarial duties, as far as I understand."

"No, it's a courtesy title if anything else, and you were very polite to use it. And indeed my work for the Guilds doesn't really involve writing things down and storing them for later use."

"You're a spy, then?" Rondei concluded.

"Not exactly that, either. As I said, I gather information. But not necessarily always for the Guilds themselves."

Rondei noticed that Ardelei was standing slightly back from the conversation, probably doing what she always did when meeting a new person she couldn't quite figure out. Her cousin was using her magic to listen to Master Taraskil's song, and to decide whether he could be trusted. By the look on Ardelei's face, Rondei suspected that the first impression hadn't been altogether positive. She, too, focused on the secretary again.

He saw her looking. "Mistress Galsi, if you don't mind my inquisitiveness, I would be really curious to know how you managed to get yourself to Valja so quickly."

"I am sure you would be. And I do mind."

"Understandable. This is not an interrogation. Anything you say will remain within these walls. As I said, I am merely curious."

"Rondei is under the protection of Sir Ebarilla Olvite," Ardelei said in her ringing voice. "As am I. Does that satisfy your curiosity?"

He responded with one of his cryptic smiles. "Not really, Mistress Jolama. I knew of the Gesaian meddling already. And I'm not that convinced that the Duchess is ready to vouch for just any revolutionary, even if you ask her."

"I said nothing about the Duchess," Ardelei continued, just as steadily.

Seisikei, who had been circling around the three others all the while, spoke up. "Master Taraskil, if you are quite done, I am going to have to ask you to leave. Even if Sir Olvite will not acknowledge my friends, I do, and they can claim sanctuary in this house should they need it. If the Guilds want more information, tell them to come straight to me — officially this time. Have I made myself clear?"

He bowed. "You have, Mistress Gimse, and you have been most forbearing. However, I feel that I have not made *myself* clear to your esteemed guests." He looked at both Ardelei and Rondei in turn. "If you want to help your friend, it's not the Gesaians you should turn to. It's the Siblings themselves." He bowed once more, and walked straight-backed out of the room.

As soon as they heard the door slam, Seisikei asked, "Is he really gone this time?"

"He is," Ardelei said.

"My apologies," their hostess continued. "I'm so used to having servants keeping an eye on people that it never even crossed my mind that I'd need to show this man out before he started eavesdropping."

"No harm done, I think."

"What are we going to do?" asked Rondei, who didn't feel quite as sanguine as her cousin. The strange visit had been a shock enough, but now that the man was gone, his words were beginning to sink in. "Can we believe him?"

"No," said Seisikei.

"Perhaps," said Ardelei at the same time. "How well do you know of this person?" she asked their agitated hostess.

"Clearly not as well as I would like," Seisikei said, still shaking her head. "I knew he was officially employed by the Guilds, and that's one of the reasons why I've cultivated a kind of friendship with him. Over the years, he's kept me up to speed with trade negotiations and other important business; in return, I've rewarded him with some small things I know." She met Ardelei's scandalized eye. "Don't you dare start lecturing me. We both know how our trade works. It's all give and take. Am I not right?"

"You're right. Let's just say that your methods are not my methods," the mage said with a sardonic wave of her hand.

"Anyway, Beljone Taraskil is an enigma and a half. No one seems to know where he comes from. He speaks the Valja dialect as fluently as the next person, but there are no other Taraskils here that I know of. He works at the Guildhall, but he has a tendency of disappearing for long stretches of time, and turning up in the most unexpected places."

Rondei pressed her forehead with her fingertips, willing her brain to work faster. "So, whose side is he on?"

"The gods know. If I had to give a simple answer, I'd say he's on everyone's side – which means that ultimately, he's on no one's side. He doesn't work like we diplomats do, and not exactly as a spy, either. He just likes to have a finger in every pie, and to profit from the information he gathers."

Ardelei pursed her lips. "That's not how any of this works, and you know it. It's not possible to play for every side, particularly if you're passing on sensitive information. There must be someone protecting him, at least."

"I didn't say there wasn't. I just haven't been able to figure out a better motivation for what he does. And frankly, in the past, I haven't really needed to. As you could hear, he's always giving away information quite freely."

"There's profit in that, too," Ardelei said, sitting down with a thud. "Everyone knows that Valja is headed for another period of unrest. Why not stir up just a bit more trouble to make everyone mistrust everyone else, and to make life just a bit more uncomfortable?"

"Who do you think it is, then?" asked Seisikei.

"You know better than that," she wagged a finger at her colleague. "Jumping to conclusions is for amateurs."

"Well, if you want to turn this into a diplomacy lesson, I don't mind. It's been a while since I've been able to pick that brain of yours, and I notice that I've been getting a bit set in my ways, which is not a good trait in our profession. So, let's think together. You too, Rondei," she sat down next to her. "You of all people should come equipped with fresh ideas. Tell me, who stands to gain from the downfall of the Guilds?"

"The Siblings, and the Cause," Rondei answered promptly.

Then, understanding the scope of the question, she faltered. "I mean, that is the obvious answer. You are looking for the less obvious ones; I do not think I am very good at this game."

"Don't be ashamed. The idea of this exercise is to get all possible ideas out in the open, no matter how trivial or unexpected. And I agree, the Cause is the first to benefit should they manage to topple the Guilds. Let's think inside the city as well as outside. There are lots of personal animosities involved as well."

"You know much more about those than we do," Ardelei pointed out. "But I'm still of the opinion that having a local agent of chaos wouldn't be a very clever idea, and the agent himself would be aware of this. If Master Taraskil is risking his neck, who in Valja would be willing to save him, given that he's been double-crossing every which way?"

"Good point," Seisikei conceded. "We all know that Gesaians are involved, and that Beljone at least claims to have known of their meddling already. What's in it for them that Valja goes up in flames?"

Again Ardelei answered. "As far as I know, The Duchess hasn't had any problems with the Guilds, and is most likely waiting for the situation to settle. After all, a revolt wouldn't be beneficial for the trade, and there have been enough disruptions in the past couple of years. Yet," she paused to think. "Ondala din Rettimiso isn't the only one who wields power in Gesaia. And Ebarilla Olvite isn't the only one with informants in Valja, either."

"Damn," said Rondei. "Do not say he is working for the Brotherhood."

"I didn't," Ardelei said, leaning eagerly forward. "But I wouldn't disregard that option, either. What made you say that?"

Thus, Rondei had to summarize her meeting with Professor Dubele, and to flatter Ardelei by saying that he had mentioned her in particular. Since then, Rondei had had other things on her mind, and had, if not exactly forgotten, laid aside the urging of her academic friend to keep her eye on the bigger picture, and on the Brotherhood of Light in particular.

"How intriguing," Seisikei said. "But not too surprising, either. The Brotherhood has got a lot more active since the plague, or at least some parts of it have."

Ardelei poured herself a glass of wine. "So what's this about them trying to supplant the Linduvans? Is there any truth to it, do you think?"

"Not that I know of. But I agree that it is becoming a problem that we don't have a central authority to turn to anymore. I mean, I've always been more or less independent, but I've still been able to call myself Linduvan all the same."

"And you don't anymore?"

"Frankly, I haven't been in a situation yet where my authority has been challenged. But that time will come, and I'm not sure how I'm going to respond. I've never been a particular friend of Darbei Kusvin."

Rondei watched her cousin's face. Even now, Ardelei didn't seem upset by any of the information she'd received so far. Yet, it was easy to see that she was making an effort to appear composed. "What are *you* going to do?" Rondei asked her. "Are you going over to the Gesaian side for good, now that you have the chance?"

"As far as I'm aware, there's no one Gesaian side. You told me yourself that the Brotherhood is vying for influence on Ederai as well. When I took my diplomat's oath, I swore to stand for the whole island equally, and to only work with outside powers if that benefitted Ederai as well. I'm still standing by that oath."

"Do you think you can compete with the Brotherhood alone?"

"No. Not alone." She blinked, and paused for a moment — clearly making up her mind. "It takes a lot more people to keep them out of the Eastern Isles. Seisikei," she looked at her colleague. "Should it come to it, will you help me resist them?"

"You didn't even need to ask."

"I know. But we might need to go even farther than that."

"I'm aware of it. Whatever resources you need, I'll gladly give. I'm not thrilled with the new direction the Linduvans are taking, but I've taken the same oath, and will not let the Brotherhood trample all over our interests."

"Rondei," there was a fragility in her cousin's voice she'd rarely heard before. "I'd like to have your expertise on this as well."

It only took three seconds to decide. After all, Ardelei was only asking for her expertise on the matter, not her entire focus. She also agreed with Seisikei that things were complicated enough without the outside meddling of the Brotherhood. "I am not sure if I am good for much, but you will know where to find me if you need help."

The Gimse house was as far away from the Old Town as you could get within the city walls. Thus, opening the window, Rondei couldn't hear anything unusual from the street below. The heat rose to meet her like a blanket; yet, that, too was completely normal for a summer's afternoon in Valja.

"Nothing?" Ardelei asked.

"Nothing, as far as I can tell."

"I haven't heard the curfew bell, either," Seisikei was saying. "It looks like they're still pretending to have things under control."

"Perhaps they don't need to pretend," said Ardelei. "You yourself remarked on the absurd number of guards in the streets earlier."

"Are you absolutely sure you want to do this?" Seisikei asked Rondei. "There are other ways of getting in touch with the Skovos."

"I did not come here to twirl my thumbs," Rondei snapped back. "And you heard the man. If we want to help Meropat, we need to ask the Siblings for advice. And it seems to me that there is not too much time to lose."

"I'm coming with you," said Ardelei, in a tone that brooked no opposition. "Two pairs of ears are always better than one."

Normally, Rondei would have argued, if just out of habit. This time, she only said, "Very well. But I want to speak to the Siblings alone."

"Agreed."

Before venturing back into the streets, Ardelei took advantage of Seisikei's generous wardrobe — and unerring sense of style — to change into a less conspicuous set of clothes. Rondei, too, helped herself to a pair of tight-fitting sandals and a sand-colored scarf to make the journey across the city more comfortable.

"I wish I had some weapons to give you to protect yourselves, but I'm afraid Serkinel's taken our only functioning crossbow."

"Don't be absurd. We're much better off with no weapons," Ardelei said, padding her pocket with a small smile. "Visible ones, I mean."

"You remember the route?" Seisikei continued to fuss over them.

"It is all in here," Rondei assured her, pointing at her temple. She'd taken a look at the detailed map of the Brewers' Quarter, and that look had been enough to fix the position of the safe house in her memory.

When they stepped into the street, the heat took their breath away. No wonder the citizens preferred to remain indoors even on an unusual day like this. Despite the sturdy sandals she'd borrowed, Rondei could feel the scorching cobblestones beneath her feet. She rotated the map she'd memorized in front of her mind's eye. To get to the opposite side of the city as safely as possible, they'd need to keep to the narrowest of alleyways. Despite adding complications to their route, this plan had its advantages. The canyons between tall houses would at least give them some protection from the sun, as well as from the prying eyes of people.

They set off slowly. Ardelei was getting her bearings, and scanning the nearby streets for movement. After they'd crossed Cooper Street, and met no one on the way, she made a sign to Rondei to speed up her steps. As the lazy afternoon wind changed direction, the smell of smoke suddenly pervaded the air. Coughing discreetly, the two women plunged into the network of narrow streets and alleys that was the heart of the Brewers' Quarter, grateful for the excuse to move farther away from the source of smoke.

While the Old Town was the historical heart of the city, overseen by the Guilds, and the Cobblers' and Boyers' Quarters boasted some of the most modern buildings in all of Sendal, the Brewers' Quarter had a decidedly less organized feel to it. Born with very little planning, and apparently even fewer means, it was a maze of small workshops, baths, and rooming houses that seemed to have haphazardly sprouted out of the damp soil of the city. Many of the buildings were tall and narrow, the more ramshackle ones ready to topple over from the sheer weight of added stories and balconies.

Navigating the labyrinth, Rondei wondered who had gone through the trouble of mapping the entire quarter in such loving and timely detail. Seisikei had said that the small map was a recent acquisition, and indeed it showed all the places where houses disappeared during the turbulent plague years. Had the thieves of Valja commissioned the map? It seemed to her that no self-respecting criminal would want to learn their trade routes from a beautifully printed piece of paper. The guard, on the other hand, would most likely buy such items in bulk.

Traversing the malodorous maze, they soon found that they weren't the only ones on their way to the northeastern side of the city. Rondei often caught movement out of the corner of her eye. Someone walking or running soundlessly just ahead of them, or disappearing around a corner behind them. Their journey had not gone unnoticed by the inhabitants of the Quarter. Here, compared to the more genteel Bowyers, it was much more common to stick one's head out of the window and confront any unusual event directly.

Not for the first time, Rondei wished Serkinel Gimse hadn't decided to take her crossbow with her. Although she wasn't much of a shot, a conspicuous weapon tended to make navigating densely populated spaces easier. It also lessened people's interest in asking intrusive questions.

"No, we don't," Ardelei was saying. "We're on our way to see a friend, that's all."

The person interrogating her was a broad, light-skinned woman whose head had appeared out of a ground floor window — along with an impressive knife-blade.

"Not your usual time for social calls," the woman said.

"Indeed not," Rondei replied. "Do you have any regards for the Siblings you would like us to take along?"

The woman's pale eyes widened. "I... I don't think so."

Rondei gave her a reassuring gesture. "That is quite all right. I rather think they will be busy today. Good day to you."

"Was that absolutely necessary?" Ardelei hissed at her as they once more launched themselves into the tangle of alleyways.

"I suppose not, but I was curious to see the effect that name would have on an ordinary citizen," she said after a while. "And I do not see why we should be hiding our affiliations, either. After all, it is not probable that any ally of the Guilds would be lurking in the Brewers' Quarter right now."

"Speak for yourself," her cousin answered. "My affiliations have never been on show, and I don't intend to start now." She accelerated her pace, leaving Rondei to stumble after her in her borrowed sandals.

The house they were looking for wasn't exactly conspicuous, particularly as it hid among similarly anonymous neighbors. Indeed, the building would have been impossible to locate among streets full of graying edifices had it not been for the occasional signaling whistles and discreet raps and knocks the two women had to follow and respond to on their way. Also, if it hadn't been for the rather ghostly noises around them, they would have thought the entire area deserted. So far, they'd gotten used to shuttered windows and barred doors. Still, in the parts they'd passed, there was always some small detail that betrayed the presence of people: a well-tended pot plant, a crowing rooster, or a barrel brim-full of water.

Here, everything was deadly quiet and dry. Ardelei's face grew troubled as she listened to the song of her surroundings.

"Something ugly has happened here," she said in a barely audible voice, pressing her palm to her diaphragm. "Not that long ago."

"So there is no one here?" Rondei asked, ready for disappointment.

"I wouldn't say that." She turned around slowly, trying to locate any living beings nearby. Then she let out another whistle.

They retreated to the shadow of the nearest house to wait for a reply. The sun continued to seek them out with its relentless gaze. The wind that had picked up earlier had died down again. Rondei, who had spent the last two summers in the relative coolness of Daurbar, began to think she'd soon faint, or else melt into a gloopy puddle in the middle of the street. To distract herself from such disgraceful eventualities, she kept her eyes on the wall of the opposite house, and started counting the bricks.

She'd only gotten to sixty-four when Ardelei perked up. Behind them, one of the street level basement windows opened a crack.

"They're not here," a small voice said.

Ardelei thrust her foot into the crack a moment before the unseen person tried to close the shutter again. "We need to see them. This is urgent."

"That's what everyone says. But they're not coming back. The guards raided this place last night, and it's not safe anymore."

Ardelei crouched down and continued in her most soothing tone. "I'm sorry to hear that. Do you know where they've gone?"

There was a long pause. Then, to her horror, Rondei realized that the person in the cellar was crying. It wasn't the sound of a distressed adult, either. This was a child, wailing with abandon, not caring if anyone heard them.

"I can't get out," the child was saying. "They told me to stay here, but then the door collapsed. I've tried to break the shutter, but it's too high up for me to reach."

"Are you alone in there?" Ardelei was asking.

There was another disquieting pause. "There's... someone else here. I don't think he's breathing."

"Gods," Ardelei said, mainly to Rondei. "We have to get them out."

The shadow above them was diminishing. Soon, the sun would dip lower, glaring at them with its full ire. "Is that wise?"

"We came here so that we could help save someone's life. Turns out it's a different person, but the situation's the same. Are you seriously suggesting we leave this child here?"

Rondei bit her lip. She was still focused on the plan they'd formulated earlier. Deviating from it seemed like utter madness. "The cellar seems to me as safe a place as any, knowing the circumstances. We can bring them something to eat and drink, and return to check up on them once we have achieved our original goal."

Ardelei seemed ready to slap her across the face. "In the name of all..." She drew a sharp breath, and seemed to grow more solid somehow. "Fine. You go on, and try to achieve whatever goals it is you came here to achieve. I'm going to do my best to get at least one living person out of this cellar."

Rondei leaned against the wall, again focusing her eyes on the opposite building. Theirs had been a flimsy plan to begin with, ready to fall apart at the first crossroads. And, who knew, perhaps the child would be able to tell them something important about the Siblings — or, more likely, the half-collapsed cellar might still hold some relevant documents or maps that might help them get a clearer picture of the revolt the Skovos had been planning.

"Very well," she said, not meeting Ardelei's eyes. "I will help you. But how exactly did you plan to open the cellar door without bringing the entire building down?"

Her cousin gave her one of her infuriating grins. "I wasn't planning on anything like that." She crouched down again. "Listen, we're going to try to break this shutter from the outside. Is there anything in there that could be used as a tool?"

Chapter 12

Sendal - Meropat

The Old Town was burning. At first, Meropat had tried to stop the smoke from pouring into their cell, but had soon realized the futility of the effort. There was no holding back the reeking fumes. By blocking the narrow windows, they'd effectively cut off the entire air supply, making the already stifling space even more uncomfortable. Thus, they moved close to the door, hoping that some cooler air would float their way, despite the iron bolts that held the portal fast. As time went on, they found themselves sliding lower and lower along the wall. Even without the fires, the cell would have been unbearably hot. Now, as the temperature continued to rise, their heart was pumping furiously, sending overheated blood all over their already tortured body.

This wasn't the death Meropat had imagined for themself. A duel after a heated argument, getting crushed by a mob of over-enthusiastic admirers, or being slowly embalmed alive by expensive Paishnali wines. Those things would have been acceptable, if not necessarily welcome at their relatively young age. Suffocating to death in a dingy prison while a full revolution raged on outside was an embarrassing way to go — in addition to being drawn-out, solitary, and really quite painful.

They were beginning to ponder how they could at least manage to leave their corpse in a more dignified position when a strange metallic noise made itself heard. It was as if someone was walking along the corridor, carrying all the tools of a blacksmith's workshop, and possibly dragging an anvil behind them for good measure. Meropat got to their knees, and heaved themself to their feet. Whoever was making their way to the cellars had to be a courageous person. All the guards had been called away ages ago to quench the spreading fires which were by now threatening the Guildhall itself. In the meanwhile, prisoners were trying desperately to break out of their cells — and by the sound of it, some of them had already succeeded.

The sound of the smithy got nearer and stopped just outside of Meropat's door. They had just enough time to scramble towards the middle of the cell when something heavy hit the door with a jarring boom. The sound was repeated four more times. On the fifth, the highest bolt shuddered and fell to the floor with a clank. It didn't take long for the rest of the door to be demolished and finally kicked off its hinges.

All this while, Meropat had tried to work out the identity of the two people so determined to get into the cell. It wasn't at all clear whether this was done in order to rescue them, or to do away with an inconvenient prisoner while the backs of the citizens were turned. The apparel of the two strangers didn't help, either. In the smoky gloom, Meropat could only make out grayish garments. The faces of the newcomers, when Meropat could make them out, were mostly covered with a damp cloth. To help them breathe in the smoky corridor, they guessed, but also to disguise themselves. This reassured Meropat: murderers rarely bothered to hide their identity from their victims.

"Come, quickly," the smaller of the two said as soon as the door had crashed to the ground. "Can you walk?"

"I think so," Meropat said, not entirely truthfully. The mere act of standing still was making them uncomfortably trembly. "Who sent you?"

"You need to ask?" the taller one said.

"In the present circumstances I don't think that's necessary," they admitted. "But it would be nice just to be sure."

"We're friends," the first person said. "I think that's enough."

In the end, they had to drag Meropat out between them. The last days in the jail — this final one with no food or water — had been enough to weaken their otherwise robust constitution, and the smoke had done the rest. The two hadn't abandoned their assortment of tools and weapons, but had tucked them back into their various belts with admirable expertise. The only thing they'd left behind was their makeshift battering ram.

"You have come prepared," was all Meropat could say.

"We knew what to expect," the tall person said, rather laconically. "Now, let's get out of here before any of the guards decide to come back."

It soon became clear that there was little fear of encountering anyone on their way out. As they got to the ground level, they could see that the Guardhouse was deserted, apart from those unfortunate prisoners who hadn't been broken out of their cells. Outside, it was still full daylight, but the afternoon had taken on a grayish hue. Meropat stood still for a long while, drinking in the cleaner, freer air.

When they finally looked up, they could see people running — some fleeing, some pursuing, some just hurrying from one place to the next. Some were carrying torches, others buckets. When these two groups met, there were inevitable clashes.

"Can you walk now?" the smaller person beside them asked. At the same time, she took off her makeshift mask to reveal a thin, determined young face.

"Just give me a moment to catch my breath." Meropat didn't need to exaggerate just how winded they were. "You wouldn't happen to have anything to drink? I'm absolutely parched."

The second person had also taken off his mask. He was darker of skin, but otherwise bore a close resemblance to his companion.

"That's all we have," he said as he handed Meropat his water flask. "We'll fill it up on the way."

"Where are we going?"

"The less you know, the better," the young woman answered.

"Where have I heard that before?" Meropat said in an undertone.

Thus began their nightmarish journey out of the Old Town, and out of Valja altogether. Meropat stumbled after the Cousins (as they soon began to call the two young people in the privacy of their own mind). The pair had a hard-won pragmatism about them, and a very familiar lack of empathy as well. Although they often glanced back at Meropat, and gave them sparse encouragement, the Cousins made it clear from the start that the pace they'd chosen was the only possible one.

Meropat understood why. The three of them had to keep constantly swerving into doorways and alleys to avoid either the enraged mob, or the armed guards. In addition, there were many citizens desperate to defend their property. Here and there, fire crews were pulling down houses to keep the fire from spreading. As far as Meropat understood, the flames were mostly confined to the oldest part around the Square. Apparently, the smoke that had poured into their cell earlier had come from a hastily erected bonfire, not from the Guardhouse itself.

They were trying to catch a glimpse of any members of the inner circle of the Cause. After all, the thing the Skovos had had in mind was more of an organized protest, rather than a destructive riot. At some point, it seemed the more violent elements had taken over, and were now wreaking havoc within the walls of the Old Town. Meropat passed looted shops with their shutters hanging askew and their merchandise spilling out into the street. They could hear the frantic barking of guard dogs and the shrieks of frightened children.

The walls of the Old Town were sturdy and high. During the plague, when there hadn't been much else to do, the Guilds had volunteered their time and money to repair and reinforce the weaker parts, and to fix the eight gates as well. On a normal day, the gates were open from dawn to dusk. Unlike the city gates, which followed a similar schedule, these weren't regularly manned, or even very carefully closed for the night.

Today, however, the ancient defensive mechanism had been put to its original use. The four western and southern gates, Meropat's companions told them, had been heavily guarded since dusk, and still held against the rioters. Two of the others had been breached, and at some point, one of the eastern gates had been held by the Skovos themselves. That, at least, was the rumor. Meropat's new friends freely admitted that on a day like this, reliable information was as scarce as snow at the end of summer.

"We might as well head for the nearest gate," the woman said, wiping her brow. "See what's going on. No use stumbling around blindly."

The young man looked down at Meropat, who had slumped against a dry fountain as soon as they'd stopped. "Are you sure you can make it?" His tone indicated extreme reluctance to remain in one place for too long.

"It would help if I could eat something." There was an insistent buzzing noise in their head that grew louder with every step they took.

"Wait here," the woman said, and disappeared behind a corner.

She came back at a half-run, carrying a huge, white loaf and a bunch of grapes. Meropat accepted these gratefully. Only after half of the food was gone did their brain start catching up with the recent events.

"Where did you get these from?"

She gave a derisive laugh. After they continued staring at her, she said, "Can you do nothing but ask stupid questions?"

Meropat drew a breath. "Forgive my slowness, my friend. I

have to admit that being starved half to death in a cell and then dosed with smoke and unbearable heat for half a day have not done wonders for my mental faculties. Also, I still don't know who I'm dealing with. You obviously know who I am. I've never met you before, and am, therefore, at a disadvantage."

"That's fair enough," the young man said, a conciliatory note in his voice. "I'm Aisdote, and this is Olaiga. The Siblings have told us so much about you. When we heard that you were held prisoner, we started looking for ways to break you out."

Meropat wasn't exhausted enough not to be flattered. Apparently, their fame was already so well-established that it was enough just to hear about their accomplishments to light a flame of admiration in the souls of simple people like Aisdote and Olaiga. Meropat also understood that, so far, they'd managed to let their admirers down in the worst possible way. Instead of exhibiting their sparkling wit and unavoidable charm, they'd acted like a bumbling fool with two left feet and a birch-bark tongue. It was no wonder that both of their saviors were now having second thoughts about accompanying them out of the city.

Revived by the fresh air and victuals, they drew themself up to their full height and gave a bow that would have caused them to be laughed out of any Gesaian court. In the dim Valjan street, however, it managed to dazzle its targets.

"Dear friends, I beg your pardon. Your names are well known to me. It is only your faces I did not recognize. Of course, the Siblings have talked about their most loyal followers to me many a time. Often enough have I asked to see a miniature, but you have been cautious enough never to have gotten one painted. I salute your astuteness! My problem is that half of Valja knows my face, and the rest have at least heard my name."

Aisdote's face was radiant. If before Meropat had doubted his affiliations, they couldn't continue to do so now. Not even a Paishnali playactor could have produced such a reaction of genuine, childlike pleasure. "We completely understand. And you must forgive my sister. We are all somewhat short of temper right now."

"Completely understandable," Meropat said. "And I couldn't be more grateful to you both. Before we go on, could you give me a rundown of today's events?"

Olaiga shrugged. Her expression had grown softer. Unlike her brother, however, she wasn't entirely overwhelmed by Meropat's charm. "I think you can work it out yourself. The plan was to disrupt the Oath-taking today. When the entire ceremony was cancelled, the Siblings decided to go on with the disruption anyway. However, the situation got out of hand pretty quickly. It would have been easier to harass people in the town square, and to target guards who would be standing around. Not so easy to pester some innocent people on their way home, or to defend oneself against fully armed mercenaries."

The last word cut Meropat to the quick. They thought it best not to show their consternation. "So what did the Siblings do?"

"We don't really know," Aisdote said. "By the time the burning and looting began, we decided to try and break as many people out of the cells as possible. We knew that you were kept in the lowest story, and had prepared some tools beforehand."

Meropat took another calming breath. "So the Siblings didn't order this?"

"No, this was our own idea. The Siblings have been so caught up in the planning of today's campaign that they haven't had any thought for anything — or anyone — else." He made a wide gesture. "You know how it is."

So the Skovos had truly thrown them over. Perhaps it was for the sake of practicality. The entire Cause couldn't stop for one person, as there were numerous others who had suffered the Guilds' displeasure. Most likely, however, it had to do with Meropat's own rather lackluster participation in the planning of the revolt, and their lack of willingness to carry sharp objects about their person. Without the mad determination of these two young people, they would already be dead in their cell, their contribution to the Cause all but forgotten.

"Friends," they smiled at them. "I think it's time we got out of Valja. The nearest safe exit is always the best one."

The two eastern gates, however, wouldn't let them out easily. They'd guessed this long before they could get a clear view down Moneyers' Street, past the rubble and smoke of what, not so long ago, had been a group of houses. The colors of the Guard were conspicuous all over the eastern part of the Old Town, although at the moment most of the gate guards seemed to be busy with righting an upended horse cart. The message was clear, however. The route that would have led them out the fastest, and given them access to the least guarded section of the city walls, was blocked.

"North we go, then," Olaiga said.

This wouldn't be a safe route, either. As the fighting had started in this part of the city, most of the chaos was still concentrated here. On every street, something was burning — a house, an abandoned market stall, another improvised bonfire. The air in the narrow streets was nearly unbreathable, at least to Meropat who'd already had too many lungfuls of smoke for one day.

The other problem was the continuing heat. The small gusts of wind only made the situation worse, as they fanned the fires, scattering sparks and soot all around. Many of the stone houses could resist the flames, but stores and stables weren't that lucky. The streets crackled with heat and there wasn't a speck of shadow to be found, even between the taller buildings. Often, the three of them had to duck into a doorway just to get a moment's respite from the stupefying presence of the sun.

Unfortunately, there were perils lurking within the houses themselves. The owners weren't going to watch the destruction of their property calmly. In many cases, they'd come out to put out fires or to carry more vulnerable items to safety. Many affluent houses had guard dogs, and small armies of aggressive servants who were ready to club any potential looter over the head. A couple of times the three of them had barely gotten away before a shower of crossbow bolts started raining from a balcony above.

"Aren't there any of our people about?" Meropat asked as another angry shout sounded behind them, forcing them to stumble down the street once more. "Someone with a bow wouldn't go amiss. Or a really big shield."

"They're all probably gathering around the Guildhall," Olaiga said. She, too, was looking pale and drawing in air in painful gulps. "That, I think, was the main target."

"What do you mean, target?" It had clearly been a while since Meropat had taken part in the meetings of the inner circle.

"You know," she raised one shoulder. "We need to make a point, loudly and concretely. No use just running around, shouting slogans at random."

Meropat didn't want to advertise their ignorance any further. And anyway, they had a good idea of what "making a point" meant for the Skovos. All this time, the Siblings had been talking about workers' rights and the fairer distribution of property, but the methods for achieving these things had been only alluded to in coded terms. Thus, what Meropat had taken for speculation and philosophizing was actually an incitement to violence.

The first of the northern gates was already in view. As far as the three of them could tell, it was unguarded, and indeed nearly deserted. The only person they saw was a young woman who was pushing a teetering wheelbarrow through the gate toward them. An annoyed-looking goat was being towed behind her, at turns leaping forward and stopping dead in the middle of the street.

"Come on," said Aisdote, as the two others stopped to enjoy the spectacle. "It's not safe here."

Meropat shrugged themself back into the present moment. Whatever waited on the other side of the old walls couldn't be much worse than what they'd already witnessed within. Still, as they caught the eye of the young woman, they asked her, "What's happening out there?"

"Ha," she said, pulling the end of her headscarf out of the goat's mouth. "It's madness, pure and simple. Most people are scared to even look out of their windows. Those who are out in the street just go about breaking things and setting them on fire. Revolutionaries, they call themselves! Criminals, I call them. If they're on the side of the common folk, they should try and respect our lives and our property."

"The situation's much worse here," Meropat warned her, sidestepping the goat. "I hope you've got a safe place to stay."

"Oh, it's safe enough," she tugged on the rope once more. "My family has a large cellar. Good luck trying to burn that down."

They made it out of the gate and onto Roofers' Street, one of the broadest and best-kept roads in Valja. As the woman had said, there weren't that many people about. Meropat, whose survival instincts were good but rather imprecise, raised their hand.

"There's something strange going on here. Why were all the guards all over the eastern gates, and no one has thought to come and secure the others?"

"Why should we care?" Olaiga said. "We made it. Now, we just make our way through the Brewers, cross the river, and we're safe."

"Easier said than done," Meropat said. "I for one would much rather avoid the Brewers' Quarter right now."

"We can't make any detours now, if we can help it," said Aisdote reasonably, putting his hand on Meropat's shoulder. "The Boyers won't be any safer. There's bound to be more guards there. This is our territory. Just follow us, and you'll be fine."

They chose the first alleyway leading in a northerly direction. First, they walked cautiously, peering around corners and starting at the smallest of sounds. Soon, they began to relax. The Brewers protected its own. Although the inhabitants of the disgusting labyrinth weren't going to step in to help anyone, they had no reason to impede their progress, either. What was more, Guild guards would hardly dare to show their faces here in full daylight. The sun, however, was dipping ever lower behind the houses, and shadows were beginning to lengthen.

Meropat got a feeling that something was seriously wrong. The stillness that had met them outside the gate suddenly descended on the alley as well. They were also experiencing a terrible sense of déjà vu. Something similar had happened in the same place not so long ago, with decidedly unpleasant consequences. They were being pursued, but the pursuers had no need to make themselves conspicuous — at least not yet.

"Be careful," they said to Aisdote, who was following a few steps behind. Olaiga, as usual, was too impatient to wait for them, and had already disappeared behind a corner. "I don't like the feel of this place."

"I think I agree with you," the young man muttered back.

They came to a place where five branching alleys met. Any sensible person would have stopped there to wait for her companions, and to negotiate the way forward. So far, Olaiga had struck Meropat as a sensible person. Yet, she was nowhere to be seen. They tried calling her name discreetly, and peering into each alley in turn, but she had seemingly vanished into thin air.

"This isn't like her," Aisdote said. He was trying to remain calm, but his voice betrayed his growing panic. "Maybe we should split up and look in different directions. I don't think she's gone far."

"That's the most dangerous thing we can do. Whatever it is, we're better off facing it together. You've got the weapons, remember," Meropat said. "And the strength to use them. I don't fancy my chances on my own."

"Right. You keep watch, then."

The silence was getting more and more oppressive, as if a glass dome had been placed over the alley filtering out all noises, except for the ones made by Meropat and his clinking companion.

Meropat tried to think like a guard — or a mercenary. If there was hostile magic involved, it was probably used to trace people, while keeping the pursuers silent to their prey.

They stopped and caught Aisdote by the hand. "We need to make as little noise as possible," they whispered close to his ear, and patted the nearest knife-belt. "And we need to get out of this wretched maze. Lead on. If we can make it to Scribe Street, I know my way from there."

Both of them realized soon enough it was no good. They'd already gone too far north to be able to trace their way back to Meropat's home quarters in a reasonable amount of time. The awareness of being pursued made it hard to remain silent. And anyway, no matter how slowly they walked, the sound of their breath alone would have given them away to anyone listening for human noises with magically amplified ears.

So far, Meropat had been walking on sheer willpower alone. Now, seeing that Aisdote, too, was beginning to flag, they got an almost overwhelming urge to sit down and wait to be discovered. After all, if they were going to get caught anyway, what was the point of wasting precious energy and wearing out their good shoes? This time, they definitely weren't going to put up much of a fight, and didn't care very much where they ended up, as long as it was a place where they could lie down and rest for a few hours.

It did cross their mind that it might be the spell's influence making them think this way. The Guild guards had a very limited repertoire of magic, and there were serious restrictions on the kinds of spells any mage was allowed to use within the city walls. Mind-bending spells would definitely be among these. Yet, many rules had already been discarded in the interest of so-called public safety: it wouldn't have surprised Meropat to hear that the Guilds had brought in extra mages from outside the city, and let them use any spells they deemed necessary.

The pair emerged into a small square, which Aisdote recognized immediately. "We've come quite a way west," he said. "From here, we can either go directly toward the river, or keep to the alleys and make a more diagonal way northeast." There was a moss-covered stone bench and he sat down on it with a heartrending sigh.

"Which do you think is the better route?"

He looked pained. "I wish Olaiga was here. She always knows what to do." He choked back a sob. "I just wish –"

"I know," Meropat said, sitting down next to him and patting him on the shoulder as he started to cry. "Maybe she just got scared of something and ran away instinctively. We'll meet her at the river later on."

"Olaiga doesn't get scared. Not like that. Whatever it was she would have stayed there to fight, or at least would have called to us for help." He dropped his head into his hands. "Oh gods. I wish I knew what to do."

"Listen," Meropat said. "Can you hear anything?"

Without a pause, the young man said, "No. The whole place is dead."

"That's not what I meant. Earlier, when we were in the alleyway, it felt as if the whole world had been silenced. There was no birdsong, no human sounds, no wind, nothing. Right now, it feels normal again." They looked up. "See, there's a pigeon on the roof." The bird fluttered its wings with a small scuffling sound and then settled down to coo with its neighbors. "Maybe we're no longer being followed."

After Meropat had explained their suspicions to Aisdote, they both agreed that they needed to get out of the narrow alleys as quickly as possible. Whatever was happening — illegal or Guild-approved — would be less likely to happen out in the open with more potential witnesses. This, at least, was their hope.

"I wish we could get rid of some of your weapons," they said to Aisdote. "That way, you would look less like a revolutionary."

The young man gave them a sideways look. "*I* look like a revolutionary? If anyone asks, I'm just on my way to help a cousin whose house has been robbed. My face hasn't been plastered all over the city."

"What do you mean?"

It was then that Meropat learned that over the past few days, their name and face had started appearing on the lists of dangerous criminals. This information was exhibited at the front door of the Guildhall, but also on notice boards and pub entrances all over Valja. It was a common pastime to try to spot one's enemies or neighbors in these announcements, which were usually only taken down after the criminal had been convicted.

Meropat couldn't help but be somewhat pleased at this unexpected notoriety. "Where on earth did they get the engraving from? Is it a good likeness?"

Aisdote gave them another sideways look. "Good enough. But I have to say that I wouldn't have recognized you just by that woodcut alone today."

They looked down on their dusty clothes. The gods knew what their face looked like. They hadn't had a look in a mirror for days. "I must look a fright."

"That's good," he smiled. "The Guard is looking for this well-groomed, flashily dressed person. You're wearing the perfect disguise."

"What excellent good fortune," Meropat said.

They resisted the temptation of following Cooper Street all the way to the river. Although the main thoroughfare looked unusually deserted, traversing its broad expanse would have left them vulnerable to not only being spotted, but to being shot to death there and then. The billows of acrid smoke that hovered above the street wouldn't have given them enough cover, either. Meropat had also realized that they were now effectively running away both from the guard and the Cause: thus, it was even more important to keep their head down and trust no one until they were far away from Valja.

Aisdote led them down a side street, towards a place that boasted numerous public wells and fountains. Finding water had suddenly become another priority, one that was beginning to trump all others with every step they took. Even the setting sun showed them no mercy. The parched, fire-licked streets would continue to shimmer with heat long into the night. Getting to the river wouldn't be of much help in this predicament, as its water wasn't particularly drinkable. Thus, it made sense to drink deeply, and fill their water flasks at the closest fountain, even at the risk of being recognized.

The problem was that every other person finding themselves in the Brewers seemed to have gotten the same idea at exactly the same time. Not all houses and workshops had their own wells, and the lodgers of rooming houses preferred to get their water from the public fountains rather than the often hastily dug shallow wells.

Aisdote peered behind a corner and then leaned back. "It's no good. The whole street's packed. People are fetching water for their evening cooking. Most of them probably want to take a bath as well."

The mere mention of bathing made Meropat itchy. They contemplated stealing a bucket: that would serve both as a drinking vessel and an emergency tub. Then, remembering their memorable appearance, they abandoned the notion. "Right. We need to move on then, water or no water. We can't wait for the street to clear. Do you know any other fountains on the way?"

"I do, but the situation will be the same everywhere. The entire city's parched." He rocked back and forth on his feet for a while, undecided. Then, he said, "It would be safer if I went alone. I mean, I can leave some of my weapons with you. That way I'll be much less conspicuous, and can move faster as well. I don't think people will ask questions. They've seen me around."

Meropat was about to object, but stopped themself. The young man was right. After all, they wouldn't get very far without water. "Fine. You go. But if there's anything suspicious at all, you turn straight back. We need a drink, but it's no good dying over a drop of water."

Aisdote disappeared behind the corner, leaving Meropat to wait in the shadow of the alleyway with their heart in their throat.

They weren't that confident that the young man would be allowed to pass unchallenged: known or not, compared to the other well-goers he looked unmistakably like a rioter. Meropat would have liked to keep an eye on him, but couldn't go on peering into the street like an actor in a fourth-rate Zeiroan comedy.

They kept their back to the wall and waited, counting breaths to calm themself down. Waiting had never been a forte. Neither had sneaking around, but it was always easier to move about than to do nothing at all. In truth, they didn't know how far they could trust Aisdote's stealth, either. The young man was way too earnest to excel in the art of deception. Also, despite having left two of his longer knives behind, he was still wearing far too much steel to pass for an innocent bystander.

Minutes crept by, as if dipped in syrup. People passed Meropat's hiding place, lugging buckets or pushing laden wheelbarrows. Everyone else seemed to have gotten their share of the city's water supply. Still, the regular to and fro of people was a good sign. It was easier to blend into a large, active crowd than into a trickle of folk. More people did mean longer queues, however, and Aisdote was certainly taking his time.

Meropat gritted their teeth. When they couldn't hear any approaching footsteps, they risked a quick peek towards the fountain. Aisdote was placidly waiting for his turn, and seemed to be drawing no undue attention to himself. It appeared that the citizens of Valja had seen enough upset for one day, and no one was minded to pick a fight. Everyone kept their heads down, filled their buckets and went on their way again, scarcely stopping to exchange greetings with their neighbors.

Another long moment passed. Meropat was having trouble standing up. Black spots danced before their stinging eyes, and their head rang like a great brass bell. If they didn't get something to drink soon, they would only be able to leave their hiding place at a crawl. They were cursing their short-sightedness regarding their supplies. Clearly, every group needed a person like Olaiga —

bold, straight-talking and practical. She would have filled their flasks every time she had the chance. After all, Meropat and Aisdote had passed fountains before, and only taken a few mouthfuls of water to quench their thirst. Now, perhaps neither of them would have the opportunity to learn from this experience.

Meropat perked up, alert despite their discomfort. They felt the change in the atmosphere before they heard anything. It was as if suddenly everyone in the piazza had stopped in their tracks, and fallen completely silent. The air tensed, and seemed to grow colder. Even the constant chirping of sparrows ceased.

Then the first shot was fired. A crossbow doesn't make a lot of sound. Neither does a bolt when it hits its target. A human receiving a crossbow bolt in the thigh, however, will make a great deal of noise, and their distress will provoke the people around them to make noises, too. The succession of sounds hit Meropat like an electric jolt. Their body reacted instinctively and stood upright and trembling, ready to run away.

The first victim wasn't Aisdote. The wail had been that of an older woman caught completely off guard while filling her barrel. The second voice, however, Meropat recognized all too well. They took quick looks into the piazza that by now was a tumult of moving bodies, rolling buckets, and flying arrows. Most of the bolts seemed to be raining from above. Another peek showed a masked person on a nearby roof with a large crossbow, tracking the movements of the defenseless folk below.

Then, only a few moments after it had begun, the scene calmed down. Those who were able to run had already made their escape. Those who had been wounded were being pragmatically hauled into wheelbarrows and pushed away. Those who were dead were left to bleed out onto the cobbles. Aisdote was among the last group. He lay slumped against the rim of the fountain, an arrow sticking out of his throat.

Meropat recognized a dead person when they saw one. There was nothing to do but retreat via the safest route possible. That every rooftop might host an archer did cross their mind at that point. They chose the narrowest of alleys at first and kept close to the walls of buildings. Spurred on by sheer terror, their exhausted body carried itself at a surprising speed for a while, not even tripping over stray cobbles or fallen pieces of wood that at times appeared on their path. They were also aware of the direction they were going: north, and towards the river. After all, the Rugolatas were survivors who only surrendered to panic as a last resort.

Soon, however, their parched system began to lag again. Thirst burned in their throat, and breath came in ragged gasps. They were aware that they were making far too much noise and stopped for a while. Blood roared in their ears, but a moment's pause indicated that they probably weren't being followed — at least at street level. Unfortunately, the roofs in this part of the Brewers offered an almost equally smooth and noiseless passageway as the alleys did for those in the know.

Had they been younger, Meropat might have chanced the rooftop route themself. Now, however, the spring had disappeared from their knees, and the bounce from their jumps. They kept one hand trailing along the walls they passed; it was increasingly difficult to walk straight, or even keep their eyes open. The sun was setting, and the sky was turning from luminescent purple to pitch-black. In this part of town, people rarely wasted money on lamps, and most of the illumination they used was reserved for the indoors. Blundering about in the maze of alleys wasn't the best of ideas. They might end up going round in circles, or even worse, returning back to where they'd started from earlier in the day.

They sat down with an undignified thump. Their legs were simply refusing to carry them any further. Meropat tried to rub some life into their shaking limbs, but soon found that their arms were growing numb, too. Although there was still some light in the sky above, they couldn't make out the silhouettes of the houses around them.

This is not how I'm going to die. Not in this dank alley that stinks of piss. Get up. Now.

But their body didn't care. There had been too many shocks that day, and too little sustenance. A mouthful of water would have taken them to the river, perhaps, but the nearest fountain was a two-minute walk away. They were going to die here with no ceremony, no music, no one to hold their hand.

Just as they slipped into unconsciousness, they felt a jarring kick against their leg. Someone had nearly stumbled over them, and was even now trying to regain their balance, swearing like a Gesaian sailor.

"It's a person!" she was saying. "No, I don't think they're drunk. Rondei, come and give me a hand."

Chapter 13

Sendal - Ardelei

"I **still** do not think this is a good idea," Rondei was saying, her voice tense with barely repressed anger. "We should have left the city when we had the chance. Now we might never get out."

"It's not like you to be so dramatic," Ardelei answered. "We only had a fool's chance, anyway. Much better to wait for the situation to cool down a bit before trying to get out. There are enough places to hide within the city walls for all of us."

"How's the child?"

"Still sleeping. No wonder. Imagine having to spend a day and a night in a cellar with only your dying brother for company."

Neither of them mentioned Meropat. There was no need. Ever since the two women had managed to manhandle the poet into their lodgings, they'd shown no sign of waking up. Ardelei's song-sense told her that they were very much alive, and suffering mainly from shock and exhaustion. The blood they'd found on Meropat's face and clothes turned out to be someone else's, and there had been no visible injuries anywhere.

"They are a lucky scoundrel. Always have been," Rondei had remarked, pulling off Meropat's cracked shoes, and tossing them as far away from her own person as possible. "Imagine breaking out of the most carefully guarded cell in Sendal amid a full riot, and escaping with only some scratches."

"Some people lead a charmed life," Ardelei had agreed. "But not all charms lead to happy endings."

Lijana hadn't been so lucky. They'd managed to extract the girl from the stinking cellar moments before another part of the building came rumbling down, choking the cellar even further. Once out on the street, she had looked impossibly small and frail. They could tell by her tattered tunic that she and her brother had been sleeping rough for some time. The parents, it soon became clear, had perished when the plague had reached their village, leaving their five children to fend for themselves. The eldest girl had taken their tools, determined to continue the family business. The rest had left to seek their fortune in nearby Valja.

What had happened to the other two siblings Ardelei hadn't yet found out. Lijana could remember little of the time she'd spent with her parents, and the events of the past couple of months were fast becoming blurred in her young mind. At some point, her brother had fallen in with the Cause, and through the older apprentices had been given the job of guarding the cellar and its contents. As far as Ardelei understood, sister and brother had mainly kept body and soul together by stealing food from market stalls or begging on the riverside. Valja, unlike most other Sendali cities, was reluctant to provide for its poorest citizens.

Rondei's present lodgings were far from luxurious, and definitely too cramped for four people. Yet, the little girl had exclaimed with pleasure at seeing the narrow bedroom.

"A real bed," she'd said, her dark-rimmed eyes fixed on the only piece of furniture in the chamber. "Is it all yours, Mistress?"

"It is mine," Rondei had said with her characteristic stiffness; yet, something in the girl's earnest pleasure touched her, and she'd added, "And you can sleep in it tonight."

That was before they'd found Meropat, and had hauled their limp body through the door. Lijana hadn't even woken up when

Ardelei had picked her up and transferred her onto a makeshift pallet in the kitchen.

Rondei sat down on a creaking chair in what could charitably be called the drawing room. The Skovos had originally suggested this apartment, and she'd occupied it with some reluctance. Now, she was holding onto her forehead as if she feared a part of her brain might fall out.

"We need to get a message to Seisikei, or someone else equally sensible," she said. "There is no way we can turn this place into a field hospital."

Ardelei made a small sound at the back of her throat. They were both desperately tired and quickly running out of patience with each other. "It's risky to send messages without a carrier pigeon. I was hoping Lijana would wake up, so we could send her out on errands. She looks so innocent that no one would ask her questions."

"I would not trust that child with a broom handle," Rondei scoffed. "She is too young. She would get lost as soon as she turned a corner. No. Let her sleep. Children are usually the least trouble that way."

"You're right," she sighed. "Is there anything left to eat?"

"An onion, a handful of dried peas, and some sunflower oil," Rondei rattled the list off by heart. "Half a bottle of the disgusting wine. Nothing else. I would kill for a fresh loaf of bread," she said with an innocent cadence.

Ardelei stretched out her arms. Neither of them had had more than two hours of sleep last night. First, taking care of their two new charges, and then listening to the continuing noises outside. The fear of spreading fires was still keeping them alert. "How did it come to this?" she asked. "The riot was only meant to last for one afternoon. Is no one in charge?"

Understanding the rhetorical nature of the questions, Rondei only said, "It is easy to light a spark. Slightly more difficult to get a fire to actually take. But nearly impossible to control it once the flames start to rise."

"Is that from one of your pamphlets?"

"It could be. If I ever have the heart to write another one."

"So you've turned pacifist overnight?"

"It is not as simple as that. But I admit that seeing the chaos yesterday made me reconsider my attitude towards large crowds of people. Like wildfires, they are impossible to control, and act with no consideration for the property or safety of others. Stupidity gets concentrated in mobs. That is what I learned yesterday."

"You do realize we are in deep trouble?" Rondei continued into the dense silence. "The guards will be looking for Meropat, and will recognize them in a heartbeat."

"I am aware of that," she said, staring at the floor, tired of the sound of her cousin's voice. "And you're free to seek safer lodgings if you feel that you don't want to be implicated in Meropat's crime. I came to Valja expressly to find them, and to help them any way I can. I cannot leave them now."

"And the girl?"

"Perhaps Seisikei will find her a place. After all, she's short of staff right now. A small girl like that will be easy to train."

"You would put her into service, just like that?"

"Where else would I put her?" she shot back, meeting her cousin's eyes. "Service is as honest a trade as any. Better than most, as there's every chance of promotion, and a roof over one's head at all times. And for someone like Lijana with no family that we know of...?" she made an illustrative gesture.

"There is the orphanage," Rondei said quietly.

"Have you been there? No? I have. I wouldn't punish the child of my worst enemy by putting it into the hands of the people who run the place. As far as I know, it's connected to the Brotherhood as well. Charity to cleanse the soul and all that."

Rondei perked up. "How is it that wherever one goes nowadays, the name of the Brotherhood keeps popping up?"

"A valid question, cousin."

"Are you still minded to impede their progress?"

"Let's get out of Valja alive, first," she said. "But yes, eventually I'd like to investigate the workings of the Brotherhood, and the extent of their plans."

Rondei yawned. "Is it still the old man, l'Oremel, who is in charge?"

"On paper, Eriai l'Oremel is still the High Priest of Ipira. However, over the years, the Brotherhood has developed some offshoots that aren't directly under the High Priest's supervision."

"Such as?"

"Such as the branch that has started sending would-be diplomats all over Ederai. The last time I spoke with Gesaian representatives they professed to know nothing about this. Nothing official, that is."

Rondei leaned back in the chair, which emitted another painful croak. "Where do you want to start looking?"

"Ideally, here. In Valja. After all, it was here that Beljone Taraskil saw fit to communicate with us. In my experience, people like that don't work alone."

Minutes passed, and slowly turned to hours. They heard a group of guards walking down the street. No one else would have had the audacity to tramp so loudly on the cobbles. In the kitchen, Lijana shifted under her linen sheet, but then settled into deep sleep again.

Ardelei envied the simplicity of a child's world. A bed meant sleep. Friendly adults meant trust. "I'm supposed to report to the guard at the city gates today. Otherwise, my documents will be invalid."

Rondei rolled her eyes at her. "The gates are closed. Everyone knows that. There will be no one there to stamp your papers."

"I'm aware of that, but if any guard should check my documents and find them unstamped, I'll end up in prison."

"You will have to avoid the guards, then."

Sometimes Rondei, too, seemed to live in a childishly simplistic world. Still, her suggestion had its own relentless logic behind it. If there was no way of getting a stamp on her documents, what was the point of even seeking out the gate guards? "I wonder if Master Rankomai ever got to Judge Laikova's office."

"I doubt it. The fighting started in earnest in the Old Town. He is lucky if he never left his lodgings in the first place."

"Do you know where they are?"

"I have a rough idea." Rondei waved her hand in a vaguely northward direction. "As I said, we had to part ways before entering the city."

Ardelei rubbed her stinging eyes. "I'm just trying to think of people who could help us, and Meropat. I can't impose myself on just anyone at a time like this."

"Not even Seisikei?"

"Seisikei's different. We're colleagues. But I have a strong suspicion that her house will be watched even more closely than usual."

Rondei blew out a long breath. "One of us will have to go, guards or no guards. There is no other option if we want to survive. We need food and proper medicines, and we need tidings. Ignorance, too, can be fatal."

Ardelei waited until the sun had passed its zenith, and the afternoon lull was beginning. This afternoon, it looked like the city was willing to settle down for some true rest. The tramping of boots had ceased. The smell of smoke was also beginning to subside, or perhaps she was just getting used to it. Peering out through a crack in the shutter, she could see no one passing the building, apart from a pair of pigeons making their jerking way across the cobbled street, cooing loudly as they went.

She felt slightly ridiculous as she wrapped the sand-colored scarf loosely around her head and shoulders. Anyone on the lookout of a former Linduvan mage would pick her out of a crowd easily. Yet, Rondei was right. Isolated, the four of them had only a fool's chance of survival. Even in a city like Valja, people relied on their families to provide help in troubled times. As far as Ardelei knew, none of them had any relatives in the capital.

She had long since abandoned her birth family for the Arrikan community, and through her profession, had established ties almost as binding as those of blood. She knew Seisikei wasn't going to be overjoyed to find her on her doorstep once more. Still, the two women had helped each other so many times before that it was impossible to say who owed more favors to the other.

First, of course, she'd have to make her way back to the Bowyers. This time, she was hoping to take the straightest possible route. But to do that, she needed to measure the mood of the quarter. It would have helped to know who was truly in charge. That, however, was one of the things that couldn't be deciphered from the song of the city alone. She'd need to use all of her senses to get a more detailed picture of what was going on.

As soon as she plunged into the street, she could not only hear but *taste* the change of atmosphere. The sky was overcast, and a brisk wind was blowing in from the west. Fortunately, it seemed that the fires of the day before had burned themselves out, and were reluctant to be fanned into life again. The bad news was that with the freshening of the weather, people were likely to keep their siestas short and begin assessing and repairing the damage as soon as they could. Ardelei moved along the street slowly at first, mainly to get her bearings, but also to attract as little attention as possible. The quietness of the streets was deceptive. Even though the guards had stopped their ostentatious parading, she could hear human notes drifting her way from somewhere close by. The clarity of the music confused her for a while. There was no one in the street, and yet she could sense the presence of another person as if they were standing next to her.

She glanced up. Of course: the citizens of the Brewers' Quarter had long used rooftops as a quick way of getting around the quarter and away from less savvy intruders. Brewers natives knew exactly which roofs turned slippery in the rain, and which householders placed spikes in their gutters to discourage any traffic upon their property. It wasn't particularly easy to navigate the highway. From above, the city looked and sounded very different, and it was easy to get lost as most familiar landmarks were either invisible or unrecognizable.

Ardelei deliberated. If the children of innkeepers and cobblers could learn the tricks of the pigeons and sparrows, so could adults. The more nimble among them could easily cut off a fleeing criminal — or a pursuing guard if they knew their way around the quarter. It wouldn't take much of a bowman to shoot someone from above. She suddenly understood what Meropat had been trying to tell them when they found their nearly lifeless body in the alleyway.

"Look up," they'd said in a cracked voice. "Outsiders."

At the time, both of the women had taken their words as the ramblings of a muddled mind. Now, the three small words opened up a frightening possibility.

Ardelei pressed herself against the wall of the nearest house. It didn't take long before a faint shuffling sound approached her. Someone was walking in soft shoes across the roofs on her side of the street. The sound stopped almost right above her. She strained towards the person, trying to get some sense of their music. Guards usually exuded confidence, or at least a sense of purpose. This person's music, however, was different. It was quieter, to begin with. It was also more complex. The mission they were on wasn't straightforward guarding business. This was the song of a hunter stalking their prey.

Gradually, she became aware of a questing magic. Something very like her own, albeit less subtle. She slammed down her defenses, dampening her own music to almost nothing. This, hopefully, would lead the mage on the roof to conclude that she was indoors, or otherwise farther away. She drew long, careful breaths to keep her panic at bay.

What in the name of all hells are they doing here?

She hadn't been expecting to encounter such blatant magic on the streets of Valja. *Outsiders*, Meropat's voice whispered in her head, and she reluctantly agreed. As far as she knew, the Guilds had never resorted to mercenary mages before. They'd always considered themselves above such underhand foreign tactics. Indeed, Valja had some extremely strict laws regarding the use of magic written into its very constitution. Even Ardelei, every time she entered the city, had to read and sign a declaration stating that she wasn't going to use her music to meddle with the minds and bodies of Valjan citizens, or try to make a profit with her skill.

And yet, this was exactly what the mage above her was doing. Not only were they profiting from their magic, they had rendered themselves invisible so as to sneak up on unsuspecting citizens. Or non-citizens, in this case. Ardelei wondered if this was a coincidence. Perhaps the mages had been specifically set on people like her and Rondei. That way, no laws would be broken. Which didn't matter all that much anyway in the present situation, she thought sourly, as the Guilds could just rewrite all legislation, having given themselves almost unlimited power during the plague years.

A small eternity passed. Ardelei remained pressed against the wall, hardly daring to breathe; the person above her stayed equally still, determined to wait her out. It was only the return of the pair of pigeons that defused the situation. As the birds bobbed their way past Ardelei's sandals without even casting a glimpse at her, the mage on the roof seemed to finally make up their mind that there was nothing more to see below. In a few minutes, their music was moving across the rooftops in a southerly direction.

Ardelei blew out the breath she'd been holding, thinking she'd need to leave out some breadcrumbs for the pigeons later. Right now, it was time to move on. Going back indoors wasn't an option. If she closed the door behind her now, it would take a while before she'd have the nerve to open it again. She couldn't stay within the safety of the familiar street, either. Sooner or later, the siesta would come to an end, and the neighbors would start wondering about the stranger hugging the wall of an otherwise unremarkable house.

She closed her eyes for a moment to get a clearer idea of the sounds of her surroundings. The mage gone, the only people she could sense close by were Rondei and the other inhabitants of the houses behind her. She knew the quarter well enough to start devising a route that kept her out of sight as much as possible. That, of course, went in complete contradiction to her earlier plan of getting to Seisikei quickly. But that couldn't be helped. Right now, she was too full of indignation to care too much about her change of route.

Whose gang had the Guilds hired? Over the years, Ardelei had had her share of run-ins with mages who sold their skills to the highest bidder. Often, this was a matter of survival, and wasn't any more insidious than an herbalist or a midwife charging for their expertise. Then, there were the organized mercenary groups which, when times were rough, often took to terrorizing remote villages and farmsteads for food and protection money.

It was very rare, however, that a city would stoop to hiring these law-breaking ruffians. During the first plague months some Zeiroan towns had tried something similar, putting together groups of "volunteers" who patrolled the gates and turned back anyone who looked like a potential carrier. Some of the makeshift guards were mages who said they could use their powers to detect and repel the disease. It didn't take long, however, for the people to realize that magic could do no such thing, and to send the mages packing.

The established mercenary gangs rarely settled in one city, or even one country, for more than a few months. The most notorious of these — named after their founder Hasaure — moved unimpeded between Sendal, Nebe and Zeiroa, resorting to a spot of highway robbery when times were lean. Personally, Ardelei had a kind of nostalgic fondness for the Hasaure gang, as during her first year as a fully-fledged Linduvan diplomat, she'd been called to a Sendali village that wanted to negotiate a treaty with the mercenary mages. The person leading the negotiations on the villagers' behalf was a man called Beldor Amsta. She'd been deeply impressed by his cool competence, which in the end had won the villagers their freedom from the mercenaries.

She wished she could talk to Bel now. Not so much to ask for advice, but to hear his measured response to her troubles. He had a way of seeing the bigger picture, and not getting bogged down by the smaller human complications which often tripped Ardelei up. Many times she'd found this trait frustrating. It was, after all, the human emotions and complexities that she was defending. But she had to admit that over the years he'd taught her almost as much about negotiations as her teachers at Arrika had. Had she ever told him that?

She arrived at a street corner. All around her, the soundscape was serene and spoke only of everyday things. A pump creaked into life nearby. A group of children ran giggling over a yard, dragging a bucket behind them. Dogs barked lazily at the commotion, then at each other, and gradually fell silent again. Ardelei concentrated on the top layer of this music, but still couldn't hear anything out of the ordinary — just the rising wind whistling across rooftops, and getting trapped between tall chimneys.

It was her cautious nature that saved her once more. Just as she was about to make a dash across the small piazza ahead she heard a clean sound, as if a small stone had just pinged off a terracotta tile. She withdrew soundlessly back into the alleyway. For a while, nothing happened. Knowing the methods of mages, she now focused her magic directly above her. Just as she'd anticipated, two pairs of feet moved carelessly downwards on a low roof – and thumped down onto the street level only a few armspans away from her.

She'd relaxed her guard for a while to listen better. Now, her defenses were up again. Luckily for her, the two mages weren't expecting to meet any fellow magic-users at this stage of their mission: otherwise, they would have been much more careful with both their presence and volume, and much more vigilant about their surroundings.

"That's it," one said. The language they spoke was a curious mixture of all the major Ederaian languages. The grammar was mainly Zeiroan, but the words came from all over the Eastern Islands. "I'm not going any farther today. If the captain wants to comb the city for more lawbreakers, she can do it herself."

"Yeah, I don't see her crawling over rooftops from dawn to dusk, with no breaks in between," the other replied. "Besides, they've all gone back underground if you ask me."

"Like the rats they are," chuckled the first man.

"Back to the base?" This in a hopeful tone. "I'm gasping for a beer."

His companion clearly agreed, and the two mercenaries continued their chatty way southwards. Ardelei's heart was hammering in her throat. The encounter had been an uncomfortably close one. Still, the near collision had confirmed at least some of her suspicions. The lingua franca spoken by the mages was familiar enough. The only people she'd ever heard use a mixture quite as breathtaking as that had been members of the Hasaure gang, who made a point of never reverting back to their native languages — not even in the company of outsiders.

With the voices of the two men bouncing off the walls behind her, Ardelei kept her defenses close and stepped across the piazza. What was happening around her clamored for more than one head to puzzle it over.

"What do you think they meant, 'lawbreakers'?" Seisikei asked, handing her a cup of chilled, spiced wine.

"I wish I knew," Ardelei sighed. "To me, that's an oddly general term. If they'd been on the lookout for the Skovos or their associates, I'm sure they'd have called them 'revolutionaries' or something similar. Personally, I doubt these people are here to hunt down just any pickpocket or match-carrier."

"I agree," said Albister. "Why not hire more guards in that

case? These mercenaries are notoriously expensive, as they work for the highest bidder."

When Ardelei had finally arrived at Seisikei's door, she'd been relieved — and also pleasantly surprised. Mistress Gimse was in a much calmer mood, and in no way irritated to see her colleague again. Most of the shift could be attributed to the arrival of another acquaintance of theirs, Albister Aniata, who had presented himself at the Gimse residence almost as soon as Ardelei and Rondei had left it.

Albister was a Zeiroan mage, and somewhat older than the two women. He'd taught both of them briefly in Arrika, but their friendship had truly started when all three of them worked on Ederai and often came into contact with each other through their diplomatic activities. Recently, Albister had landed a rare and desirable position: he was in the employ of the Zeiroan government, representing his native country as an official ambassador and occasional diplomat.

"So, I'm assuming this isn't an official visit," Ardelei had concluded as soon as she'd disentangled herself from their long hug.

"Your assumption is correct," Albister had smiled at her. He looked exactly the same as the last time they'd met. Round-faced and sleek, like a well turned-out seal, in his expensive silk suit. "Let us just say that if it had been up to me, I would not have come to Valja voluntarily during this warm season."

Seisikei had led them to one of the smaller rooms on the ground floor and closed the door behind her. She was a woman who learned from her mistakes. "I must confess that I'm feeling exceedingly slow-witted today. What is it that the Zeiroans and the Gesaians know that we don't?" She had nearly dislodged her turban by pulling on a strand of hair and tucking it behind her ear.

Now, the three of them were pondering the sudden appearance of mercenaries upon the rooftops of Valja. According to

Seisikei, nothing official had been said about their presence – and nothing like this had happened before.

"Which means that most people won't even know the mercenaries are here," said Ardelei. "And won't recognize one when they cross paths in the street."

"And most likely, will never even find out that they were here," Albister commented. "Are you certain that this is the first time they have been called over?"

Seisikei raised an eyebrow. "Now, my magic isn't as keen as Ardelei's, but my networks are near faultless. *Someone* would have heard something, and that information would have percolated its way to me, sooner or later."

"I believe you," Albister nodded, resting his large hands on his mound of a belly. "Which, then, begs the question: what are the Guilds afraid of? What is going on now that has not been seen before? I for one do not believe they would risk their reputations for the sake of the Siblings. Valja, of all the northern cities, has seen its share of rioting and has not suffered too greatly from it, in the long run."

Ardelei finished her wine. She deliberated – and then decided. "Have you heard of a person called Meropat Rugolata?"

Her colleague furrowed his brow. "It is possible."

"You would know them if their name had been mentioned in a professional context," she smiled. "They're a Gesaian poet. Used to work here as a printer's apprentice for a while, and in the evenings wrote revolutionary songs for the Skovos." She paused to think. "I've heard only one of these songs, but its power is unmistakable. Meropat has a talent that seems to distil raw magic into memorable lyrics."

Albister leaned back on his divan, studying his fingertips. "Interesting. Where has this person been trained?"

Seisikei let out a bubbling laugh. "By the sound of it, in every tavern backroom and dingy alleyway Ederai can offer. The gods know what they did back in Gesaia."

"Pretty much the same things, as far as I know," Ardelei

admitted. “But they hail from one of the most influential families in Mandiora. I’m surprised the name doesn’t ring a bell,” she said to Albister, who only shrugged. Bankers were of little interest to someone who drew an annual salary in solid Zeiroan silver. “Recently, Meropat was imprisoned under highly suspicious circumstances. I’ve heard Hallerians mentioned as part of the events that led to their capture. I went to see Judge Laikova yesterday, just to generally announce by presence, and also to flaunt the name of Master Rankomai in her face. She didn’t appear particularly bothered.”

“She never does. I don’t admire her tactics, but I am in awe of her personality. But you said that there have been further developments,” Seisikei said.

Ardelei summarized the developments, emphasizing the coincidence that had led her and Rondei to bump into Meropat on their way back to their lodgings. Her companions listened to her in silence: both of them had been trained in the art of diplomacy, which mainly consists of learning when to ask questions and when to refrain from speaking altogether. Their faces, however, were a study in amazement and polite shock.

“I agree,” Albister said as soon as she’d finished. “We need to get your friends out of that place, as soon as possible.”

“Are you suggesting you bring them here?” asked Seisikei, almost as quickly. “I’m not sure that’s a good idea.”

“I agree,” Ardelei said. “The girl would perhaps be safest under your protection, but the others need to get out of Valja — or indeed out of Sendal altogether. Any suggestions?”

Seisikei gave her another of her dazzling smiles. “I hear Jirda is very pleasant at this time of year. And, as it happens, we have boats going that way regularly.”

“How I love a happy coincidence,” Albister beamed at them.

Chapter 14

Sendal - Rondei

Rondei gripped the side of the boat so hard that her knuckles turned white. The reaction didn't stem from fear. She wasn't partial to traveling on water, but had gotten used to it as one of life's minor inconveniences.

No. Rondei was livid. "I cannot believe you could just go over our heads like that," she hissed at Ardelei, not even deigning to look at her cousin.

"What would you have me do?" Ardelei answered in the tone she used to calm people down, and which always made Rondei even more irritated. "Leave the three of you to be flushed out by mercenaries? Or burned to death in the next outbreak of accidental fires, or just elegantly starving as all supplies run out?" She waved her hand in exasperation. "Anyway, we're not in the clear yet. You might just get a chance of getting back to your beloved Valja, after all. In chains. And you can be sure that this time, I won't be there to bail you out."

When Ardelei had left in search of food and medicines, Rondei had enjoyed a rare moment of solitude. Meropat and the little girl were asleep, and would, by the looks of it, remain in that state for the foreseeable future. Therefore, she'd been able to stretch out her legs and close her eyes, thinking back to the frantic days that had preceded that moment , and trying to plan for the equally perilous times ahead.

Left to her own devices, Rondei would have been content to remain underground, relying on the Skovos and their numerous allies to keep her victualed. After all, the Siblings had shown their gratitude to her in similar ways before. There was little cause for them to stop caring for her now, at the cusp of achieving their goals.

The quietness around her had brought on an almost insuppressible urge to write. She was a creature of habit, and during her cloistered time in Daurbar she'd worked to a rigid schedule that might seem tedious to an outsider, but for her created the perfect circumstances for creative endeavors. Doing the same things at the same time every day left a part of her mind always free, so that she could ponder the less mundane questions of life while carrying out those daily actions.

She was also one of those people who think best on paper. She could come up with perfect sentences and groundbreaking ideas while walking, or doing her hair, but the train of her thought was always at its clearest when she could trace it down on paper right from the start, correcting its course and tweaking its length if necessary. Thus, her present inactivity was making her anxious. The ideas and memories floating around would need setting down soon, or they'd be gone for good. After all, she was living through some truly interesting times — full of events to be evaluated, written down, and saved for future generations.

Before entering the city, she'd toyed with the idea of keeping a diary. Such a journal would be priceless in the days to come. She'd brought a loosely bound notebook and a brace of pencils for that purpose; yet, those implements had been left lying idle at the bottom of her bag. Since her arrival, there had been little time for writing, and even less for coherent thought. Even during this quiet afternoon hour, sitting with her hands on her lap, she couldn't muster the energy for picking up the notebook and coming up with a captivating way of telling the story of the past two days. She'd also come to the realization that committing evidence to paper might not be safe at the moment.

When Ardelei had rushed back, full of news, ideas — and, most annoyingly of all — a plan of escape, Rondei had at first felt relieved. Once again, someone else had taken from her the burden of work. She could throw herself into the course of great events around her, and only piece together a coherent story afterwards. She could postpone the painful moment of staring at a blank page, deciding how best to fill it.

Very soon, however, the relief turned to anger. Who were these diplomats to play god over other people's lives? Who were they to decide who should stay, and who should be shipped off to Nebe like so many sacks of flour? Her annoyance grew when she realized that Ardelei wasn't even listening to her. The plan had already been settled on. The ambassador Albister would knock on their door at sunset, and the four of them had to be ready – Lijana to be transported to the Gimse house, and the rest to start their journey towards Jirda.

"I am not going," Rondei had said as soon as the weight of the plan settled on her. "I agree that Meropat will be safer out of Sendal, but there is no reason for me to leave Valja right now. I have enough friends here to look after me."

Ardelei had drawn a deep breath. "I wish that was an option. Albister can only take us as far as the river. From there on, I'll need someone to help me carry Meropat. You've seen how they are: I can't manage on my own all the way to Jirda."

"There will be hands enough on the boat."

"There'll be hands enough to get the boat and the goods to Jirda and back. I promised Seisikei that we won't inconvenience the crew if we can help it. They'll be taking a big enough risk as it is."

Her cousin had been right about the hands, at least. The Gimses ran a tight operation, not wasting space or sailors on shorter trips like this one. Indeed, the crew had had to remove a few bales of cloth to make room for the three extra passengers. By their undertone comments, Rondei could tell they weren't at all happy about that particular development. Ardelei was having to pull all of her diplomatic weight to get on the good side of the sailors even before their journey had begun.

While Meropat slept a drugged sleep below decks, and Ardelei tried to work her magic on the crew, Rondei sat on deck, gazing at the flat landscape ahead. As the sun rose higher, the yellowing cornfields and motionless windmills came into better view. No people or animals yet moved in the riverside villages. Rondei had to admit that being able to breathe in clean country air, and to generally go about her life unafraid of stray arrows or rampant fires felt liberating. She almost felt like taking out her journal and jotting down the beginnings of what was surely going to be a masterpiece in journalistic observation.

However, as Ardelei had said, they weren't yet in the clear. After bundling the four of them into a narrow dog-cart, Albister had been able to steer his course to the riverside unimpeded. A rumor ran that all gates were to open again at sunrise. Thus, there was so much coming and going in the streets that the guards on night-duty hadn't been able to check every passing vehicle – nor did they seem particularly interested in the task. The Oath Day and its aftermath had taken its toll on even the most fastidious of guards.

The rumor turned out to be true. After an agonizing wait in the pitch-dark hold of the Gimse riverboat, Velvet, Rondei had heard the dawn bell, accompanied with the pained creaking of chains. The eastern water-gate was open, and they were soon on their way down the Ruoke. Again, the exhausted guards only glanced at the vessel and its documents before waving the Velvet through. Merchants like the Gimses were a force to be reckoned with and didn't take kindly to any impediments to their trade, particularly when all their documentation was known to be in impeccable order.

Albister had mentioned that another rumor was making its rounds in the city. That both Siblings had been caught, along with their inner circle, and that the revolution had been quenched for the time being. That would explain the sudden opening of the gates, at least. Yet, all of them knew not to take the information too seriously. Urban rumors bred like lice in bolsters, and fed themselves on people's love for scandal.

Rondei and Ardelei were also painfully aware that even though they'd made it out of Valja didn't mean that they couldn't be stopped farther down the river. The rest of Sendal usually cared little about the troubles of the capital city, neither did the other communities take kindly to Valjan meddling in their affairs. Still, the Guilds had their representatives elsewhere in the country, and merchants in particular had to follow common laws and rules. Spot-checks weren't unknown, particularly in times of unease.

Rondei knew that she could just demand to be put back on land there and then, and make her way back to Kaldona on foot. And, if it had just been her cousin on board with her, she would have done just that. Indeed, returning to a peaceful, independent existence seemed like the best policy altogether at the moment. However, the presence of Meropat impeded her from making such rash decisions. Although she didn't believe in fate, she couldn't help thinking that there was something meaningful in the two of them meeting in such extraordinary circumstances after all these years. As they hadn't had a chance to talk yet, she decided to remain on the boat. After all, it was a similar chance meeting that had led to rather unusual events the last time they met.

She woke up abruptly, with a sensation of falling from a great height. Ardelei's face was looming very close to hers. "What time is it?" she asked. The hold of the boat was dark. Rondei would have much preferred traveling on deck, but had agreed with the crew that both she and Ardelei were rather too conspicuous at the moment.

"Midday, or thereabouts." Ardelei glanced behind her. "Meropat has been getting more restless. It looks like they'll wake up soon."

"And you wanted me to witness this spectacle?"

"They might want to use the chamber pot," Ardelei smirked at her. "Easier to do with two helpers, I always find."

Rondei tried not to show her exasperation. Nevertheless, she couldn't help but be disgusted by the minutiae of Ardelei's daily life. Rondei had chosen to live mainly in her mind. Her cousin, on the other hand, was much more at ease with the corporeal world and its varied functions.

Ardelei's mind seemed to be moving along a similar track. "I still don't understand how you could have turned out to be such a squeamish creature. After all, we both were born of the same Nebian muck, and had to live in it for an equal number of years."

"That may be true, but I decided that there is life beyond Nebian muck, and elevated myself above it."

"Well, there are certain things that can't be avoided, no matter how elevated your position." She turned to look at Meropat who had made a small groan. They didn't seem to be willing to wake up, however, and sank back to their torpor with a deep sigh.

Rondei understood them only too well. "This tub seems to be taking an awfully long time to even get out of Sendal. If we had the Gimse fleet at our disposal as seems to be the case, we should have taken the northern route on the Strait. The distance is equal, but a sailboat would have made it to Jirda in a matter of hours."

"We chose a heavily laden vessel on purpose. Who in their right mind would try to escape on a riverboat at this time of year, when you'd get to Jirda much faster on foot?" Ardelei said. "Also, the Strait itself might be the faster route — which I agree it is, when the weather's favorable — but getting there would mean getting through the Sendali customs, as well as other random checks they might have decided to run at the docks. The river route is more relaxed. And as far as I know, none of us has pressing appointments in Jirda, or indeed anywhere else."

"I trust we have a safe house when we get there?"

Ardelei flashed her another of her grins. "We'll think of something."

"It would have been handy if the route to Luneken were still open." She couldn't help the small dig at her cousin, just to puncture her confidence a little.

"I'd never have taken either of you there. Arrika is not a sanctuary, you know that. The only way we've been able to maintain our neutrality is exactly this: that we don't bring in any fugitives or political prisoners. Once you let one person in, you'll never stop."

Rondei raised an eyebrow. "From what I hear, things may be changing."

"If they are, I know I've played no part in that." She looked down for a moment, drawing a few calming breaths. "It might be that the Arrika I had the luck to live in was only a dream, held together with flimsy bonds. That sooner or later it would dissolve into disagreements, just like any other community of its kind will."

The two women lapsed into an uneasy silence. Above them, the crew worked to a lazy routine, trying to stay away from the midday sun as much as possible. Now and then, they exchanged greetings with people on the riverside and on other vessels passing by. For them, this was a regular route, and most likely they'd soon stop at some familiar inn for their midday meal. Rondei wondered if it would be possible to place an order. She had a sudden craving for fried fish.

She stared into the half-darkness. As her eyes got used to the low light, she started to distinguish the outlines of the hold and the expertly packed goods it contained. Stray sunbeams dappled the space, highlighting random objects here and there.

"Why are you suddenly so anxious to get to Jirda, anyway?" Ardelei finally asked her.

"Whatever gave you that idea?" she scoffed. "The last time I looked, I had no say in any of the decisions that were being made about the route, or indeed the schedule. I am just quietly looking forward to the moment when my life is my own again."

"Do you think that will happen soon?" Ardelei's tone was light, yet her words were deadly serious. "After all, you did promise to help me find out what's truly going on in Valja. Now that the mercenaries are involved with the Guilds I, for one, can't just turn my back on the capital and go back to blithely brokering peace."

"I had not forgotten," she said in a quiet voice. "I just had not imagined that aiding you would be the only goal of my life from this day onwards."

"You make it sound like a prison sentence. Why do you find collaboration such an anathema? Or is it just me?"

"It is mainly you," Rondei had to smile. "I suppose I just value my freedom after having worked under the Stainerau yoke for so long."

"But what's the point of working, if you only do it for yourself?" Ardelei asked. "None of us is truly independent: even a hermit needs a community to distance themselves from." This sounded like one of the trite sayings they taught in Arrika.

"I have never said that I would not want to work for a greater cause, if that is the term we want to use. I just work best on my own. There is a difference. Do you see it?"

"I think I do." After a while Ardelei said, "In order for this venture to succeed, we'll need free agents like you. People who are free to move from place to place, and who don't need someone to give them orders constantly."

A clamor of voices approached, and the two women stopped to listen, startled out of their own debate. After a tense moment they understood that another riverboat was making its way towards them, and the two crews had begun exchanging news in the traditional song-language as soon as they were within earshot. In the dim hold, the women remained silent, listening to the rapid, half-coherent explanations the sailors of the Velvet were giving, and the confused questions of the other crew. It seemed that the tidings of Valja's unease hadn't yet spread as far as Nebe.

"When is the last time you went back?" Ardelei asked as the repetitive melodies finally began to subside.

"To Nebe? Or to my family?"

A careful pause. "I didn't know that you were still in touch with your family."

"I am not. That is why I asked. I have been to Jirda, not that long ago. Strictly business. I ordered my printing press there before I left for Haller."

"I haven't been back, either," Ardelei said, even though Rondei hadn't asked her. The lives of their rural relatives had ceased to be of interest to her long ago, when she'd found that there was a different life to be led as far away from them as possible, among people who loved words on the printed page far more than the yearly accumulation of wheat and chickens.

"We both have found new communities elsewhere. People who admire us for the things we do, and for the things we might yet achieve," Rondei said. "Why should we return to a place that has never appreciated us?"

"A damned good question, that," said a third voice from the corner.

Meropat had been awakened by the singing sailors, and was understandably confused about their present circumstances. Ardelei gave them some lukewarm tea, and began to explain the events of the past two days.

"Jirda?" Meropat asked, in a tone that made Rondei smile in sympathy. "We're certainly playing it safe, ladies."

"Playing it safe felt like an intelligent thing to do, given the circumstances," Ardelei said. "I for one have had quite enough of risking my neck for the time being."

"Besides, Jirda is a port city," Rondei felt obliged to add. "You do not need to stay there any longer than is absolutely necessary."

There was a short silence. "So I wasn't dreaming, after all. It was your voice I heard, Rondei Galsi. Come closer so I can see you." They paused. "If you dare."

As Ardelei lit a lamp, Rondei made her slow way to Meropat's bedside. The uneven light showed only half their face. Despite the years that had passed, the poet still looked the same as the last time they'd met, and their eyes had the lively sparkle that made them appear even younger. Rondei had no illusions about her own appearance: every passing season added a line or two to her face, and deepened the permanent grooves around her mouth. It wasn't vanity that made her hesitate: it was the flood of memories that the sound of Meropat's voice had suddenly unleashed.

"Hello, Rondei," Meropat said, holding her hand and slowly bringing it to their lips. "This was an unexpected pleasure."

"The pleasure is all mine," she replied. A true courtier's reply, which this time was entirely true. The cadences of the voice she'd once known so well wiped away the intervening years and brought back their shared time in a heartbeat.

Ardelei must have caught some of the intimacy of their greeting, as she didn't go on with her usual nurse's routine of asking meaningless questions about Meropat's bodily functions. Instead, she took a long look at Rondei and said, "I'll be frank with you, Meropat — I'm sure I can call you that?" After an affirmative gesture, she went on, "As we're all friends here, I can tell you that ours was a very quickly made up plan, and, like all such plans, it's leaky at the seams. Jirda is a much friendlier city than Valja, and Rondei and I will have some immunity there, being Nebians by birth. You, as I understand it, have no such connections, or any of the required travel documents."

"Papers can always be acquired," Meropat said calmly. "I'm sure our crew will know willing forgers in the docks."

"I'm sure they will. As do I, for that matter. And we aren't entirely devoid of funds." A pause. "I think for the time being it'll be safer to stick together — but a group like ours is always going to attract attention."

Meropat closed their eyes for a while. "We'll think of something."

"Of course," Ardelei touched their hand. "I'm sorry to spring this on you. You've been through a lot in the past days."

"Yes, it's been an eventful summer, even by my standards," they grinned, growing solemn just as quickly. "I just wish I could skip the last part of it altogether."

Luckily for the three of them, the crew decided to have their luncheon onboard the Velvet; thus, their journey went on at its mind-numbingly ponderous pace. Rondei found that despite her previous craving for river fish, when the mealtime came she didn't have much of an appetite. Below decks, the temperature began to rise steadily, and the stink from the bales of cloth around them didn't make the atmosphere conducive to eating at all. She nibbled on some fruit. Meanwhile, Ardelei negotiated some wine-soaked bread into Meropat, all the while recounting what she knew of the situation in Valja, and elsewhere on Ederai.

"So you don't know what happened to the Siblings?" Meropat asked. "If they're still alive, at least?"

"Nothing for certain. We don't even know if they were still in Valja when the rioting started. Let's say that they didn't make themselves conspicuous at any stage."

"I think I heard their names mentioned at some point. There was a battle at one of the gates. The Skovos were leading the attack." They closed their eyes again. "Although that's a rumor, too. How is it that when something momentous like this finally happens, a city full of printers and writers can only produce gossip and half-truths?"

"I wish I knew," Rondei said, having wondered the same thing. "Perhaps because no one can be in every place at once. One needs to decide which source to trust, and eyewitness accounts are unreliable. People are always thinking about their own concerns, and do not pay enough attention to the events around them. If you ask the witnesses of a robbery what the accused was wearing, they will all say something different."

Meropat opened their mouth to take in another piece of bread. After some meditative chewing, they said, "I'm so glad the muses chose me as their conduit. No matter how difficult it is to write poetry sometimes, I'd never make it as a journalist, or a pamphleteer. All that truth — or the search for it — just bogs you down."

"I have never found that," Rondei said. "And truth is rarely the most interesting thing about an event or an argument. It is more the different sides in any given situation. The different viewpoints people have, and the way they give their grounds."

"But however we look at it, the Cause has failed," Meropat said. They didn't sound disappointed, or even resigned.

"I wouldn't say that," Ardelei opined. Her tone indicated that she was mainly making the argument for argument's sake. "Even though the Skovos have been imprisoned; even if they've both been killed, and every one of the inner circle likewise, I'd say that their martyrdom would only add fuel to the fire they started by creating a lasting myth around their name. And if they are alive, as I very much think they are, they will keep up their fight. The Siblings don't strike me as naïve. They've prepared for setbacks like this. I rather think they've counted on them and used this first attack as a testing ground for both their people and their ideas. The Guilds were never going to take these riots lying down. The way they've hit back at the slightest provocation means that the Skovos were right all along, and that there's something rotten at the heart of Valja."

The poet was silent for a while. Rondei rather wished they'd fallen asleep. That way, she could have gotten used to their presence more easily. However, their mind was still mulling over the new information, "So, what are you going to do about all of this?" Meropat asked the mage.

"Me? As it is, I don't even have any official standing in any of the Ederaian states at the moment," Ardelei admitted.

"Which country do you have an official standing in, then?" Meropat hadn't lost their acuity, Rondei was glad to find.

"I'm currently in the employ of the Duchess. But even that isn't official."

"Interesting," Meropat said. Then, "Do the Guilds know that you're spying on them on the behalf of the Gesaian government?"

Ardelei smiled wryly at their attempt at intrigue. "I wish I had that kind of authorization." She met their eyes. "I'll be frank with you, Meropat: a couple of weeks ago I was approached by Sir Ebarilla Olvite. Do you know who I'm talking about?"

"Unfortunately, yes."

"He asked me to find you, and to extricate you from the mess you'd gotten yourself in. His words, not mine."

Meropat looked at Rondei, who could only shrug. She didn't know why Ardelei had chosen to show her hand so early in the game, either. "I see. And I'm assuming that all this talk about Jirda was sham, then."

"It's not a sham. I'm under no orders to deliver you to Sir Olvite, or indeed to anyone else. As far as I'm concerned, my work is done. You're free to go wherever you please. I'd just very strongly advise you against returning to Valja right now."

"Why should I believe you?"

"That's for you to decide, really," Ardelei made a rhetorical gesture. "I've seen only a part of the intrigue you've managed to entangle yourself in. And in a remarkably short time, may I say. I assume that the Guilds aren't the only ones who'd like to get their hands on you. Yet, as far as I can see, the Gesaian goals are less personal than they are political. It's in the best interests of the Duchess to get all of her citizens out of Valja before truly ugly things start happening."

Meropat was about to speak, but Rondei got there first. "What do you mean, ugly things? What did Sir Olvite tell you?"

"He told me nothing, of course. No spymaster worth his salt would. Neither has the Duchess seen it fit to communicate her suspicions to me. But let us just say that I've played this game long enough to see a crisis when one is due. People like Ondala din Rettimiso don't send their spymasters to help just anyone. Meddling with the judiciaries of other countries is an action that can potentially lead to conflict. As we know, the Duchess avoids conflicts at all costs."

"That doesn't sound like the Duchess I know," said Meropat.

"Foreign conflicts, at least," Ardelei amended herself. "I know that her domestic reputation is very different."

Rondei leaned back. Things were circling back to topics she'd much rather avoid right now. Yet, she couldn't help asking, "What does Ondala din Rettimiso know that we do not?"

"Let's not go there," Ardelei answered with some asperity. "That is a game we can play for the rest of our lives. But I see what you mean. She's seen the trouble in Valja coming for weeks, perhaps months, and has acted accordingly. Of course, this wasn't the first riot in the history of Valja. It wasn't even the first spot of trouble since the plague. Yet, things haven't gotten this serious in decades — and somehow the Duchess's instincts once again proved true."

"Perhaps you should get in touch with her?" she suggested. "If we have someone with that amount of foresight, I for one would like to take advantage of it."

"I will get in touch with the Duchess as soon as we get to Jirda safely. There are too many things that are converging around one city, and any scrap of information would help us right now."

"Who's 'us,' exactly?" Meropat wanted to know.

"No one," Rondei said quickly. "Ardelei is just keen to get back to her diplomatic meddling."

They crossed the Nebian border under the cover of darkness. They'd just made it to the last Sendali checkpoint by sunset, and were again screened from close scrutiny by the sheer number of other travelers, as well as by the members of the Velvet's crew. All of their faces were known to the border guards, and no one was minded to check their tedious little craft when another day under the hot sun was about to come to an end. There didn't seem to be any particular anxiety regarding Valjan vessels or the unexpected passengers they might hold; thus, the travelers assumed that no news about their escape had yet reached this part of the country.

Rondei heard the sailors exchanging routine jokes with the guards. No one felt obligated to laugh, but the relaxed nature of the conversation reassured everyone that there was nothing out of the ordinary about the Velvet's errand. In a week or so, the same sailors would make their way past the checkpoint again, this time most likely jesting about their feigned eagerness to get back home to their families.

Rondei had to admit that despite her apparent absentmindedness, Seisikei Gimse had known exactly what she was doing. She was also beginning to understand how many hidden messages — and passengers — must make their way along the river route between Valja and Jirda every year. The relaxed way in which the crew treated their presence onboard was an indication that none of this was new or surprising to the sailors.

As the banks of the Ruoke had disappeared into the darkness, the sailors had started looking for a place to moor the boat, and Ardelei had made her way on deck. Rondei had ached to follow her, but seeing her cousin's furious glance, she had quickly suppressed the impulse. Instead, she'd checked on the sleeping Meropat and had sat back down in the small corner she'd claimed for herself, wishing she'd brought a change of a shirt at least, as the current one was sticking to her back.

Her clammy clothing was the least of her discomforts, however. She understood perfectly well why Ardelei wasn't talking to her. After everything they'd been through together, and all the promises of mutual aid, Rondei had gracefully turned around and let her cousin down at the first opportunity. She did wonder how easily the words had slipped out of her mouth.

There is no us. Even though she wasn't the most communal minded of people, it wasn't like Rondei to be so blatantly callous.

Most likely, if it had been just the two of them, talking about their plans for the future, she'd never have said those hurtful things. The presence of Meropat was a welcome one, and Rondei had no regrets of having agreed to help them out of Sendal. Yet, their effortlessly charming demeanor made Ardelei appear pathetically threadbare in contrast. Whereas the poet was content to drift through life in a haze of cheap wine and compliments, her cousin was ever grasping for more influence and intrigue, not caring how desperate she appeared to the people around her.

It was perhaps this new desperation that had made Rondei hesitant about joining forces with Ardelei. Before, her cousin had been a diplomat of high standing. Someone whose very name made people stand up straighter in any room. Now, with her Linduvan immunity gone, she was just a middle-aged woman with no formal occupation, no community to back her — and what was even worse, no family to go back to.

Although having ambitions above one's birth was definitely seen as admirable, the thing that mattered most to all Ederaians was their lineage. The village and the family they were born into, and the name they bore as a sign of this inheritance. Having no family meant lacking a clear past, but it also signified having no viable future. Breaking blood ties happened often enough, but most people sought a similar community to unite themselves with, either through work or marriage. Independent agents were viewed with deep suspicion. Being able to leave one's family meant having very loose ideas about loyalty in general.

Rondei had wrestled with similar feelings often enough. Unlike Ardelei, she'd never had the opportunity to join a formal community of professionals. Instead, she'd served various apprenticeships, befriended book printers and writers, and even for a brief while toyed with the idea of marrying one of their number. Her one regret about leaving Vejel's father had been tied to the fact that her son would grow up deprived of one half of his inheritance, and a definite place to put down roots. To give her son those things, she had thought long and deeply about wedlock before coming to the conclusion that a wayward, drunken father was more detrimental than no father at all.

Time had shown her another route and given Vejel a chance to enjoy some of the things he had been denied before. Lord Stainerau would be obligated to provide him with a livelihood in Daurbar. Rondei was confident that her son would eventually find his place in the tight little Hallerian circle, and that he would be much happier there, instead of being constantly lugged around by his itinerant mother (or, by the gods, ending up onboard some leaky Nebian vessel). In Daurbar, Vejel would also be free of her associations with Sendali politics — at least for the time being. As Rondei was beginning to learn, politics was a complicated game with ever-changing rules and board designs, and a number of unexpected players and pieces dropping in and out of the game at will.

As the air began to cool, most of the crew settled down for the night. Rondei, too, gradually fell asleep. She was just drifting into the beginnings of a dream when some disturbance jolted her awake. At first, she wasn't sure what had intruded on her rest. Meropat was still slumbering in their narrow bed, and apart from the habitual creaking and popping of the vessel, everything seemed perfectly peaceful onboard the Velvet. A few minutes later, however, she heard it. A muted squeak that came from the other side of the planks she was leaning on. The splash of an oar. An order given in a low voice, in a language she half-recognized.

She was on her feet before she could form a coherent thought. Stumbling up the ladder onto the deck, she realized right away that the crew of the Velvet was unaware of the approaching danger. All hands had luckily remained onboard, despite the fact that they had moored the boat close to a small village. On all Gimse boats, the sailors were expected to guard the cargo they were transporting. Thus, in theory, one-third of the crew remained on duty at all times. Tonight, after a stressful night and a strenuous day, most of them were taking advantage of their peaceful surroundings to get a bit of extra rest.

In the dim starlight, Rondei nearly tripped over a man's legs. As he looked around groggily, ready to mutter some half-baked excuse for his inattention, she took him firmly by the shoulder and explained the situation in as few words as possible. She also opined that it would perhaps give them a small advantage if the attackers thought they were raiding a sleeping vessel. The sailor agreed, and crept towards the first mate — the only other crewmember awake.

Rondei found her cousin at the prow, fast asleep against a coil of rope. Again, she didn't have a lot of time for niceties. She put her hand lightly against Ardelei's lips so that she wouldn't make a sound waking up.

"It is me," she said.

The mage was wide awake in a heartbeat, and instinctively alive to the danger around them. "What's happening?"

"An ambush, sounds like. Another boat has sneaked up on us. The crew speaks cant, if I heard correctly."

"Shit." She got up, lithely like a cat, and cast around with her magic. "Oh yes, there they are. Are our sailors prepared?"

"They are, just about."

All around them, the sailors were in various stages of preparing their defense. Homemade weapons of various kinds — knives, hooks and sickles — glistened in the starlight. The captain, a squat middle-aged Zeiroan called Arrenterio, was loading a crossbow. The clockwork precision of the crew convinced Rondei that this wasn't the first time someone had tried their luck at robbing the vessel at night. No commands were spoken, and none were needed. Everyone moved around on silent feet, keeping an eye on the position of their comrades, and the possible entry points of the attackers.

Rondei wasn't sure, however, if the sailors had encountered these kinds of mercenaries before. It certainly took them by surprise when the darkness was suddenly rent by a lightning-flash of a spell. A young lad fell screaming, clutching at his stomach. Ardelei let out a roar, casting a shielding spell around her and rushing forward.

"Magic!" she shouted. "Keep clear of the sides!"

The sailors knew an order when they heard one. They stopped in their tracks, waiting for the mercenary mages to show themselves. The captain handed the bow to his first mate, and walked over to Ardelei for a quick consultation. Rondei started retreating back to the hold. Ardelei understood her intention, and gave her a gesture of approval. Then another spell seared across the deck, and Rondei had to drop to her hands and knees for the rest of her journey towards the hold door.

Below decks, the smell of dye was as oppressive as ever. Meropat had woken up, and was struggling with a tangled sheet. Rondei explained the situation in a few words. Both of them had by now understood that the intruders weren't after the cargo at all. They had another, much more lucrative, quarry in mind.

"Help me dress," Meropat said.

"You are not well enough to get up," she commented, while tying the strings of their shirt with trembling fingers. "And definitely not well enough to fight."

"I know that, but if it's a choice between getting killed in my bed, and dying in a shipboard fight with mercenaries, you know which one I'll choose any day."

"I see," Rondei knotted a garter as elegantly as she could in the swaying light of a single lamp. "Under the circumstances, there might not be anyone to write your epitaph."

"Oh, the epitaph's already written," they grinned, stretching out a leg to admire her handiwork. "But I would like a commemorative hymn sung at the stone ceremony. Thirty stanzas at least. One for each of my virtues."

"Ever the optimist," she responded to their smile.

Judging by the muddle of sounds coming from above, the deck was now host to at least twice as many people as the Velvet usually held. It was impossible to know who had the upper hand; yet, from the occasional flashes of light, Rondei guessed that the mages and their accompanying brutes hadn't been scared off, or even subdued, by Ardelei's efforts.

"Why do they keep doing that?" Meropat asked, looking up, as another spell flashed above their heads. "You'd think that it would be more efficient to use invisible magic, instead of advertising your position with every spell you cast."

"Now, I am no expert — and if we are lucky, you will be able to get a proper lecture on this topic from Ardelei," she said. "But the way I understand it is that some types of magic are easier to learn and require less energy than others. The kind my cousin uses is subtle, and takes years of practice to master so that it does not drain the mage completely. These kinds of electric pulses, on the other hand, can be taken out of the very air around us, and are also easier to learn to control. Plus, they are surprisingly effective, particularly when fighting at night. It is not easy to tell whence a spell comes when you are suddenly blinded, and surprised and frightened to boot."

"Fair enough. So it would be a good idea to have some illumination to fight these mages, would you say?"

Rondei, not yet understanding where Meropat's ruthless mind was going, only said, "Yes, at least theoretically. Yet, the other mercenaries are bound to have crossbows. It will not be a very intelligent move to make oneself a visible target on deck, either."

"Well, I wasn't really thinking of going on deck." They looked around them. "Do we have some more lamp oil? Could you bring it over?"

Rondei groped around until her hand met the container of oil she'd seen before. In the heat, it hadn't even crossed her mind to light more lamps than was necessary. Her eyesight was good, and she could move around in the hold by the light of the small lantern hanging over Meropat's bed. She watched with mounting horror as the poet pushed themself off the bed, and gingerly holding the container, made a beeline towards the bolts of cloth stowed tightly around them.

They sprinkled the nearest bolts with oil, making sure some of it also ended up on the floor. Then, reaching up, they carefully took hold of the lamp, and tipped it over so that its already heated oil poured over the fine Paishnali silks. The flame that had been struggling in the confines of the lamp flowed greedily into the open, bursting up and outwards in a few heartbeats.

The first bale of silk took some time to yield to the lapping flame. However, the heat from the burning oil soon persuaded the cargo to catch on fire – tentatively at first, and then in a sudden roar of flame. Rondei gagged. The smell of burning hair emanating from the bales was nearly overpowering, and billows of greasy smoke filled the small space in a matter of seconds. Meropat sat on the bed, surveying the destruction of the Gimse property with grim satisfaction.

Rondei, still coughing, took them by the arm. "You will burn the entire boat down! Is this a wise idea?"

"My dear, I have never aspired to wisdom. A long life, however, is always a thing worth pursuing, don't you think?"

Chapter 15

Nebe - Meropat

Just before being rudely awakened, Meropat had the most delicious dream. They were reclining in a fragrant Gesaian garden, with gently swaying branches silhouetted against a honeyed sky, and a cool stream tinkling somewhere in the distance. Birds fluttered by, settling to sing heartbreaking melodies just out of sight. There were other people in the garden, too. Young, lithe, and attractive, now and then glancing in Meropat's direction with their gazelle eyes, coyly inviting them to join in whatever new game they had devised.

The air carried the scent of apricots and rosewater. Whenever they reached out their fingers, a glass of cardamom wine or a sweet, fluffy cake appeared. After a while, they were beginning to wonder if they had died, and this is what the afterlife looked like. This was a disconcerting thought, but they couldn't help smiling to themself. Dying young was a tragedy, but perhaps it was more so for those left behind. Meropat was beyond pain, and fully minded to explore all the pleasures eternity had in store for them.

Then an ugly sound came tearing through the fabric of this most perfect of scenes. A voice — a decidedly living, corporeal voice — called out their name. Something cold and wet was slapped across their forehead, and in a few moments, an infernal shaking began, rattling their teeth and jostling their aching bones.

Meropat struggled to open their eyes. That action did little to elucidate the situation. All of their sensations bled into one overwhelming feeling of discomfort. "What?" they managed to ask the air around them.

"Oh, you just lie there and enjoy the ride," a voice said from somewhere above them. "We're not there yet."

No further explanation was forthcoming. Gradually, the mass of unpleasant sensations started to separate into more comprehensible portions, and their senses remembered their proper jobs. By turning their head ever so slightly this way and that, Meropat began to work out what was happening to them. The feeling of confinement and the incessant shaking were due to the fact that they had been placed in a small dogcart. Evidently, the vehicle and its unwilling cargo were now trundling along some picturesque country road. The smell of dung from the surrounding fields soon confirmed this.

The hinge-like, heavily accented voice they'd heard belonged to the driver of the cart. Although she didn't appear very talkative, now and again she hummed to her dogs to encourage them. Meropat had very soon decided against turning their head, as the smallest movement brought on twinges of pain all down their spine. Thus, the only thing they could see was a patch of lightening sky and the occasional dusty tree branch. The wet cloth that had been placed on their forehead was also impeding their vision, as well as giving off an unmistakable whiff of goat. As the journey dragged on, they tried lifting their right arm in an experimental way. But it seemed that their body had stopped following the orders of their confused mind.

After a while, they cleared their throat. "Excuse me?"

A long silence. "Yes?"

"Where are we going?"

"Oh, just to the village. We're not there yet."

"I see. And why exactly are we going there?"

Another reflective pause. "Why? Because I'm the only one with a cart big enough for your bulk, begging your pardon."

Seeing that conversation with this unseen entity would have frustrated even the most stoic of contemplative philosophers, Meropat said, "No offence taken. In my line of work, it's considered an advantage to be conspicuous."

In most cases, merely hinting at their occupation would have elicited an enthusiastic response and a slew of questions. The driver, however, remained stolidly unimpressed. Thus, there was nothing left for Meropat to do but to stare at the pearly sky above them, and try to understand the chain of events that had led to them being transported, alone and by land, towards the closest village — wherever that was.

They remembered a boat, and a sudden fire. There had been many people — Rondei Galsi and the mage Ardelei among them. The peril of the night seemed to have passed. But if they could travel this openly, and slowly, along a public road, where were their two companions? They also soon realized that they had no way of knowing how much time had passed since the moment they had decided to set the riverboat Velvet on fire.

Their memories of the night were patchy to say the least. Having only recently emerged from their previous bout of ill health, Meropat's system hadn't been able to handle the sudden high heat and the acrid, poisonous smoke that had engulfed the hold of the boat and nearly blinded them and Rondei. Their survival was indeed largely due to Rondei's quick thinking and dogged determination – as well as her strong arms that had mercilessly hauled Meropat out of bed and onto the smoking deck before the flames overtook them.

As Meropat had hoped, the violent fire had dampened the mercenaries' enthusiasm to continue the attack. The sailors, too, had suddenly found a different set of priorities. At first, they had tried to save the boat and as much of the cargo as possible, but the ravenous hunger of the fire soon made it clear that the best thing to do was to ensure that everyone escaped with their lives. As far as Meropat had seen, the mercenaries had jumped overboard like so many rats, desperate to save their own vessel from the all-consuming flames.

From that point onwards, their memory started to get unreliable. They remembered seeing Ardelei's soot-streaked face as she had tussled with a crewmember who tried to get below decks. Together with the first mate, she had finally convinced the young man that there was nothing heroic in getting himself burned along with the already doomed cargo, and managed to get him off the boat in time. By that time, the riverbank was alive with people. Most of them were crewmembers, but some light sleepers from the village had also made it to the site remarkably quickly, and were trying to understand and aid in the chaotic situation.

Why Meropat had still lingered onboard at that point, and how they had managed to finally escape the flames were questions they were unable to answer. They remembered the nearly overpowering coughing fits that had stopped them from being of any use to the crew. They had tried to stay out of the way as the sailors tossed their valuables to the shore and jumped after them. They, too, would have liked to follow the crew's example, but had feared the roiling water more than the cracking flames. Meropat didn't remember seeing Rondei at this point, but guessed that she had something to do with them still being in the land of the living.

As the jolting journey continued, they were beginning to question the point of their survival. If that morning's dream had been a glimpse of the world to come, what was the point of suffering indignations such as this? Particularly if they had sustained some unsightly injuries during the night. There was only one thing worse than losing their looks, and that was losing their mental capacities. But how could they continue to write inspiring poetry if their physical charm was ruined for life?

As it happened, their morbid musings were cut short by the sound of voices. The entire village was by now wide-awake and out of doors. Meropat could imagine that in such remote locations, exciting accidents like this took place perhaps only once in a generation. Also, Nebians were known for their hospitality. No doubt each household was preparing to open their doors and larders to the devastated crew of the Velvet.

The cart stopped, and a face appeared just above Meropat's. The familiar sight was enough to make them laugh out loud.

"Oh good, you are awake," Rondei said, somewhat sourly. "How are you feeling?"

"It's hard to say," Meropat said, truthfully. "I'm sorry I laughed. This whole situation is just too absurd, and I was so relieved to see you. I can't feel my hands."

"Oh, that is because of the bandages." Seeing their panicked expression, she quickly said, "Do not worry, nothing is broken as far as we can tell. You caught the falling mast with your bare hands. Do you remember?"

"I wish I did." They tried to get up again, but couldn't get enough leverage against the mattress at the bottom of the cart. "Listen, could you help me sit up? This is a rather undignified position to make an entrance."

Something dark flashed in Rondei's eyes again, but in the end she only smiled and said, "Certainly. Let me give you a hand."

In hindsight, sitting up may not have been such a good idea after all. Meropat's head was still reeling from the smoke, and the knock they'd gotten falling down with the burning mast. They kept their eyes closed and listened to the unfamiliar voices of at least half a dozen people negotiating Meropat's near future with Rondei. One of the first things they noticed was that Rondei spoke a Nebian very different to these villagers. It was much easier to understand her than the lilting tones of the locals.

"The Bulvis have promised to take you in," Rondei said at last, gesturing ahead of her. "They have a big, comfortable house at the other end of the village. I will check up on the others first, and then join you there."

"But," they had time to say before the printer stalked away. "What's happening? And where's Ardelei? Is she –"

"Ardelei is fine. She's always fine," she said. "But two of the sailors did not make it. The captain among them. We need to get word to their families, and to the Gimses."

"Ye gods. Was it... the fire, or...?"

"The captain collided with a spell and then took a knife to his gut. Ardelei said that there were at least three magic-users among the mercenaries. They were all either trying to get to her, or to work out where the two of us were. The second casualty was a young man who stopped one of the mages from getting into the hold. With his life."

Meropat only now realized that Rondei's right arm was in a sling. "And this?"

"A damned inconvenience," she grimaced. "But no major bones are broken, they told me. Should be fine in a couple of weeks."

Thus Meropat had a lot on their mind as the dogcart trundled through the village of Rekava. In addition to being paragons of hospitality, Nebians were also tremendously proud of their dwellings. Even the humblest houses they saw were in immaculate shape: shutters intact and gleaming with fresh paint, fences straight-backed and holding freshly shorn sheep or intently scratching chickens, and kitchen gardens and fruit trees beautifully pruned and bursting with ripening apricots and pink peaches. To the casual observer, it looked as if the plague had taken one look at the perfection of Rekava and decided to move on to less insalubrious surroundings.

The old woman driving the dogcart didn't seem particularly impressed with her native village, or at least didn't see the need to offer any commentary on it. Most of the houses were strikingly similar, and thus it didn't make a lot of sense to list the people living in them to a complete stranger. Perhaps it made even less sense to talk about those houses with discreetly boarded-up windows and hatted chimneys.

They passed the main piazza. Clean and orderly, with a dry fountain and a wooden statue of four women at its center.

Meropat had to ask. "Who are they, then?"

The old woman woke slowly from her reverie. "Ah, the carving, you mean? Just some local women. You wouldn't know them."

Fascinated by the slow circles in which their guide's mind was revolving, they persisted, "But they are significant somehow, seeing that they've been immortalized in this way, for the whole village to see."

"I suppose so." She leaned forward to sing to her dogs again. Then, "There was a flood. A big one, I mean."

"Ah." Perhaps no use asking when. In places like this, years and centuries soon blended into each other. The only real measure of time was the endless cycle of sowing, harvesting and preparing for the new growing season. "And these four saved the village?"

The driver let out a howl of laughter. Once she'd gotten her breath back, she said. "Saved? Who said anything about saving? They stole a boat and stuffed as much of their neighbors' things into it as they could, while the rest of the villagers were trying to save their crops from the rising water. Then they just floated downstream and sold the stuff in the first town."

Meropat blinked. "And did they get caught?"

"Not as far as I know."

"Did they become rich in the city?"

"How would I know? No one heard a word from them afterwards."

"So riddle me this, Nebian," Meropat said to Rondei later that day. They'd been given a very comfortable bed in the Bulvi house, and had already managed to charm the two eldest daughters to wait on them hand and foot. Indeed, the arrival of Mistress Gelsi had caused some pointed glances to be thrown in her general direction.

Rondei leaned back in her chair — a movement she immediately regretted, as it jolted her sprained arm. "Ow. There is very little to riddle. In most places, people make carvings and commission paintings in order to commemorate a remarkable person or an important event. It would seem that to the inhabitants of this particular village, the theft of a boat during one of its history's biggest floods is something to commemorate."

"Yes, but what's the moral of the story? Are the four women heroes or villains in the minds of the villagers?"

"That depends on your point of view. If it was your boat or valuables they stole, they are very definitely villains. Then again, they showed great courage and foresight in their actions. In one version of the story I've heard, the women were young sisters who had no other family to care for them. Thus they took the only route they could see to better their lives, leaving behind a village that could not, or would not support them."

The bedroom door opened without a warning, and Ardelei stepped in, wearing her habitual graceful air. The sleepless night only showed in the shadows around her eyes; yet, there was a stillness about her that hadn't been there before. She had borrowed a loose, white robe from someone in the village; the flowing garment made her look decidedly magical. She greeted Meropat warmly, and asked after their health. She didn't say anything to her cousin. Indeed, she didn't even look at her.

"Any tidings?" Rondei asked her nevertheless.

"The other wounded sailors are going to live, although one of them may lose a leg. This is a bad season for deep wounds." She met Meropat's eyes. "Is there anything I can do for you? I have some painkilling herbs, but for more specific needs you'll need to turn to the village herbalist."

"I'm all right," they said, truthfully. The only thing they really needed was some rest. And that didn't seem forthcoming in the present circumstances, or in their present lodgings. "Did you manage to capture any of the mercenaries?"

"None of them alive. They moved quickly, and with a small troop. Perhaps they thought our vessel undefended, or this was just a preliminary attack to get us onto dry land."

"Or just a ruse to frighten us," Rondei opined.

"That, too, is an option," the mage answered dryly. "The villagers have promised to get in touch with the sailors' families, and I'll send a coded message to Seisikei if I can find a trustworthy messenger. She'll find out about the fate of the boat and crew soon enough. The villagers are saying that there might be an official enquiry, and the sailors agree."

"Even though we are on Nebian soil? Is that even legal?" asked Rondei. There was definitely some coolness between the two women. Both of them addressed their remarks more at Meropat, never directly at each other.

"It is legal enough. This is a Gimse vessel, and involved in international trade. Also, as the aggressors were mercenaries from all over Ederai, this will most likely involve both Nebian and Sendali officials."

"Oh, good," Meropat said under their breath.

Ardelei responded with a sardonic grin. "Which is why, I think both of you agree, we need to talk about the next stage of our journey."

There was a reflective silence. Ardelei was clearly expecting her cousin to speak her mind, but Rondei hung back, worrying the fabric of her already frayed sling with her left hand. Thus, it was left to Meropat to break the awkward silence.

"It would seem to me that the river is now out of the question."

"For the time being, yes," the mage said. "The good news is that we are definitely on Nebian soil. Any Sendali official who has claims on our freedom doesn't stand a strong chance of dragging us back across the border. Officially, at least."

"Yes, that's what I'm worried about as well. That this isn't official business anymore."

"There is always Zeiroa," Rondei said with a quiet voice. "It might not make any sense to try for Jirda anymore, but the river does flow southwards as well."

"But not all the way across the border," Ardelei reminded

her. "I thought you weren't too fond of mountains, or of the proximity of Hallerians, either."

"I for one would rather avoid that direction," said Meropat, giving an involuntary shudder. "In Valja I was nearly caught by a Hallerian band of ruffians, and I must say that I didn't much enjoy the experience."

Rondei brightened up. "I had heard of this. Did they make any demands?"

"They didn't say, exactly. One of them pretended to befriend me. They clearly thought that the two of us had been in touch recently. That through me, they'd be able to catch sight of you. Or something like that. As I was fleeing from them, I was apprehended by the city guard. This seemed like a strange coincidence at the time. In the cells everything just got more muddled, as no one told me anything, and I began to doubt my own memory."

Ardelei had been following her own train of thought in the meanwhile. "I could get in touch with Bel. He could find a safe house for the two of you, for the time being."

"And not for you?" Rondei asked quickly.

"I have things to do. People to see. This business with the mercenaries is getting too serious to just let slide."

"So you are anxious to shed the two of us, and let us molder away in your lover's little cabin in the woods, as you go back to your diplomatic friends?"

Ardelei took a deep breath — and then another. Meropat could tell that at that moment she'd gladly launched a fireball at her cousin, but being aware of the people around her, controlled her anger. Even now they could hear their hosts moving back and forth across the house, no doubt anxious to catch any thread of gossip that was thrown their way by these exotic visitors.

"Let me remind you, Rondei, of the things you said to me not that long ago, and in full possession of your famous wits. You denied having any interest in joining me in my mission to get a deeper understanding of the undercurrents of politics and magic on Ederai, particularly when it comes to the possible link between the Brotherhood of Light and the mercenaries that we've come across quite a few times now. You've also expressed, on several occasions, the desire to return to your peaceful existence in Kaldona, among the academicians and booksellers you love so much. Despite the fact that such a public existence may have become completely impossible to you under the current circumstances. You would agree, however, that despite your selfish leanings, you do feel some loyalty towards your friend Meropat, and are concerned for their well-being. Is that correct?"

"Yes," Rondei said, drawing a deep breath.

Before she had the chance to explain herself, Ardelei stepped on her cousin's tongue, making a forceful gesture. "I think we all agree that in their present condition, Meropat isn't able to look after themself. Both of you are in need of a secluded, safe space to recover from your injuries and to hide from the Sendali authorities. I know such a place not far from here. That it is also the abode of a good friend of mine shouldn't cause any inconvenience. Apart from the fact that you, Rondei, have never liked Beldor Amsta, and indeed have never even tried to hide that dislike from me." She drew another breath. "I can live with that state of affairs. I'm just wondering if you can live without relaxing your rigid sensibilities for a moment, and accepting the aid of a person who is so distasteful to you."

"I have never said that he is distasteful," said Rondei stiffly. "Indeed, I do not know him well enough to call him anything."

"Yet you sneer at our friendship at every turn."

"Perhaps I am just wondering that if your so-called friendship is as deep as you say it is, why do you make a point of avoiding Beldor so much."

"Meaning, why I haven't set up a cozy home with him?" She laughed mirthlessly. "So it was about that, after all. You, of all people, should know that relationships are never straightforward. Particularly between people who are not entirely free."

Silence descended, dense enough to be cut with a knife. Meropat, who enjoyed good scenes as much as the next person, was just as averse to their aftereffects. Thus, it was up to them to defuse the situation. "I know Bel," they said in a mild voice. "And Heather. He does frighten me a bit, but then again, he's also saved my life at least once. I wouldn't mind staying at his place, if that is among the options. Also, if we want to understand what just happened to us, we can't afford to stray too far away from Valja right now. I for one am getting desperately tired of running away. That only makes trouble chase you faster."

Ardelei flashed them another luminous smile. "You know, I'm in complete agreement with you, Mistrum Rugolata."

Rondei looked from one face to another. "I see," was all she said.

Their stay in Rekava was going to be cut unexpectedly short, despite the village's welcoming atmosphere and intriguing folklore. When dealing with people and situations she knew well, Ardelei didn't hesitate. She contacted Bel through whichever magical means she possessed, and declared that her lover was ready to welcome them in his house as soon as the three of them could find a way to travel to him.

But no matter how determined they were to leave, Meropat's rather shaky condition meant that they still needed help in moving about. Hiring a dogcart would have been the simplest solution. The villagers, however, were in the middle of a grain harvest, and neither dogs nor carts were available for the foreseeable future.

"Of course, we can always go on foot," Ardelei shrugged. "In my opinion, moving slowly is better than not moving at all. Everyone knows about the attack on the Velvet by now. It's a wonder no more curious strangers have come to Rekava to gawk at us."

"How are your legs?" Rondei asked Meropat.

Meropat took a meditative breath, aware of the weight of the question. "There's nothing wrong with my legs. It's just that my head seems to be too heavy for my body, if you know what I mean. Every time I try to get up I feel dizzy. Even sitting is uncomfortable sometimes."

"Hm," said Ardelei, measuring their body in a few swift glances. "We might be able to do something about that. If you're willing, that is."

Fascinated by the mage's use of the plural, Meropat made an enthusiastic gesture. "At the moment, I'm willing to drink live eels if there's a chance that it makes me feel better. I'm tired of being bedridden. It's much more entertaining when there's a crowd of anxious followers behind one's door asking about one's health every half hour."

Seeing that, despite their flippancy, Meropat was actually serious, Ardelei asked Rondei to leave the room, and keep any curious onlookers out as well. Although the coolness between the two women was beginning to thaw, it was clear that the mage didn't trust her cousin to witness her more intricate magic, or its potential failure.

"Relax," she smiled. "This isn't going to hurt — and there won't be any eels involved. First, I just want to understand what's wrong with that head of yours."

They became aware of the awkward position in which they'd been sitting, and shrugged themself free of any tension. "Of course. I'm just not used to this kind of thing."

The mage laid her hand on Meropat's forehead. "No one is," she said. "Even in Arrika, magic is rarely used in healing this directly. And, as I said, I'm not a healer. I know the extent of my powers, but I really don't know how your body will respond to my magic."

Her hands were pleasantly cool against their skin, and Meropat took a deep breath as they'd been instructed to do. "I trust you."

"Good: keep breathing," she said at length. "If at any point you feel discomfort or pain, let me know. I'm trying to open up the communications between your limbs and your brain. That should happen as painlessly as possible." She touched their hand briefly. "Are you ready?"

"As ready as I'll ever be."

She walked over to the window and closed the shutters. The only illumination in the room came from the tiny cracks in the door and the wooden shutters, and a bunch of slightly malodorous rushlights burning in front of the fireplace. Ardelei had explained that this made it easier for both of them to concentrate on the music that was going to link her mind to Meropat's. She'd also talked about her magic in more detail, but Meropat's tired mind couldn't really take in the sophisticated concepts.

"Anyway, it doesn't really matter whether you understand everything that's going on. The main thing is that you trust me. Let yourself feel light and protected. Rondei is keeping watch outside the door, and I'll be right here beside you. The music you'll feel is a healing music, but it also resonates on a deeper level. In order to open the right pathways in you, I'm using the song of the elements: the air we breathe, the river-water that flows past us, the ancient soil this house rests on. You'll most likely feel overwhelmed at some point, but I'll make sure that you won't be overtaken by this music. Yet, you should also be aware that an encounter of this kind always changes both people involved in subtle ways, and often in ways we least expect." She took Meropat's hand in hers again. "Do you want to do this?"

"I do," they said, touched more by the poetry of the mage's words than the actual concepts she talked about.

"The effects of the magic won't necessarily be physical. Your mind and your spirit will respond to it in their own ways. As you know, healing doesn't depend on the body alone. If the mind resists, nothing will happen. Thus, if there are some thresholds to cross, you might find yourself feeling some mental discomfort as well. Do you understand?"

"I do," they said.

"Then we begin."

At first, nothing seemed to happen for the longest time. Meropat tried not to fidget. They remembered Ardelei's instructions, and kept their eyes closed and their ears open. The sounds in the small room came mainly from the two of them. Meropat could hear Ardelei's soft breathing, as well as their own. In a while, they began to hear their own heartbeat, as well as the regular gurgle of their stomach. This was rather disconcerting, and they decided to concentrate on the sounds coming from the outside instead: the chirrup of birds, the swish of wind in the branches, and the distant barking of dogs across open fields.

They drifted into a doze, and through it, they could somehow feel Ardelei's presence more keenly. The mage didn't move, nor did she make a sound. Yet, it felt as if she was leaning closer, watching Meropat's sleep and directing it. As the mage had talked about the different songs of individual people and places, Meropat had expected the healing to take place through actual music. They began to understand that Ardelei had been talking metaphorically. The connection that her magic created was like a song in that it was invisible and intangible, but still a clear form of communication between people.

Soon, they could feel an eddy of energy swelling up at the foot of the bed. The sensation was cool and curious, and without hesitation Meropat opened themself to it, willing the spell to touch their skin and to move gradually up their body. As a poet, they were always looking for similes to explain what they felt, yet, they'd never experienced anything like this. Stepping into a swift river was similar in some ways, but the current moving in and around their body was nothing like water. It had a presence of its own, and had Meropat so wished, it would have been denied entry to their body.

But Meropat had never been a person to say no to new experiences, no matter how disconcerting they appeared at first. Any new drug, any new person or position offered, they grasped it with both hands. They had an unquenchable appetite for novelty. But more than that, they had a craving for things that could be turned into art afterwards. Even though a new partner wasn't particularly skillful or even attractive, their very essence could serve as a part of a satirical poem on love, or something they said could be used in a tragic play. A potent wine or a heady herb could leave nasty aftereffects which could be used as a part of their poetic palette of pain.

Some time passed. Meropat had become so intertwined with the magic that it was impossible to tell where their body ended and the spell began. They didn't feel Ardelei's physical presence anymore, but sensed her through the currents of the song she so skillfully manipulated. None of it felt invasive. The air one breathes doesn't feel invasive, nor does sudden darkness at the end of a long day. Fleetingly, they thought whether dying would feel like this. Relinquishing oneself calmly to whatever came afterwards, as one does when falling asleep.

While they lost awareness of their own body, they were beginning to sink deeper into the undercurrents of their thoughts. At first, this was a pleasant enough experience. Fleeting images of people and places passed across their mind's eye. Snatches of songs and conversations rushed past their ears. Gradually, the happy memories began to give way to decidedly painful ones. They traveled further and further into the past. The deeper they went, the more grating grew the undertone of these interactions.

Look where you're going, clumsy child!

Useless, you are — and always will be. What were the gods thinking when they gave me this lump of a grandchild?

If you'd stop to think about something other than your belly for a moment, you might learn something worthwhile.

Oh yes. I knew you would get in this kind of trouble. That seems to be your only true talent, does it not?

People leaned over them. Tutors and servants, relatives and neighbors – even people who they'd regarded as friends. All of them tangibly disappointed and disillusioned with Meropat's very person. For once, their famed tongue remained mute. Their face contorted into a mask of rebellious shame.

They floundered, desperate to escape the flood of images and voices, but there was nowhere to go. The memories were more physical. They tasted of iron, and fastened ever-tightening bands around Meropat's chest. Their heart beat frantically, as if trying to break through their ribs. It was getting harder to breathe. It was impossible to speak. Although they knew that the person being berated wasn't their adult self, the same indignant helplessness that had gripped them as a child now descended on their body with overwhelming force.

There was pain — and there was only one way to escape it.

Ardelei laid her cool hand on Meropat's sweating brow. Through her song-sense the mage could feel some of the struggle that had taken place behind the closed lids, and understood Meropat's need to shut themself away from it — and from the world at large.

"I told you this wasn't going to be easy. One's past has a habit of sneaking up on one, and you were right. Running away isn't the wisest option. I know you're strong enough to confront it. I just wish you knew that, too."

She got up and closed the door lightly behind her.

Chapter 16

Sendal - Ardelei

A **slow** drizzle began to fall. The forest around them seemed to pause in anticipation before opening itself up to the precious drops of water. The whirr of cicadas stopped; birds landed on branches to shelter from the rain. The path under Ardelei's feet was dusty and knotted with roots. Soon the surface would turn to a slippery mire, making their progress even slower.

She turned to her companions. "Let's stop under that oak there and have a bite to eat. We've come a good way already, I think." She tried to check the false heartiness in her voice, but didn't quite manage it.

Rondei only glanced at her, and after a while nodded. She put her arm around Meropat's shoulder, whispering something encouraging in their ear. The poet didn't look up. They continued walking listlessly — just like they'd done all day.

"Listen," Ardelei said to her cousin as they'd finished their frugal meal. "Healing takes different paths for different people. The mind and the body are intrinsically linked. Trying to fix one without the cooperation of the other gives only short-term results. Meropat knew this, and they still wanted to go ahead."

"You have taken their spirit away," Rondei said, her eyes growing darker. "That is what it seems to me."

"It breaks my heart, too, to see them like this. However, I can tell that behind the silent façade, there's a lot going on. Meropat's spirit is still very much there – it's just otherwise employed at the moment. Trust me, they'll surface soon. Most likely eager to write an epic poem about the experience."

"You take all of this very lightly," Rondei said, regarding her fingertips. "Do you feel no responsibility at all?"

"All healers feel enormous responsibility at all times, mainly because it's not just the patient themself they need to deal with. It's their loved ones as well, and often those people are much more difficult to handle. That's one of the reasons I chose not to pursue that particular career. I don't like my choices challenged over and over again."

Rondei didn't speak. Ardelei knew from the timbre of the silence that the conversation wasn't over. She took a sip of water and watched pewter-colored clouds chasing each other across the leaden sky. The rain was abating, but the wind coming directly from the mountains had a keen bite to it.

"I do love them," Rondei said at last.

"I can tell," she said.

"It is not easy to explain, even to myself. It was not easy to accept at first. I am not sure I accept it entirely even now." She paused to think, lightly raking the ground with the fingers of her good hand. "I suppose that when it comes to the people I love, I am very possessive. Meropat, however, is a free agent, always will be. I thought it would be all or nothing. Now, I am thinking that remaining friends is better than not seeing each other at all." She pressed her hand over her trembling lips. "I do not know why I am telling you this."

She embraced Rondei briefly, mindful of the sprained arm. "I'm glad you did. And I do understand at least some of what you're saying. People like clarity: clear borders, written-down rules, unambiguous relationships. I suppose that's why most people marry and settle down to live together. That way, their lives are much easier to explain — to themselves and to other people." She met Rondei's eye. "But then there are relationships that are much more difficult to delineate. Most friendships aren't definite. They're not based on a contract, or shared blood or property, or even on an easily defined feeling. They're not dependent on time or proximity. You can meet someone once every five years, and still consider them a good friend. Friendships are not possessive; that's why I've always preferred them to any other relationship. They're more flexible — much more forgiving than a romantic relationship, and less demanding than a familial one."

"That is because you are freer than most. You have had opportunities most people can only dream of. You do realize that?"

"Of course. But so have you."

"I suppose so. But in my line of work a certain respectability is expected. I cannot live like Meropat, even if I was so inclined."

"I know what you're talking about. My line of work used to be similarly restricted. And I'm not talking about just sleeping around with anyone, and calling them friends. I'm talking about a bond that develops naturally between people who are fond of each other and who often have a lot of things in common, but who don't want to put an official seal on that relationship. Who appreciate freedom over commitment."

Both women stopped to glance at Meropat, who had made a curious noise. All the while, they'd seemed completely unresponsive to the world; all through the preparations for the journey they'd sat on their bed, staring at their feet. Once goaded out the door, they'd followed Rondei like a particularly dull sheep. Not once looking around them, or exchanging farewells with the villagers who'd come to see them off. All this time, they hadn't uttered a word, or tried to express themself in any other way.

Even though they'd not said a word, it was clear that they'd heard and understood the conversation. Meropat's face was a study in compassion; a single tear rolled down their cheek. But when they saw the two cousins looking, they wiped their nose with a tired hand and continued staring into the distance.

"I know you can hear us, Meropat," Ardelei said. All the while, she was using her music to carry them, to soothe them, and to make them feel less isolated. She could feel their own song responding to hers, even if reluctantly. "You're not alone: you're among friends."

"I – I do not know what to say," whispered Rondei, still visibly moved. "Perhaps I have said too much already."

"You haven't. Whatever happened between you two in the past is now gone. Both of you have built your lives independent of each other, and most likely will continue to live apart after this. Yet, I don't believe this meeting was a coincidence." She spoke instinctively, and the words seemed to flow from some deeper place within her. "All this time I've thought that it's the two of us who should work together for the good of Ederai. Perhaps I've been wrong. Perhaps it's the two of you. Meropat is a poet. You are a printer. Together you can truly move the hearts and minds of people anywhere."

Rondei was shaking her head. "I do not believe in coincidences. That does not mean that there is no weight to our meeting at this most unpredictable of moments. There are larger forces at play that are drawing like-minded people together: it does not need to be any more significant than that. And for that reason, I do not believe that the two of us need to work separately." She looked fearlessly into Ardelei's eyes. "I am not a particularly brave person. I always seek to save my own skin, and to cover my tracks just in case. That is why I told you the other day that I was not interested in this venture of yours. I was deeply afraid of how it might affect me and my career. I realize now that there is no going back to my sheltered, isolated life. That is the worst thing I can do to myself right now. No one can truly work alone, not even a writer. Particularly a writer."

"I agree."

"I have also been a hypocrite." She drew a deep breath to steady herself. "I have been trying to distance myself from the Skovos and their desperate little revolt. For a while, I felt ashamed of my association with them. But you are right: I chose my path long ago, and I need to walk along it with my head high, accepting the travel companions who are also taking this tortuous route. I cannot expect to receive money from the Guilds with one hand while writing against them with the other."

A blue hawk circled the edge of the forest. Ardelei watched it hover effortlessly on the restless air, and then plunge down in a heartbeat. When it rose again from the long grass, it was carrying a mole in its beak.

Rondei had also witnessed the hunt. "We need to go back to Valja, do we not?"

"I think so. Eventually, at least. But first we need to hear the latest tidings, and decide whether we are truly needed there."

"It would not surprise me if the Guilds have decided to close the gates again. That, at least, would give everyone time to think twice about the efficacy of rioting as a form of protest."

"It could also give rise to a lot more discontent," Ardelei argued. "The situation was very different during the plague. Then, everyone in the Eastern Islands was more or less living under the same strange rules, and became much more tolerant of uncertainty. Now, only Valja insists on following those rules, and restricting their own citizens."

"The Cause will need some time to regroup, too," said Rondei after a while. "Particularly if the Skovos are now out of the picture. They do not strike me as people who have planned so far ahead to name deputy leaders."

"There'll always be people clamoring to be leaders. Also, the Siblings have more foresight than you think." She got on her feet. "But once I get you two to Bel's place, I'll start making my enquiries. It's the fate of the Skovos that interests me the most."

Meropat said nothing. Yet, for the first time during this journey, they got up without any prompting from their companions.

They arrived at the small lake by sunset. This time, too, Heather had managed to track down Ardelei, and was enthusiastically guiding them home. The cabin was in total darkness, and there were no signs of recent habitation anywhere nearby. There were no discernible paths across the yard, and tufts of grass were beginning to push themselves through the porch. Yet, Ardelei found a broom leaning against the door: a message to anyone passing by that the occupant was away, but would return soon. Heather, too, was eager to come indoors, and it was this sign that most reassured Ardelei of Bel's imminent return.

The kitchen was well stocked, and after some bickering, Ardelei agreed to take on the cooking responsibilities. Meropat had again turned their attention to their toes, and Rondei pointed out that having only one functional arm, she wasn't the best choice for a cook.

"Anyway, I do not much care what we eat, as long as it is warm." She thrust her hands towards the fireplace that was flickering to life.

"I remember vividly you caring very much, on numerous occasions," Ardelei said in an undertone; yet, there wasn't much rancor in her answer. She was happy that Rondei had trusted her enough to confide in her — a rare occurrence in their long relationship.

Heather was watching her intensely. Now and again, the dog's ears would flick sideways, and her nose would twitch. From these signs, Ardelei could tell that Bel wasn't far away; otherwise, the dog would either have gone out to look for him, or would have lain down to sleep in the meanwhile. Thus, she wasn't at all surprised when someone walked across the porch with a light step, and the door creaked open.

"Well," Beldor said, pausing on the doorstep. Heather was in his arms in a flash, licking his face and moaning with puppyish abandon. The dog's unrestrained emotion made the humans feel less self-conscious in turn.

Ardelei put down her ladle and reached her arms around Bel. They rarely met in the company of other people. Yet, it felt completely natural to kiss him on the mouth in full view of her two other companions. "It's good to see you. And I'm glad that we could come here on such short notice. Things have been somewhat... unpredictable lately."

"I can see that," he grinned at her. "I don't think I've ever seen your hair this long. Something drastic must have happened to make you so slovenly."

She touched her head, which did feel unusually woolly. "I might borrow your razor tomorrow, if you don't mind." Then she turned to Rondei. "You two have met, haven't you?"

"We have," her cousin said. "And I want to thank you, too, Beldor, for extending your hospitality to us."

Bel touched her outstretched hand, and muttered something about his host's duty. His eyes had already fallen on the hunched figure of Meropat.

"Meropat has had the most difficult time of us all, so you must forgive if they don't get up to greet you," Ardelei said. "They still need some time to process what's happened."

"I understand," he said. He walked to Meropat's side and put his hand on their shoulder. "I've heard only some scraps of tidings from Valja, but what I've heard tells me that this person has achieved great things in a very short time." He met Ardelei's eye. "And also that they are keenly expected in the capital."

"Expected by whom?" Rondei wanted to know.

"By friends and strangers alike. Also, as I understand, by the Skovos."

"So they are alive after all," said Ardelei. She wasn't surprised. People like the Siblings tend to land on their feet. "How do you know all this?"

"I have my sources." At her irritated gesture, he continued,

"Since the gates opened, people from the nearby villages have started making trips to Valja to sell their wares. Mainly so that they can listen in on the city gossip, and gawk at the ruins of the burned buildings. I doubt many of them have sold anything. The Guilds don't let just anyone hawk their wares openly. Also, it's not wheat and apricots the citizens want, but good clean glass and solid bricks so that they can start rebuilding their houses and shops."

"So have the Skovos actually been seen?"

"They seem to be fairly conspicuous around the city, aye. Definitely bolder than they were before. Bolstered by their battle scars, and the new songs that they've taught everyone to sing." Once again, his eyes were on Meropat.

"And what songs would those be, then?" Ardelei had to ask, even though she already knew the answer.

"There's one song in particular," he said with a strange cadence. "It's called 'The Last Harvest'. A farmhand sang it to me, fresh out of Valja. That blasted song hasn't left my ears since."

"Well, the tune is well known," Ardelei tried.

"So it is. But it's not the tune on its own. It's the whole song, all twelve stanzas of it. The words fit the melody perfectly, and to follow each other so naturally that it only takes one hearing to learn the whole thing. Also, it seems that once you've heard it, you can't get it out of your head." They cast a dark glance at Meropat. "That's a spell if I ever knew one."

Although Ardelei had been initially keen to travel to Valja, once she and her companions had settled in the cabin, she found herself reluctant to leave. Bel had brought them tidings enough. They knew that the capital had opened its gates, and was trying to appear as unruffled as possible. There were guards in the streets, and everyone's documents got inspected on a regular basis. There was no talk of the foreign mercenaries whatsoever. The Siblings were, again, mustering their followers. And this time they were much more reckless in their rhetoric. Everyone who had heard their latest speeches knew that they weren't afraid to challenge the Guilds head-on. And there were a lot of speeches, some of them on piazzas and other public spaces. There were also more traditional methods of getting the message through to the citizens.

"It's still illegal to print and distribute political pamphlets," Bel was saying, "and to spread anti-Guild news through the press. However, that's never stopped people before, and it definitely won't slow the Skovos down now. You can copy texts without a printing press. You can broadcast messages by whistling them from the rooftops, or just tapping them out on the walls of buildings." He glanced at Meropat. "Of course, the most effective way of all is to put your message into song form, and to teach it to everyone you meet."

The poet didn't answer. While they were slowly recovering their speech, they still didn't like to talk about the Cause, or their own involvement in it.

Rondei was wiggling the fingers of her injured hand. The talk of printing clearly reminded her of the nimble work she was capable of. "Surely, the guards all got eyes and ears, too?"

"It's not possible to be everywhere at once, or to arrest everyone. The citizens have also grown less tolerant about the guards' interference, and have been known to fight back if they think they're being unjustly treated. And even though the Siblings themselves are bolder, many of their followers are still secretive and careful with their own safety, which is clever. That way, the guards have no way of telling how many people are actually involved."

"It's the mercenaries I'd be more worried about," Ardelei said.

Bel's informants had had no information about the unofficial guards. No one had reported meeting any rogue magic on the streets of Valja. Then again, it often took a mage to recognize another. "What are you planning to do about them?" he asked.

"Me?" she scoffed. "Alone, nothing. Particularly as I have no official standing in Sendal, let alone in the eyes of the Guilds. I've also managed to aggravate one of the highest-standing judges in the land. I think the rest of the judiciary won't be too happy to work with me, either."

"You're still thinking like a Linduvan," Bel said, raising an eyebrow. "You're still following the rules."

"It's hard to stop after all these years," she said. Yet, she understood his point. As a freelance mage, she'd need to start thinking outside the official code of her order. "But I believe I still have some friends who can help us. People who know the rules well enough to be able to break them at will." After a while she added, "And I don't think I need to be in Valja to investigate where these rogue mages come from. In fact, it may be an advantage to be able to roam outside the city gates for once."

"Do you think the Duchess would be interested?" asked Rondei, who had always been fascinated by Ondala din Rettimiso, and who seemed to find an opportunity to introduce her into every conversation with Ardelei nowadays.

Meropat scoffed at her. "That woman is only interested in money." Their voice was lower and huskier than before, which added a certain gravitas to their words.

"When was the last time you met her?" asked Ardelei, not unkindly. "She is a skilled politician, and politicians need to be thinking about finances at all times. Without taxes there is no state. And without a state there are no politicians. However, I've also found her interested in the lives of her people in a way that many rulers aren't. People, after all, are even more important to the state than taxes."

"Exactly," they said. "She looks after her own taxpayers. Why should she be interested in this puny island, then?"

"She's interested in Ederai because this island and hers are stuck together. The Strait doesn't divide us; it brings us together as long as there are ships to navigate it." This was a rather elementary piece of political theory; thus, she thought it better to elaborate. "Ondala has always kept a keen eye on the way our negotiations work, and has implemented some of our tactics in Gesaia as well, as you well know. A peaceful neighbor is a boon to a country whose main interest is in trade. Thus, if that peace is threatened from within — or worse, by Gesaian agents — then it's no wonder that the Duchess should want to extend her interest farther into our politics."

"So you're saying that it's the Brotherhood of Light that's been causing all of this havoc?" Bel asked her, in his infuriatingly calm voice.

She, too, put on her best diplomat's demeanor. "I'm suggesting that some of this havoc might be caused by outside agents. But not by the entire Brotherhood, by any means. There's nothing in their code that would justify meddling with the running of foreign countries. Eriai l'Oremel is ever swearing his neutrality, and his wish to dedicate his life to his faith. I for one believe him."

"So where do we start?" Rondei asked, looking into each face in turn.

Ardelei rested her head in her hands for a moment. "A few days ago, I was ready to rush back into Valja to see how things stood there. Now, I'm not sure if that's necessary. It's very easy to get sucked into the concerns of the capital when you're inside the city walls, and forget what's going on outside. We've also learned that it's very easy to get sucked into a revolt once you're in close proximity with rebels. Valja is not the best place to think, or to negotiate. Nor is it the best place to understand how the different strands are connected." She stared at the tabletop. "But wherever we are, we need more people and information. I'd like to get in touch with Ebarilla Olvite, for one."

"Do you think he'd tell you anything?" Bel had had his run-ins with spies before. "You may end up doing his bidding, rather than the other way round."

"I did what he asked me — or what the Duchess asked me, which is effectively the same thing — and although I've already been paid for my services, I'm confident that I could get something relevant out of him in return."

Meropat was drawn into the conversation again. "So it really was the Duchess who wanted you to follow me. What else did she want?"

"Nothing," she answered simply. "I told you before: she only wants you safe."

"And I told you before that there's always more to that woman than meets the eye. And to Master Olvite, too." They laced their long fingers together nervously. "They both want me back in Gesaia — back under their watchful eyes."

"They'll find a way to keep an eye on you, wherever you go. And that's not necessarily a bad thing, considering your circumstances," Ardelei said. "Although you've tried to shed your family ties, you can't shed who you are."

"None of them understand who I am," they said, defiantly. "They never did."

"Who are you, then?" Rondei asked in a quiet voice.

Meropat looked up at her, surprised. Behind the simple question lay a quite serious challenge. Then, licking their lips, they said, "I just meant that I'm not the person my family expected me to be. Rugolatas have always been interested in money and power. Nothing else matters. Marriages are contracted on the basis of wealth and status alone. Children are only appreciated if they're worth something to their parents. Friendships are fostered only among like-minded and equally wealthy people." They took a deep breath. "From very early on, I realized that I was made differently. I had an inner drive to express myself through means other than money. I had a talent that couldn't be quenched by the people around me."

"And you had magic," Ardelei said. This was a statement, not a question.

Meropat took it as such. "Yes. I suppose you could call it that. I've always had this flame burning inside of me that has made me more sensitive to the finer things in life. Again, my family didn't understand it, or was unable to measure its worth. Thus, they tried to extinguish it. Through any means possible."

Rondei lay her hand on theirs. "Is that not one of the tenets of the Brotherhood, too? That most magic is harmful and should be discouraged?"

"It is," Meropat said. "Although my family has never claimed to be particularly religious. But they did find ideas like this useful."

Ardelei said, "I don't agree with the Brotherhood in that magic should be stamped out of secular life altogether — mainly because that's impossible. But from what I've seen, I also know that rogue magic is truly harmful. If not to other people, then at least to the person who bears it in secret. Have you ever had any training in how to control this power?"

They scoffed. "Who would have trained me?"

"So you've suppressed it?" At their assenting gesture, she went on, "As you said, you've probably used it to fuel your creativity — and, may I say, your rather excessive lifestyle." She smiled to show that she wasn't entirely serious. "I mean, not everyone can lead a life of such extravagant self-indulgence well into their middle years and get away with it. Yet, you look like a person barely out of school."

"How old are you, exactly?" Bel wanted to know.

Meropat glanced down, abashed. "That is a rude question, even among friends." In a smaller voice, they continued, "I was born in the spring of the year 200."

"You're only two years younger than me!" Ardelei exclaimed. Then, narrowing her eyes at the poet, she said, "Yes, there's definitely some spellcraft at work here." Seeing Meropat's continuing embarrassment, she added, "None of this is your fault — I'm not saying that it is. You've perhaps found the safest way to burn off excess magic. Some people turn aggressive because they can't handle the aimless energy. Some dull their senses with drugs. You make beautiful things for people to enjoy."

They beamed at her.

"And yet," she said. "This song of yours shows that magic can very easily get out of control. There are laws in many countries against spells like this. And even if they're legal in Sendal doesn't mean that this kind of behavior should be encouraged."

"It is just a bit of poetry," Rondei tried.

"You're cleverer than that, cousin. It's a piece of propaganda. It's a call to a revolt. And it's inciting the people of Sendal as we speak." As no one answered, she went on. "There are also other risks — more personal ones. You've probably had moments when you've felt that your creativity has abandoned you altogether, and not understood why?"

"Only once," they admitted. "This summer. It was strange: my mind has always overflowed with ideas, and it's only been a matter of sitting down and getting the words onto the page fast enough. Then, suddenly it was all gone. I mean, I could still write mediocre things when I absolutely had to, but the true inspiration was gone."

"I'd rather say that your well of magic had run dry for the moment," Ardelei said. "And like a physical well, it needed time to refresh itself. A trained mage knows how to regulate this flow."

"Or maybe someone had tried to poison the well," Bel said, only half-jokingly.

"I wouldn't be surprised," she answered. "Yet, magic is a natural resource. You can only extinguish it by extinguishing the mage."

Meropat placed a hand at their throat. "That did nearly happen, too."

Later that evening, Rondei went around the cabin, lighting candles and adding oil to the lamps. Her narrow face, illuminated by the unsteady flicker of the flames, showed deep grooves around the mouth. Yet, her coal-dark eyes glittered with a new fire.

"We have a lot of work to do, cousin," she said.

"You seem happy about it," Ardelei replied.

Rondei laid another candlestick on the table. Both of them knew what Ardelei had left unsaid: *For a change*. "I suppose I am. But then, I am used to working — having my hands full at all times."

"Do you feel ready to start writing again?"

"I am not sure." She sat down opposite her cousin. "I feel that right now, no matter what I write, my texts will have little impact. Particularly to the members of the Cause. They have chosen their path, and will not step off it at my command."

"What about the academicians?"

"What about them?" she scoffed. "They have always regarded me as their little pet, as someone to show off to their foreign colleagues. A self-taught writer who fancies herself an academician! No," she shook her head. "I have trod that route, too, and it has proven an empty diversion. I want to do something more... original," she said.

"If you ask me, everything you do is original," Ardelei smiled, briefly touching her hand. "But I see what you mean. So far, I've had the support of the Linduvans to fall back on – but I've chafed against their rules at times, too, as well as the usefulness of my own contributions to the greater good. If there even is such a thing. I don't think I can settle down to serve another cause, or a community — at least not before I've carefully weighed my own place in the world. There is a myriad of ways of making a difference."

Rondei cracked open a book. Still, Ardelei could see that her eyes kept following the same line over and over, and she didn't once turn the page.

Finally, she looked up. "Are you going to write to the Duchess soon?"

"I think I must. All the roads seem to be leading to Gesaia this summer."

"Good," Rondei said, the corner of her mouth twitching. "I have not been to Gesaia."

Chapter 17

Sendal - Meropat

T**he night** was wondrously still. The lake reflected the splendor of the starry sky; not a ripple marred the silver perfection of its surface. Now and then a bird called from deeper within the woods, its voice soft and soothing like the sound of water itself. The trees lifted their tired branches towards the heavens, their leaves tinted with various shades of gray and blue. There was a curious dusty smell to the cooling air that mingled with the scent of some late-blooming flowers.

Meropat breathed deeply, drinking in the peacefulness of their surroundings as if it were a healing potion. All the while, they were trying to keep themself open to the scene, waiting for their inner magic to connect with the enchanting world outside. Ardelei would have told them that magic didn't work like that. It wasn't possible to tap into a landscape as one tapped a barrel of wine for its matured contents.

Yet, Meropat was a poet, and their very soul responded to the lyrical scene with instinctive greed. Had they been asked, they would have written a circular Zeiroan sonnet about their lakeside experience in a matter of moments. They'd always thought this was merely an expression of their inborn talent, honed to perfection by years of practice. A gift from the gods, if you like, polished and kept razor-sharp for daily use. A part of them had suspected that there was more to this flow of language than met the eye. Still, they'd suppressed that voice, leaning into the praise and the patronage, and wilfully forgetting that the flame that burned so brightly within them could one day turn into a raging wildfire that destroyed everything they held dear.

They stretched their fingers, and then slowly dipped their right hand into the midnight lake. The water was like velvet against their skin. Although they were still feeling the aftereffects of all the violence they'd been subjected to, their physical body was healing at a remarkable rate. This, too, Ardelei attributed to their inner music, and the way it ran uninterrupted through their veins. A less fortunate person, they knew, would have been laid low for months, perhaps never to rise again. Meropat felt tired and sore, but otherwise unhurt.

This, however, was only true of their body. Their mind had taken a more severe battering – and also a heavy reshuffling at the hands of the Linduvan mage. For the first time in years, they'd been forced to confront the voices that had implanted themselves in their head, constantly telling them that they were worthless and hopeless — too clumsy, too loud, too much for anyone to take. Definitely too ungainly for anyone to love.

Although they'd been able to suppress these voices over time, they were never fully driven out. Sometimes, in the night, when they'd just fallen into the deepest of sleep, a fragment of a memory would leak from its careful isolation and jolt them into wakefulness. A half-seen face, or a half-heard voice could throw them straight back into their Gesaian schoolroom, making them feel the pain of humiliation all over again.

A large bird flew across the lake with heavy wingbeats. Meropat didn't recognize the bird. They'd always enjoyed nature in its abstract form, not in its grimy particulars. They'd always been a city person, anyway. In a city, the only live birds you learned to recognize were the pigeons and the sparrows. It was more important to develop an appreciation of the different types of poultry on your plate, and learn the best sauces and wines to go with each one.

They dried their hand on a tattered trouser leg and hunched forward. Despite its breathtaking beauty, there was something depressing about the expectant emptiness of the scene and the monotony of the birdcall from the woods. The austere silence of the cabin wasn't much better. They missed the chaotic jolliness of the boarding houses of Valja, where people of all kinds kept dropping in, bringing their songs and stories with them. Even during the hardest plague months, there had always been someone to talk to, or to sing with, even if it was through the paper-thin walls of the by-then then private bedrooms.

Ardelei had been right, however. Although they could always return to the bustle of a city, and claim their place in it, there was no going back to their old carefree habits. They weren't a young person anymore. Although years still hung lightly on them — most days, at least — they were aware of the inevitability of middle age. They'd seen enough powdered, tinted old people to know that trying to mask the effects and responsibilities of time doesn't make a person young: it only makes them ridiculous. It was much better to learn to carry one's age with pride. After all, the past ten years of their life had been the best so far. Who could measure the delights that were still to come?

There was also the other, much more delicate issue — the knowledge that they could even now only touch with a fingertip, to peer at around a corner. Through their magic, they'd unleashed something uncontrolled into the world. A poem, a piece of magic, written on a scrap of paper and pushed through the window of their prison cell. A piece of propaganda so catchy that anyone who heard it had to sing it from start to finish, and then teach it to someone else.

In a way, this was what they'd always dreamed about. Fame and recognition. The creation of a poem so powerful that it gripped the heart and mind of anyone who came across it. But as always, the real-world embodiment of a dream was somehow more grotesque than its imagined original. It hadn't been their intention to force people to listen to this wretched rhyme, let alone sing it at street corners night and day. The words may ring true, but the message hadn't come from their own heart. It was a cunning piece of spellcraft that rode on someone else's passions. Meropat didn't even know who'd picked up their desperate message and thought of setting the poem to the best-known tune of the day.

While they sat and pondered their future, there was a curious sound from the trees, as if the entire forest had decided to fall silent at once. The reason for this silencing soon became obvious. Heather made her way to the lakeshore and drank noisily, sending widening ripples towards the middle of the water. She was aware of Meropat's presence, of course; the night-gray dog sauntered lazily up the deck, and then unceremoniously pushed her wet muzzle into their face.

"I do beg your pardon," Meropat chuckled as they wrestled the dog's head away. "I'm not your personal handkerchief." Then, as she continued rubbing herself on their person, they changed register to the colloquial. "Heather: ew!"

The dog settled down next to them with a dramatic sigh. She sat gazing at the lake for a while, and then lay down, huffing out another long breath.

"I do envy you sometimes," they said to the dozing dog, caressing the rough pelt on her back. "You know who you belong to, and what your duties are. Bel loves you like few people love their children. You rush off into the trees after a scent, but always come back as soon as he calls. No wonder why people admire your kind so much."

Heather, as was her habit, didn't answer. Yet, there was something in her silence that suggested that she didn't entirely agree with Meropat.

"Yes, I see your point," they said after a moment's reflection. "You live in a world of smells and sounds we humans can't possibly decode, or even sense. I suppose there's poetry in that world as well — and conflict."

The dog twitched her ears. The two of them shared the silence for a while.

Then it was Meropat's turn to draw a deep sigh. They continued talking, as if their point continued logically from the previous one. "I think I'd quite like to settle down. Or at least at the moment it feels like it, you know? Moving around all the time has been good fun, but it's getting harder and harder to part from the people and places I've grown fond of. Even now, I long for Valja. Even though the city I used to know doesn't exist anymore. It's funny. During the plague, I dreamed of the day when the gates would open and I'd be free to travel again. I swore that I'd never even piss in the direction of that wretched city. When that day came, I really didn't know where to go. At first, it didn't feel safe. Then, it just didn't feel right. So I stayed on. Now, the world is wide open to me." They paused. "Or at least most of it is. I can go anywhere. I still have a lot to learn, and a lot to give. And I don't want to be stuck in a provincial town like Valja for the rest of my existence."

"There are worse places than Valja," Bel said. He had also stalked noiselessly out the forest, and sat down on the other side of Heather, who greeted him with a low, contented growl before falling straight back asleep. "But I see your point. Now, I'm not an artist myself, but Sendal doesn't strike me as a particularly nurturing place for those who like to think for themselves, or try out new things."

"But you need people like us to teach others how to think," Meropat said. "Of course, that's often less rewarding than getting constant praise from people who claim to understand your every word." As Beldor didn't go on, they felt confident to add, "I really enjoyed my time with the Siblings and their followers. They might not be the most sophisticated of people, but there was an almost childlike openness among them for new ways of thinking and being. You understand how rare that is, particularly among the working folk?"

"I do. But then again, there are people like that everywhere, even among the workers. Particularly now, when many of us are questioning the old rules and practices." He rubbed his bristly chin. "Valja is a good place for an open revolt, as there are the Guilds and their laws to revolt against. Having a clear enemy unifies any group of people in a matter of moments." He tossed a pine cone into the lake with a plop. "It wouldn't surprise me if the Siblings' ideas would start spreading across the country – but not every community has such inflexible rules to rebel against, and such strong walls to batter down."

"So you're saying that change is impossible."

"Not impossible: never that. Change is inevitable. Steering its course, on the other hand, is like trying to divert a river by throwing a single stone in it." He reflected for a while, and then elaborated on the metaphor he'd invented. "But if you throw a stone in the same place every day, you might be able to build a dam in a few years. If all the people in your village do the same, you'll get results faster."

"You might just flood the fields if you're not careful."

"There's always that risk," Bel grinned. "And that's the risk you take every time you seek to change the course of your life — or the lives of others. No one can foresee the future. Not even the most astute of Linduvan mages have been able to work out a reliable method of divination."

Meropat rubbed their eyes. The metaphysical topics were starting to weigh on their already harassed mind. "So, what about your future? Will you and Heather stay here for long?"

"Who knows?" the diplomat said. "I go where I'm needed. Some years ago I made a bargain with the people of the nearby villages that I would act as their negotiator. I've continued to honor that agreement. Still, the things I've heard recently have made me question my own standing here." He took a careful breath. "And the things Ardelei has told me have made me even less certain that I want to tie myself down for much longer."

Meropat shifted carefully. They'd rarely heard Beldor talk

about their own life or plans at this length. It was perhaps the expectant silence of the night that made both of them eager to reflect on their choices. That, and the fact that the two cousins were now constantly speculating and arguing about the best course of action. "Are you going with Ardelei, then?"

He was silent for a long time. This was the Beldor Meropat knew better: the man who always weighed his words carefully, and only spoke when there was no other option. "I might. It depends on where she's going. Heather's not too keen on boats."

At the sound of her name, the dog wagged her doughnut of a tail.

"Do you really think she'll go to Gesaia? To serve the Duchess?"

"You make it sound like some sort of betrayal. Ardelei and Ondala din Rettimiso have known each other for a long time, and they've built their relationship on mutual trust and mutual usefulness." He met Meropat's eyes. "Just because you've grown wary of your homeland doesn't mean that everyone else should avoid going there altogether."

"Is that one of your diplomat's phrases?" they teased.

"No. But if you pay me enough, I can give you a few to make you feel better. You're an artist," he continued with a friendlier tone of voice. "You only need to consider the needs of your current patron. We diplomats learn to keep an eye on the bigger picture at all times. Follow currents of thought. Sniff out patterns in the movement of people. Ardelei is an excellent diplomat, and she's keen to follow her instincts on this matter."

"I may be just a humble poet, but as you said, I understand matters of patronage. And as I see it, Ardelei Jolama is without a patron at the moment."

"You fear she might start working exclusively for the Rettimiso house? I find that hard to believe. Ardelei is a woman of strong loyalties, and one thing she's always held dear is her connection to this land. Even when she lived on Luneken, she was Ederaian through and through. That, as I understand it, is the foundation of her magic."

Meropat decided to drop that particular topic, as the mention of magic made them falter nowadays. It was also clear that even with his few words, Bel was able to run rings around them rhetorically. They could feel the warmth of his body in the cooling night. A small part of them wondered if they should take advantage of this rather intimate situation. They'd never been particularly attracted to Bel — the woodsman type didn't really do it for them — but they'd been remarkably celibate for weeks now. Yet, whether it was Heather, gently twitching in her sleep, or something that had shifted in their own self, they decided not to get carried away by the still night and the silvery light of the stars.

Or perhaps it was just middle age creeping up on them. The thought made them snigger out loud.

"What's so funny?" asked Bel, eventually.

"I'm just in a merry mood," Meropat said. "It's getting a bit chilly. Should we head indoors?"

They'd expected Ardelei to make up her mind quickly, and to head off into whatever political direction she deemed most wise. Still, the midsummer days mellowed into weeks. Fruit ripened on the trees, and the lake developed an unappetizing green sheen over it. The five inhabitants of the cabin settled into a routine that seemed to please at least four of them. The two women got up early, ate a brisk breakfast, and then disappeared into the forest for long foraging walks. Bel, as was his habit, slept little, and was often away on errands he didn't see necessary to explain to anyone. Heather basked in the shared attention of her new extended family, sometimes going with Bel, other days deciding to accompany the women.

In the evenings there was much fuss over the day's spoils, and a lot of chopping of herbs, mixing of oils and boiling of fruit. This caused Meropat to wonder aloud whether the cousins intended to stay put for the rest of the year: there was only so much jam a sensible person could carry around with them. This had only earned them scornful looks, and a long explanation on the importance of having things to barter – and the necessity of finding enough medicinal herbs to tide over all foreseeable emergencies.

"If it was not for Ardelei's medicine bag, you would not even be able to stand upright as we speak," Rondei chided them.

They understood where she was coming from. Yet, they were unable to join in with the housewifely joy the cousins shared at every filled pot and sewn-up sachet. Unlike Rondei and Ardelei, they'd grown up in a household where there were servants for these kinds of tasks. Their mother had certainly never chopped mint, or bloodied her hands on a prickly pear.

Instead, they tried to busy themselves with things they were more comfortable with. At their request, Bel brought them a sheaf of paper and some inks, so that they could compose poetry whenever the muse decided to light on them. So far, nothing had happened. At first, they felt nauseous just looking at the inkpot on the table. A few days later, they sat down, planning to write something more free-form just to get themself going after the unusually long creative pause. Perhaps a memoir of their time in Valja, complete with some quickly sketched images. A first-hand account of the revolt. A dramatic retelling of their journey down the Ruoke.

Nothing. They took walks along the lakeshore, and sought solitude in the woods. Yet, the exercise only made them hot and bothered, and earned them painful blisters and an entourage of mosquitoes. One evening, as they sat in the glow of a lamp, furiously scratching their arm, Rondei sat down next to them.

"It is all right. I find that taking an occasional break from one's writing is the best service one can do to one's skill. It is important to keep one's quill sharp, but it is equally important to know when to lay down one's tools for a while. One cannot force inspiration."

"I don't think I'm exactly forcing things," they wailed. "I'd *like* to write something. It's not as if I have a shortage of ideas."

Rondei picked up a quill and twirled it in her slender fingers. Meropat had always found her hands irresistible. They were a study in the elegant strength that characterized the woman herself so well. "I am wondering," she said.

"Go on." It wasn't like her to require so much goading.

"Is it the song?" she asked, in a voice so low that Meropat had to nearly read her lips.

They knew immediately what she meant, and recoiled. "No," they said. Then, "I don't know. It might be, partly." They glanced out of the dark window. There was absolutely nothing to see, but they kept staring at it anyway. "I mean, that's the most powerful piece of poetry I've ever written. And I don't know how I did it. I fear I might not ever be able to write something like that again. And again, I'm afraid that I will."

"I do not envy you," she said. "In fact, I have been thinking what I would do in your position." At Meropat's encouraging gesture, she went on. "Well, in my experience, there are only two things you can do. Either walk away from your craft and find something else. Or to learn to live with what you did, and hope to learn to understand it better."

They did envy her clear, linear mind. "That might be true. But both of the options are untenable, frightening. I could try to perfect some of my other skills. I know I can do that, if I must. But having worked as a printer's apprentice, I know what it's like to compete with people at least five years younger than myself. And you know me: I couldn't possibly try my hand at unskilled labor. I just don't have the constitution for it."

She gave them a sideways glance. "It is a shame that the Linduvan community decided to cut itself off from Ederai," she said eventually. "That might have been a neat solution."

"Perhaps so," they said, hesitating. "Did they ever accept... older people among their ranks? As novices, I mean?"

"You will have to ask Ardelei. As I understand it, anyone wishing to join the community was welcome to do that, as long as they brought something with them. Either a skill, or a talent, or some money, for instance."

"Well, as you say, that's not an option anymore. Any place that's stupid enough to throw out Ardelei is better off without me, too."

"That leaves you with the second option."

"I suppose it does. And that's what I've been trying to do. Yet, I seem to lack direction somehow. Perhaps I'm so used to having a patron to work for that I've forgotten how to write for myself. I mean, very few people can even afford to do that."

Rondei slid her hand along the rough tabletop. Then she said, "Is that all it would take? To have someone to pay you?"

Again, they understood her meaning immediately. "I couldn't take money from you, Rondei. That wouldn't be right."

"But it would not be from me," she said, not quite meeting their eyes. "Ardelei and I – I mean, this thing we are about to do, this foolhardy journey we are about to start on..." Meropat had rarely seen her struggle to express herself. "It is nothing definite as yet. It keeps changing every day, as we talk about it. It keeps getting bigger, too. But whatever it is we end up doing, we will need more people around us. I am not quite sure how much you are used to getting paid, but..."

Now it was Meropat's turn to glance away, embarrassed. "Well, one's fee depends often on the generosity of the patron." In truth, during the plague years they'd scarcely been paid at all. That was one of the reasons why they had needed to turn apprentice at such an advanced age. "And there's never full payment before the work is done."

"So you would be willing to work for us?"

"I'm still not sure I understand what it is you'll be doing.

And what would be asked of me. I'm not a diplomat, and I'm definitely not a mage."

She picked up a piece of paper and started rolling it in her fingers. "You know we have talked about how to best oppose the Brotherhood of Light and their like here on Ederai. The first stage is gathering information. Bel and Ardelei are already doing that, and what they have found out seems to support our initial suspicions. We have also known from the beginning that we cannot do this by ourselves. Whoever is behind this outrage, they have spread their tentacles all over Ederai by now. We need to contact people we trust, and we need to persuade them of the magnitude of the threat." She looked up. "This is where you could help. Writing letters, meeting people – you are much better at this than I am. And perhaps helping to spread the word in other ways that you think best. We could pay you for such work. Ardelei and I have savings, and Bel is not exactly poor, either."

Seeing the earnest pleading in her eyes Meropat suddenly felt ashamed of themself. "I couldn't take money from you, Rondei."

"But you said yourself —"

"If you can give me a bed to sleep in, and a plateful of something warm twice a day, I'm yours," they said. At that moment, they felt it, too. Living together with the three extremely driven people had felt annoying — but only because they felt like the only lazy, useless member of the household. Given a more equal standing among the group, they felt that they could go on living like this — even in this gods-forsaken hovel next to a stinking pond.

They couldn't quite understand why Rondei's eyes suddenly welled with tears. Blinking rapidly, she gave a small, embarrassed laugh and said, "All I am asking is that you think about it, Meropat. We would be so pleased, all of us, if you decided to join us."

"I'll think about it," they said. Then, as she grasped their hand in hers, they drew a deep breath. "Who am I kidding? If I don't join you now, I'll regret it for the rest of my life."

"You might still end up regretting all of this."

"Well, then at least I'll know that it was something I chose to do. Besides, if I'm not here, who's going to eat all that jam?"

Rondei laughed, and kissed them lightly on the cheek.

Also by Anne Karppinen

The Songs of Joni Mitchell

The Songs of Joni Mitchell examines recorded performances from Mitchell's first nine studio albums, and the contemporary reviews of these albums in Anglo-American rock magazines. In one of the only works to discuss Mitchell's recorded performances, with a focus that extends beyond the seminal album *Blue*, the book explores the craft of Mitchell's songwriting and her own attitudes towards it, as well as the dynamics and politics of rock criticism in the 1960s and 1970s more generally.

Available on Amazon

About the Author

Anne Karppinen is a university teacher, writer and musician. She holds a PhD in Contemporary Culture, and studied Creative Writing in the UK as a part of her studies. She has been teaching writing – both academic and creative – for over ten years.

Karppinen writes speculative and historical fiction; her short stories have appeared in various publications, including *Not One of Us*, *Wyldblood Magazine* and *Toronto Journal*. Her non-fiction book *The Songs of Joni Mitchell* was published by Routledge. She lives in Central Finland with a collection of weird folk music instruments.

https://www.annekarppinen.com/

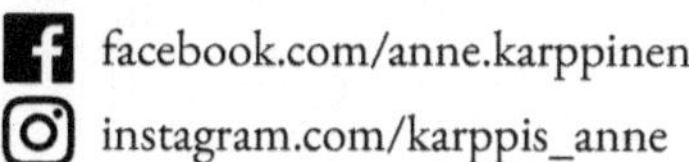

Also by Inkd Pub

Anthologies - Fantasy, LGBTQIA+, Science Fiction, Mystery, Horror

The DRC Files Contemporary Fantasy

The Phoenix DRC Contemporary Fantasy

The Khimmer Chronicles Contemporary Fantasy

The Sorrowborn Trilogy YA Adventure Romance

Miss Fitz's Classroom of Arcane Magics: The Gray Domain Middle-grade Fantasy

When Spirit Speaks: True Paranormal Investigations

And more at InkdPub.com

www.ingramcontent.com/pod-product-compliance
Lightning Source LLC
LaVergne TN
LVHW091107080826
845145LV00008B/1838

* 9 7 8 1 9 6 6 8 4 8 2 0 2 *